DANCING JAX
FREAX AND REJEX

ROBIN JARVIS

HarperCollins *Children's Books*

First published in hardback in Great Britain
by HarperCollins Children's Books 2012
HarperCollins Children's Books is a division of HarperCollinsPublishers Ltd,
77-85 Fulham Palace Road, Hammersmith, London W6 8JB.

Visit us at www.harpercollins.co.uk

1

Text copyright © Robin Jarvis 2012
Illustrations copyright © Robin Jarvis 2012
ISBN 978-0-00-744802-9

Robin Jarvis asserts the moral right to be identified as
the author and illustrator of the work.

Printed and bound in England by Clays Ltd, St Ives plc

The Baxter Blog

Warning the World

YET ANOTHER NEW blog. How many sites have I been kicked out of now? There aren't any UK-based hosts left that aren't under *their* control. I'm having to use a Dutch server. That isn't a clue as to where I am though, so don't bother trying to find me, Mr Fellows. You won't.

So – it's been how many months since that foul book was published? I can't and don't keep score any more. I won't waste time or space here by doing the whole 'told you so' routine, but I want you to know I did my best. I tried – we tried – to warn you. Some listened, but not nearly enough – not until it was too late and it had gotten too strong a hold.

Just look at the state of the UK now. The anger and the protests and curfews have stopped because there aren't enough of you left out there with your own minds. Somehow they got to you; somehow you were made to read, or listen, or ate that foul muck and now you're the same as the rest of those brainwashed sheep.

For those of you who are still resisting (I know there are still a scant few) by whatever means, either through strength of will or simply because you're just naturally immune to that madness as I am, I urge you to get out, as soon as you can. Leave the country; there's nothing you can do there now. Britain is finished. But you can help stop the evil spreading across the world. Find the escape route – the links are out there on the Web.

If you can satisfy our agents you're genuine, you'll be given instructions and directions and real help. Apologies for the hoops you've got to jump through, but we have to protect ourselves. *They* are watching; *they* will stop at nothing to catch us. Good luck!

Martin Baxter

1

REGGIE TUCKER HOISTED his rucksack on to his shoulders. It was time to leave the park. Crawling from the safe cover of the rhododendrons by the far wall, he joined a path and hurried along. He clamped his mouth shut tightly as he passed through a cloud of fat, buzzing flies. A stink of decay hung heavily over this gloomy corner. The weird, repulsive plants that had first appeared several months ago were firmly established now. They had taken over the rose beds and their bristling trailers stretched through the railings in search of fresh soil.

Reggie stepped over them carefully then quickened his pace. The smell from the ugly grey flowers caught in his throat. He glanced back in disgust at the swarms of bluebottles that clustered round the sickly petals and hastened on.

Keeping his head down, the boy avoided eye contact with a dog walker and a small group of people sitting close together on the grass. They were reading intently from a book, rocking backwards and forwards as they uttered the words aloud. He didn't need to wonder what book it was. There was only one book now.

Reggie hoped nobody would notice him, or if they did then the low-numbered playing card he had pinned to his coat would be enough to satisfy any curiosity.

He was desperately hungry. He had eaten the last of his hastily packed rations yesterday. There was money in his pocket, but he was too scared to go into a shop to buy food.

He was tired too. For three nights now he had been sleeping rough. So far he had been lucky. It was a warm, dry April and no one had spotted the twelve-year-old boy skulking around empty back streets, trying to gain entry to deserted buildings or hiding in a burnt-out van that had blazed during the recent riots, or under some boards in a skip.

And yet, at that moment, Reggie wasn't thinking about his stomach or lack of proper sleep. He was anxious and worried, but not for himself. It was late afternoon now. Where was Aunt Jen? They had arranged to meet here at midday, but she hadn't appeared. He knew she was being watched, yet surely she would have texted if there had been any problem slipping away? He checked his phone once again. There were still a couple of bars of charge left and a good signal, but no new texts from her. The last had been yesterday morning.

From: Aunt J
Will meet 2moro at 12. U know where!
Plz be careful. X

Reggie tried to ignore the other texts that had come in since, but his eyes couldn't help flicking over them.

From: Mum
You won't get far

From: Dad
Filthy aberrant!

From: Mum
I hope they kill you

There were others from his sister and the lads who used to be his best friends. It was all the same: vicious threats and insults. Reggie marvelled at how unmoved they left him. Was he really so used to it now? Before this madness started, he had never even heard the word 'aberrant'. For the past month it had hounded him wherever he went, at home, at school, in the streets around town. Strangers yelled abuse and spat at him. Then last week the first stone was flung. The bruise was still there on his leg. Others had bloomed across his body since.

The twelve-year-old thrust the phone back into his pocket. Aunt Jen was the only other person he knew who had not been taken over. For some reason, just like him, that mad book hadn't affected her. Uncle Jason and her two kids treated her with contempt because of that and she was ready to go. She and Reggie had planned this escape in secret. They had intended to make a run for it at the end of this week, but Reggie couldn't stick it out at home any longer and had fled. It had ruined their careful plan. She was going to steal the family car on Friday, drive the forty miles to his house and then they would make for the coast. She had contacted someone on the Net. There were people out there who could help, unaffected people like them, who could get them out of England, away from this country that had gone insane.

"Hey, you!" a voice called suddenly. "Blessed be!"

Reggie looked up. A young girl, no older than seven, was twirling around on the grass. She was wearing what had been a Disney princess costume, but the outfit had been customised so that the sleeves now hung emptily from the shoulders and her arms were slipped through holes cut beneath them. Ribbons and tasselled curtain ties had been sewn to the bodice and around the skirt for a more medieval look.

"That's a little number!" she cried, checking the playing card on his coat as she skipped towards him. "You're only a three! I'm a six. I'm better than you."

The boy looked around nervously. Where were her parents? But then families weren't the same any more. They wouldn't worry or even care if she was missing all day long, especially if it fitted the character she was playing from the book.

"Read to me!" she demanded.

"I have to be somewhere," Reggie muttered, continuing along the path.

"Read to me!" she commanded again in a louder voice. "You're just a three. I have to get back to the castle, but I don't know the big words. Read to me now!"

"I don't have my book with me," Reggie explained hurriedly.

The girl stared at him in surprise. She had a pale, pretty face and her mousey hair was plaited into a stubby rope. Her grey eyes were glassy but questioning and her lips and chin were stained with the livid juices of fruits like those he had just passed.

"Everybody has a book," she told him. "Mine is over there. I get it. You read it me."

She was about to return to where she had left her copy of that horrible book, but Reggie called her back.

"Let me go get mine," he said quickly. "It's at home. I forgot to bring it with me. I'm on my way there now."

The girl put her head on one side and looked at him quizzically. Something about the boy was wrong. There were no stains around his mouth and the dark centres of his eyes were too small. She started to back away. Then her young features scrunched up and she screamed at the top of her voice.

"ABRANT!" she shrieked, pointing accusing fingers and shaking her head violently. "ABRANT!"

Reggie reached out and tried to shush her, but she jumped clear – still screaming.

"ABRANT!"

Reggie looked back fearfully. The group of readers were rising to their feet. One of them was checking an iPad. The boy knew the online list of UK aberrants was being consulted. It was updated daily so his picture was sure to be there. His mother had probably provided his last school photograph. Yes, he saw the man with the iPad look up sharply. He had to get away, fast.

The readers began running towards him. The dog walker came hurrying back along the path and, with the girl's shrill screams in his ears, Reggie legged it.

The street where Aunt Jen lived wasn't far from the park. He had spent the past few days making his way here. It had been slow going, trying to keep out of sight, but he had been pleased and surprised by his own resourcefulness. It had brought him so close. But why hadn't she shown up?

Reggie ran until the people in the park had been left behind and he was sure no one else was following. Slowing down, he caught his breath. He walked for another half a mile, but felt sick from hunger and leaned against a garden fence as he looked around cautiously.

This was a pleasant, leafy suburb. The housing estates were agreeable groupings of detached homes, each one different to its neighbour, with well-tended front lawns and faux leaded windows. His aunt's house was close, just two streets away. Reggie knew it was stupid to go there, but he had to find out what had happened. Besides, where else could he go now?

Setting off again, he noticed how eerily quiet it was here. No sound of traffic. No music or noise coming from the houses, not a single person in sight. It was all so still and deserted that when a magpie came swooping down from a tree and landed on a lawn nearby, it startled him so much he jumped sideways into the road.

Reggie began to wonder if these streets had been evacuated due to an emergency, perhaps a gas leak or something? That would explain the forsaken emptiness of the place. It might also explain Aunt Jen's silence, if she had been forced to leave the house suddenly and in the rush had left her mobile behind...

"That must be it," he told himself. "She's had to clear out with everyone else. So why am I still going to the house? Why don't I turn round and get out of here as well? It might be dangerous. It might be poisonous – or explode."

He frowned and turned the corner into the street where his aunt lived. "But then everywhere's dangerous now," he told himself grimly.

His aunt's house was almost in view. Reggie gripped the straps of his rucksack and continued, taking short, sampling sniffs of the air as he went. He couldn't smell gas, just the faint reek of that horrible plant. People were growing it in their gardens now.

The boy's imagination began inventing other explanations for these empty streets.

"Radiation," he suggested fancifully. "A dirty bomb has gone off and this whole area is contaminated. Or… a chemical spill in the water supply? Subsidence? A big hole might've opened up in one of the roads and the houses aren't safe. Plague! All these houses are filled with dead bodies; it kills instantly and turns you green – with huge spots full of pus. A lion might've escaped from a zoo, though there isn't one anywhere near here…"

Reggie grimaced. He knew that whatever had happened was bound to be because of that book. He almost wished there had been a chemical spill or radioactive fallout – or even a crazed killer with an axe. At least they were things he could understand.

There were no garden fences or hedges in this street. The lawns sloped gently up from the pavement and paths edged with solar-powered lamps led to the front doors. Soon the boy was standing outside number 24. It was large, detached and half-heartedly half-timbered. The lamp post outside was hung with long coloured streamers like a maypole. He saw that the driveway was empty. Then he stared at the front door. It was ajar.

Had they abandoned the place in such a hurry that they hadn't bothered to close it? Was someone in there?

Reggie looked left and right, up and down the street. There was still no sign of another human being anywhere around. Should he chance going inside? He had come this far – besides, there would be food in the kitchen and he was starving.

The boy sprinted across the lawn and pushed the door wide open. The hallway was neat and tidy. There was no sign of any hasty evacuation. He stepped inside and his heart beat faster. Moving warily through the hall, he peered into the living room. Everything looked normal: sofa, plasma TV, cork coasters on the coffee table, family photos on the wall. A framed print hanging above the fireplace caught his attention. That was new. The print was of a white castle, the one featured in that book.

The boy shuddered and looked away in disgust. He quickly made his way to the kitchen where he tore into a bag of bread and stuffed a soft white slice into his mouth. Then he pulled open the fridge and gave a grunt of satisfaction as he gazed on the illuminated contents. Grabbing ham and cheese, he threw them into two more slices and ate them so fast he almost choked. Then he found a can of Coke and guzzled half of it down in one swig. He checked the fridge again. There were some sausage rolls. He wolfed one down and shoved two more in his pocket.

Chewing greedily, he knew he should take as much as he could fit in his rucksack. Removing it from his back, he set to work. There were some things though that he didn't dare touch: yoghurt, juice cartons and a fruit pie. The packaging bore the logo of that book and contained the pulp and juice from the foul-smelling plant.

Once that was done, Reggie turned his attention to the cupboards. Fresh stuff wouldn't last long. He should take some tins as well. Two lots of beans, an oxtail soup, macaroni cheese, they were all his bag could take.

"Tin-opener," he told himself sharply. He yanked open a drawer and began searching through the cutlery. A knife and spoon went clattering on to the tiled floor and the unearthly silence was broken.

Reggie froze. Why hadn't he been more careful?

"Who's there?" a voice called suddenly.

The boy turned.

"Who is it?" the voice called again.

Reggie's stomach flipped over. He knew who that was! His face broke into a huge grin and he rushed to the hall and clutched at the banister as he glanced up the stairs.

"Aunt Jen?" he cried. "It's me – it's Reggie."

"Oh, Reggie!" the voice answered faintly. "I knew you'd make it."

The boy ran up the stairs. His aunt sounded tired. What had his uncle done to her? Had she been locked in a room? Perhaps she was tied up.

"Why didn't you come to the park?" he called when he reached the landing. "Why didn't you meet me? What's happening here?"

He looked quickly into the bathroom, then in his cousins' bedrooms. They were all empty.

At the end of the landing his aunt and uncle's bedroom door was half open. It was dark inside.

"I couldn't, Reggie," his aunt answered from the darkness. Reggie's relief and joy disappeared. Dread and fear took their place.

"Why?" he asked.

"It's no use, Reggie," Aunt Jen replied.

The boy took a step closer. "Why didn't you text me?"

"I couldn't."

"Why not? What did Uncle Jason do? Where is everyone?"

There was no answer. Reggie put his head round the door. The curtains were drawn, but the light of the April afternoon leaked in at the edges. At first he thought someone was slumped on the bed then he realised it was only a mound of clothes. The drawers and wardrobes had been ransacked, their contents strewn about the room. Then he saw, in front of the curtains, a figure sitting before a dressing table mirror, gazing at her reflection in the gloom.

"Aunt Jen?" he ventured. The person didn't move.

"Jen?" he said again.

Reggie didn't want to go any closer. He shouldn't have come here. He could just make out that the woman's head was covered by a veil of black lace.

"I expected you here hours ago," she said, still staring into the mirror.

Reggie took a step back. The figure did not move.

"I thought something had happened to you," the boy muttered. "Something bad."

"Something did, Reggie," she said softly. "But it was good not bad – so very, very good." The woman rose from the chair and turned, lifting the veil from her face.

Reggie let out a sob of dismay and stumbled out of the room. Aunt Jen came striding after. Leaving the darkness, she stepped on to the landing. Reggie blundered backwards, retreating to the top of the stairs.

His aunt was wearing a long gown of black tulle and taffeta that rustled like dead grass when she moved. Long gloves of black silk reached to her elbows and a necklace of jet beads glittered about her neck. Her once friendly face was now set in a scowl. Raven-black lips made her mouth ugly and her eyebrows looked like they had been inscribed with coal. At her bosom she had pinned a playing card and upon her cheek she had painted a large black spade.

"Not you!" Reggie cried. "Not you!"

"I am the Queen of Spades," she told him. "Last night it happened. At long last the way opened for me. I was drawn beyond the Silvering Sea and awoke in the great castle of Mooncaster and finally knew this grey world for what it was, a flat dream. I am one of the four Under Queens. That is my true life."

The boy shook his head. "No, it isn't!" he shouted, but he knew it was no use arguing. He had lost her, just like he had lost his sister then his parents. He had to get out of there.

"It is not too late for you, Reggie," she said as he hurried down the stairs. "The woman Jennifer was fond of you, her nephew. I will entreat the Holy Enchanter. He may be able to help. You cannot remain an aberrant. Join us."

"Not on your life!" he spat as he raced through the hall and into the kitchen to retrieve his rucksack. "You and the rest of them can stick it."

"Aberrants will not be tolerated," she said as she came swishing down the stairs.

Reggie closed his eyes tightly and drew a deep breath. He had to control himself. There wasn't time to grieve for her. That could happen later, when he was safe, if he could ever be safe. Right now he had to run.

He rushed back into the hallway. The woman he had known as Aunt Jen was standing on the bottom stair, a black-feathered fan in her hand.

"You cannot leave," she said, tapping it lightly against her gloved palm.

"Watch me," he growled.

Reggie barged out of the front door then staggered to a halt. With despair and defeat in his eyes, he gazed around and a deathly cold clasped him. The street was filled with people. A crowd of several hundred residents and neighbours had gathered silently in front of the house. They were all dressed as some medieval fairy-tale character and every one of them wore a playing card on their home-made costume. Close by, on the lawn, stood his uncle and his cousins.

Uncle Jason was wearing a smock and apron. Pewter tankards were hooked to his belt. He was supposed to be an innkeeper, but he merely looked ridiculous. His sons, Tim and Ryan, were also dressed up. One was a page, the other a kitchen boy.

Reggie felt his courage disappear. He was trapped.

"Aberrant," his cousins said.

"Aberrant," his uncle repeated.

"Aberrant," spat the voice of Aunt Jen in the doorway behind him.

The word spread through the large crowd until everyone was chanting it like a mantra, their faces twisted and angry.

"We must not suffer an aberrant to live!" Uncle Jason shouted.

"Burn him!" Ryan called out.

"Burn him!" echoed the crowd.

Reggie stared at them in horror. Yes, they would do it. They would burn him alive. The madness had gone that far.

"Lock him in the shed and set light to it!" Uncle Jason cried.

"No," Aunt Jen commanded. "It must be done properly, as we would burn the Bad Shepherd in Mooncaster. Build a bonfire. Bring wood and fuel."

The crowd gave a mighty cheer. Many went running to their homes to fetch anything that would burn. The rest came surging towards Reggie and closed in around him. There was nothing he could do, no chance of escape. Strong hands grabbed at him. He was hitched high off the ground and carried to the road.

The beginning of a bonfire was swiftly thrown on the tarmac. Chairs, tables, empty bookcases, shelves ripped from walls, tied towers of newspaper from recycling bins, anything that a flame could bite was brought there in euphoric haste. A man emerged from his house with a chainsaw and immediately set to work, carving the furniture into useful, stackable pieces.

Reggie was paraded around the mounting timber pyramid like a living guy. He saw a pensioner gleefully throw his walking stick into the midst of the growing pyre and watched a woman come laughing from her garage carrying a can of paraffin. She looked up at Reggie and he saw the joyous expectation on her face. Dancing around the woodpile she sloshed the paraffin over it with carefree abandon.

Reggie was held so tight he could not even struggle. He knew there was no way out of this. He tried to shout, to tell them they were insane, that the book had possessed them – that they were about to commit murder. But nobody listened and they sang the stupid songs from those evil pages all the louder. This was it. He was going to be burned to death.

And then, suddenly, a siren cut through the excited babble of voices and, to Reggie's overwhelming relief, two police cars came roaring down the street, screeching to a stop in front of the bonfire.

"Oh, thank you, thank you!" Reggie yelled.

"Break it up, break it up!" the officers shouted as they slammed the car doors shut.

The crowd grew quiet. One officer moved forward, his hand poised close to the firearm at his hip. Since the beginning of the protests and street violence some months ago, the British police force had been armed.

"Put the boy down," he ordered.

There was a moment of hesitation, but the mob could tell he meant business. The men carrying Reggie lowered him to the ground.

"Step away from him," the officer instructed.

The crowd obeyed, grudgingly, and the boy ran over to the squad cars.

"I can't believe it!" he cried. "I thought you were all got at. I thought you were all taken over by the book! These nutters were going to burn me!"

The policeman ignored him. "Who's in charge here?" he called out.

"I am," Aunt Jen's voice rang out.

The crowd murmured and parted, forming a path for her to come forward. Fanning herself, the woman sauntered regally through them.

Reggie glared at her and countless accusations blazed as fiercely in his mind as the bonfire would have done. But before he could speak, the officers did something that caused his newfound hope to shrivel and die.

Every police officer removed his cap and dropped to one knee before the Queen of Spades. Reggie knew that somewhere, under their stab-proof vests, they too would be wearing playing cards.

"Majesty," the policeman said. "I am Sir Gorvain of the Royal House of Diamonds."

"You are come just in time to join our revel," the woman greeted him. "This day we burn one who defies the Holy Enchanter, a foul malefactor in league with the Bad Shepherd."

"Grant me the honour of escorting the fiend to the flames."

The Queen of Spades slapped her fan shut and pointed over the policeman's shoulder with it. "First, Sir Knight," she said crossly, "you shall have to catch him again."

Everyone turned. Reggie had seized his chance and was racing down the street. The crowd jeered and booed. The boy had discarded his heavy rucksack and was running faster than he had ever done before. He knew the bonfire was blocking the way of the police cars. They wouldn't be able to chase him. He might just manage to get away. There was still a slender chance!

Two shots were fired, but Reggie only heard the first. A moment later, he was on the ground. At last he had escaped, to a place where the evil of the book could never catch him.

The crowd cheered. Sir Gorvain waved his gun with a flourish and took a bow as they applauded. Then one of them began to sing, another played lute music loudly on a mobile whilst someone else shook a tambourine and a courtly dance commenced. The colourful streamers hanging from the lamp post were taken up and the courtiers skipped around it, laughing. Others took out their copies of the book and began to read aloud in unison.

What a glorious April evening it was.

The woman who had been Aunt Jen gazed impassively down the street where the body of the young aberrant lay. Then she snapped her fan open once more and joined the dance.

2

"As many of you out there may be aware, something strange is happening across the pond in good old Blighty. You might have seen news reports or read about it on the Internet, but do you really understand, in the name of all that is sane, just what those Brits are up to? I've been trying to follow this phenomenon, but frankly it's clear as chowder to me. Here's Kate Kryzewski, reporting from London, England, with the Jax Fax."

The VT rolled and the news anchor leaned back in his chair.

"Damn crazy little ass-end country," he said, shaking his head dismissively. "Let them keep their crappy books to themselves this time. We don't want it. Am I right?"

A make-up girl darted in from the side and dabbed at his glistening forehead.

"How'm I looking, Tanya?" he asked, almost purring.

"Just wonderful, Mr Webber," the professional and pretty Tanya answered.

"You don't think I need a little tuck and lift round my eyes then, huh? Still holding up well, yeah?"

Tanya wisely refrained from telling him she knew he'd already undergone two procedures for the eye bags and the crows' feet. It was good work though, probably done here on the East Coast where politicians go for the subtle stuff, not the Californian waxwork-under-a-blowtorch look.

"So you want some sushi after?" he asked, switching on his best bedroom eyes. "I know a great place where I won't get mobbed and we'll be left alone – just me, you and the wasabi."

"That would be a no, sir," she declined for the sixteenth time that month.

"Always with the no," he said with a shrug of his Armani-suited shoulders. "A good-looking, successful guy could lose confidence around all those noes. I had enough noes when I was with my wife, until the divorce. Then it changed to yeses. Yes, she wanted my apartment, yes, she wanted my cars, yes, she wanted my alimony checks, yes to all nine pints of my O negative. I was lucky to get out with both my… ahem… 'wasabi' still attached."

"Still a no, Mr Webber," Tanya said, ducking out of shot behind the camera.

"Would a little bit of raw fish be so offensive?" he entreated, staring at her departing chest.

"It's not the fish, you dick," she muttered under her breath.

Harlon Webber cast around for someone else to engage with, but the crew knew him well enough to only catch his eye when they needed to. Reluctantly he turned his attention to the monitor and watched the pre-filmed item that was going out.

The whole of the United Kingdom had apparently gone nuts. Five months ago a children's book called *Dancing Jax* had been published and had sold a staggering sixty-three million copies, at least one for every member of the population. It had completely taken over everyone's life in that country.

Reporter Kate Kryzewski was speaking over footage of violent clashes in Whitehall between opposing factions. Police officers in riot gear could be seen battling on both sides, most often fighting against one another. A bookshop burned to the cheers of a mob, petrol bombs were hurled against the gates of Downing Street and an army tank rolled through Trafalgar Square, scattering the incensed crowds. In Charing Cross Road water cannon and tear-gas grenades were deployed against a tide of protesters.

"These were the alarming scenes here in London just seven weeks ago," Kate's voice-over said. "Similar pitched battles were being waged right across the UK. It seemed that all-out war had broken out, here in the home of fish and chips and the Beatles. The cause? An old children's book of fairy tales first published in 1936. Unbelievable as it sounds, this nation was bitterly and brutally divided between those who had read it and those who refused to read it. The angry protests have since died down and peace has returned to the British Isles. Why? Because just about everyone has now read this book. So, what is it about *Dancing Jax* that could have triggered such an extreme reaction? I haven't read it and won't until I find out more, so I went on to the streets to do just that…"

The report continued with her interviewing random people around London, against such familiar touristy backdrops as Buckingham Palace and Big Ben. They all praised the book and what it had brought to their lives.

"It *is* my life," said a distinguished man in a dark blue suit outside the Houses of Parliament. "You might as well ask what it's like to breathe. No question about it. I have to have the book with me always because I can't bear to be away from Mooncaster for very long. In fact, I've got five spares dotted about in case of an emergency. It's market day there and I shouldn't be messing about playing politics here. I've got to get the stall ready and set my wares out…"

"Excuse me, sir," Kate said, "but you don't strike me as someone who would be interested in that kind of role play."

"Role play?" he snorted indignantly. "I don't have time for games, madam. Only the Jacks and Jills can indulge in idle sport."

The picture cut to the main entrance of Selfridges on Oxford Street where an overly made-up elderly woman, decked out in countless necklaces and three earrings per ear, was staring aghast at the reporter. "You haven't read it?" she cried in disbelief. "Oh, you must, dear. Get a copy this very minute. Don't do anything else – go right now and get it!"

"Why is it so important to you?" Kate asked.

"Important?" the woman repeated in bafflement. "It's just everything, dear, simply everything. 'Important' doesn't come into it – it gets me back home, out of all this."

"It makes this bumhole of a place bearable, dunnit?" a black cab driver said to camera as he leaned out of his window.

"And how many times have you read it?" Kate enquired.

"No idea, darlin', but there'll never be enough, never. My real life there is sweet as a nut. Look at that bloody bus, thinks he owns the bleedin' road! Why the hell can't I bring my longbow with me into these soddin' dreams, eh? I'd soon have him."

Back in the studio Harlon Webber threw his hands in the air for attention.

"Why are all those schmucks wearing playing cards?" he asked anyone who would listen. "Is it some kinda cult of Vegas?"

Nobody answered. They, like the rest of the world, were bewildered and intrigued as to what was happening in the UK and were watching the report closely.

"Hey, Johnny," Harlon called, squinting into the gloom behind the cameras. "Didn't you say you got a kid sister over there? Weren't you worried about her a while back?"

Jimmy the cameraman was used to the jerk getting his name wrong. It used to bug him, but now it didn't matter.

"She's just fine, Mr Webber," he answered flatly. "It's all just fine."

"Kate's looking trim there, isn't she? Hey, anyone here nailed her? I don't normally dig redheads, but I've been trying for two years. Maybe I need to wear army fatigues. Yeah, I bet that's why she goes to all them war places. She must have a thing for jarhead grunts. One of those power broads who has to feel superior the whole damn time."

No one in the studio answered him.

"Hey, hi!" a young American student said into the lens outside the British Museum. "I'm Brandon from Wisconsin – or that's who I'm supposed to be when I'm here, right? I'm really a farm guy in the Kingdom of the Dawn Prince and hey, you just watch out for that Bad Shepherd. He's been sighted over by the marsh and that's just way too close, man. He's like real bad news and if he goes anywhere near my goats, I'm going after him with my axe and getting me some shepherd brains. He tore the hearts clean out of Mistress Sarah's geese last fall, every one…"

"If I could just speak to you as Brandon for a moment," Kate interjected.

"Sure, that's cool. That's why I'm here, right? To be Brandon and rest, so I can be stronger there – awesome."

"What do your parents make of all this, back home in the US?"

"Yeah, I like Skyped those guys the other day. It's real weird having a set of folks in this dream place, when my true mom is back in our cottage right now, teasing the wool, or out in the field pulling up the turnips."

"But your family in Wisconsin, what do they think?"

"Oh, they don't understand, man. They don't have a copy of the sacred text so how could they? They're nice people an' all. Not their fault. They were like freaking out and stuff."

"Because of your devotion to *Dancing Jax*?"

"Just ignorance, dude, that's all. They'll know real soon though. I FedExed them a copy yesterday."

"You sent one of these books to the United States?"

"Sure, I can't believe it's not out there already. Wake up, America!"

"Thank you, Brandon."

"Hey, blessed be, man."

Kate Kryzewski, a no-nonsense breed of reporter who had been to Afghanistan and Iraq, seemed genuinely disturbed by what she was hearing.

She turned to camera and stared at it gravely.

"'Wake up, America,'" she repeated. "That's what the young man said and I couldn't agree more. Every person I have met here in London has been obsessed by this seemingly ordinary and old-fashioned children's book. When I say obsessed, I use the word quite literally. These people aren't just ardent fans. I would go so far as to say they've been possessed by it, so much so that they have assumed the identity of a character from the story. They aren't interested in anything that doesn't relate to it. They read and reread the stories whenever they can and the British government has just passed new legislation for seven fifteen-minute intervals throughout the day when everything will stop so mass readings can take place. Apparently, the reading experience is best shared. Can you imagine this happening in America?"

"Damn freaky, that's what it is," Harlon stated, leaning back in his chair and slapping the news desk. "Wackos, the lot of them. That's what warm beer and bad restaurants do to you. Last time I was there they tried to serve me beans for breakfast. I was like, 'You frickin' kidding me? Get that redneck pig slop outta here!' Dumb, backward, Third World douches."

"… And in every garden and park," Kate continued, standing in the Palm House at Kew, "are these strange new cultivars of trees and fruiting shrubs called minchet." The camera panned past her to zoom in on a row of ugly and twisted bushes that had strangled and killed most of the exotic plants.

"This plant features in the book and just be thankful we don't have smell-o-vision because these things stink of swamps, halitosis and damp basements all in one. And yet the British have developed such a taste for this fruit that they've started to put it in juices, sodas, cosmetics – even candy. You can buy a MacMinchet Burger, a Great Grey Whopper and there are now *twelve* herbs and spices in the colonel's secret recipe. No doubt you're thinking there's some addictive substance at work here – that's what I suspected too – but we've had it tested and there's absolutely no trace of anything that could account for this behaviour."

The report cut to the exterior of the Savoy Hotel and Kate was wearing her most serious face.

"At the centre of these strange new phenomena is the man responsible for bringing *Dancing Jax* to the attention of a twenty-first-century audience. He too has assumed the identity of a character from those very pages, that of the Ismus, the Holy Enchanter. He's the charismatic main figure in these fairy tales and I have been granted an audience with him. So let's see if he can explain just what is going on here…"

The scene changed to the plush interior of a hotel suite where a lean man with a clever face and perfectly groomed, shoulder-length dark hair listened to her first question with wry amusement. He was dressed in black velvet, which made the paleness of his skin zing out on camera.

"No, no," he corrected, "*Dancing Jax* is not a cult. Cults, by definition, are small, hidden societies of marginal interest."

"Then can you explain to the millions of Americans, and the rest of the people around the world, just what is going on with this book?" Kate asked. "And why you Brits are so hooked on it?"

The man stared straight down the lens.

"*Dancing Jax* is a collection of fabulous tales set in a far-off Kingdom," he said. "It was written many years ago by an amazing, gifted visionary, but was only discovered late last year…"

"Austerly Fellows," Kate interjected. "He was some kind of occultist in the early part of the twentieth century. There is evidence that suggests he was, in fact, a Satanist, a founder and leader of unpleasant secret sects, and controlled a number of covens."

"Malicious rumours spread by his enemies," the Ismus countered. "Austerly Fellows was without equal, a man far ahead of his time, an intellectual colossus, bestowed of many gifts. Jealousy and spite are such unproductive, restraining forces, aren't they?"

"What I don't understand is why such a man, Satanist or not, would even write a children's book."

"It is merely the format he chose in which to impart his great wisdom. The truths *Dancing Jax* contains have enriched our country beyond all expectations. It speaks to you on a very basic, fundamental level."

"So you're saying it's a new religion."

"No," he laughed. "It is not a religion. It is a doorway to a better understanding of life, a bridge to a far more colourful and exciting existence than this one."

"But don't you have two priests dressed as harlequins in your entourage and isn't there a woman, called Labella, who is a High Priestess?"

"There are many characters in my retinue."

"But surely these mass readings that are scheduled to take place… might they not be viewed as a form of organised worship?"

"Only if you consider breakfast the organised worship of cornflakes."

"I'm a black coffee and donut person myself. Can you explain the significance behind the playing cards that readers of the book wear?"

The Ismus smiled indulgently. "If you'd read it yourself, you'd know," he said. "But it isn't giving anything away to say that *Dancing Jax* is set in a Kingdom where there are four Royal Houses which have, as their badges, Diamonds, Clubs, Hearts and Spades. The numbers indicate what type of character the reader identifies with, so a ten of clubs would be a knight or noble of that house, whilst a two or three would be further down the social scale – a maid or groom. Perfectly simple."

"But the harlequins I mentioned earlier, and the priestess, as well as certain other characters in your entourage, I notice they don't wear a card. Why is that?"

"They are the aces; they are special. They don't need to."

"I don't see a card on you either. Does that mean you're an ace?"

He laughed softly. "No," he told her. "I suppose you could say I'm the dealer."

"Yeah!" Harlon Webber quipped in the studio. "You look like one, pal!"

Kate continued. "But could you ease the growing fears and genuine concerns that we in America have about this book and its inexplicable power over the people of Britain? Can you understand why it would be viewed as strange, even menacing and sinister, from the outside?"

"Of course it must appear odd to any outsider, but let me allay your fears and concerns. There is nothing to be afraid of. The benefits it has brought our society are endless."

"And yet, just under two months ago, there was civil unrest in all your major cities. People were protesting against this very book, in scenes reminiscent of the clashes in the Middle East. We all saw the CNN footage of those battles in the streets and the Internet was disconnected throughout the UK for almost three whole weeks. How do you account for that? Were there not also several deaths?"

"There are no riots now," the Ismus assured her. "Those misguided crowds were agitators who had not read the book and did not understand why it was important they should do so. The deaths were regrettable accidents, no more. Such violence could never occur again."

"Because the anti-Jax groups have now read the book and are under its, and therefore your, control?"

"Like I said, there are no riots now. In fact, across the board, crime isn't just down – it's non-existent."

"I can't believe that."

"It's true. The last reported crime was over a month ago, that's all types of crime. Just doesn't happen now."

"That's incredible."

The Ismus grinned at her.

"Isn't it?" he said. "Then there's the sale of prescription drugs such as Prozac and Valium – down to nil. People don't need that junk any more. They don't need any type of drug, legal or otherwise. Drug and alcohol rehab are things of the past; every former user and addict is now completely clean."

"I'm finding this very hard to accept, Mr Ismus."

"Just Ismus."

"You're saying clinical depression has been cured by this book? That violent and petty felonies have been wiped out by this book? That dependence on hard, Class A drugs such as heroin has been totally eradicated by this book?"

"You should take a look inside one of our maximum-security prisons. Now they've each got four teams of Morris Men and their own internal league."

"That really is astonishing."

"It's just one of the joys of *Dancing Jax*," the Ismus told her. "It has united this broken country. Made it into a better place."

"So can you explain just how that has happened? What exactly are the readers of this book getting from it? What is the power it has over them?"

The Ismus looked into Kate's eyes until she found it disconcerting and uncomfortable, but she wasn't going to let him intimidate her. She'd interviewed more powerful people before – or so she thought.

"It gives them order," he said. "That's what people want, but are too conditioned to admit. They want to believe in a simpler world where the burden of choice doesn't exist, where they know who they are and how their jigsaw life fits into the larger pattern. To know and to belong…"

"The burden of choice?" Kate interrupted. "Excuse me, but *freedom* of choice, free will, freedom of speech are what define us, especially we Americans; our constitution is founded upon that. How can you call it a burden?"

He waved a hand in airy dismissal, which she felt insulted and antagonised by. "What a pretty illusion that is," he said. "The choices you think are yours are just smoke and mirrors. What choice is there in this world where all the shops and food outlets are the same? Take the Internet, for example; where is the choice there?"

"I don't see what you're driving at. There are an infinite number of choices on the Internet."

His face assumed a pitying, patient expression. "Millions of people online," he said. "You'd think there should be unlimited choices, unlimited options open to them. But that isn't what they want."

"It isn't?"

"Too much choice is confusing. As I said, they want order; they want to be told what to buy and from whom. People need herding. That's why the chaos of the Internet is being tamed and moulded, by every one of their sheeplike clicks of the mouse. They're building boundary walls within infinity because they're terrified at the prospect of something so limitless and arbitrary."

"I can't say that I agree with…"

"It's a waste of your spearmint-scented breath to deny it. There is only one place to download music, one auction site, one social network site, one search engine, one place to share your videos, one place to buy books, one encyclopaedia and one way to pay for it all… and you say you believe in the illusion of choice? Come now, are attractive women still pretending to be less intelligent than they are to get by in what they see as a man's world?"

Kate refused to let herself get nettled by him any further and switched back to the book.

"And what about the people here who haven't been seduced by *Dancing Jax*?" she asked.

"Interesting word choice. Yes, there are a very few sad individuals. Less than a fraction of a per cent of the population who just can't appreciate the power and beauty of *Dancing Jax*."

"Is it not true that those very people are now facing discrimination, persecution and violent oppression?"

"That's profoundly untrue; they deserve our pity and understanding, and get plenty of both."

"Not according to my sources."

His eyes locked on her and Kate, despite being a veteran of war reporting in some of the most dangerous hot spots of the world, felt a stab of fear unlike anything she had ever experienced.

"Now I wonder what those sources can be?" he asked.

"I can't disclose that."

"You don't have to. I can guess. Tell me, do you always give credence to paranoid conspiracy theorists with personal grudges? Martin Baxter is just a jealous, embittered maths teacher from Suffolk. His grievance isn't with *Dancing Jax*. It's with me. His ex left him to become my consort. Her son is also with me; the boy is one of our four prime Jacks – the Jack of Diamonds. Martin Baxter just doesn't know when to let go. I feel sorry for the man, I really do. He should move on."

"Is that why he's in hiding?" she pressed. "Is that why he's too afraid to even meet with me and communicates via email only? He is very outspoken and critical of what you and your book have done here."

"The guy is delusional and a militant agitator. He's wanted by the authorities here for stoking the very unrest you were talking about earlier. His accusations against me and *Dancing Jax* have been totally discredited and condemned and the papers uncovered some very unpleasant, shameful details about his personal life. Why would you even listen to someone like that?"

"Sir, what I'm more interested in is the treatment of the people who haven't embraced your book. What is happening to them?"

The Ismus looked down the lens again and continued. "I intend only to help those people, to try and enable them to come join the rest of us and reap the same incredible rewards from this amazing work. Just as I hope to share it with other countries, yours included."

"Sir," she repeated without any respect in her tone. "The rest of the world is watching what is occurring here, watching extremely closely. Washington will not permit this controversial book to be published in the US if it provokes such heated demonstrations and turns citizens into brainwashed zombies who think this life is not their real existence. I really don't think you can expect the book to be published anywhere else but here."

The Ismus grinned at her. "And yet," he said, "earlier this month, at the Bologna International Book Fair, *Dancing Jax* was sold to many different countries. At this very moment it's being translated into nine languages. I can't wait to see those foreign editions, I really can't. The words of Austerly Fellows are going global."

The interview ended on his crooked smile and the picture cut once again to Kate Kryzewski outside the Savoy.

"And so there you have it, the current situation in the United Kingdom. I still can't begin to understand it, but I will say this and once again echo the words of Brandon from Wisconsin: 'Wake up, America'."

The camera did a slow zoom on her face.

"Do not permit this book to get a foothold in our country," she warned. "Do not let it take root; do not let *Dancing Jax* brainwash our citizens, our precious children, as it has here. Never let the Land of the Free become subject to the tyranny of this insidious book. If you receive a copy from a relative or friend over here, destroy it immediately. Don't even leaf through the pages. Don't give it a chance to hook you in. America, I love you. Be vigilant. This is Kate Kryzewski for NBC Nightly News, reporting from London, England."

The familiar environment of the studio snapped back on air. With eyebrows slightly raised, Harlon Webber appeared as calm and professional as ever and ready to introduce the next item.

Suddenly a voice yelled out in the studio and Jimmy the cameraman ran in front of Camera Two. He raised his right arm, brandishing a copy of *Dancing Jax* for millions of Americans to see.

"Hail the Ismus!" he roared, flecks of spittle flying from his mouth and dotting the lens. His eyes were wide and the pupils dilated so much that hardly any iris could be seen. "Hail the Ismus!" he continued to bawl until Security dragged him away. "Hail the Ismus! He is amongst us!"

3

EARLY MORNING AND it was overcast, almost chilly. Not quite the glorious sunshine they were hoping for in the first Friday of May. Perhaps later on it would brighten up a little, in time for the special arrivals. Still, everything else was perfectly in order.

The man now known as Jangler, or the Lockpick, after the gaoler character in *Dancing Jax*, ran through his checklist one last time and twirled his fingers through the neat little grey beard that sprouted from his chin. Meticulous and methodical in habit and training, he made a bluff mumbling sound under his breath as he satisfied himself he had missed nothing. Everything was organised, nice and tidy. Turning, he glanced up from his clipboard and peered over his spectacles at the holiday compound behind him.

Up until three months ago, this idyllic retreat in the heart of the New Forest had been a favourite place for hostellers and school parties on outward bound trips. The main block housed the kitchen, refectory and lecture room, while seven lesser buildings were dormitories. They were designed to resemble log cabins, with various degrees of success, but the cumulative effect was not unattractive. They looked sufficiently picturesque and rural, surrounded as they were by trees and bedecked with spring flowers in a myriad of pots and window boxes and fluttering heraldic banners and bunting. It looked good on camera and that was the important thing today.

Jangler drew a tick on his list. He enjoyed drawing ticks. They signified something had been completed. It was a leftover habit from his previous existence as a solicitor in a drab, file-filled office in Ipswich. Before the power of *Dancing Jax* had taken control, his former name had been Hankinson, but he hardly ever remembered that now. He had spent that entire former life waiting for this. Through the generations, his family had been disciples of Austerly Fellows and were entrusted with keeping the documents and secrets of that incredible personage safe down the decades.

He continued to twiddle with his beard and checked the list once more.

The news crews were assembled inside the main block for the press conference that the Ismus had convened. With two exceptions, everyone there was in the thrall of *Dancing Jax*. Reporters were dressed in medieval-type clothing, with a playing card pinned somewhere on their outfit. They showed a nauseating deference to the personage of the Holy Enchanter when he came striding in. The lecture hall popped and flared with white light as camera flashes went wild. The Ismus paraded up and down, so that everyone could get a great photo, and the tails of his velvet jacket whipped about him as he strutted before them.

Five chairs were lined up at the front, facing the press. Occupying four were the Jacks and Jills, the teenagers from Felixstowe who had become the embodiment of the lead characters in the book. They were now the most famous teens in Britain. Their faces appeared everywhere, endorsing products that suited their royal personalities. No magazine or newspaper was complete without photographs of them and there were endless articles about the minutiae of their lives in this drab world. Each had their own reality TV show.

Currently, the one featuring the Jill of Spades had the highest ratings. The girl had been responsible for the Felixstowe Disaster the previous autumn, in which forty-one young people had died, and the consequences of her confession were most entertaining to watch. At the moment, she was out on bail and her trial was due to commence in two months' time. It promised to be a total circus. The Audience Appreciation Index figures for her programme were unprecedented. Her sly, devious ways made it unmissable viewing. The British public were hooked, not only on *Dancing Jax*, but also on her outrageously amusing antics in this world.

Kate Kryzewski and Sam, her unshaven cameraman, waited for the applause to die down as the Ismus took the vacant seat in the middle. His bodyguards, three burly men with blackened faces, stood behind him and two Harlequin Priests assumed their positions at either end.

"Blessed be to you," the Ismus addressed everyone.

Again Kate and Sam were silent while those around them responded.

The Ismus smiled.

"My loyal subjects," he began, "I crave pardon for summoning you, but I wished to explain the events taking place here this weekend. It has come to my attention that in this Kingdom of ours there are certain children who have not yet found their way to the Realm of the Dawn Prince. The words of the sacred text have as yet been unable to reach them."

The news teams began to murmur and some people spat on the floor in contempt.

"Do not be hasty to judge and denounce them as aberrants," the Ismus chided gently. "Some paths meander and veer deep into shadowy woods before rejoining the true way. We must practise patience and show kindness to these sad wretches. Consider how isolated and empty their unhappy existence must be. To be locked in this drabness with no waking in the real world and no sight of Mooncaster's white towers to set their hearts a-racing. They are to be pitied and must be guided to the right path. Have faith that, given time, the hallowed text will heal them of their ignorance. We are going to give them the weekend of their lives to atone for any sorrows they have endured. Glorious Mooncaster-themed fun, packed with games and feasts worthy of Mistress Slab, the castle cook, interspersed with communal readings led by our finest Shakespearean actors."

The assembled press clapped and cheered at this most charitable intention. The Jacks and Jills joined in. Even the Jill of Spades seemed moved by this benevolence.

"Excuse me," Kate interrupted.

"Miss Kryzewski!" the Ismus greeted her. "We meet again. How good of you to accept my invitation back to these shores."

"It wasn't easy," she replied. "There are no direct flights from the US to Britain any more. Not since planes started to land back home with every passenger and crew member having been inducted into this... whatever you want to call it, somewhere over the Atlantic. Sam and me had to fly to France and come here on the Eurostar."

"I hope the regrettable misunderstanding between our two countries will soon be resolved," he said. "It must be very inconvenient for so many people."

"The 'misunderstanding', as you call it, will stay in place for as long as your book continues to pose 'a clear and present danger' to our citizens. Since our last meeting, there have been outbreaks of violence across Europe. In the cities where *Dancing Jax* is being translated there have so far been two murders, one suicide and a German publishing house was the scene of an all-out battle between the staff. Do you still insist this book is anything but a negative and destructive force?"

"Change is always resisted," the Ismus replied. "Every advancement mankind makes is met with suspicion and mistrust. Man's first instinct is to smash what he fears and doesn't understand. Luddites hatch faster than bluebottles, but their lifespan is just as brief."

Kate hadn't come all this way to hear the same old tunes. With this latest report, she was determined to cut through the tinsel and tights of this unhealthy mania and expose the man behind it as the pernicious dictator he really was. She wanted to put the Holy Enchanter right at the top of America's Most Wanted List. The American Ambassador and his staff had been recalled from London, but they too were under the book's insidious spell. They, together with the passengers and crews of the planes she had mentioned, were currently being detained at Vandenberg Air Force Base in California and undergoing psychological testing. Last week in Illinois there had been a tragedy involving three families who had come into contact with just one smuggled copy of the book. There had been five separate incidents in other states.

So far the President was dragging his feet over 'the UK Issue', as it had become known, and his procrastination was infuriating many. The Republicans were calling it a 'Jaxis of Evil'. Kate intended her report to put even more pressure on him to finally initiate strong, maybe even military, action. She was going to provide irrefutable evidence that *Dancing Jax* was a weapon of mass mind destruction.

She was aware the other news crews around her were shifting in their seats, casting hostile glances in her direction, but she took no notice and continued to goad the Ismus. If she could get that soft-soap façade to crack just a little…

"So let me get this straight," she said. "You're rounding up all the minors who haven't yet been brainwashed and bringing them here? Is that correct?"

His face might have been made from marble. "Only those between the ages of seven and sixteen," he explained. "Any younger would be unthinkable. We are not barbarians."

"And over the course of this weekend," she carried on, "you'll be hoping to work your voodoo on their impressionable minds? Isn't that more than a little sinister?"

The Ismus laughed at her. "It is no more sinister than one of your Renaissance Fairs!" he said. "But a hundred times more authentic and joyful – and with a greater purpose."

"So what happens after this jolly weekend? What happens to those kids who still haven't found their way to your narrow idea of paradise? What will you do to them then? Have them put away?"

"That is why the gentlefolk of the press are here," he answered suavely. "To inform their audience to treat such individuals with compassion."

"That would certainly be a change from what I've heard…"

"You will insist on listening to scurrilous rumours. I assure you, and the rest of the world, that my only desire is to repair any wrong or hurt that has befallen them and usher in a new age of kindness and consideration for those little ones who, through no fault of their own, are shut out. They are still a precious part of the Dawn Prince's flock, remember – and our future after all."

Kate folded her arms. She wasn't buying any of this snake oil.

"Sounds like a blatant PR exercise in damage limitation to me," she said. "It's got 'desperate stunt' stamped all over it."

The Ismus's eyes glittered at her.

"Why don't we go outside," he suggested, "and see what delights we have planned, before the children arrive? I'm sure your readers and viewers would find it most fascinating. The world should see what merry times are to be had in this, united, kingdom. There is nothing for them to be afraid of."

He rose and his entourage moved with him to the doors. The crowd of press followed.

Kate hung back with Sam.

"I thought he was going to set his goons on you just now," Sam said, lowering the camera. "Don't push him too far, Kate."

"He may be a crazy-assed sociopath," she replied, "but he's not stupid. He needs to keep us sweet right now. His grand plan isn't going as smooth as he expected. He's more anxious than ever to show the world his warped vision of Merrie Olde England."

"I don't get why he asked you back here in that case. You're never going to give him a glowing testimonial."

The woman agreed. "Just remember what I told you," she warned. "Eat and drink only what we brought with us. If someone offers you anything, don't touch it, not even if it's an unopened can of soda."

"Sure thing! Hey, do you think it's true the Queen of England thinks she's a miller's wife and now bakes all the bread in Buckingham Palace?"

"Nothing would surprise me any more. OK, let's go out there and do our job."

The sun was finally attempting to break through the cheerless clouds and the spring flowers threw out their deepest colours. Four horses, arrayed in the pageantry of Mooncaster's Royal Houses, were standing patiently by one of the cabins. A group of mummers were rehearsing and the narrow road outside the compound was already lined with cars and vans. Musicians and brightly dressed folk in the best replicas of Mooncaster apparel had arrived to make this an extra special celebration.

Here and there, in the gathering crowd, snatches of song could be heard and toes were pointed as steps of courtly dances were practised and instruments were plucked, or strummed or blown into. One of the horses leaned forward and grazed idly on the cascading blooms of a hanging basket.

With this in the background, Kate recorded an introductory segment to camera, explaining the farcical pantomime that was being put on today for the world to witness.

It was another forty minutes before the first cheerfully painted coach came lumbering up the forest road. The Ismus and his tame press crews stepped forward to welcome the weekend's special guests.

"Here they are!" he declared, holding his arms wide. "Our lost and lonely lambs. What a time they shall have; what pleasures and adventures lie in store for them."

Pulling Sam through the crowd, Kate Kryzewski ploughed her way to the front and directed his lens up at the coach's windows as it slowed to a stop.

Dozens of young faces were pressed against the glass.

"Oh my God," she whispered. "Those poor kids. They look shell-shocked."

No one would have believed the children in the coach were coming for a "glorious" weekend. Their little faces were sombre and still and a measure of fear dimmed every eye. Some had been crying. The adults who sat beside them had not bothered to wipe those tears away. Kate scanned along the wide windows. There was a mix of ages. Some appeared as young as seven but, here and there, were sullen teenagers who refused to look out and were staring morosely at the headrest immediately in front of them. Only the adults in the coach seemed excited to be here. They were all grinning and pointing and waving and laughing.

The door of the coach slid open.

At once the musicians struck up a joyous tune and the carollers sang a Maying song from the book.

"Welcome!" the Ismus called. "Welcome, one and all!"

The parents of the children rushed out, keen to breathe the same rarefied air as the Holy Enchanter and see the Jacks and Jills who were now seated upon the horses and were saluting and nodding in greeting.

Kate hadn't even tried to interview any of those four. They were too deeply immersed in this madness to shed any light on it. They were living puppets, enslaved to the wishes of the Ismus, and had almost forgotten their original identities completely.

But at that moment she wasn't thinking of them. She urgently wanted to speak to these stunned-looking kids. Impatient, she waited for the adults to leave the vehicle and, when no child came following, she jumped on to the coach, dragging Sam with her.

Right away her nostrils were assaulted by the rank stink of that foul plant and she saw that the seats and floor were strewn with stalks and well-chewed fibrous lumps. She knew the slimy debris was down to the adults. Minchet didn't work on these kids. That was why they were here.

Seventeen children were still sitting in their allocated seats, dotted evenly down the length of the coach. The younger ones stared up at her, confused and unsure, cuddly toys clenched in desperate headlocks.

It had been a long journey. They had been collected from across the southern counties and hadn't been allowed to sit together or talk to one another for the entire trip. Kate doubted if they even wanted to. They looked so withdrawn and unwilling to make eye contact with one another.

Kate was moved in the same way the grieving families of Gaza, Baghdad and Haiti had moved her when she reported from there. But she was a veteran at detachment. She had an important job to do and she trusted Sam to capture and linger on the children's frightened, damaged expressions. It would make striking footage.

"Hi," she began quickly. "My name is Kate and I'm a reporter for American TV. This scruffy guy with the camera is Sam. You don't have to be scared of us. We're your friends. We haven't read that book. We haven't tasted that minchet stuff. We're on your side."

Someone at the back hissed through his teeth. Kate looked over to where a pair of Nike trainers poked between two headrests, but whoever it was had slouched too far down and she couldn't see who they belonged to.

"If I could have a few words with some of you," she continued, fiercely aware that this precious time alone with them was limited. She was amazed no one had already come running in after her to shepherd the children out. A cursory glance through the window told her the Ismus was being mobbed by the kids' parents and his bodyguards were being kept very busy. Good.

"Please, Miss," a girl of seven near the front piped up in a timid whisper. "I've been sick."

Kate went over to her. "What's your name, sweetheart?" she asked.

"Puke-arella!" a boy of twelve said before she had a chance to answer.

The girl's face crumpled, but she didn't cry.

Kate glared at the boy. "Hey, watch your mouth, wise-ass," she told him.

The boy looked up at her with an anguished, jumbled expression of gratitude and helplessness on his face. Then he burst into tears. That one rebuke was the most normal interaction he'd had in the past few months. Kate bit the inside of her cheek. Dear God, this was tough. These poor kids were totally messed up and traumatised.

"It's OK," she told him in a gentler tone. "You're going to be all right. My report is going to show the whole of America what's happening here. You'll be fine. I promise."

Another dismissive hiss sounded from beyond those Nikes at the back.

"Christina," the girl who had been ill voiced meekly. "My name's Christina."

The front of her dress was soaked in a spectacular display of sick. It was cold and Kate wondered how long her parents had let her sit like that. How could they not care? How could they forget all the love they must have had for her before the pages of that book ruined everything? Which of those hyper couples, now fawning over the Ismus and capering around the Jacks, trying to get their autographs and have their pictures taken with them, were her mom and dad?

"Well, don't you worry, Christina," Kate said, taking hold of her small hand and squeezing it comfortingly. "We'll find you clean clothes and have you feeling better in no time."

"The cases are in the luggage hold," a new voice piped up. It belonged to an older, studious-looking girl, with short, mouse-coloured hair, wearing a shapeless, apple-green cardigan and faded, baggy jeans. "You really think *they'll* let you broadcast this? You're a deludanoid."

Kate ignored that for the moment. "Hi," she said. "And who are you? Where's that lovely accent from?"

"Jody. From Bristol. Could you be any more patronising?"

"Hello, Jody. And what would you like to say to the Americans watching this?"

The girl looked away. "Not much," she answered flatly. "They'll find out soon enough I reckon."

"I'd really like to hear your story, Jody," Kate persevered. "I'm sure it's a fascinating one."

Still gazing into space, the girl shook her head. "Nothing to tell," she answered. "'Cept I've been in this cattle wagon for eight hours an' there weren't enough bog stops."

"What about *Dancing Jax*? How has it affected your life and that of your family and friends?"

Jody shrugged. It was obvious she was afraid to criticise any aspect of the book. "Just didn't work on me, that's all," she answered evasively. "It didn't work on none of us in here. We're duds – rejects."

"That isn't true!" Kate said sternly. "You're the innocent victims of some mass hysteria, a nationwide sickness that we haven't been able to understand yet. But it is containable. I'm going to use this report to ensure you all get away from this country, to places of safety where this won't ever touch you. The UN is going to intervene and begin putting everything right."

The older children turned their eyes away. They had experienced too many crushed hopes in recent months to invest in any more. The younger ones, however, grew excited. One of them punched the air and another cheered.

"Raindrops on roses, whiskers on kittens," Jody mumbled with weary sarcasm.

Kate knew exactly what she meant. Pity and promises weren't what they needed. But first things first…

"This is what's going to happen," she told them. "Sam is going to walk down the middle here and I want each of you to look into the camera and state your name, age and where you're from. Speak up nice and clear – you'll be famous the world over."

Again the hiss sounded at the back.

The reporter liked whoever that was. At least one of these kids had some fight left in him. She'd get to Nike boy soon, but first she told Sam to start. She knew it was of vital importance to get a record of the kids. Heaven knows what the real intention of the Ismus was, but it certainly wasn't to give them a fun weekend. She'd stake her life on that.

As Sam moved down the coach, they heard the noise of another vehicle approaching. Kate stared out and saw a second coach driving up the forest road.

"More rejects," Jody observed.

It turned into the compound and parked close by. Again eager parents came piling out first. Kate saw more wretched young faces left behind in their seats.

Sam concentrated on the task at hand. The older kids gave their names grudgingly; the ones of around ten and eleven did it with stilted shyness. Most of the youngest stood up to do it, with emphatic nods. Others had to be prompted to speak louder.

"Daniel Foster, nine and a quarter, Weymouth."

"Beth McCormack, Marlborough, twelve."

"Patrick… Patrick Hunter, eight… ummm Horsham – twenty-three Elm Tree Grove."

"Christina Carter, I'm seven and a half and… I've forgotten."

"Never mind, honey," Kate reassured her.

"Jody, fourteen, Bristol and you're wasting your time."

"Mason Stuart from Ashford, eleven."

"Brenda Jenkins, ten, Epsom."

"Rupesh Karim, Upton Park, nine."

The next child was a thin, frail-looking boy with an ashen face. There was a large bruise on his forehead. Sam made sure the camera picked that up. The boy stared dumbly into the lens, like a startled baby bird.

"And what's your name, little buddy?" Sam asked.

The boy mouthed something inaudible, then murmured a bit louder, "I'm seven."

"Tell the folks in the US who you are," Sam coaxed.

The boy took a breath and the bruise crinkled as he frowned with concentration.

"I think I was called Thomas Williams," he began in a bewildered, faltering voice. "But now… now…"

"Now? What do your mom and dad call you?"

"Punchbag."

Sam choked. He laid the camera down and put his arms round him. Other children craned their heads round the seats to see. From their envious stares, Kate realised they were completely starved of affection and had forgotten what a hug felt like.

She clenched her teeth, but banked the anger for later. She'd seen and heard enough. The crass PR stunt that Ismus creep had planned to pull today had blown up in his arrogant face. What good press was he hoping to wring from these abused and neglected kids? One thing was certain, they weren't going to spend another day in this malignant, twisted country. She'd get each one of them out somehow.

"It really is Julie Andrews time," she said, taking out her mobile. "I'm calling Harry. He'll know who to yell at or put the squeeze on to cut through the red tape and BS. We're out of here, Sam, and the kids are coming with us – if it means sending in the goddamn marines."

She found her producer's number in New York and pressed the phone to her ear, waiting for it to connect. Suddenly a shrill squeal filled the coach and she dropped the phone as if it had bitten her. The screen went blank, no signal – no nothing.

"Sam," she urged. "Get your cell. Call Harry."

The cameraman obeyed hurriedly. The same piercing shriek blasted from his mobile.

The younger children stared at them. Jody grunted and muttered under her breath. At the back of the coach the hiss was replaced by a mocking snort.

"Has anyone got a cellphone?" Kate begged. "I need to speak to people who can get you out of here, away from this."

Several hands rose slowly. Then, at the back, the trainers withdrew and the angry face of a black youth reared up from behind the seats.

"What is wrong with you?" he shouted at the reporter. "You terminal stupid or something? *They* won't let you call nobody. They'll burst every phone you try."

"He's right," Sam said. "They're jamming us. We can't call out – we can't contact anyone."

Kate clenched her hands. She should have expected something like this, but even in the most remote places of the world she'd always managed to get her reports back to the network. Still, she wasn't overly worried yet. She should have been.

"Thanks," she addressed the boy at the back. "What's your name?"

"You don't need my name, lady and I ain't interested in yours, cos you and Spielberg there are the biggest fools I seen in a long while. What you even doing here? You're a couple of turkeys who don't know it's Christmas. You don't know nothin'!"

Thumping the headrest, he dived back on to his seat, pushed in his earphones and turned up the volume of his MP3 player.

"My laptop's in the hire car," Kate told Sam. "I'll go email Harry and get things moving."

"You think they won't be jamming the Internet as well?"

"That's what I admire about you, Sam, always so positive. If they're doing that, I'll just have to drive till I'm out of range."

"I'll come with you."

"No, stay here and finish what you're doing. Then get over to that other bus and do the same. It's important."

She clapped her hands. "Listen up, kids," she said. "I need to leave for a little while, but I'll be back. Sam is staying and I want you to start talking to one another and make friends. OK? You're in this situation together now. You have to pal up and begin looking out for one another. You hear me?"

The muted responses were not encouraging.

"Oh my days!" Jody observed sharply. "What Top Shop travesty is assaulting my eyes out there?"

She was staring out of the window at the second coach, where a teenage girl dressed in a pink and white leather outfit was looking expectantly about her, searching for the news crews and smiling widely for any cameras.

"Tanorexic Barbie spawn," Jody commented. "With an IQ lower than the dead animals she's wearing. What plastic planet is she on?"

Kate Kryzewski was too focused on composing the urgent email she was going to send to even look. She turned to hurry back to the door. Then she halted and drew a sharp breath.

There was the Ismus. His lean, velvet-clad frame ascended the two steps into the coach and he broke into a crooked grin. The younger children shrank down into their seats.

"Welcome, my pretty pigeons," he greeted. "Time for you to fly into the sunshine and see what delights and marvels have been prepared. Such fun you shall have."

He prowled closer to Kate and brought his face uncomfortably near. "We wouldn't want them to miss a moment of what's in store for them, would we?" he said, breathing dead, stagnant air upon her.

4

THE TEENAGER IN pink and white leather was oblivious to the sneers directed at her from Jody in the first coach. She was too busy flicking her blonde hair extensions back and casting a critical eye at her reflection in the glass of the vehicle's door. Her mother was just as eager to meet the Ismus and the Jacks as the other parents, but she had resisted the powerful urge and remained with the girl.

"Make sure you get your face on camera as much as possible," she instructed. "Soon as the rush dies down, we'll move in. You latch on to his Lordship and hang in there like a limpet."

The girl nodded. "I know," she said. "Like he's a Clooney or a Rooney. Aww, I made a poem, innit!"

"And remember, you're here to learn as well as get your face in the papers and glossies. I don't know why the book hasn't worked for you yet, but I'm sure there's a good reason. Just taking a bit longer with you than the rest of us."

"It's not cos I'm fick, Ma."

"I didn't say you was. But this is your big chance – don't cock it up. What has your mother always said? 'You have to turn every setback into a lesson to do better next time.'"

"You ain't never said that! You always told me to act dumb and common cos no one likes a clever bird."

"Well, I'm saying it now. There might not be a next time after this. You've got to grab this chance by the curlies and make the most of it. You're gonna wake up from this miserable dream world sometime this weekend and find out you're royalty – a Jill or higher, not a three of clubs laundress like me. Can't be nothing else with that pretty face."

"I'm a princess, innit," the girl told herself. "You an' Uncle Frank always said I was."

Her mother gave her an appraising look then prodded her chest. "You got those chicken fillets in? Should have used ostrich's. Put your shoulders back so they stick out more."

"Do they have things like these in Mooncaster?" the girl asked. "I don't wanna be no flat-chested munter when I wake up there. I wanna good boob rack."

"Don't you worry about that. We've got corsets and bodices to show off our milk puddings a treat. It's Boots' make-up counter I miss when I'm there and those other silly fripperies they have here in my dreams. I'm not sure about sleeping with raw bacon on my eyes to keep the crows' feet at bay or rubbing goose fat on my poor chapped fingers. If I could afford some of the Queen of Hearts' concoctions, I would, but laundresses don't earn many sixpences – silver coin isn't easy to come by. I'm not complaining – that's just how life is there and it's a bushel better than here, I promise you."

"You don't half talk funny since you been goin' there. It's mad. Like you're in an old film about history, like that *Shakespeare's Got Love*. It's not fair the book hasn't worked on me. It should of. You know how hard I been tryin'. You know me an' readin' don't get on, unless it's *Cosmo* or *Hello* or a catalogue or Garfield or a text message. That book's the longest fing I ever read in my life. Took me over a month solid an' I've done it dunno how many times since – and had that sloppy minchet stuff in all my Slim Fasts an' mixed in with my avocado salads, but I'm still bleedin' here! What's that about then?"

Her mother shushed her. The Black Face Dames had emerged from the first coach, leading a straggly line of unhappy children. The musicians played with even more gusto and dancers came skipping forward to perform. The Ismus was there, accompanied by a woman and a straw-haired young man who was busily filming the last few children emerging from the vehicle. The black youth at the very end pushed the lens out of his face and gave him the finger.

"There's His Highness, the Holy Enchanter!" her mother exclaimed. "And there's a camera – perfect moment. Get in there!"

The girl didn't need any persuasion. She tottered hastily over the grass in her pink diamanté heels, making a beeline for the Ismus.

Kate Kryzewski was wondering how she could get away from him and his bodyguards and make it to the car without being noticed, when the girl and her mother bore down on them.

"Your Lordship!" the woman cried, bobbing into a curtsy. "I am Widow Tallowax of the wash house. A lowly matron, though of good character, far beneath your notice I'm sure. After a long day at the steaming coppers, when I nod off on my comfy rocker by the ingle, I find myself here where I am this girl's mother. The pity of it is the poor mite can't find her way back to the castle so we've no idea who she really is, but she's a rare beauty and obviously a personage of quality and standing whom no doubt the Limner will be sure to paint a likeness of."

The Ismus listened with faint amusement.

"And what is your name here?" he asked, addressing the girl directly.

"Charm," the teenager said, nodding perkily and pushing her shoulders back. "Charm Benedict, but we dropped the last bit. It were goin' to be Charm Bracelet for my modellin', but Uncle Frank, he's my manager, said that were a bit naff. I really liked it, but he said brands work best with just one word and he's right when you fink about it. So it's just Charm now, innit?"

The girl thrust her arm through his and ran a hand over his sleeve.

"This velvet is well lush," she said enthusiastically. "You look well elegant. Ooh, that sounds funny! Is there such a word as 'welegant'? There should be."

"Thank you, now if I may…"

"I bet you're an After Eight!"

"A what?"

"You know… them skinny square chocs at posh dinner parties. See – I reckon everyone has their own flavour. You're classy, right – like an After Eight. There it is, nice and slim in its special little bag fing, all dark chocolate but wiv a minty cream fillin'. Smoove an' sleek on the outside, zingy like toothpaste in the middle. Hidden Depps – like the actor."

"She's always putting flavours to people," her mother added, beckoning to Sam to bring his camera over. "It's just one of the pretty quirks she has. I'm cookie dough apparently. Tell them what you are, Charm, go on."

The girl managed to flick her hair back and swivel both herself and the Ismus round so that the camera was fully on them.

"I'm a rainbow sherbet," she said with a perfected smile. "Mixed with that space dust stuff, so I froth and sparkle with sweetness on your tongue."

"Effervesce," her mother corrected in a muttered aside. "Froth makes you sound like you've got rabies."

The Ismus tried to disentangle himself, but the girl wasn't going to let him escape that easily.

"I am well looking forward to this weekend!" she declared, clinging on with determination. "I'm so excited I could wet my knickers. This is what I've been waiting for, ever since the book come out and I couldn't get my head round it. There's no one who wants to go to Mooncaster more'n I do. Me ma's told me so much. Sounds amazin'! I am going to work so hard and make sure I get there. I'll do anyfink I will. Look what I had done soon as I knew I was coming here."

She unzipped her leather jacket and lifted a skimpy T-shirt to show the heart-shaped, pink diamanté stud that pierced her navel.

"You getting that?" she asked Sam, angling her midriff so the diamanté glinted in the sunlight. "Matches my Dolce Gabbanas as well, see. Course I don't know what I'll be when I wake up in the castle, but I hope it's Hearts, cos I luuurve 'em; them's the prettiest, but I don't mind what I am – honest. I can change this for whatever. Diamonds would be well good."

Sam kept the lens on her. The teenager's attitude was the weirdest he had encountered so far. She babbled away like a Valley girl, not letting the banal chatter drop for a moment. She fired off questions then gabbled over the answers and her mother chipped in whenever there was a pause for breath. The longer this went on the better, thought Sam, because Kate had slipped quietly away.

Kate Kryzewski made it to the hire car without any hindrance. Market stalls displaying food fit for a medieval banquet had been set up right in front of it. This ye olde bake sale formed the perfect screen. The car was completely hidden from view.

Once inside, she quickly typed the explosive email that would jump-start America and the UN into action.

"Blue touchpaper well and truly lit," she told herself as she clicked on send. But there was no wireless signal.

"Failure to launch. Damn you, Sam for being right."

The reporter frowned and thought calmly. Maybe there just wasn't any coverage in this nowhere place anyway. She slid across into the driver's seat and turned the engine over. She'd drive to the nearest village or town, until that little graphic began to blink on her laptop.

Kate glanced in the mirror to reverse out, but braked sharply. While she had been typing, a large wooden wagon loaded with hay bales had been wheeled directly behind, blocking her in.

"Unbelievable!" she seethed impatiently.

There was nothing for it but to get out of the car and get the wagon moved. But there was nobody near it and no one she asked had seen who put it there.

"The carter'll be having a mug of ale, most like," a pie-seller told her. "Try asking over yonder, at the brewer's stall. There's a tidy crowd there."

Kate glanced across, but it was too close to where the Ismus was being monopolised by that teenage wannabe.

She returned to the wagon and pushed against it. The thing wouldn't budge. How did it even get here? There had to have been a horse pulling it. She ran back to the pie-seller. He was a big, beefy man with thick forearms and looked strong as an ox.

"Hi again," she said, with her most winning smile. "I wonder – could you please do me a massive favour? I don't want to disturb the wagon guy if he's having a beer. I'm sure if we both push, that thing'll move out of the way and I can get my car out."

The man stared back at her blankly.

"I can't leave my pies unattended," he told her. "Not when the Jack of Diamonds is about. He'll nab the lot soon as my back is turned. Beggin' your pardon, Mistress, but you won't find none here in the market who'll neglect their wares whilst Magpie Jack's around."

Kate understood. No one was going to help her. The wagon had been put there deliberately to keep her inside the camp.

"Fine," she uttered. "Just fine – dammit."

But it wasn't fine. The unspoken menace here was mounting. She'd been in tight spots before, but this, this was something else. She wished she'd brought a truck full of US troops with her instead of one laid-back Californian cameraman. Why did she always think she could handle any situation on her own? Why did she think she was Teflon-coated?

For the first time in too long she thought of her father. He had served in the military all his life. By the age of nine, she had lived in half the US army bases in the world. Kate hadn't spoken to him in three years. Their political views were poles apart and the last row had been nuclear with lots of fallout. Still, if he was here now, he'd have broken the Ismus's jaw before those blacked-up bodyguards had guessed what was coming. At that moment, Kate would have given anything to see that. She smiled faintly at the thought and promised herself that, after this, she'd make the first move and call Lieutenant Colonel Pete Kryzewski and say, "Hi, Dad."

She took off her jacket, retrieved the laptop and wrapped it inside. Holding them under her arm, she cast a careful glance towards the coaches and moved quickly but discreetly through the bustling people. Everyone under the influence of that book appeared to be having the time of their lives. Carollers were singing and the minstrels were filling the spring sunshine with lively music. Kate kept to the edge of the crowds and wove her way towards the main gates. If she ducked around the far side of the second coach, she could reach the forest road without being spotted.

The urge to run was strong, but she forced herself to walk as nonchalantly as possible. The children and teens from this other coach were now standing in front of it, bewildered and ill at ease. Kate saw the same traumatised expressions on them as before. She didn't dare stop or speak to them. It was vital to get this email sent.

She ducked round the side of the vehicle and sprinted along the length of it. Then she checked her pace and sneaked out of the camp gates.

The narrow forest road stretched in front of her. Kate looked searchingly at the lines of cars parked on either side. She couldn't keep darting to and fro, checking every car. Someone would be sure to spot her. Choosing the left-hand verge, she hurried past the cars parked there, trying the doors.

"Come on," she whispered urgently. "Show me some keys! There's no larceny in this country any more, right? No reason to worry about auto theft. Why do you Brits have to be so uptight, even when you're all nuts? Just one set of keys in the ignition. I'm not fussy – doesn't have to be a Porsche."

It was no use. Every vehicle was locked. Finally she understood why. The owners had known the Jack of Diamonds was going to be here today. His character in the book was cursed with itchy palms. He couldn't help himself. He stole anything he took a liking to. The drivers weren't taking any chances with that roguish Knave at large.

Kate uttered a curse of her own. She would have to reach the nearest village, or wherever she could get a signal, on foot.

Half running, she set off down the tree-lined road and tried to recall the journey that morning. Sam had been driving and she had been concentrating on her notes, so barely noticed the landscape they passed through. Sam had commented at the time that this place wasn't his idea of a forest. Sure, there were lots of trees, but they were clumped in many separate areas of woodland, interspersed with open tracts of heath and pasture. His idea of an English forest was based solely on Robin Hood and King Arthur movies and some of them were cartoons. Still, she remembered he had pointed out several riding centres, hotels and restaurants along the route. Surely they couldn't survive without Internet bookings?

It took her ten minutes to reach the junction where the narrow road joined a wider way. Kate knew they had turned right off there. Staying close to the trees, she began retracing their journey and unwrapped the laptop from her jacket.

Still no signal.

She swore under her breath and hastened on.

Behind her, in the camp, a horn sounded a warbling fanfare and a great cheer went up. She wondered what that meant – the call to a mass reading or a free-for-all at the pie stall? She hoped Sam would have the sense to get in the car whilst any reading took place. She'd briefed him on it enough times before they arrived. It was too dangerous to risk hearing just one sentence from that infernal book.

Suddenly she stopped walking and whipped her head around. She could hear the thudding of horses galloping along the road and the whooping of the following crowd.

"Oh, Jeez," she breathed. "They really are totally insane."

Now she understood why that horn had been blown. It was the start of a hunt, and they were hunting her.

Kate clutched the laptop tightly and ran. She was in good shape – female reporters had to be or they didn't get on TV. She went to the gym three times a week and did plenty of cardio: rowing machine, bike, stepper, always finishing with half an hour on the treadmill and when she didn't go there, she jogged.

She had to get off this road. So far, the riders hadn't emerged on to the main road and she wanted to be out of sight when they did. The trees on the other side grew sparsely and she saw a stretch of open heath beyond them.

Kate dashed over and jumped into the thin woodland opposite. She had seen a car in the distance headed this way. She hoped the driver hadn't spotted her, or if they had, wouldn't be suspicious of a woman haring across the road. It was a ridiculous hope.

Not looking back, she plunged into the trees and then out over the green expanse of coarse, scrubby heathland.

The Jack of Clubs' horse was the first to clatter out on to the main road. He reined it around, looking right and left for the fleeing reporter. Presently the other riders were alongside him.

"Where is she?" the Jill of Spades asked. "Did you mark where she went?"

Jack shook his head. "We must divide our number," he instructed. "You come with me; we shall take the left way. The others must ride yonder!"

"Why can I not go with you?" the Jill of Hearts asked. "I like the look of that left way better."

"Are you sure it is the *way* you prefer the look of?" the Jill of Spades asked pointedly.

The girls exchanged spiked glances. By now the car was almost level with them. It slowed to a stop and the driver, a woman in her fifties with a five of clubs pinned to her coat, got out and sank to her knees.

"My Lords and Ladies!" she exclaimed, elated beyond measure. "A mighty honour this is, to find you here, in my grey dream – of all places! 'Tis really you! Our dear own Jacks and Jills, right in front of me, here in this nothing place! How blessed I am!"

The Jill of Spades sneered at her and the Jack of Diamonds leaned over to whisper in the Jill of Hearts' ear. They laughed together.

"Good mistress," the Jack of Clubs declared, with a charming smile. "We are hunting one who has defied the Holy Enchanter. Have you seen sign of her?"

The woman nodded her head vigorously. "Just seconds ago!" she cried, delighted to be of assistance and pointing with excitement back down the road. "She ran across that way, through those trees!"

The Jack of Clubs thanked her and they spurred their horses on.

"Blessed be!" the woman shouted after them.

She rose to her feet just as a black SUV, with impenetrable tinted windows, pulled out of the forest road, flanked and followed by a crowd of stern-looking people.

"These dreams are so peculiar," the woman said, getting back into her modest hatchback.

Kate Kryzewski was over halfway across the heath when she heard the horses' hooves leave the tarmac and come thumping on to the grass behind.

Another area of woodland spread out ahead. If she could reach that, the riders might not be able to follow. But, as she ran nearer, she saw the trees were too evenly spaced to prove any obstacle to her pursuers. Her efforts would be wasted. Undeterred, she sped on. One thing those early years growing up in army bases had taught her: you never gave up.

The galloping came closer and closer.

Kate sprinted past the first of the trees and looked around wildly. Filtering through new spring leaves, the warm sunshine caused the bluebell-carpeted floor to glow. It was an enchanting, idyllic place, but its beauty was lost on the reporter. Escape was all she could think of.

Some distance away there was a dense thicket of young birches. No horse could get through there. With renewed hope, she tore off diagonally towards it.

The four riders came charging into the wood.

Before *Dancing Jax* had ensnared them, not one of those teenagers had ever ridden a horse. The book had made them masters of the saddle. Now, flushed with the thrill of the chase, the Jacks stood in their stirrups and urged their steeds on. The Jill of Spades applied her riding whip and the horses thundered through the bluebells.

Kate called on her last reserve of strength. The birches were almost within reach. She might just make it.

"Bring the peasant down!" the Jill of Spades cried, pulling a dagger from her belt and waving it threateningly.

Kate felt the ground shudder. The horses were almost upon her. A snorting breath blasted against her neck. She yelled and, with an extra spurt of energy, flung herself forward. The horses shied and reared behind her as she stumbled into the cover of the birches. She heard the Jacks call out in anger and frustration and she gave a rueful grin before hurrying on.

As she ran, she discarded the jacket and fumbled with the laptop. To her overwhelming relief and surprise, the wireless symbol was blinking. She couldn't believe it and staggered to a stop. Her fingers were shaking from exertion and fear and it took two attempts to reopen the email.

"Go…" she blessed it breathlessly. "Get this party started."

But the email was never sent. At that moment, a violent blow punched into her spine. The laptop flew from her hands and suddenly she was on the ground – her face buried in bluebells.

Almost immediately she flipped over on to her back and there was the Jack of Diamonds standing astride her, looking very pleased with himself. He had leaped off his horse and come tearing after her.

Having just turned twelve, he was the youngest of the Jacks. Kate knew everything about him, who he had been before the book had taken control.

"You're Paul," she panted desperately. "Paul Thornbury."

"Be silent, serf!" he commanded. "You must not address me so."

"I've spoken to Martin Baxter. You remember him. You and your mother lived with him in Felixstowe, remember?"

"I am the Jack of Diamonds!" the boy retorted haughtily. "Son and heir of an Under King. I will not heed such untruths from so common a ditch trull as you!"

Kate shook her head in exasperation. He was too profoundly lost in the book's power. There wasn't time for this.

"In dances Magpie Jack," the boy began to chant, the expression draining from his face and his eyes staring fixedly ahead, the pupils dark and glassy. "So hide what he may lack. In his palm there is an itch and the spell he cannot crack. Jools and trinkets he will…"

"Oh, shut up, Your Royal Jackness!" the woman snapped. With an angry yell, she brought her legs up and kicked him in the chest.

The boy cried out in astonishment and tumbled backwards, hurled off balance.

Kate scrambled to her knees. The laptop was still open and lying upside down, just out of reach. The woman lunged for it, but the heel of a riding boot slammed her aside. Then she felt a steel blade press against her neck.

"You dare strike out at a Prince of the Royal House of Diamonds?" the Jill of Spades snarled. "You will die for this, serf!"

Kate twisted around and saw the fierce expression on the girl's face. She knew that was no empty threat.

"Emma Taylor," the reporter told her. "Your name is Emma Taylor. Think before you do this. You're Emma Taylor!"

"I know who I am in my dreams!" the teenager scoffed. "What business is it of yours?"

"This isn't a dream! This is the real world. There is no White Castle. There is no Mooncaster! You're caught up in some mad delusion. If you use that knife, you'll be committing murder."

The teenager snorted with scorn.

"The girl Emma is already guilty of so many crimes," she boasted. "What is one more? It will make good viewing for her reality show here."

Behind her, the Jack of Clubs and the Jill of Hearts were dismounting and the Jack of Diamonds picked himself up, brushing grass from his doublet.

"Is it proper for serfs and thieves to affront and assail us so?" asked the Jill of Hearts. "Dispatch her quick and let us return to the merrymaking."

The Jill of Spades grinned cruelly and turned the dagger in her hand, admiring the sunlight flashing over the blade.

"Hold!" the Jack of Clubs ordered. "The Ismus wishes her unharmed."

"That Ismus is a sick, psycho wack-job!" Kate blurted. "You kids don't know what you're doing!"

The teenagers ignored her. Everyone had heard a car approaching. They turned and saw the SUV stopping at the edge of the wood. The three Black Face Dames got out and strode towards them.

The bodyguards seized Kate roughly. They pulled her to her feet and dragged her over to the car. There was no point trying to struggle against them.

The Ismus was leaning casually against a wheel arch, his arms folded.

Behind the vehicle, a large crowd, dressed in their Mooncaster best, was waiting in expectant silence. The reporter saw many parents of the newly arrived children among them. She wondered what was happening back at the compound. What was the Ismus really up to? What did he really plan to do with those poor kids?

"Miss Kryzewski," he hailed her. "How ill-mannered of you to leave the festivities without bidding adieu."

"Oh, gee," she replied sarcastically. "Did I forget my goody bag?"

"You left before the reading commenced."

"Yeah, well, that's one treat I can skip. Thanks for having me. I had a real swell time. Now tell your Jolson homies to let go of my arms."

The man merely smiled back at her and held out his hand. One of the Harlequin Priests stepped from the crowd. With a reverent bow, he handed him a copy of *Dancing Jax*.

"The plan was for you to hear the sacred text read by one of our greatest Shakespearean actors," he told her. "In a more intimate, cosy setting than this. But I do believe yours is the better choice. Let it be alfresco. It's such a lovely day."

He nodded to the crowd and every single one of them took a copy of the book from a large pocket or bag and turned to the first page in unison. It was the most chilling and sinister sight Kate had ever seen.

"You can't do this!" she shouted. "I'm an American citizen! You have no idea how severe the consequences of your actions here will be. My country will instigate full and major punitive measures on your skinny ass!"

The Ismus chuckled mildly. "After the glowing report you're going to send in about this wonderful weekend?" he asked. "I very much doubt that, Miss Kryzewski."

"They having snowball fights in hell today? Cos that's the only time I'll be doing anything you want."

The man's chuckle turned into a full-blooded laugh.

"If you only knew how droll that was," he told her. "But no, you will do just as I ask. Why else do you think I invited you back?"

Kate pulled and tugged at her arms, but the bodyguards gripped her more fiercely than ever.

"Now shall we begin?" the Ismus asked. "Are you comfortable? Perhaps not, but you will be very soon. I promise."

The woman glared back at him. "You won't convert me so easy," she growled. "Come on – bring out your best Shakespeare guy, let's see what he's got. Personally I always thought your actors were overrated, only good for playing bad guys in dumb action movies. I'm a Pacino girl through and through."

"I guessed as much," the Ismus replied. "That is why I thought it would be more amusing to have someone more familiar read to you."

He rapped his knuckles on the SUV's roof. The rear door opened slowly and a tear rolled down Kate's cheek when she saw who got out. She screwed her face up and turned away.

"Hello, Sam," the Ismus greeted him.

5

THE YOUNG CAMERAMAN smiled shyly, the lids of his glassy eyes blinking sleepily. Then he tore another impassioned bite from the grey, slimy fruit in his hand. The livid juices had already stained his chin.

"Here's the book, Sam," the Ismus said. "It's time for Miss Kryzewski to join us in the Realm of the Dawn Prince."

Sam shoved the rest of the minchet in his mouth and chewed it urgently. Then he wiped his hands and took hold of *Dancing Jax*.

"Don't do it, Sam!" Kate pleaded. "Please don't."

The fair-haired man swallowed the fibrous lumps in his mouth and grinned. "It's all right, Kate," he assured her. "It's just like they said. We were dead wrong. This place, this crap – it isn't real. We belong in Mooncaster. You'll see."

He lowered his eyes and began to read.

"Beyond the Silvering Sea, within thirteen green, girdling hills…"

The assembled crowd muttered along with him, following the words as he read them aloud. The Jacks and Jills came to join them and everyone began to nod their heads in time to the rhythm of the sentences.

Kate Kryzewski felt the day darken around her. The sunlight dimmed and a faint buzzing sounded in her head. She tried to think of something else, anything – it didn't matter what.

The hairs on the back of her neck prickled and the skin crept on her scalp as something drew close to her.

She blotted out Sam's voice and flooded her mind with her most vivid memories: a child searching the rubble of Haiti for her mother, the smoking wreck of a bus after a suicide bomb in Gaza, a rocket attack over Baghdad that made the night bright as day, pouring a glass of Merlot over Harlon Webber's hair plugs when he made a pass at her at the Emmys, the crooked smile of the Ismus…

Frantically she shook that last image out of her head. Sam's voice filled her ears. She couldn't blot it out any more. She couldn't fight any longer. She had to listen. There was nothing else.

Before the darkness rushed in, one final thought of her own flickered briefly.

"Poppa, I'm so sorry!" she cried.

The Ismus's stark white face reared in her mind. His lean, hungry features were triumphant and she felt her will, her spirit, everything she was, spiralling out of her – till there was nothing left. She threw back her head and her eyes fluttered open. The tall white towers of a magnificent castle stood against the bright blue sky. She gasped in amazement. Then the Black Face Dames let go of her arms and she sprawled on the ground. The grass tickled her hands like feathers.

Columbine looked up from the goose on her lap and wiped her brow, leaving a faint smear of blood behind. Her fingers returned to the dead bird and she continued to mechanically rip the snowy feathers from its body. The goose's head dangled and jerked to the motion of her hands.

The kitchen was unusually quiet that wintry afternoon. Mistress Slab was in the slaughterhouse across the courtyard, elbow deep in a basin brimming with a bloody mixture. That pink, sticky mash of minced pork, breadcrumbs and herbs would soon be fed into empty lengths of pig intestine. The Mooncaster cook would not permit anyone else to learn the secret recipe of her sausages and always barred the slaughterhouse door when she was busy at this task.

Ned and Beetle, the kitchen boys, were in the village, bringing fresh loaves from the miller's wife in a barrow. Columbine was completely alone.

It was a huge kitchen, much larger than the four others that prepared the meals of the Royal Houses. It was kept at a constant summer heat by two great fires. Their flames shone in every copper pot that hung on the limewashed walls and sweat splashes were an ingredient in every dish that Mistress Slab prepared.

Columbine was used to the fires by now and she dressed in loose, ragged garments, patched and mended with more squares of cloth than a quilt. She was a young, red-haired girl whose face was only clean on high days or when the pranking kitchen boys carried her to the horse trough and threw her in. She went about her endless chores barefoot, for it was good to feel the cool flagstones under her soles and trail her grubby toes through the straw or cinders.

She never complained when Mistress Slab beat her with the largest wooden spoon if she found her idling. The girl knew how privileged she was to work in the castle and in rare free moments she would creep up the kitchen stairs and peep out at the finely dressed courtiers going by in the Great Hall. What a feast for the eyes they were, so sumptuously dressed and lordly. During the revels, when the music came filtering down into the kitchen, she would close her eyes and twirl in time to the dance, imagining herself draped in the finest gowns wearing slippers of golden silk.

But Mistress Slab's bear-like voice would always summon her from those reveries: the onions needed peeling or the grates needed sweeping or the spit needed turning or peas needed shelling or the butter needed churning.

When the goose was plucked naked, and looked faintly embarrassed to be in such a state, the girl sat back on the stool. She reached for the second bird she had been instructed to denude before the cook returned.

High above, on the battlements, a trumpet sounded. Down in the kitchen, Columbine heard and knew it heralded the return to Mooncaster of the Jack of Clubs from the day's hunt.

A delighted smile flashed over the girl's dirty face. She leaped from the stool and raced up the stairs to the passageway that linked to the Great Hall.

At the end of the passage a carved wooden screen hid the entrance from view of the nobles within. Columbine waited there, peering eagerly through the fretwork. Lords and their ladies came sweeping by, speaking of the day's adventure and how the Jack of Clubs had the almond hind in his sights at least twice, but refrained from loosing his bow. The Jill of Spades was most scornful. His love of beast and bird was well known, but such displays of mercy were foolishness.

Hearing their chatter, the girl grinned and moistened her lips. The Jack of Clubs always took a long time to enter the Great Hall, for he would not suffer any groom to stable Ironheart, his splendid horse. He did the work himself, speaking to it like a lover, and often slept in the stall for it was the last of the untameable steeds and there was no finer beast in the land.

Columbine stroked the back of the screen with her rough fingertips, impatient for a sight of the handsome youth. He was the pride of Mooncaster, the hero of many hearts, and his golden hair and steadfast voice were always capering through her dreams when she was away from this place.

The gossip of the Court fell to a hush and the Jack of Clubs came striding through the main doors. He laughed with the Jill of Hearts, who stepped forward to try and capture him with her beauty, and shared a pleasantry with his father, the King of Clubs.

Columbine drank in every detail: his curling hair that was likened to a ram's fleece bathed in the sunset, the soft, wispy moustache that curled at the ends and heightened his beguiling smile. The sleeves of his shirt were rolled up past the elbow and she clasped herself in her own grubby arms, breathless with imaginings. She closed her eyes and shivered with secret pleasure.

Suddenly a real hand closed tightly round her arm. She gasped in fright as a tall, portly man came sidling further behind the screen.

"Haw haw haw," he chuckled softly.

It was the Jockey, the one courtier whom everyone in Mooncaster feared. He played unpleasant tricks and games on them, always seeking to cause mischief and strife between friend and neighbour. Even the Ismus found his presence unsettling and ungovernable.

He brought his stout bulk closer and the caramel-coloured leather of his tightly buttoned outfit creaked and strained. Columbine tried to pull away, but his grip was fierce.

"You set your eyes on too high a trophy," he told her. "But what eyes they are, as green as the stone in the head of a wishing toad. How they flash and glare at me. Such hate, such pride in one so low."

"My arm!" she protested. "You hurt, my Lord."

"Haw haw haw," he laughed. "No bruise will show through the filth on your flesh!"

"I shall cry out."

"Then do so. None shall attend. The Jockey's ways are never questioned."

Columbine pushed at his paunch and his fingers loosed on her arm. She spun around and darted back along the passage and down into the kitchen.

The creaks and squeaks of the Jockey's costume followed her. He came tippy-toeing down the stairs.

The girl ran to her place and the heap of goose feathers whirled up into the air.

"And where is Mistress Slab?" he asked, stealing closer. "Why is she not broiling over her pots?"

"She is in the slaughterhouse," the frightened girl replied.

The Jockey laughed. "Ah, yes, 'tis sausage day. How the Punchinello Guards adore them. How readily they accept them as bribes. Would that you were so easy, my dirty scullion. Still, now we are quite alone, with only dead geese for witness and they shall not honk any secrets."

"Keep back," Columbine begged, reaching for a knife. "Else there will be one more fat pig stuck this day."

The man hesitated. Yes, she would dare do it and that inflamed him even more.

"My glance has oft been your shadow ere today," he said as he paced warily from side to side. "Your hands are coarse as an ox's tongue and your smudges and smuts rival only the midden-man. And yet... I have observed you long and I am enamoured and enslaved by you. The dirtier you are, the more like a queen you appear. A celestial goddess, come down amongst us, disguised in rags and ashes. My Lord, the Ismus, would bring you to his bed only if you were soaped and scrubbed by the tiring women till you shone like a shield. But I... I would have you as you are, all grimy from your base toil, with mutton grease and straw in your hair, soot etched in every cranny and aglow with sweat that smells of pepper and freshly sliced onions. I would tongue-bathe every inch of your fire-bronzed skin, baste you with the juices of my mouth and rip those rags from your shoulders and hips, as you have torn the feathers from that goose. You are a banquet I intend to gorge on and my appetite will never be sated."

"No closer," she warned, brandishing the knife.

"You have already pierced my heart, my pretty slattern. Bitter steel would only relieve me of that keen pain. Jab away, prick me, fillet me – shred my being even more than your grubby beauty already has."

He lunged forward. She struck out. The blade sliced into his reaching palm. He yelled in anger, slapped her with the back of his other meaty fist and smacked the weapon from her grasp. It went clattering across the flagstones.

Then his strong fingers were around her throat and she was pushed against the table. He leaned in and licked the sweat trickling down her cheek. The cut on his palm dragged a vivid scarlet wake over her skin.

"The Jockey rides everyone at Court in the end," he hissed into her ear as she struggled. "One way or another. You must give him his due."

His frenzied paws snatched at her rags and tore them. Her bare shoulders glistened in the firelight and he buried his florid face into her dirty neck as his bloody fingers went roving.

"My Lord Jockey!" a voice called suddenly.

The man snarled and glared round at the stairs. The small, dumpy figure of the Lockpick was standing at the top of them.

"What business have you here, Jangler?" the Jockey demanded angrily.

Jangler bowed. "His Highness, the Lord Ismus, would speak with you," he said.

"His Highness can wait."

"On a matter most urgent."

The Jockey ground his teeth. His eyes shone as fiercely as the fire in the grates. Then, reluctantly, he stepped away from the girl.

"Do not think I am done here," he told her, clenching a fist till the blood squeezed between his fingers. "I shall be back; the Jockey will have his sport."

Columbine watched his stout figure go skipping up the stairs after the Lockpick. Then, shaking, she covered herself with the tatters of her clothes and sank down on to the feather-strewn floor where she sobbed quietly. What was she to do? There was no escaping the whims and fancies of the Jockey and she was now the next game he was determined to play. Who could she turn to for protection? Nobody would dare stand against him. If she tried to run away from the castle, he would surely loose the hounds and hunt her down like an animal.

Lifting her face, she saw the glint of the knife he had knocked from her hand.

"Next time I shall not fail," she told herself. "Before he lays another greedy finger upon me, I shall let out every last gill of his blood. There must be a whole hogshead's worth swilling in his veins."

At that moment, a gentle but insistent tapping sounded upon the kitchen door. Columbine wiped her eyes before answering. She did not want Mistress Slab, Ned or Beetle to see she had been crying.

A draught of sharp, wintry air came biting in when she opened the stout oak door. Standing upon the frost-glittering step was the bent figure of an old woman, wrapped in a thin shawl that was no defence against the icy wind. A large wicker basket sat heavily on her crooked back and the wide brim of a black straw bonnet hid her downcast face. In her cold, pinched hands she carried another basket. When the door swung inward, she lifted it in greeting.

"Chestnuts," her cracked and weary voice said. "And apples, as sweet and juicy as last autumn when they was picked off the bough."

Columbine did not recognise her, but there were many strange folk who dwelt in the woods and forests. She wondered how far the woman had walked that day. Even the effort of lifting the basket seemed too much. For a moment, she forgot her own predicament and pitied her.

"I cannot buy your wares," the girl answered apologetically. "I have no purse and my mistress is busy. She would box my ears if I disturbed her. Have you called on the lesser kitchens in the castle? Or down in the village?"

The old woman's shoulders sagged even more.

"Slammed doors and curt words are the only blessings Granny Oakwright has been given this bitter day," she said unhappily. "I must return to my hut in the Haunted Wood, where no fire, no crust and no cheer await me."

She turned to leave, looking more hunched and feeble with each shambling step. Columbine could not bear it.

"Wait!" she called. "I haven't any pennies, but there are no warmer hearths in all Mooncaster than here. Come you in, old dame, and thaw yourself."

The woman shuffled about and entered the kitchen, muttering her thanks. Columbine guided her to the stool by the largest fire where she eased herself down and removed the basket from her back.

"Oh – my old bones!" Granny Oakwright exclaimed, holding her mittened hands towards the leaping flames. "Granny can feel her chilblains resurrecting! What a tingling in her knobby fingers!"

Columbine smiled then ran to the larder, returning with a thick slice of mutton pie and a wedge of cheese. She knew Mistress Slab would beat her for this charity, but what did that matter?

"Here," she said kindly. "'Tis a meal fit for the Lord Ismus's table and you shall have hot spiced ale to wash it down."

The old woman gasped in astonishment and clapped her hands at the sight of such princely fare.

"What a virtuous, generous child you are!" she cried, with her mouth full. "The most unselfish heart in the whole Realm – and a pretty face to match."

Columbine busied herself with adding cinnamon, cloves and nutmeg to a mug of the best October ale. Then she plunged a glowing fire iron into it, causing a ribbon of fragrant steam to hiss upwards as it bubbled and foamed over the sides.

When she handed the hot brew over, the old woman had already finished the pie and cheese and was dabbing at the crumbs on her shabby kirtle.

"I could wrap more cheese in a scrap of muslin for you to take home," the girl suggested. "If we had any bread, you'd be welcome to that too, but the kitchen boys are fetching it from the miller's even now."

Nursing the steaming mug in both hands, her guest took appreciative sips whilst regarding her keenly. Two dark little eyes, webbed with age, shone out from the shade of the bonnet's wide brim.

"I would rather eat poisoned snake livers than the finest table loaf baked by Gristabel Smallrynd, the miller's wife," she said with sudden vehemence. "Threatened to set her wall-eyed dog on me this day she did and swung a stick at Granny's head... but she'll come to rue that."

Her warty chin moved from side to side as she glugged the ale down. Then, with a contented sigh, she said, "I will take no cheese. Though I thank you for the offer of it. You have been open-handed enough already – and with such victuals that will be missed, which I wager you'll be punished for. No other in Mooncaster would show such tenderness to a wizened, friendless crone such as I."

"I could not see you hobble from this door, on so cold a day as this, tired and hungry."

"Then I must repay you, child. Is there aught you would ask of a grateful forest hag? Granny is in your debt and that must be settled at once."

Columbine almost laughed, but checked herself in time so as not to bruise the old woman's feelings. What could one so steeped in poverty afford to give her?

"I wish for nothing," she said.

The old woman leaned forward and her dark eyes glinted.

"Yet your face tells a different tale," she said. "Tears leave loud tracks upon cheeks smirched with soot and ashes. And there are bloody stains

71

of violence upon you. How came ye by such gory daubs? What troubles you so sorely? Tell Granny your woe; she may find a way of easing your burden."

And so Columbine told her what had happened, how the Jockey had caught her, peeping out at the Jack of Clubs, and his unwanted attention afterwards.

"He has sworn to return later," she said. "But I will not surrender unto him. He or I will die."

To her surprise, the crone began to chuckle. It was the last reaction she had expected.

"I mean it!" Columbine cried. "I would rather jig a deserving dance at the gibbet than have that fat villain steal my maidenhead."

Granny Oakwright slapped her bony knees and laughed all the louder.

"I see no merriment in this!" the girl shouted angrily. "My plight is most hopeless and grim. Is this how you reward my kindness? Be still and silent, old dame! How can you laugh so cruelly?"

The woman's mirth eased and she fixed the girl with a glare so powerful that Columbine caught her breath and took a step back.

"Large in heart thou mayest be, child," Granny Oakwright said, her voice now harsh. "But thy wits are shrivelled for balance. Let this be an end to play-acting. No more pretence, no more poor old grateful Granny."

"I do not understand…"

The old woman's face became sour and severe. "Dost thou truly believe any aged dweller of the forest would brave this deadly frost and tramp the many leagues from their squalid hovel to beg at this door? Hestia Slab is renowned for her parsimony. She is too mean to bait the traps. I can hear a mouse even now, over by the salt sack. No empty-bellied wretch would come a-knocking here."

"Then…?"

"I am no peasant!" the stranger proclaimed. "I am no starveling, scratching a life in the wild wood. I am she whose name is whispered with awe and dread, with powers enough to challenge even the Holy Enchanter."

Columbine gasped. "Malinda!" she blurted. "Malinda – the Fairy Godmother!"

"Malinda?" the crone shrieked with indignation. "Malinda of the clipped wings and mangled wand? Idiot girl! Malinda is no more than a mere dabbler and a faded one at that! That spangle-dusted amateur gave up knocking on doors and granting hearts' desires to silly young maidens many years ago. I am not she!"

"Then who are you?"

"I am Haxxentrot!" the old woman announced and, when she spoke her name, the nearby hearth roared and the flames blazed violet, shooting high up the chimney.

"The witch of the Forbidden Tower!" Columbine uttered fearfully. "Why are you here? What do you want?"

"To see with mine own eyes how the peoples of Mooncaster are faring," the witch replied. "Though I own many spies, it pleases me to walk amongst the village folk from time to time and relearn why I despise them so. When I have toppled the Holy Enchanter and the White Castle is a smoking ruin, there is not one whose wretched life I shall spare."

She tapped her foot irritably on the flagged floor.

"Thus I must be in no one's debt!" she told the girl as she took two chestnuts from her basket and spat on both. "Place these as nigh to the fire as ye dare. Consider this one to be thine own self and this… he is the Jack of Clubs. If the scorching heats cause them to burst and fly into a thousand pieces, thy secret yearning will ne'er blossom and bear fruit. Yet if they ignite and burn together with steady flame then ye shalt become lovers and remain constant evermore."

Columbine obeyed. She had heard many stories of the fearsome old witch who hated the Ismus and the inhabitants of Mooncaster. Haxxentrot was always seeking new ways to bedevil and inflict pain upon them. Warily the girl put the chestnuts as close to the fire as she could manage. Haxxentrot muttered some words under her breath and they waited.

Presently the two chestnuts began to smoulder. Then they both crackled and were wrapped in a pinkish flame.

. "Behold!" the witch declared with a satisfied, matter-of-fact nod. "Thy future is clear. Great love 'twixt thee and the Knave of Clubs shalt surely come to pass."

She took up the straps of the other basket and prepared to haul it on to her shoulders once more.

Columbine stared at the burning chestnuts in disbelief. An overwhelming sense of disappointment took hold of her.

"Wait!" she cried. "Is that it? Is that all?"

"All?" the witch repeated. "What more could there be? Hast thou not lain awake, many nights, aching for his embrace? Now thou knowest it will surely happen."

Columbine felt so cheated she could barely speak. Then her resentment found its voice and any fear she had of the witch was swept aside.

"What sort of magickal reward is that?" she demanded. "Was that the best you can do? This is not how kind deeds are repaid in old tales. Where are the wishes? Where are the magickal gifts? The gown of gold, made with cloth so fine it fits into a walnut shell! Where are the enchanted slippers to make the wearer the daintiest dancer in the Realm? Where is the jug of moon dew that bestows shining beauty on whoever bathes in it? Where is the potion to make he who drinks it fall into a stupor of love for me? Where is the mirror that shows any view I desire?"

"Ye modern maidens expect too much," the witch observed with a sniff.

"I expect more than two musty old nuts and a bundle of hollow pledges! You call that a debt repaid? You're naught but a hoodwinker. *Hoax*xentrot should be your name!"

The witch rounded on her.

"A morsel of hard cheese and a slice of day-old mutton pie are not equal to a feat of high magick!" she snapped. "That pastry was like elm bark and what meagre specks of mutton it housed were a chewing chore of fat and gristle. Witchery is no exchange for a hard seat with no cushion and a night of griping gut-groan."

Before Columbine could think of a fitting retort, the kitchen door flew open. The sudden draught gusted through the goose feathers, driving a ticklish blizzard against the girl's face. She spat out the ones that had blown into her mouth and wafted the rest aside. Then she saw. Standing on the step was none other than the Jack of Clubs.

Surprise, excitement, wonder, adoration, hope and fear played equal parts in the confusion that seized her in that startling instant. Haxxentrot turned her face away and sat down quietly on the stool.

Jack looked even more handsome than before. Silhouetted against the bleak winter light, he seemed no ordinary being. Here was a hero of legend, made flesh and living.

Columbine gazed on him. How fine he was, how noble and fair, how strong. Why was he here? Princes of the Royal Houses never visited the kitchen. Perhaps he was seeking Mistress Slab on a matter of oats for his fabulous steed? Only the best would suffice for that beast. Or perhaps he wanted Ned or Beetle to help the grooms? Or perhaps…? Columbine could feel her heart thumping. No, she must not allow herself to think such fanciful things in his presence. She clasped a hand to her bosom. Surely he too could hear the mighty pounding of her heart? It was louder than the steady, rhythmic clamour of the smithy, only here she was the anvil and the Knave's unwavering glance was the hammer. Into what shape would this dreamed-of moment be fashioned?

The Jack of Clubs said nothing. His blue eyes stared back at her. With long, purposeful strides he entered and approached. The servant girl stood as still as stone. Her own eyes grew increasingly wider until the pride of Mooncaster stood before her. The corners of his mouth lifted and the gentle smile made him even more charming and adorable. Then he pointed a toe and made the most perfect, courteous bow.

Columbine felt faint as she dipped into the answering curtsy. Here was her every desire, unfolding right in front of her at last.

"M…my Lord!" she finally managed to stutter.

He reached out and placed a fingertip against her lips. This was not a time for words. Taking her dirty hands in his, he held her close. From somewhere, maybe it was merely inside her own head, Columbine thought she heard music. Clasped in each other's arms, the prince and the kitchen maid began a slow dance. The cool flagstones beneath her feet might have turned to clouds for all she could feel of them. Around and around they danced. His eyes locked on hers and the air almost sparked between them. She would embed this beautiful moment in her memory forever more. Her jubilant heart flew up through the ceiling, up through the beams and stones of the castle and up into the clear sky.

Still lost in the devoted stare of her prince, a movement in the corner of her eyes caused them to flick aside. There was Haxxentrot, perched on the stool, hugging herself in amusement. In the shock and joy of what was happening, Columbine had completely forgotten about the witch. And there was something else…

She looked across the kitchen, over Jack's athletic shoulders, to where the copper pots and pans gleamed on the walls. The rippling reflections that glided over polished lids and swollen curves made her frown. Those imperfect, broken echoes of she and her gallant knave were twisted, molten likenesses that flowed from one surface to another. It was difficult to recognise the fractured, merging figures and she began to peer at them intently, to try and untangle them. Yes, there was her own revolving form, with arms held out. But Jack's shape looked so odd, even the colour of his velvet jerkin was wrong. She could see no scarlet or gold in those copper surfaces. What was that teetering tower of four white globes that followed her wherever she twirled? Columbine could not decipher it until finally, in a lightning flash of comprehension, her mind unpuzzled what she saw.

The girl shrieked and leaped away.

Standing on one another's shoulders, four Bogey Boys sniggered and mocked her. The illusion was broken. Here was no Jack of Clubs, just these ugly creatures of Haxxentrot. They were her stunted servants, with large, white, wobbly heads and mouths crammed with baby teeth. Their yellow eyes were ringed with ginger lashes and their noses were upturned. The one at the top had an adder coiled around his brow. The one beneath wore a necklace of living spiders. Below him was a wig of rats' tails. The Bogey Boy at the bottom was the fattest of the four and had powdered his shiny cheeks with green pigment and blackened his thin lips with ink.

fig. 24

The Bogey Boys
The four servants of Haxxentrot, the evil witch, are called: Jub, Hak, Rott and Crik. Tis said they are the four lost sons of the North King, who were stolen away as infants and turned into th

Their hideous appearance, coupled with their snaky laughter, revolted Columbine and she snatched up a ladle to smite them and knock them down.

"Jub! Crik! Hak! Rott!" Haxxentrot commanded. "Enough!"

The creatures stopped sniggering and leaped from each other's shoulders. The witch lifted the lid of the larger basket. Leering at the girl and making insulting gestures, they hopped inside. Haxxentrot closed the lid and patted it.

"Now is pie and cheese repaid in full," she stated flatly.

"Repaid?" Columbine objected.

"Thou hast experienced thy heart's great dream! Thou canst not deny thou had much joy of it. I saw thy rapture."

"It wasn't real! It was false and ugly."

"Love is always thus," the hag observed with a dismissive shrug.

"It isn't good enough!" Columbine protested. "I gave you food and warmth and all you do is trick and deceive!"

"The food was not thine to give!"

"The bruises I'll get from Mistress Slab will pay for it and more!

Malinda would not have treated me so…"

"I am not Malinda!!" the witch reminded her hotly. "The lover's heart is a region unmapped by me! I do not deal in longings and gladful ever-afters. Seek out that wingless Fairy Godmother in her cottage, deep in Hunter's Chase, if thou wouldst procure a philtre to turn a prince's head, but ask it not of me! Venom and curses and ill deeds are all I know."

She was about to lift the basket on to her back again when she paused and gave Columbine a sidelong look.

"And yet," she murmured, "there is one gift I could grant unto thee. A present more useful than the way to a Jack's heart."

"What could you give me?" the girl asked sceptically.

Haxxentrot tapped the wicker lid. It creaked open and a Bogey Boy's white face appeared beneath.

"Jub," the witch ordered. "Fetch me the timbrel."

The face vanished and the lid closed once more. A moment later, a small hand appeared, clasping a tambourine. Haxxentrot took it and rattled it in front of her with a flourish.

"What use is that?" Columbine asked.

"Patience provides every answer," the witch answered tetchily. She placed the tambourine on the table then sorted through a leather pouch hanging at her waist.

"Here," she said, removing a small velvet bag and emptying it.

Columbine uttered a cry of disgust at the thing that fell on to the instrument's circle of taut parchment. It was a human ear, dried and blackened and scabbed with old blood.

"What horror is this?" the girl demanded.

Haxxentrot's crabbed mouth broke into a depraved grin. "'Tis the only relic of Sir Lucius Pandemian left above ground or uneaten by wolf, gore toad, marsh snake and battle crow," she explained. "A valiant questing knight was he. Most courageous in Mooncaster."

"I've never heard tell of him."

"Hast thou not? How easy the denizens of Mooncaster forget. How my hatred festers for them anew. 'Twas many long years past, when the Dawn Prince's exile was still fresh in mind. The Realm was plagued by countless terrors, dreader fiends than they who abide in the dark forests today. One such was the Lamia. She harried cattle and carried off infants in her claws, devouring them in the ivy-choked ruins of the Black Keep, nigh to mine own tower."

Haxxentrot snorted with displeasure and her face became more twisted with rancour than usual.

"A noisesome neighbour was she," she grumbled. "Entry to the vault, wherein she slept during the hours of day, was granted only by the tolling of a great bronze bell high above. This bell couldst not ring lest she commanded it. Three deafening clangs and the marble cover stone would slide aside. Then out she would fly – on webbed wings. Never was so deafening a clamour as that bell heard in the land. Deathknelly the peasants named it, in their usual vulgar fashion. When its fearsome voice shook the night clouds, they would flee to their homes, cowering till they heard it resound again ere dawn when all was clear."

Columbine cleared her throat and held up her hand to interrupt. "How does that lead to this foul object?" she asked, grimacing at the severed ear.

"'Twas Sir Lucius who pursued the Lamia back to the forest one rain-lashed night," Haxxentrot said. "His spear pierced her side and she did drop the latest child victim from her claws. Bellowing in pain and fury, she swooped upon the knight, seizing his horse by the head and bearing both beast and he aloft. Over field and treetop she carried them and all the while he hewed and grappled with her, fending off her blows and fangs till his shield shattered. And so he raised his sword for one final thrust, but she cast his mount from her grasp and horse and rider fell from the sky. At the very entrance to the Black Keep they came crashing. The steed burst on the forest floor, but he fared a little better. Though one eye was torn from his head and his body was slashed by twig and talon, still he lived. He saw the Lamia come screeching down to rend his limbs and feed on his noble flesh, but luck had not yet deserted Sir Lucius. In that very instant, as his death seemed writ and certain, the sun pushed above the eastern hills. The Lamia screamed and rushed to the safe darkness of her lair. The mighty bell clanged direct over the brave knight's head and his ears bled. Marble grated back in place and the vault was closed. Then Sir Lucius knew what must be done."

The witch paused and regarded the blackened lump of skin with almost tender eyes.

"Wounded, ripped and broken, driven half mad by the bone-jarring sound, he climbed the ruined keep – up to the lofty pillars where the monstrous bell did hang. Without its voice, the tomb could ne'er open again so he reached into Deathknelly's mouth and removed its tongue. Yet the thing was so grievous heavy and he so beaten, he could not bear the weight and so he toppled."

Haxxentrot took up the ear and held it close as she inspected and stroked it.

"I found him there, late that day, crushed 'neath the bronze bell tongue. Already the forest creatures had been at him. They are such busy, eager workers. This I took in token of a brave man, the best in this putrid Kingdom. He had rid me of a rival scourge and for that I was grateful. The Lamia has ne'er been heard of since. The sealed vault became her tomb."

Her voice faltered and she stared at the gruesome souvenir intently.

Columbine shuddered. "And you think I would want that as a gift?" she muttered incredulously. "Are you as mad as you are ugly?"

The witch did not answer, but put the hideous thing to her withered lips and kissed it. Then, before Columbine could prevent her, the crone lunged forward, pressed the ear against the girl's shoulder and rolled it in the Jockey's still glistening blood. She called out strange words, picked up the tambourine and slammed the two together.

At once the hearths erupted. Torrents of green and purple fire exploded into the kitchen. The flames whooshed and roared about Haxxentrot and Columbine and fiery stars went zinging about the room, ricocheting off pots and plates. One struck a large glazed jug and it shattered into dust.

Another shot into the salt sack and the precious grains came streaming out. The air screamed. The witch spun around shrieking an incantation. Columbine yelled for her life. The coppers shivered on their hooks. Tables juddered across the floor as the flagstones trembled beneath them and the big basket quaked as the Bogey Boys rocked with wild laughter within.

Then, abruptly, it was over. The fireplaces crackled cheerfully once more and the kitchen was as normal as ever.

Shaken and afraid, Columbine stumbled away from the witch.

"Begone, foul hag!" she cried. "Leave now, before I call the Punchinello Guards."

Haxxentrot gave a throaty cackle. "I am done here, my pretty pie-giver," she said. "Here is the magickal gift thou didst demand of Haxxentrot."

She held out her aged hands and presented the tambourine. Columbine stared down at it.

"It cannot be!" the girl exclaimed.

"And yet thine own eyes say it is so," the witch replied. "They tell no lies this time."

In the centre of the drumhead, where moments ago there had been only blank parchment, there was now a human ear. The two were fused together, with no visible seam. The ear was no longer black and shrivelled, but the same hue as the stretched skin to which it had been joined.

"What have you done?" Columbine breathed. "And why?"

"Sir Lucius Pandemian was the last to hear Deathknelly's strident voice," Haxxentrot told her. "Just as the final image is retained in the eyes after death, so the din of the great bell was locked inside his ears."

She waggled the tambourine experimentally and looked very pleased with herself. "To thee and me, 'tis but a harmless jingle," she said. "But shake this timbrel when the Jockey comes a-leching and the thunderous voice of Deathknelly shalt awake and resound in his head, for it is bonded to him by blood. One shake will send him reeling and yowling from thy presence. Another will cause his own ears to gush as freely as the fountains in the Queen of Hearts' garden. One more and his oafish head will crack like a hen's egg and the yoke of his brains shalt bubble forth. So, child, is this not a most marvellous recompense for pie and cheese? What say thou? Art thou not most adequately repaid for thy kindness to Granny Oakwright?"

Columbine received the instrument in amazement. She was too stunned to know what to say.

Haxxentrot nodded with pride and rubbed her bony hands together.

"You have saved me," the girl cried at last. "He will never get close enough to touch me again!"

She was so delighted she capered around, smacking the tambourine against her hips and over her head.

"Be certain to keep the timbrel with thee always," the witch cautioned. "Do not let it stray out of arm's reach or thou shalt suffer the consequences."

Columbine swore she would carry it with her wherever she went.

"Let me help you on with your pack," the girl offered.

Haxxentrot refused. "No more kindnesses!" she said. "Or I shalt be obliged to thee for another gift, ye greedy girl. Dost thou truly…"

Her voice trailed off. She was staring into the far corner, where the salt had leaked freely over the floor.

"Mistress Slab will be in such a rage!" Columbine cried when she saw the mess. "Its value is great! I must sweep it into another sack and hope she…"

The witch grabbed at her arm. "Hold, child!" she snapped. "Canst thou not see? What marks are those?"

Then Columbine noticed the shapes sunken into the spilt salt.

"They are footprints," she murmured in astonishment.

"Just so," Haxxentrot said. "Yet neither of us hath ventured thither this whole while."

The girl turned a frightened face to her. "Then what made them?" she asked.

"'Twould seem the mouse I heard was no mouse. There is an eavesdropper here. A trespasser who veils himself from our eyes."

"But who in Mooncaster can do such a thing? Is this some new torment of the Bad Shepherd? Is he here now? Are we to be butchered and slain?"

"That is what I shalt discover!" the witch declared. "Jub! Crik! Rott! Hak! Jump out! Hunt down the unseen spy!"

The lid of the basket flew up and the four Bogey Boys leaped out.

"Arm thyselves with knife and skewer!" the witch commanded. "Sniff out the shadow-wrapped sneak. Bring it down! Kill it!"

The Bogey Boys gave frenzied yells and dashed about the kitchen, snatching up weapons. Then they began questing the air and, one by one, their yellow eyes turned towards the pantry door.

"The skulker is cornered!" Haxxentrot shouted. "Hack it into invisible collops!"

The four creatures shrieked shrilly and raced towards the pantry, brandishing their cleavers, pokers, slotted spoons and knives.

A chair suddenly lifted into the air and was hurled at the attacking Bogey Boys. They yowled and dived out of the way. Then pewter dishes came sailing from the shelves and went spinning at them. One struck Jub on the forehead. He screeched and somersaulted backwards, losing his rat-tail wig. There was the sound of footsteps, running towards the kitchen door. Crik, Hak and Rott whirled around and went charging after. The door yanked itself open and the footsteps went echoing out into the courtyard.

The Bogey Boys flung their weapons after them in frustration. Jub sat up and uttered a string of curses as he jammed the wig back on to his shiny white head. Haxxentrot rubbed her warty chin.

"Well, now," she said, sucking her gums. "Mooncaster hath a new terror to dread. One to make the Holy Enchanter's head ache most grievously. Yea, and the rest of us also – it hath entered the Kingdom at last."

"What manner of fearsome monster is it?" Columbine murmured in dismay.

The witch narrowed her eyes and answered gravely, "Ye shalt find out soon enough, aye – soon enough…"

Kate Kryzewski heaved a sharp, gulping breath, as if surfacing from deep water. She stared about her in shock. The vibrancy and colour was gone. The sunlight was pale and weak and her pupils dilated to compensate. How flat and grey this world was. Already she ached to return to Mooncaster.

"I am the Two of Hearts," she exulted, rolling back on the grass. "I am Columbine! Praise to the Holy Enchanter and the glory of Mooncaster! I am Columbine! Blessed be this day!"

The crowd around the SUV cheered and applauded and Sam came rushing over to help her off the ground. The reporter jumped up and hugged him. Then she turned to the Ismus and lowered her gaze respectfully as she curtsied.

"My Lord," she said in a worshipful whisper. "Your commands are my joys. Bid me and I will obey. The report to the network shall be just as you wish."

The Ismus was barely aware of her. He was gazing distractedly at the copies of *Dancing Jax* in everyone's hands and for once his gaunt features looked troubled.

"Another manifestation," he muttered to himself. "Another trespass. It is happening ever more frequently."

He cast a shrewd glance back across the heath. Doubt and uncertainty moved over his face. His thin lips pressed together and the shadows deepened beneath his brows. A dark, speckling blemish appeared on his forehead.

His devoted followers shifted uneasily. They had never seen him in this humour before. The Harlequin Priests pointed to the blue patches on their motley robes and the Black Face Dames did not know what to do. The Jacks and Jills drew close to one another. No one understood what ailed their Lord.

Then, abruptly, the Ismus tossed his head back. The crooked smile returned and the blemish faded.

"Why do we delay here?" he announced, casting off the disconcerting mood. "We should be giving those precious children a rousing welcome. We must make their stay here one they will never forget… for as long as they live."

6

JANGLER HAD WATCHED the crowd hurrying from the camp, chasing after that bothersome American reporter, with only the mildest of interest. There was still much to do on his timetable and this would be the perfect opportunity to show the newly arrived children their accommodation.

With his clipboard under his arm and the iron hoops at his belt clinking and rattling with large keys, he marched over to both groups. The winkle-picker shoes he wore, to go with his medieval gaoler's outfit, were new and he hadn't had time to break them in. They pinched his toes and chafed his heels. It was spoiling his enjoyment of the day.

"Now then, if I could have your attention," he began, in his usual officious manner. "While His Highness, the Holy Enchanter, is otherwise engaged, I will show you where you are to be billeted."

The children were looking anywhere but at him. The older ones were pulling their bags from the luggage holds in the coaches while the youngest were gazing around the camp, unsure and afraid. They eyed one another shyly. Trust had been ripped from their lives, but they were desperate for friendship and company. They were damaged and wary, but soon the first hesitant smiles were exchanged.

It was more difficult for the teens.

"That's my case there, that pink one – and that one!" Charm's voice shouted. "Careful – they're genuine Louis Vuitton repros!"

A sandy-haired lad, with a guitar slung over his shoulder, shrugged in bemusement. "You planning on stoppin' here permanent?" he asked dryly. "How many frocks can a body wear in one weekend?"

"These is just me basic essentials," she replied, pulling up the handles and trawling the cases back to where her mother was waiting.

Another boy, in a pale blue Hackett polo shirt with the collar turned up, stared after her, inclining his head to one side.

"Now that's tasty," he said appreciatively.

"I dinnae eat plastic," the other lad commented.

"Afford to be fussy, can you? Even now? You're wrong though, matey. That there would have been top trophy totty even before *DJ* ruined everything."

"You reckon? Did you no hear her and her mother yakking on the coach all the way here? I can do without that earache."

"Trick is not to listen to them, amigo. Just nod when they look at you and flirt a bit with their mums. Works a dream."

"Dinnae call me amigo."

"What then? I'm Marcus. Do you play that guitar?"

"Aye, you look like a Marcus. And no, I just carry this with me to use as a paddle in case I get washed overboard my luxury yacht."

"No need for the attitude. We're in this cack together."

The Scottish boy considered him a moment. He had seen Marcus get on the bus at Manchester. He was about fifteen, the same as himself, but a type he would normally never associate with, in school or out. He was far too cocky, sporty and wore casual clothes that had never been chucked on the bedroom floor after use. He probably folded them before putting them in the laundry basket and ironed his socks and underwear. He certainly spent way too long in front of the mirror and too much money on self-grooming products, if his painstakingly arranged hair, moisturised skin, pungent shower gel and aftershave were anything to go by. Before that book had taken over and changed all the rules, he must have been a swaggering fish in his own little north-west pond. But, despite those unappealing traits, this Marcus was undoubtedly right. Aberrants such as themselves faced enough battles out there without picking quarrels among their own kind.

"Alasdair," the Scottish boy muttered, extending his hand. "Just dinnae call me Al, Ally – and if I hear a Jock or a Jimmy, at any time over the next few days, I will have to kill you."

Marcus grasped the hand and shook it, too heartily in Alasdair's opinion. He was like a teenage estate agent or used car dealer.

"Nice to talk to another normal person for a bloody change!" Marcus said.

"Whatever normal is, aye."

"Not being a raving Jax-head, that's what I call normal."

"I wouldnae know any more. It's been so long."

"It's mental. I still don't get it. Soon as that ruddy book came out, every girl I know… knew, cracking pieces they were, no rubbish, dumped me and chased after some scrawny loser just because he had a ten of clubs on his Primark anorak. I was like, *what*?"

Alasdair glanced at the branding on Marcus's shirt and smiled to himself. In Scotland the word 'hacket' meant ugly.

"Aye, well," he said. "If your own parents can kick you out as mine did, there's no many surprises left."

If he had expected Marcus to sympathise or ask him about it, he would have been disappointed. He wasn't.

"So," Marcus continued, reverting to his favourite topic, "if you don't fancy that hotness, it's a shame to let it go begging. I'll have a crack at her. I am having one hell of a dry spell. Before they brainwash me this weekend and do my head in good and proper, I'm going to cop off with a fit bird one last time."

Alasdair seriously began to wonder if this boy's brain actually was located in his underwear.

"Did you check out that other coach?" Marcus continued. "No talent at all in that. Just more kids and a definite 'Avoid' in a manky green cardy. The blonde bit is the only thing worth chasing."

"You're wasting your time," Alasdair told him. "Yon plastic dolly'll no be interested in you. Fancies herself way too much that one."

Marcus pushed the short sleeves a little higher up his biceps and picked up his case.

"No skirt in its right mind can resist the Marcus magnetism," he boasted as he sauntered after Charm. "When I shift into fifth gear pulling mode, I'm the Stig's knackers."

Behind him, Alasdair winced.

"Total tool," he muttered.

Jangler was irritated and his feet were throbbing. No one was taking the least bit of notice of him. He cleared his throat and clapped his hands. Eventually he called one of the minstrels over and banged crossly on his drum.

The children's heads turned his way. The teenagers dug their hands deep into their pockets or folded their arms. Charm stood to attention and waited politely, posing her head this way and that, as cute and as coy as she knew how, all the while wondering where the cameras had disappeared to. Marcus positioned himself behind her and admired the view. Jody sunk her chin into her chest and huddled into her cardigan. Alasdair looked at the pompous little man, staring over his spectacles at them, and hummed the theme to *Dad's Army* to himself. For all his medieval costume, the Lockpick reminded him of Captain Mainwaring and in spite of everything, the Scottish lad couldn't stop smiling. At the back, Nike boy hissed through his teeth and kept his earphones in.

"As there are thirty-one of you," Jangler addressed them, "eighteen girls and thirteen boys, I'm going to call out your names in groups and assign each group a cabin. Make your way to it, unpack and freshen up, and we will foregather here again in one and one half hours to commence the weekend's revels – won't that be nice? Now females first…"

He began to read from his clipboard. The younger children looked confused. Their parents had trailed after the Ismus, but help was at hand in the form of women, dressed as serving maids, who found their bags and cases and ushered them to the right cabins.

The camp had only been open a couple of years so these dormitories were modern, comfortable and pretty spacious inside, considering. Usually they slept five, but extra frames and mattresses had been fitted into them for this special weekend. The girls were allocated three cabins.

The boys were crammed into two.

Shaking her wet hands, Jody Barnes emerged from the toilet and returned to the bed where she had dumped her holdall. She looked around her. The place was clean, if spartan. She assumed the prints of painted Mooncaster landscapes had been hung on the walls for their benefit, but there was also a TV and a games console.

Each cabin was laid out the same. This ground floor housed four beds and there were two more on the small, partly enclosed mezzanine area up the stairs. Jody should have raced straight up there and bagged one of those bunks for herself, but her bladder had decreed otherwise. Two of the younger girls from the other coach had claimed them instead. Still, she didn't mind; this wasn't so bad. After so many months being the only person in Bristol shut out from the world of *Dancing Jax*, it was going to be a breeze sharing this place with other rejects, even if they were mainly kids.

The only downer was that Charm creature. She'd been put in here as well. Her mother was still fussing around her and Jody felt a pang of jealousy. Her own parents were outside with the Ismus somewhere. They only came today so they could meet him. They took no interest in her any more. They were bored of having to be her mum and dad in this world. Five months on, the pain of that rejection was still there and induced tears if she picked at it, so she never did. Jody turned away and her attention rested on the child sitting uneasily on the corner of the bed next to her own.

It was little Christina Carter. Her dress was still covered in cold sick.

"Where did the nice TV lady go?" the seven-year-old asked when she saw Jody looking at her.

"As far away as she can if she's got any sense, which isn't very likely," Jody replied.

"She said she was going to take us with her," the little girl said, staring down at her feet. "I don't like it here."

Jody pitied her. This new life must be so much worse for the very young ones. If she couldn't understand what was going on, how could they?

"Open your bag," she said. "Let's get you some fresh togs out. Then come with me to the bathroom and we'll clean you up. How does that sound?"

Christina's answering grin was the widest she'd ever seen and they made a game of searching through the little girl's bag to see what had been packed for her.

"We should have them two beds upstairs," Charm interrupted them, addressing Jody, hands on hips. "We're like the oldest in here, innit? I'm gonna kick them kids out. What do you say?"

"You're orange," Christina told her.

Jody's nostrils widened as she suppressed a laugh. "I'm fine where I am," she replied. "It's only for two nights. Let those girls enjoy themselves for a change. They must have a miserable time of it back home."

"I want to sleep up there," Charm insisted. "And I'm gonna. Them kids've gotta shift. If you won't help then I'll do it on me own, makes no difference. But don't expect to kip up there when I've sorted it."

Jody squared up to her. Although she was a year younger than this painted gargoyle, she knew she was stronger and wasn't afraid to smack the lipgloss clear off her face.

"You leave them alone," she said forcefully. "They got there first, so the penthouse is theirs. If you try to evict them, I'll drag you down the stairs by your extensions so fast, you'll slide out of your tan like a snake sloughing its skin. You got that?"

Charm glowered at her. Jody half expected her to throw a tantrum.

"Come away, child," Mrs Benedict interjected, shooting Jody a scolding glance and drawing her daughter back to where the pink suitcases were waiting. "Don't you mingle with the likes of that common sort. Naught but a lowly two at the most, I'll wager, if she ever makes it to the castle, which I doubt. What a surly face. I've seen prettier sights round the backs of cows and what comes out of them. We don't want her kind in Mooncaster. A proper dirty aberrant and no mistake."

Jody snorted. That was the most fun she'd had in months and she promised herself a weekend of Barbie baiting.

"I know what her flavour is," Charm told her mother in a deliberately loud voice. "Old cabbage and sprouts!"

Christina stuck her tongue out at her. Then the seven-year-old's attention was arrested by a strange circular object, fixed high on the wall. She pointed to it and asked Jody, "What's that?"

In the boys' cabin that had been fitted with seven beds, Marcus was looking at an identical device and wondering the very same thing. It resembled an old-fashioned radio from the 1930s, being made of brown Bakelite, with a central dial and a brass grill. But it was too large and didn't match the rest of the interior decor. He dragged a chair over from the TV corner and stood on it for a closer inspection.

"It's bust," he announced to anyone listening. "These knobs down the side don't do anything and the needle doesn't go round the dial. It's just for show. It's junk."

A slightly younger boy gazed up at it. "Maybe it's just a speaker?" he suggested. "To wake us up in the morning and tell us when to go for breakfast and make announcements."

Marcus looked down at him. The boy wore what he could only describe as "geek goggles" and was going through the first flush of puberty, if his crop of zits was anything to go by.

Back in the pre-*Jax* days, Marcus wouldn't have even noticed the likes of him. His posse consisted only of the cool kids, at the top of the school food chain. It was a pity that Alasdair dude hadn't been put in this cabin as well. He didn't seem so bad. If he was here, they both could have avoided talking to dweebs like this.

"There's no wires connecting it to anything," he said, jumping off the chair. "And why the phoney dial?"

"Was only an idea."

"So who're you, know-all?"

The boy hesitated. He'd got out of the habit of speaking to people who weren't possessed by the book and was now always on his guard.

"Er... Spencer," he said with some awkwardness.

"Herr Spencer?" Marcus scoffed. "You German?"

"No, just Spencer."

Marcus punched him playfully on the shoulder.

"OK, Herr Spenzer," he laughed. "You zee any pretty Fräuleins, you zend them to Marcus, ja?"

"I'm not German," Spencer reiterated, rubbing his shoulder. "I'm from Southport."

"Just teasing ya!" he said, flicking the boy's spectacles so they sat at an angle on his face. "Take a joke."

Spencer backed away, adjusting his glasses, and returned to his bed. He sat there protecting his bag, in case Marcus thought it would be funny to run off with it.

The older boy groaned. What a useless bunch of kids he'd been lumbered with. Every one of them could win a misery guts contest in ugly town.

"Oh, lighten up, the lot of you!" he called out. "This has got to be better than what you left behind at home, hasn't it?"

Five sullen faces stared back at him. He rolled his eyes and knocked his knuckles on his temple.

"Hopeless!" he uttered. "Bloody hopeless. Right, I'm going to grab a shower. I've a feeling I'm going to get lucky, not that any of you can possibly understand what that means. If you need a wazz, go now while I get my towel. Just a wazz though; if you want to drop a log, tough – you'll have to wait till I'm done."

He went up the stairs to the mezzanine. At least he'd had the sense to be first up here and take ownership of one of those beds. He wouldn't have to sleep down there, which would be an airless pit of sweaty socks, bad breath and BO by tomorrow morning. Herr Spenzer's zits probably glowed in the dark too.

At the top of the stairs Marcus stopped. The other bed up here had been taken by the black lad from the other coach. He was reclining on the covers with his earphones in, puffing away on a cigarette. The grey smoke had gathered in a ghostly canopy overhead.

Marcus scowled. "Hey, dude," he said. "You wanna take that outside? I don't want me or my stuff to stink."

Nike boy's eyes opened and appraised him slowly, up and down. Marcus folded his arms so he could push the biceps out a bit more. He wasn't going to be intimidated. Still, that lad was stocky, not gym-toned but naturally brick-wall solid.

"You just call me 'dude'?"

"Take your cancer sticks outside, man," Marcus told him.

"You don't get to tell me what to do, white boy."

"Oi, don't start that!"

The lad rose from the bed and Marcus saw he was a good bit taller than himself. He stood his ground as the other approached, the cigarette hanging on his lip.

"I will start what the hell I want," he said as he came closer. "Who is you to lay down rules in here? Lab rats don't get to say what's what. You're in the same experiment as the rest of us. If you don't like my nicotine then you better go find somewhere else to lay your head this weekend cos I *will* be lighting up in bed, I *will* be blowing smoke in your face while you sleep and I *will* be burning holes in your AussieBum panties. You better pray to baby Jesus that's all I'll do, cos I got me a blade and your pussy face could do with a few lines of interest. You hear what I'm saying?"

Marcus blinked nervously. The boy leaned into him and exhaled a dense fume of smoke. Marcus spluttered and backed away, clenching his fists in readiness.

Suddenly the other boy broke into a laugh.

"Just teasin' ya!" he roared, throwing his words back at him. "Take a joke!"

Marcus glared fiercely for a moment. Then he pushed past to collect his toiletries bag and a towel from his case. In stony silence he stomped downstairs to the shower. On the way he heard Spencer chuckling. He'd remember that.

On the mezzanine the smoker returned to his bed and stretched out on it luxuriously. "Lee Jules Sherlon Charles," he congratulated himself. "You is the last of your kind."

It wasn't too long before the drum was beaten again outside and everyone was summoned from the cabins.

Alasdair emerged feeling hungry and was glad to see serving maids weaving through the crowd, bearing trays of food from the stalls. He grabbed a large slice of ham and chicken pie and a ceramic goblet of ale and made short work of both. At least the food was good here and one thing he did admire about the world of *Dancing Jax* was the quantity of booze the characters got through. They drank ale in place of tea, coffee or soft drinks and the nobles were always quaffing wine. If that's what life was really like in the olden days, they must have been perpetually off their faces.

"Is there a vegetarian option?" Jody asked one of the wenches. "That's just a lump of death wrapped in a murder parcel that is."

At her side, now washed and in clean, dry clothes, little Christina absorbed her words and shrank away from the proffered tray.

"There is cheese and bread, Mistress," the serving maid told them helpfully.

"I like cheese," Christina declared brightly. Her very empty tummy was growling.

"It'll have been made with the chopped-up insides of a baby cow's stomach," Jody informed her.

Christina wrinkled her nose and shook her head with disgust.

"We'll just have the bread," Jody said. "Though that'll be packed full of additives and made with chlorine-bleached flour."

She took several slices of a rustic-looking loaf and sniffed them. "You wouldn't believe what they put in this rubbish," she grumbled. "There's a list of E-numbers long as your arm, trans-fats, preservatives, traces of pesticide."

Christina was too busy devouring her second slice to comment.

"Don't suppose you've got a banana?" Jody called after the departing serving maid.

A snigger sounded behind them. Jody turned to see Marcus shaking his head in disbelief at her.

"Don't you worry," he laughed. "They're going to roast a wild tofu for you veggies later."

Chuckling, he continued on his way. He was carrying two goblets of ale and was on a mission. Jody watched him push to the front. She recognised his type, and marked him down as not worth talking to.

The Ismus had returned with the Jacks and they were sitting in places of honour around a raised stage area. Cameras were snapping away and Jody saw that American TV reporter among the other news crews.

"So much for Julie bloody Andrews," the girl muttered. "Didn't take her long to get Von Trapped."

Charm and her mother had stationed themselves right by the stage. Charm had changed into a short skirt and scraped her hair into a ponytail. They were waiting for the performance to commence, or for a lens to stray in their direction. A large pair of Gucci sunglasses shielded her eyes from the afternoon sun, but she would have worn them whatever the weather.

"This has got to be the glam corner!" Marcus declared, blinking in feigned surprise as he came bowling up to them. "No one told me there was going to be a Mooncaster's Next Top Model contest going on here today. Would either of you two lovely ladies like a drink? It's not bubbly, but it's the best they're offering; the mead smells like a wino's emptied himself in it, so we'll have to make do with this. Now rev up your fun glands, the party starts here!"

Mrs Benedict pursed her lips and viewed him suspiciously as she took one of the goblets.

"I don't like your manner, young man," she said. "It's overly familiar and flippant and we don't know you."

"Call me Marcus!"

"Why? What's your real name?"

"That is my real name. I'm just being friendly. I saw you two beautiful damsels over here, on your lonesome, and thought *I have got to go over and say hello*."

He held out the other drink. Charm regarded him and the ale through her shades.

"There's more'n four hundred calories in a pint of that stuff," she said.

Marcus looked shocked. "You don't need to think about things like that!" he cried. "Not a stunner like you."

"She's been on some sort of faddy diet ever since she was nine," her mother informed him. "She won't allow so much as a Jaffa cake in the house. She'll be so much happier in the castle – there's none of that silliness there. You don't need to count calories when you're laced into a good strong bodice with a panel of wood tucked down the front."

"Well, whatever made her beautiful, I'm glad of it," Marcus said, raising the goblet and drinking a toast to them. "You're the hottest babes here."

Mrs Benedict tutted, but she was always ready to praise her daughter.

"She is most fair, isn't she?" she said proudly. "Two years ago that was *the* face of Lancashire Pickles. You couldn't eat an onion in a Bootle chippy without seeing her smile on the jar. 'Only our vinegar is sour' the slogan said."

Marcus smacked his forehead. "I knew you had to be a model!" he exclaimed. "I said so, didn't I?"

The girl's mother nodded. "Oh, yes, she's a true professional. Been doing it since she was ten, haven't you, child? This was going to be a big year for her. We had The Plan all worked out, didn't we? Still, what a prize she'll be when she finally awakens to the real world."

"Maybe we'll know each other there!" Marcus suggested hopefully.

"That would rock, knowing you here and there as well. So what is your name, beautiful?"

"Charm," she answered in a voice of lead.

"It couldn't be anything else!" he said with a grin. "I'm *charmed* to meet you."

The girl said nothing and those sunglasses made it impossible for him to read her expression. He tried one of his trademark winks. They had a pretty good success rate. The girl turned back to the stage and he thought he caught what sounded like a bored sigh.

It was time for the performance to begin. First there was a display of courtly dancing, in which the Jacks and Jills took part. Then there was a re-enactment of an episode from the book, when the Jill of Hearts was kidnapped by a Punchinello Guard, who carried her off to a cave under one of the thirteen hills. The short, hideous creature was realised by a dwarf actor wearing an ingenious costume with built-up shoulders and a large, false head jutting from his chest. The head was suitably repulsive, with swivelling eyes and, when it menaced the captured girl, the younger children in the audience covered their own. But the Jack of Clubs came to the rescue just in time. He sliced his sword straight through the creature's neck and the head went rolling across the stage.

"Oh, them fings is well vile," Charm said to her mother. "I fink I'd scream if I saw 'em."

"*When* you see them," Mrs Benedict corrected. "But don't you worry, child. The Punchinellos are usually kept in strict order by their captain, Captain Swazzle, who reports to the Ismus direct. It's the fiends that go creeping outside the White Castle and in the woods and fields that are to be feared, but you'll never have to worry about the likes of them, being of such obvious high-born quality."

"I dunno… I still wouldn't like to see them every day. Snow White always used to freak me out. When she woke up an' all them tiny old bald blokes were pervin' at her. That was well dodgy, know what I mean?"

Marcus remained silent. He heard Mrs Benedict speaking about

Mooncaster as though it was a real place, in exactly the same way everyone else he knew spoke about it. He could not understand how or why anyone could believe such infantile rubbish. When this madness had first started, he had wondered if it was a massive con and they didn't actually believe in it at all, but why they would pretend to do so was an even bigger mystery. What were they getting out of it?

In his darkest moments, and there had been many of those in recent months, when he felt utterly alone and filled with despair, he had questioned his own reason. But his ego was indefatigable and pulled him through every time. He almost wanted this weekend to successfully change him into a believer, just to see what the fuss was about, but he really couldn't see it happening. How could it? It was only a stupid book.

Elsewhere in the crowd, Christina turned to Jody and whispered in a frightened voice that she hadn't liked 'Mr Big Nose' and was glad he'd been 'deheaded'.

Jody put her arm round her. "There's no such things as Punchinellos," she assured the seven-year-old. "They're only monsters in a story; they don't exist."

"But the Jacks and Jills are in the book too," Christina said. "They're real."

"Just kids playing dress-up. There aren't any witches or fairy godmothers, no Mauger beast at the gate, no werewolf and no castle."

"My mummy and daddy say there are," the little girl uttered unhappily.

Jody glanced over to where Christina's parents were standing. Mr and Mrs Carter had forgotten about their young daughter and were transfixed by what was happening on the stage. Jody looked away in disgust. She didn't even wonder where her own mother and father had got to.

"People are the only real monsters," she said.

It was time for the reading. A distinguished actor, who had appeared in countless movies and voiced umpteen CGI characters, stepped on to the stage to appreciative applause. The serving maids made sure every child had a copy of *Dancing Jax* and the recital commenced. The actor's voice rang out, with that dry, clipped, resonant gravitas only the best Shakespearean thespians possessed.

"Dora, poor Dora the blacksmith's daughter, was a lumpen girl, built like bricks and mortar. When she was ten, she was as tall as her father, at sixteen even he could not have fought her. She could wrestle the burliest farmhand and punch out a horse's molar. The villagers of Mooncot were justly proud of her prowess, but none of them would court her. Dora, plain Dora despaired how nature had wrought her, so one bright morn she set forth – with ham and cheese and a flagon of well-drawn water. Every young maid knew of magick Malinda, so off she went and sought her. A pretty face and voice of silver was all that she was after. But Dora, dim Dora lost her way, forgetting what her father taught her. 'Don't go down the dingling track, where the toadstools grow much taller!' Down the dingling track she tramped and heard strange voices call her – to Nimbelsewskin's forest house where soon began the slaughter."

Through force of habit, Jody followed the words on the pages. She had learned very early on that rejects who showed willing were persecuted far less than those who rebelled. Marcus was doing the same. He pretended to read along with the rest, but all the while his eyes were flicking left and right.

The face of every adult was transfigured with rapture as they found their way back into the Realm of the Dawn Prince and resumed their vivid lives there. Soon they were rocking back and forth, their eyes rolling up into their heads. Only the children who arrived that day remained motionless – they and the Ismus.

The Holy Enchanter gazed out over the sea of bobbing heads. His questioning stare fixed upon each and every one of those youngsters. *Which of them?* he asked himself. *Which of them?*

He saw Charm concentrating, desperately wishing for the power of the book to swallow her up. She even tried nodding her head, but only succeeded in catapulting her sunglasses on to the stage. She let out a squeal of frustration. The Ismus looked further back, to where Lee Charles was moving his head from side to side, in time to the music blaring in his eardrums. He hadn't been paying the slightest attention to anything and wasn't even holding a copy of the book. Then the Ismus regarded Spencer. He was fidgeting nervously while trying to be as inconspicuous as possible.

A twelve-year-old boy next to him caused the Ismus to narrow his eyes. There was something unusual and furtive in the way Jim Parker was gently patting his shirt, as if he was hiding something beneath it. Nearby, Tommy Williams was still peering around like a baby bird. He and the other small boys had been put in the same cabin as Alasdair and they were now gathered about him. The Ismus considered the Scottish lad and discovered he was staring straight back. Such deep hatred blazed in those young eyes. *Could he be the one?*

When the reading ended, the crowd uttered wretched groans and gasped miserable breaths as they were torn from the blissful existence in Mooncaster and found themselves back here.

It was time for the parents to depart in the coaches. The Ismus thanked them for bringing their children on this journey. He was confident the next time they met they would have found their rightful places in the world of *Dancing Jax*.

Kate Kryzewski and Sam filmed the farewells eagerly. In spite of the neglect and unhappy home life, many of the smaller children cried when they saw their parents board the vehicles without them. Rupesh Karim tried to jump on after his father and had to be dragged clear. Jody disappeared into her cabin long before her parents thought to look for her.

There was only one sad parting.

"Now don't you worry," Mrs Benedict told her daughter. "When this weekend's over, you'll be a real-life princess – I know it."

Charm tilted her head back and fanned her eyes to stop the tears.

"I wish you wasn't going, Ma," she said. "I'm gonna miss you so much."

"S'only two days," her mother consoled her. "I'll be here first thing Monday morning to pick you up and take you back home. Don't you fret none."

"You promise?"

"I vow it, if you're not too grand for me by then. And don't you forget, when you finally wake up in the castle, come find Widow Tallowax in the wash house and spare her a silver penny or two so she can buy ointment for her poor chapped hands."

"It'll be the first thing I do!" Charm swore. "I'll buy you everyfink the Queen of Hearts has got."

Her mother smiled and stroked the girl's face tenderly.

"You're a good child," she said softly. "Your real mum will be so proud. Blessed be."

Charm wanted to tell her how much she loved her, but the lump in her throat made further speech impossible. Instead she threw her arms round her mother's neck and sobbed.

"Don't you worry," Marcus declared, imposing on this intimate moment. "I'll take care of her."

Neither took any notice of him. Mrs Benedict stepped on to the coach and Charm mouthed the words she hadn't been able to say. Her mother found a seat and waved.

When the coaches pulled away and drove up the long forest road, Charm covered her eyes with the sunglasses once more.

"If you want a great big cry," Marcus invited, holding out his arms, "my shoulders are damp-proofed and I give good hug."

Charm flicked her ponytail back and walked briskly away.

"You're a cucumber, you are," she said over her shoulder.

Marcus wasn't sure what she meant, but he called after her, "In every way except the colour, gorgeous!"

"I hate cucumber," she clarified. "It's wet and borin', pointless, tastes rubbish, keeps repeatin' an' you can't get rid."

Marcus was too busy ogling her bottom in that short skirt to be offended or discouraged. It was only early evening Friday – still plenty of time.

Jody had emerged to watch the coaches leave. Leaning against the cabin wall, she saw them turn off at the junction and disappear behind the trees in the distance.

"On my own now then," she murmured. "No change there."

A small hand slipped into hers. "No, you're not," Christina said. "You've got me."

The unexpected human contact and the simple, loving statement took her totally by surprise. Jody looked down at the seven-year-old, but the grateful smile froze on her lips. What was she doing? She wanted to tell her they would be like sisters this weekend and that she would protect her. But what about afterwards? What if Christina did get snatched away by the power of that book like everyone else in her life? She couldn't endure the pain of losing another person she cherished. She couldn't put either of them through that.

Jody shook her hand free. "Go make friends with kids your own age," she said coldly. "I don't want you hanging round me all the time. I'm not here to nanny nobody."

Christina flinched as if she had been slapped. Then she ran around the cabin, out of sight.

"You're a spiteful mare, you are," Charm said as she walked past to go inside. "That's just cruel."

Jody didn't answer, but she despised Charm more than ever for being right.

Over by the stage, the Ismus surveyed the remaining crowd. The entertainers and stallholders were milling around, enthusing about their other existence, while the younger children were either crying or staring in crushed silence at the empty forest road.

"Now the weekend can really begin," Jangler's enthusiastic voice broke into the Ismus's solemn contemplation. "Won't be long before dusk and then, in the night…"

The Holy Enchanter considered the old man gravely. He came to a decision.

"Walk with me," he said brusquely.

"It's almost time for dinner," Jangler reminded him, consulting his watch and schedule. "There is a feast prepared in the main block…"

"That can wait!" the Ismus snapped. He signalled to his bodyguards to remain and strode away.

Jangler nodded meekly; he had been looking forward to soaking his feet while the feast was going on. With delicate, hobbling steps, he followed the Holy Enchanter through the compound. What was on his Lord's mind? He seemed so preoccupied and troubled of late. In silence they crossed the grassy area behind the cabins, and passed into the trees beyond. The new leaves were rustling lightly overhead, stirred by the gentlest evening breeze.

"Is it something I have done, my Lord?" Jangler asked. "Have I displeased you? Has the day not gone in accordance to your plan?"

"It could not have passed more smoothly," the Ismus said. "Miss Kryzewski will send an enthusiastic report back to America and, while her government puzzles and dithers over it, the delay will be enough for the book to take a firm hold there. Within four months the home of the brave shall fall – to my *most* intelligent design."

"Then what disturbs you? That's splendid, is it not?"

The Ismus looked back at the compound. A blanket of soft purple shadow had stolen over it. The sun was low. Its amber light caught only the tops of the surrounding trees. None of that was reflected in the darkness of his eyes.

"Those children disturb me," he whispered.

"The aberrants?" Jangler asked in surprise. "No, no, no. They present no problem. I've never seen a more thoroughly subdued and timid lot. They'll be no trouble. They're utterly cowed and defeated, just as it should be. They're nothing, just insignificant wastage."

"You think so, do you?"

"I know it, my Lord. I've encountered disruptive elements before now; there's none in that dismal collection. They went to their chalets as compliant and docile as rabbits to hutches. Submissive and harmless dregs, that's all they are. The gullible clods truly believe they're only staying here for the weekend! They don't know what your true intent is, or what the bridging devices are for. Not the vaguest idea, I'm sure."

The Ismus shook his head. "You are mistaken, Jangler," he uttered. "One of those docile rabbits could be the greatest threat to the world of Mooncaster imaginable."

"You're having a jest with me! Nothing can endanger the blessed Kingdom, nothing!"

"One of those children back there… is the Castle Creeper."

The old man caught his breath and slowly removed his spectacles. "Are you sure?" he asked in a shocked, dismayed whisper.

"Oh, most definitely."

"But Mr Fellows doubted such a personage could exist. Theoretically it's possible, but…"

"Yes, I doubted! There was a chance! Incalculably remote, but a chance nevertheless."

"But to have been found so soon, in this country… and a child?"

The Ismus closed his eyes. The shadows of evening deepened in the hollows of his gaunt face. Beneath the enclosing trees it grew chill.

"I have sensed the incursions," he said with a slight shudder. "Felt every trespass, as keenly as a cold scalpel razoring through my skin. One of those children, one of those 'harmless dregs', has the ability to enter the Dawn Prince's Kingdom, to insinuate him or herself into my wondrous creation, yet not become a part of it. Somehow they do not assume one of the prescribed roles. They appear in Mooncaster as they are here, whilst retaining a footing in this world and, with each fresh visit, their presence gains in strength."

"Then we must kill every child in the camp at once!" Jangler insisted – appalled by what he was hearing. "Massacre them! We can set up another bridging centre in the next country that falls. The Castle Creeper is a threat to the Realm – a deadly menace!"

"Only if he, or she, strives against us. Have you forgotten what the Creeper is capable of? Must I remind you of what only they can do? What even I, even His Majesty the Dawn Prince, cannot?"

Jangler blinked and groped through his memory for the relevant passage. Then, in a voice wavering with excitement and wonder, he quoted the hallowed text.

"And who can hinder the Bad Shepherd's wild, destructive dance? None but the unnamed shape; the thing that creeps through the castle and the night."

"Yes!" the Ismus declared. "Now do you see?"

Jangler exhaled. His eyes were sparkling. "We must discover which of them is this Castle Creeper!" he said urgently. "There must be no delay!"

"It is too soon!" the Ismus warned. "That would be the ruin of this one incredible chance. We must wait, we must watch, keep those aberrants close and under scrutiny. When the Creeper is grown in strength and conceit, they will betray themselves. Then we shall know."

"What are my Lord's wishes?"

"Live up to your name," the Ismus instructed with a foul grin. "Be the gaoler of that place. When this weekend is done, you will remain. Keep the children under lock and key."

"It shall be just as you command and I shall report to you every day."

"No need," the Ismus said with a low chuckle. "I will monitor everything, know everything, before you do, Jangler."

"My Lord?"

The Ismus took three steps back and threw open his long arms.

"Dancing Jax must go out into the world and do its glorious work," he exulted. "There is much to be done and I, Austerly Fellows, must oversee the domination of every country. But I shall spare a part of me – leave a splinter of my essence – here. To observe and do what must be done."

As he spoke, dark blemishes broke out across his skin until his face was peppered with ink like spots of black mould. They bloomed and spread, foaming over his features until his head was a pulsating mass. Only his mouth was visible – a cave within a festering cloud. Mycelia branched through his hair, writhing and sprouting fresh growths. Then he arched his back and a flood of black strands and spores went shooting upward – into the leaves above. The putrid stench of decay and corruption rained down.

Jangler watched, enthralled, and he fell on his knees to worship the true form of Austerly Fellows.

The mould blossomed overhead, swelling and crackling softly, forming a thick, clotted web in the trees. And then, from within its dark heart, a malignant, bubbling voice spoke.

"Rise, Jangler. Rise, grandson of Edgar Hankinson. For three generations your family have proven their worth and loyalty to me."

Jangler got to his feet and stared adoringly up at the frothing horror clogging the shadows.

"It has been an honour to serve," the old man answered, raising his hands in adulation. "You are the Abbot of the Angles, founder of the candle faith, author of the sacred text. When I was a small boy, I dedicated my whole being to your great glory and grandeur. All my life I have venerated you."

"This shall prove your greatest labour," the voice told him. "I entrust to your safe keeping the smooth running of the camp. Fortify it. Make it a stronghold from which there can be no escape."

"Alone? Will you not guide me?"

"You will not be alone. Help shall be sent, extraordinary help. It will support and assist you."

"But the splinter of yourself? May I not come here, to this place, and consult with it?"

The mould cluster quivered as a gurgling laugh issued out. The sound filled the gathering gloom beneath the trees and the strands connecting the Ismus to the thing overhead vibrated wildly. Then they snapped apart. The hideous growths covering the Holy Enchanter's face retreated back, disappearing into his pale skin. The disembodied laughter ceased, and was immediately taken up by him. He put his arm round the old man and pointed to the repulsive, throbbing mass above. It crawled higher up the tree and hid itself among the leaves.

"I don't understand," Jangler said.

"You won't be able to consult with that fragment of myself," the Ismus told him. "Because you won't know where it is. One night this weekend, that little part of me up there is going hunting."

"Hunting? What will it hunt?"

"One of those young aberrants. That fragment of me is going to wait, out of sight, and you, dear Lockpick, will drive them in here tomorrow evening. Make a game of it. Employ whatever ruse or method seems best to you. Just see that they are all roaming this woodland when darkness falls. I shall make my selection then."

"Ho! What an amusing scheme. And what will you do with the filthy scum, once caught?"

The crooked smile appeared. "I shall hide within its body, possess it as I did the man Jezza – the previous owner of this host flesh."

"But what if your choice is the Castle Creeper? The child will be dead and its skill with it."

"One life out of thirty-one," the Ismus said. "That is a gamble I am prepared to take. Have I ever baulked at risk?"

"No, my Lord. And after you have taken possession, how shall I know which of them you are? You must make yourself known to me in a manner that will not arouse the suspicions of the others. Young people are so distrustful."

"Certainly not! I don't want you treating that host any differently to the rest. The other aberrants will know for certain if you bow and scrape every time it walks by. Your devotion would give the game away in the first five minutes. Just forget I'm there. As soon as it becomes clear who the Creeper is, I'll step forward and take command."

"Whatever you say, my Lord."

"But remember, it is only a splinter of myself which I shall view and operate remotely. I can channel no power through it. It will be no stronger than the body it animates. Do not think to call on it for help if you fail here. It is merely a direct link to me, nothing more."

"I will not fail," came the confident reply. "And I shall not even try to guess in which of them you are concealed."

The Ismus clapped him on the back. "Then let us return to our unwary little rabbits and their hutches!" he announced. "My Black Face Dames will be getting anxious. For such burly bruisers, they really are the most terrible worrywarts."

He led Jangler back towards the compound. At the edge of the wood he paused and glanced over his shoulder. High in the trees a patch of foliage rustled against the breeze. The breathing darkness within was trembling with anticipation. The hungry wait had begun.

7

THE FEAST WAS an excessive, ostentatious display of a Mooncaster banquet. The refectory in the main block had been converted to a scaled-down facsimile of the Great Hall inside the White Castle. No expense had been spared. The walls had been faced with faux stone panels, but genuine medieval tapestries, requisitioned from stately homes and museums, had been hung across them. Four long oak tables were arranged in a rectangle and laden with even more food than had been on the stalls outside. Whole suckling pigs and roast fowl of various sizes, decorated with their former plumage, added to the pies of before.

The children were shown their places by the serving maids and minstrels played as they sat down. None of the young guests looked at the food; every eye was staring at the thing that dominated the central space. Within the rectangle of tables, on a large dais of its own, was a great model of the White Castle.

Painstakingly recreated by a team of special-effects craftsmen, it was perfect, down to the smallest detail, with three concentric walls and the five-storeyed keep in the middle. There were tiny lights in turret windows, banners of the Royal Houses flew from the four corner towers, the courtyards were cobbled, and white lead miniature guards were stationed on the battlements. There was even a moat, made of clear resin – and trees, with brass-etched leaves, grew from the flocked, grassy banks.

Alasdair stared at it intently. He couldn't help admiring the workmanship and untold hours that had gone into its making, but he loathed everything the model represented.

The Ismus welcomed them with a speech about the hearty meals that would be lavished on them in here this weekend. The presence of the model was to focus their minds on their objective and to make the transition from this world to that much easier.

"Now eat, most honoured guests," he commanded, his eyes glinting in the light of the many candles burning on large iron stands around the room.

The wenches came forward bearing flagons of ale and filled the goblets on the table. The younger children were given a weak, watered-down version, but they still grimaced when they sampled it.

Marcus had changed into a Paul Smith shirt with thin vertical stripes and knew he was the sharpest dresser in the room, apart from the Ismus, but that black velvet ensemble was hardly the height of fashion. Not yet at any rate. Marcus was disgruntled not to have been seated anywhere near Charm. She was diagonally opposite him and his view of her was blocked by the castle. What was the point of looking so good if she couldn't even see him? He had hoped he could win her over by playfully throwing a grape or a rolled-up bit of bread in her direction. He didn't want to chance lobbing a missile over the castle, blind.

"I might get her in the face or in her eye," he muttered to himself. "She's not the sort to laugh at that. Probably cause a big stink about it. Does she find anything funny?" A smile tweaked the corners of his mouth briefly as he imagined getting a bullseye right down her cleavage.

He let his gaze roam over the castle in front of him. "So that's what it's all about then?" he said. "That's where everyone thinks they are when they read *DJ*. Couldn't they have just gone to Disneyland or Alton Towers?"

He jabbed his elbow in the ribs of Spencer who had the misfortune to have been placed next to him.

"Zo, vot do you zink, Herr Spenzer?" Marcus asked. "Zat ist der Colditzcaster, ja?"

Spencer ignored him and sipped at the ale as he chewed a mouthful of pie crust.

"All that lard is just going to feed those zits, dude," Marcus commented with disgust.

Jody didn't like the look of the model. To her the castle appeared grim and forbidding, a feudal fortress from which privileged nobles ruled the downtrodden lower classes. She gave her attention to the food instead and was relieved to see bowls of fruit on the table. That minchet muck was there among the grapes, pears, pomegranates and apples, but she could easily wipe its acrid residue from them. There were small dishes of almonds and hazelnuts too. She tucked in hungrily.

Christina and the other small children were mesmerised by the castle. Part of them longed to play with it, but they also knew it was a bad thing. It had taken the love of their families away from them. It was fascinating and fearsome at the same time, in the same way that fire had been when they were much smaller.

Christina glanced over to where Jody was sitting and her face clouded with hurt and resentment. Then she picked up a skewer and banged her pewter plate with it. When she was sure she had Jody's attention, the seven-year-old plunged the skewer deep into the snout of a suckling pig.

Jody started. Christina dug her nails into one of the pig's glazed ears and tore it free. Jody looked away, wishing she hadn't been so nasty earlier. She had tried to spare Christina from getting hurt, but perhaps she'd damaged her even more.

There was a remote expression on Jim Parker's face. With that detailed model in front of him, he could imagine it was a real building and he was flying above it. Jim was a lover of comic books and, since the takeover of *Dancing Jax*, had immersed himself in them completely. DC, Marvel, he loved them all, but his favourite was the X-Men. If he was a mutant with the power of flight, or maybe even just Superman, he could look down on every building like this. He smiled secretively and pressed the tip of his knife into his thumb when he was sure no one was watching. A blob of blood popped out.

"Not yet then," he murmured to himself with disappointment. "How much longer?"

Spencer felt another dig in the ribs.

"Wouldn't it be awesome if a topless dancer jumped out of that castle right now, like it was a big cake?" Marcus laughed. "I would so love that!"

Spencer didn't hear him. Something had been gnawing away at the back of his mind the whole afternoon. From the time they had been shown their cabins it had been there – a vague sense of wrongness. Of course there was the unease and dread that they all felt, knowing they were here to get brainwashed. But this was something else, something more tangible and immediate. Suddenly it struck him and he sat upright. He stared around at the other children and fizzed with the satisfaction of having worked it out.

He had to tell someone, but he didn't want to speak to Marcus so he turned to the boy on his right.

"Thirty-one!" he blurted excitedly. "There's supposed to be thirty-one of us! The Lockpick guy said so, didn't he?"

Tommy Williams dropped his fork and cowered away from him. Cringing, he waited for the inevitable punch.

"I didn't do nothing wrong!" he cried, covering his face.

Spencer was shocked at how scared he was. He couldn't begin to imagine what cruelty the boy had endured since the publication of the book. Perhaps it went back even further than that? Only Tommy knew. Spencer simply understood that he had to make him feel better as soon and as best as he could. He was too hesitant, insecure and self-conscious to put his arm round the boy and cuddle him as Sam had done earlier, so he did the only thing he could think of. He tickled him. For the first time in months, Tommy Williams laughed and laughed.

"Stop! Stop!" he begged hysterically. "I'll wee!"

It was Spencer's turn to shrink away and he turned back to his food hastily. Tommy slid down in his chair, out of breath and giggling.

"What was you on about, Herr Spenzer?" Marcus demanded. "Thirty what?"

Spencer adjusted his spectacles and twitched his shoulders.

"The Lockpick said there's eighteen girls and thirteen boys," he began. "But there aren't. Count them – there's only seventeen girls."

"So? The old git can't add up."

"Or one girl still hasn't arrived yet."

Marcus immediately became intensely interested. "Herr Spenzer!" he exclaimed, punching him on the arm. "If you're right and if she's a babe, I'll buy you some spot cream!"

Lee Charles ate in silence. He watched everyone: the little groups who were tentatively getting along, the young kids slowly opening up to their neighbours, testing those strangers with small questions and giving timid answers. He saw the Indian boy, Rupesh, staring unhappily at the food before him. He didn't touch any of the meat and pushed the watered-down ale away. Lee wondered what his home life was like now. All religions in the UK had been affected by *Dancing Jax*. Worshippers still attended the churches, mosques, temples and synagogues, but it was only through habit and the perceived need to continue acting out what they believed were their pretend lives here. How long would that continue, he wondered?

Lee's own grandmother had been a devout Christian her whole life. Her immaculate front room, which he had been forbidden to enter unaccompanied until the age of ten, was filled with her treasures such as the old radiogram as big as a sideboard, glass swans, photographs of the family and a framed print of a painting called *Christ at Heart's Door*. Every Palm Sunday she would bring home the small cross she had been given at the service and tuck it behind the print where it would remain for twelve months. This year she hadn't and the once beloved picture had been replaced with one of the many views of Mooncaster that were now in the shops. The last time Lee visited his grandmother he had discovered the print hidden down the side of the china cabinet.

He looked over to where the Ismus was sitting with the Jacks and Jills. Nothing about Lee's face betrayed the anger and hatred he felt towards the Holy Enchanter. Under the table his fist closed slowly and he imagined the weight of a gun in his hand. In his mind's eye he saw himself holding it sideways, like in the movies and music vids, and busting caps into that scrawny poser. That would be so sweet. He turned his head before the grin became too large and watched the wenches passing in and out of the kitchen. From the glimpses afforded through the swinging door, he saw that no alterations had been made in there. It was electric lights, brushed steel surfaces and magnolia paintwork.

He placed a piece of pie on his trencher, smashed it flat with the heel of his hand then slapped it on to a slice of bread, folded it over and ate it. His mind ticked steadily.

Along the next table, Charm was making cooing noises as she drank in the castle model.

"I'm gonna hang pink curtains in one of them windows when it's my turn," she promised, with a big smile to the cameras she had gathered about her. "Whoever I turn out to be, I just know I'll be painting everyfink pink. I loves it I do."

She posed and performed for the lenses then carved a slice of pheasant for herself, declaring it to be "a ropy-looking chicken" but everything else was "carb city".

"Bread, pies, beer and pasties!" she exclaimed, raising her hands in mock horror. "All the bad stuff! Go straight to my bum that would. Good job there's no spuds or I'd make a pig of myself. I love spuds. There ain't any in Mooncaster though, is there? Not invented yet or summink my ma says. God knows what I'll do without my bit of mash and gravy on a Sunday when I'm there. Have you tried them purple spuds? They is gorge –and proper purple all the way through like beetroot, no word of a lie! I tried mashing them with ordinary to make pink, but they just went an 'orrible grey. It were revoltin'!"

Scrupulously removing the "killer fattening skin" from the meat, she put a morsel of pheasant into her mouth and chewed. The instant she tasted the gamey flavour her expression changed and her eyes popped wide. A moment later, she was spitting it out and retching. Seizing the ale, she downed 300 calories in one swig.

The feast continued until nine o'clock when there was one final reading for the night. Jody rested her forehead on the table. What was the point of going on with this charade? It wasn't going to work on them now.

The other children watched in stony silence as the adults around them shivered with pleasure to be back in their other lives. Marcus folded his arms and stared fixedly at the castle model, refusing to take any notice of their slack-jawed faces. He was sick to the back teeth of it. Charm clasped her hands in front of her as though in prayer and tried to imagine roaming around those battlements or gazing up at one of the towers, willing herself there. Under one table the youngest feet nudged and scuffled one another. The playful kicks travelled back and forth in a kinetic pulse. Christina was at one end and Alasdair formed the cut-off point at the other, until he started joining in as well. The adults were too absorbed in the world of Mooncaster to notice and the mind of the Ismus was on other matters.

When the reading was over, the children were allowed to return to their cabins with promises of an even better day tomorrow.

"Lucky us," Jody mumbled to herself. "Can hardly wait."

Alasdair rounded up his group. Most of them were half asleep. It had been one long, exhausting day for everyone and their feet were dragging. He led them out and was pleased to see Tommy Williams smiling at last.

Marcus made his way over to Charm, who was put out to have lost the interest of the cameras.

"How did you like the scoff then, gorgeous?" he asked.

"It were mingin'," she answered, striding past him.

"So," he called after her. "What you up to now? It's still early! We should hang out and chillax."

"Do you ever hear yourself?" Lee asked with a shake of his head as he left.

Marcus made a gesture behind him.

When the refectory was empty of children, the Ismus thanked the minstrels and the news teams. They bowed and followed the Jacks and Jills outside. Kate Kryzewski lingered and approached.

"I trust you now have enough for your report?" he asked.

The woman looked apologetic. "I'm sorry, my Lord," she said. "It is strange for me to be out here in the Great Hall, when I know I should be in the kitchen. What will Mistress Slab say? She will cuff my head with the big spoon, I know it!"

"Peace," he told her. "Remember that in this dream you are Miss Kryzewski; you have a report to make and send to America. You are only Columbine when you awaken back in the castle. Here, you must be the best Miss Kryzewski you can be, so that you are stronger in your real life – or else how will you ward off the Jockey's advances?"

"Yes," she said, collecting herself and working with the traces of Kate that remained. "The report, what I need – what *it* needs – is to see some 'afters'. These dumb kids are the 'befores'. This piece won't pack any punch unless we get to see them after the sacred text has opened their eyes. That's the pay-off, that's what'll resonate and make Americans sit up and realise the awesome benefits of your great work. They're suckers for happy endings. If they can see these kids get turned around from surly aberrants to overjoyed at discovering who they really are, that'd clinch it."

The Ismus listened attentively. She was right and he needed to stall the US, to keep them from taking action for a little while longer.

"I agree," he said. "I promise you shall have your 'afters'. But not tomorrow. Spend that day up in London. Film in the hospitals, nursing homes, the day centres with the disabled. I can arrange for you to visit a prison to see how reformed the inmates have become. Return here on Sunday and you shall have a whole merry bunch of children anxious to tell the world of their newfound joy."

She thanked him profusely and hurried out to join Sam in the car. Jangler came over to join his master.

"Can you really turn those children?" he asked. "I thought it was impossible. That was never the reason they were gathered here – or why the other centres around the world will be needed."

"Oh, yes," the Ismus said. "It's possible. But it isn't a simple matter. I shall have to call on aid, as I did back in 1936. The night I 'disappeared'."

"That is most dangerous!" the old man cried.

"As I said, I do not baulk at risks. It will be uncomfortable certainly, but necessary. We are so close to achieving our goal. I cannot turn back now. Whatever Miss Kryzewski asks for, she gets. That is why I invited her. She is the key to America. Her report will unlock it for me."

"How many children will you give?"

"That is impossible to answer. The power I call upon is… very difficult to control. It will be like using a battering ram to gain entry to their minds. I must be careful not to cause too much damage within. Their young heads exploding would not make good footage, especially in high definition."

Jangler chuckled at the prospect then became serious.

"As long as you do not place yourself in danger, my Lord," he said.

"If I had never placed myself in danger, I would never have heard the voice of the Dawn Prince Himself, uttering my name."

"I cannot even dare hope I shall one day hear Him – or look upon His great Majesty."

The Ismus smiled. "What we do here, Jangler," he said, "will bring that glorious day ever closer."

The old man puffed out his chest proudly. "And the Lady Labella?" he asked. "Might I enquire after her health?"

"She is blooming, Jangler, blooming!"

"Most highly favoured Lady! That is gratifying news, my Lord."

The Ismus held up his hand. "But we run ahead of ourselves!" he told him. "Tonight our little aberrant rabbits must earn their carrots. That is the primary reason they are here."

Outside in the compound, a chorus of car doors and engines started. The Jacks and Jills each had a black or red BMW waiting and were driven off to the nearest five-star country hotel. The vehicles outside the camp followed them up the forest road.

Jody sat on the step outside her chalet and watched the headlights sweep over the trees and disappear in the distance. The kids inside were waiting to brush their teeth before bed, but Charm was hogging the bathroom. Most of them, including Christina, were fast asleep long before she emerged. It had been a long, exhausting and stressful day.

In Alasdair's cabin the boys had crowded round the sink together and were already under the crinkly linen of the brand-new duvets. The Scottish lad strummed his guitar in the semi-darkness for a time, lulling them to sleep with gentle tunes.

It was different and more rowdy in Lee and Marcus's hut. The boys there were older and, though tired, no one was going to be the first to admit he wanted to go to sleep. Jim was lying on his bed, rereading one of his favourite issues of *X-Men*, admiring the artistry and imagination all over again.

Spencer was engrossed in his portable media player, watching a Western. He was heavily into cowboy movies; they were as removed from the world of Mooncaster and his own unhappy, timid life as he could imagine.

Living in Southport, he had taken to roaming the seemingly endless tracts of beach and sand dunes there, pretending he was thousands of miles away, in the Nevada Desert. With classic cowboy soundtracks playing in his earphones, he would mosey on down the trail, tracking coyotes or outlaws, and practise sharpshooting with his two-finger Colt 45. Jackrabbits fled at the jingle of his spurs and the towering cacti of his mindscape were riddled with his quick-draw lead. Immersing himself in the fantasy of a lone, silent lawman, as the world around him went haywire, was the only way he had kept sane. He had even bought a Stetson off eBay and, when he was sure no one was around, would wear it on those solitary walks. Everyone had their own way of coping. That was his. He had brought his hat along this weekend as a reassuring talisman. He wasn't going to unpack it. As long as it was with him, in the bag, that was enough.

The three other boys, Mason, Drew and Nicholas, wanted to play on the cabin's games console, but Marcus had possession of the TV remote and was flicking through the Freeview channels.

"Nothing but crap on nowadays," he grumbled, hopping from station to station. "*DJ* gets everywhere. They've tarted up the Rover's Return to be an old inn and the street is pretending to be that village – they've thatched all the houses! Ken Barlow looks a right knob in tights. You can't even get *Friends* any more – you think Joey looks like me? Girls have said… Hey, we made the news! This place is on the TV. That's today, when we first got here – and there's that Charm bird all over the Ismus bloke. Talk about sucking up! Look at her! I'm still going to get in her pants though. More blah de blah from him, what else is on? How about this – *Celebrity Minchetchef*? There's no way anyone can make that vomit taste good, no matter how many chunky chips you stack next to it like Jenga. *My Big Fat Jaxy Wedding*, nope. Home shopping – get your cloaks, leather tunics and pointy shoes here, *Have I Got Jax For You*?… Oh, look, here's the black and white Nazi channel. At least that never changes. All they ever show on there is ancient stuff about Hitler. Who watches that?"

"You should, Ladies' Man," Lee said as he walked by. "You really got no idea what's going down here."

"What is it with you?" Marcus demanded, infuriated by the lad's attitude. "You've been on my case since we got here. Just what is your problem?"

"We all got the same problem," Lee told him. "But some of us is too blind or too dumb to see it yet. You think we're here to get our caps twisted? No way." He put a cigarette in his mouth and pushed against the door. "I'll take this one outside," he said as he left. "Wouldn't want you to choke in the night, Lily-lungs."

"Jerk," Marcus muttered when he was gone.

He glanced up at the mezzanine and took the opportunity to dash up and open the small window to let in some fresh air. Then he picked up his carefully folded clothes, sniffed them for smoke and checked for burns. Downstairs three boys leaped on the games console and were soon hunting flesh-eating zombies and blasting heads and legs off with sub-machine guns. They were glad that games based on *Dancing Jax* were still only at the development stage. This was what they wanted.

With the unlit cigarette still hanging on his lip, Lee strolled in front of the cabins.

"Hi," Jody greeted him, looking up from the step. "How's it going with…?" But he ignored her and continued walking.

The girl shrugged with indifference and put her chin on her knees. She had grown to accept being as noticeable as wallpaper and it only proved her earlier decision with Christina had been the right one.

"No point trying to make friends here," she told herself. "Other people only ever let you down."

Lee sauntered round the corner out of sight. The main block was before him. When he was certain no one was about, he ran across to it, veering sideways when he heard voices approaching, and crouched in the shadows.

The Ismus came striding out, followed by his bodyguards and Jangler. The men crossed to where the SUV was parked and Jangler waved them off with a flourish of his hand.

"Till the morrow, my Lord!" he called, bowing as low as his portly figure allowed.

The SUV drove through the gates and rumbled up the forest road. Jangler returned to the main block, took a hoop of keys from his belt and locked the doors.

Concealed in the darkness, Lee waited till the old man had finished, then watched him head towards the cabins.

Jody was still huddled on the step when Jangler came ambling by. He touched the brim of his floppy hat in salutation and wished her a good night.

"Are you staying here?" she asked in surprise.

He paused and a strange, unpleasant smile tugged at the corners of his mouth.

"Where else should the Lockpick be but on guard?" he replied. "You young people need someone to watch over you."

"You make us sound like prisoners."

"Prisoners?" he repeated, making a staccato noise like a cross between a cough and a laugh. "Here, in these luxury holiday chalets, with all this beautiful scenery and invigorating fresh air around you? Tut tut, what an overactive imagination."

"Shame I can't apply it to *Dancing Jax* though, huh?"

"Oho," he said. The old man inclined his head and touched his hat once more. "Sweet dreams," he added.

Jody jerked her head aside. "Fat chance," she huffed. "Been nothing but bad ones since this started."

Jangler's eyebrows lifted and the moustache jiggled on his lip. "How... distressing," he murmured. "We must see what we can do about that, mustn't we?"

Then he clicked his heels together, an action he immediately regretted because his feet were still suffering in those shoes, and continued on his way.

Something about the way he spoke those last words made Jody's skin creep. Her eyes followed him till he reached the cabin at the other end. She wondered who, if anyone, was going to occupy the empty one next to it.

Jangler hesitated before entering. He turned his gaze towards the night-shrouded forest that surrounded the camp and chuckled to himself, knowing what was lurking out there. He gave another chuckle when he anticipated what would happen later, when everyone was asleep, and let himself in.

Lee circled the main block, testing each window he came across. Finally he found one that had been left open. He climbed inside and took a slim torch from the pocket of his trackie bottoms. He was in the lecture room, where the press conference had been held earlier that day, and where Sam, the cameraman, had later been lured by the Ismus, so the Black Face Dames could hold him down and force minchet into his mouth.

Lee shone the torchlight around; there was nothing in here, nothing he could use. As silently as possible, he made his way into the next room. It was the dining hall. The tables had been cleared, but the model of the castle still dominated the centre.

The boy curled his lip at it then made his way to the kitchen.

In there the torchlight bounced over the brushed steel surfaces and sparkled in the utensils hanging on the wall. Lee wasted no time. He pulled open every cupboard, searched in every drawer. Then he rushed to another door and yanked it open. Behind was a well-stocked storeroom, crammed from floor to ceiling with catering-sized tins and packets of dry goods. None of it was Mooncaster fare.

"Sweet!" he whispered as the torch beam revealed the treasures on the shelves.

He frowned when he realised he should have brought his holdall. He couldn't carry more than two of those great tins at a time without it. Looking around, he saw, tucked under the lowest shelf, a collection of empty Tupperware containers.

"Hallelujah!" he muttered, smiling.

Taking the biggest, he put a bag of pasta and two bags of rice inside. Then he filled up the remaining space with packets of dried fruit and one of sugar. Sealing the lid back on and pocketing the torch, he carried the box through to the kitchen.

"I'll be back for the rest of you foxy bitches," he addressed the darkness of the storeroom.

It wasn't long before he was climbing back out of the window. Kneeling on the ground outside, he waited till he was sure the coast was clear. Then, lugging the container, he darted over the lawn behind the main block – towards the forbidding expanse of night-smothered trees.

Lee wasn't afraid of the deep gloom, but he almost choked at the rank smell that hit his nostrils as he pressed deeper into the wood. Was there a stagnant ditch close by? Hailing from an estate in South London, he wasn't overly familiar with the countryside. Did it always stink like this? It was stronger than the drains in July.

Although he tried to move as silently as possible, the leaves of the previous autumn crunched as noisily as crisps and cornflakes under his trainers and twigs snapped even louder. When he had gone a short distance, he stopped and took out his torch again. He had to find something distinctive, something he would recognise again. Ahead he saw a fat tree. He had no idea what sort, but its bottommost branches spread out like two arms and the gnarled bark of the trunk suggested a face with puckered lips. It reminded him of a girl he had known in the days before the book. Yes, that would do.

He deposited the box at its base and hunted around for twigs and bracken to use as camouflage. As he collected it, the sensation he was being watched began to grow in his mind and the putrid smell of decay became stronger.

Unnerved, Lee looked around. It was too dark to see; the black shadows concealed everything and he hesitated to switch the torch on again.

"That you, pussy boy?" he murmured, thinking Marcus had followed him. "Don't you try no tricks on me."

There was no answer except the listless stirring of the leaves overhead and the faintest of noises, like the soft and subtle popping of bath foam. Lee turned towards the strange sound and thought he saw a shadow slide down from above. He blinked. Trying to pierce the darkness was a strain on the eyes.

He snapped on the torch. The beam shone directly on to the bubbling mass of black mould that was rearing in front of him.

8

ALASDAIR SAT HIMSELF down on the chalet step and picked out a tune on his guitar.

"Bit miserable," a girl's voice called over to him. "But you're pretty good."

He looked up and saw Jody still on her own step.

The Scot acknowledged her with a nod.

"You get in a lot of practice when there's no anything else to do – and no pals to do it with neither," he said. "And I like 'miserable'."

"So what bands you into?"

Alasdair shook his head. "Och, no," he replied. "I'm no playing that game."

"What game?"

"Do you really have to shout? Can you no come sit here and talk civil? I've got a hut full of wee lads trying to get their heads doon."

Wrapping her green cardigan about her, the girl wandered over and sat next to him.

"What game?" she repeated.

"The 'I know more obscure bands than you do' game," he said dismissively. "That sort of music snobbery doesnae interest me."

Jody stood up again. "Oh, forget it," she said, exasperated. "I was only trying to make conversation. I shouldn't have bothered. None of you are worth bothering with. I keep telling myself I'm better off on my own; dunno why I don't listen. Stick your ruddy guitar, stick your dirges and stick your snitty attitude."

She turned to leave, but the boy asked her to wait.

"Sorry," he groaned. "When you spend months being defensive, it's a tough habit to crack and my social skills are rusty. Knee-jerk rude, that's me. Sit down… please."

"Not easy, is it?" she said, softening. "I've almost forgotten what it's like to talk to someone normal."

"Aye," he agreed. "Would you look at the state of us – it's tragic."

"After what we've been through it's not surprising: the riots, the firebombing of the bookshops, the persecution... And there's only so many times you can get the hope and trust kicked out of you. We're too scared to even try to make friends – I know I am and I can be a right cow about it."

The boy laughed.

"I can!" she insisted. "I was foul to a little girl earlier. I wish – oh, it's too late now."

"We could learn a lot from the bairns here," he told her. "They're still able an' willing to have a go at making pals without worrying it wilnae last. My lads in there are going to be thick as thieves come Monday morning."

"The day they have to leave their new friends and go back to families who don't want them," Jody said bitterly. "Provided they haven't been zombified by then."

Alasdair looked down at his guitar and played the opening notes of a song.

"Well, that's less miserable than the other one," she observed.

"'I am a Rock' by Simon and Garfunkel," he told her.

"And there's you talking about obscure!"

"Good tunes are good tunes however old they are. It's all ear food – and that one seemed appropriate."

He gave the guitar his attention once more and sang the last few lines.

> *I touch no one and no one touches me.*
> *I am a rock,*
> *I am an island.*
> *And a rock feels no pain;*
> *And an island never cries.*

"Do you have a pithy playlist for every occasion?" she asked dryly.

"Empathic jukebox, that's me," he answered with a grin. "Name's Alasdair and – *oh, no* – I'm going to make friends with you so deal with it. If I'm not brainwashed by the end of this weekend, you can even have my mobile number. Make a change having someone call it. I dinnae bother charging it up half the time."

Jody smiled with pleasure and the wall she had built around herself crumbled a little.

"Music's always been a massive part of my life," she said, gazing at the guitar. "When I was three, my mum and dad took me to Glastonbury. There's photos of me covered in the thickest mud, like some midget swamp monster. We went back every other year. The bands I've seen…"

She looked off into the darkness of the distant trees. She didn't want to think about the past. It was gone.

"Your mum and dad sound cool."

"They were," she said with a stark finality in her voice. "What about yours?"

Alasdair screeched his fingernail along a string for dramatic effect. "Next question!" he said evasively.

Jody tactfully reverted to the previous subject. "I wonder if they'll even have Glastonbury this year?" she murmured. "I was going to go without them this time, just me and my best mate, before all this happened. If they do have it, it'll probably be full of mass readings and minstrels and hey nonny nonnying."

"Do they no have plenty of that there anyway, wi' all the tree-hugging hippy caper and henna tattoos?"

Jody coughed to disguise her laughter. She'd hugged plenty of trees and had her hands decorated lots of times.

"That's only a tiny part of it!" she said. "The best, most amazing artists in the world play on those stages. It's incredible – *was* incredible."

Before Alasdair could continue, they were distracted by Marcus emerging from the next cabin. He had changed into a Man United strip and came jogging over.

"Going to do some exercise before turning in," he addressed the Scottish lad, ignoring Jody. "Want to join me?"

"No, I'm good thanks."

"Play me something to work out to then!" Marcus called, trotting to the centre of the lawn, sparring with the night air as he hopped from foot to foot.

"I do believe I'd rather catch leprosy," Alasdair remarked to Jody.

"He's full of himself that one," she said.

"Aye, well, that's probably what's kept him going. With me, it was my guitar. I dinnae know what I'd have done without it these past months. Takes my mind off it, mostly. How did you manage?"

"Books and bands. Proper books, I mean! Anything to escape from ruddy Jacks and Jills. What is it with that naff spelling of Jax with an 'x' anyway? It don't make no sense."

Alasdair had no answer for her and so they watched, bemused, as Marcus threw himself into an energetic routine, diving to the ground for press-ups, followed by crunches, then squat thrusts.

"Have you noticed the way he walks?" Jody said. "Like he's carrying two invisible carpets under his arms."

"He's no even that pumped. Thinks he's bigger than he is. And does he shower in aftershave? It comes into the room before he does and doesnae go when he leaves. Did you ever see them old Charlie Broon cartoons? There's one wee character called Pig-Pen who has a cloud of dirt about him wherever he goes. Yon laddie's the same, but his cloud's flowers and citrus notes. Ha – I loved Charlie Broon. When he's at his desk in school, you never see the teacher, you just hear this boring, droning noise coming from the front – no even proper words, just a noise. That's what I think of every time we have a communal reading of you know what."

Jody looked thoughtful. "Did you know," she began, "people use so many perfumes, deodorants and air-fresheners, the chemicals have now reached such a saturation point they can be detected in the air we breathe? Can you get your head round that? The size of this planet and we've managed to turn the atmosphere surrounding it into toxic pot-pourri. All those synthetic particles and dangerous metals soaking into the food we eat and building up in our bodies. No one knows what they'll do to us, but it won't be pleasant. Still, if a downstairs loo smells of roses and the kitchen floor is lemony fresh, it must be worth it."

"Ray of sunshine, you are," Alasdair observed. "Och, look at him jumping up and doon. What a pranny."

Jody began to laugh.

"I know why he's doing it!" she spluttered with sudden realisation. "It's so Barbie girl will see him. He thinks it'll impress her."

Alasdair knew she was right and he began to laugh as well. It was the first time either of them had really laughed in too long and the abrupt release of their pent-up fears and tensions was a bursting dam. Soon they were doubled over in hysterics. But Jody laughed too fiercely, too loudly. Tears streaked down her face; the breath wheezed in her lungs. Soon she was no longer in control. She couldn't stop and the laughter began to hurt as it escalated into a panic attack. The fear swelled in her aching chest. Her hands started to shake and she gripped the step for support.

Alasdair stared at her in alarm. Over on the grass, Marcus looked up from the set of one-handed press-ups he had started and frowned at the racket she was making.

"Slap her!" he shouted.

Alasdair ignored that, but he clutched Jody's shoulders and turned her towards him.

"Listen to me!" he told her urgently. "Calm down! Take long, deep breaths. That's it. Long, steady, deep breaths. You can do it, keep going, keep going, that's right."

The girl shuddered and he felt her go limp as the attack subsided. Her breathing eased and, trembling, she fell back.

"I thought you was about to have a seizure," he told her, relieved. "Have you no got an inhaler?"

She looked up at him through watering eyes.

"I'm not asthmatic!" she answered, gasping and confused. "I don't know what that was – you must think I'm a freak."

The boy couldn't help grinning. "Aye," he said. "A freak with a bright purple face right noo."

Jody searched for a fitting retort, but instead she burst out laughing again. This time it was a natural, carefree sound that made her feel light and good inside.

Alasdair chuckled with her.

"We're all freaks here," he said.

"Freaks and rejects," she added.

"Are you spelling that wi' two 'x's?" he joked.

Suddenly a terrified yell rang out in the distance and nothing was funny any more. Jody leaped to her feet.

"What the ruddy hell were that?" she murmured.

Alasdair rose beside her. "That was definitely no a happy noise," he whispered.

"It came from back there!" Marcus said, racing up and running round the cabin to stare at the woods behind.

"It was a person," Jody said. "A person screaming. What should we do? Call someone?"

"Like who?" Marcus snapped. "We're in the middle of nowhere."

"We could get that old guy and tell him. He could do something."

"What, Captain Mainwaring?" Alasdair said doubtfully. "You reckon?"

"Shouldn't we try? Someone's in trouble."

"You're a fine one with the understatement," the Scottish boy muttered. "To me it sounded more like they were getting their throat cut and hacked to bits. That scream was of the curdling blood type."

"Shut up!" Marcus hissed at them. "Over there – look!"

He nodded towards the trees. In the midst of that shadowy expanse, something was moving. A figure was lunging and stumbling out of them, tearing over the grass as fast as it could go.

"Who is it?" Jody asked.

It was too dark to tell. The figure came charging towards them. Soon they heard its frantic breathing and the three teenagers looked at one another nervously. Marcus began edging away. Then the unknown person tripped and went crashing to the ground. A string of expletives polluted the air.

"Oh, it's *him*!" Marcus said, recognising the voice with a mix of relief and contempt.

The other two were none the wiser, but the figure scrambled to its feet again and continued running. It wasn't long before it was close enough for each of them to identify.

Lee Charles came lurching into view, arms thrashing the air in his panic. He wasn't used to running and the sweat was pouring down his face. He almost charged right into the others, as if he didn't even see them. At the last moment, he skidded to a stop and whipped round to stare searchingly at the empty stretch of lawn behind.

"Did you see?" he demanded. "Did you see it? Where'd it go?"

"See what?" Marcus asked, folding his arms.

Lee glared at the three of them. "You didn't see nuthin'?" he shouted in angry disbelief.

Alasdair and Jody shook their heads.

"We just saw you," Marcus told him with a gleam in his eyes. "And heard you squealing like a frightened girly."

If Lee even heard that, he let it pass and turned to face the dark stretch of trees once more. He couldn't have imagined that back there. That frothing horror had been real, he knew it, and he had never been so afraid in his entire life. But what it was, he had no idea. Why hadn't it pursued him? He doubled over to catch his breath, trying to make sense of it in his head. He had escaped it – that was the only thing that mattered.

"You OK?" Jody asked.

He waited before answering. His terror was fading and cold, cynical reason flooded in to take its place, telling him he must have been mistaken. What he saw couldn't possibly exist. It was a trick of the dark and the unfamiliar. His senses were deceived, jerked around by the strangeness of the countryside at night.

"I dunno, man," he argued with himself as he straightened up. "Seemed like the real deal to me."

"What did you see back there?" Jody asked. "What happened?"

Lee looked at her vaguely and shrugged, trying to claim back any cool he had lost. "You hearing things, girl," he stated flatly. "I didn't see nuthin'."

"Didnae sound like nothing," Alasdair persisted. "If there's something dangerous out there, we ought to know."

"Leave me be!" Lee snapped angrily. "It was nuthin'!"

Pushing past them, he took a cigarette from his pocket and clamped it between his lips, but he knew if he tried to light up, they'd see his trembling hands. With a snort of impatience, he stomped back to his cabin.

"Well weird," Jody commented. "What were that about?"

"Why was he even over there?" Alasdair asked. "Running away?"

"He's dead moody," the girl observed. "Maybe he wanted to get shot of us for a bit. Can't really blame him. We're not exactly the nicest bunch, are we?"

Marcus sniffed and sneered. "His problem is he thinks he's Samuel L Jackson," he said. "Ha – you just can't get away from that word... 'Jack'. It's everywhere. You ever noticed that? Jack of all trades, hijack, carjack, Jack Russells, jackals, Jack the Ripper, Jack-in-a-box, Jack the Giant-killer, the house that Jack built – even the bloody flag!"

"So which is your favourite?" Jody asked archly.

"Jack the Lad," came the instant reply. "Just like me."

The girl wondered how often he had rehearsed saying that. It had sprung too readily from his lips. Just as readily she thought of several other types of 'Jack' that suited him better.

"S'pose I'm Jack Daniels then," Alasdair volunteered.

Marcus was bursting to come back with '*Jock* Daniels', but he bit his tongue. He'd save that one for when he knew the Scottish lad a bit better and he could get away with it.

"Well, I'm not any sort of Jack," Jody declared. "Not yet anyway. That's why we're all here, isn't it, to get turned into them? If that ever happens, which doesn't look likely to me cos so far it's been hopeless and a total waste of time. Right – I'm off to bed. See you tomorrow for more riveting fun and games – not."

"Goodnight," Alasdair called as she returned to her cabin.

"She's Jack and the Beancurd," Marcus snickered once she was inside. "Or a stone-cold Jack-et potato."

"Do ye have to be quite so unpleasant? I like the lass."

"Oh, she's not worth defending," Marcus laughed dismissively. "She's plenty capable of doing that herself. Fuglies like her – they're not much to look at so they grow up bitter and have to belittle or humiliate a bloke any chance they get. Seen dozens like it. Avoid – avoid – avoid."

"Can ye no just go away now? Seriously, I find you totally offensive."

Marcus appeared surprised. "What's up with you?" he asked.

"I'm allergic to your company if you must know. You make me boke, to be honest."

"Boke?"

"Gag, heave – cause the back of my throat to burn with bile."

"Oh, get over yourself! What are you? Some tartan saint or something? You know what, I've had it trying to be mates with you. Shove it up your sporran, Jimmy!"

He stormed off in disgust and slammed the door of his cabin behind him.

"Tosser," Alasdair muttered. "I'd forgot there were creatures like that in the world."

Then something Jody said resonated with him and he remembered that only minutes ago they had been slagging Marcus off just as harshly. No, they really weren't the nicest bunch of people. But here they were and they were stuck with each other. Whatever the weekend threw at them, they'd have to make the best of it.

"S'only two more days," he consoled himself. "I can hack that."

He had never been more wrong.

Deciding to turn in as well, he took one final look at the trees at the rear of the camp.

"I dinnae care what that Samuel L Jackson lad said," he breathed, still ignorant of Lee's real name. "He did see something in them woods – and it scared the living keech out of him."

Brooding on that uncomfortable thought, he picked up his guitar and crept into his own cabin where the younger lads were sleeping soundly. As he slid into bed, he wished he'd smuggled some ale out of the feast. He hadn't told Jody the complete truth earlier. It wasn't just his guitar that had seen him through the past few months.

The night pressed heavily over the compound.

Each small dorm was thick with the soft, sighing chorus of slumbering breaths. Even Lee had drifted into an uneasy sleep, the unlit cigarette mangled in his fist. In the next bed, remembering the threat about smoke blowing in his face, Marcus had turned to the wall.

In Jody's cabin Charm lay as still as an Egyptian mummy. She wore a pink baby-doll nightie and her face was greasy with moisturiser. A cuddly Garfield was tucked in beside her. Dreams, colours and memories drifted through the pillow-resting heads of those troubled, rejected children. One of the girls murmured unhappily. The forehead of another creased as recent events replayed in her mind. Christina squirmed under the duvet, kicking her legs as she ran in a jumbled maze of corridors lined with towering clown faces. The distorted figures of her parents retreated before her, always out of reach. One bed along, Jody's lashes were wet with the tears she denied her waking self and the eyes beneath their lids flicked rapidly from side to side.

Above the beds the air grew oppressive and smothering, like the heaviness of impending thunder. In the bathroom the light above the mirror had been left on for the young ones who were nervous and afraid of spending the night in a strange place. The door had been kept ajar, but now it closed silently and a tide of darkness engulfed the sleeping girls.

On the mezzanine, one of them cried out and whimpered. No one heard her. An unnatural, impenetrable sleep had settled. Nothing could wake them now. It coiled about them, dragging them, sliding them, down and down.

Then, in that hollow dark, a point of orange light began to glow. High on one wall it glimmered into life, accompanied by a faint but steady buzzing.

There was a crackle of static and the Bakelite device squealed as it searched and probed for signals. The central dial shone dimly and its needle quivered. Finally the infernal invention of Austerly Fellows tuned into the nightmares unfolding in the minds of the children in the beds below.

The gratis copies of *Dancing Jax* that had been cast on the floor, buried under clothes or kicked beneath beds, began to twitch and tremble. With jerky movements, they pulled themselves clear. A bedside cupboard swung open and the paperback that one of the girls had thrust inside fell out. Across the room a drawer pushed outward and the book within flipped itself free.

The buzzing grew louder. Through the device's brass grill, an old tune from the 1930s came warbling into the cabin. In every chalet it was the same. A wretched, despairing song, born of the Great Depression, went floating out across the slumbering heads of the stupefied children. A tired and downtrodden woman's voice sang about a taxi dancer in a cheap dance hall:

> *I'm one of those lady teachers,*
> *a beautiful hostess, you know,*
> *the kind the Palace features*
> *at exactly a dime a throw...*

The spine of every book creased and each *Dancing Jax* fanned open. There was a rustle of paper as the pages turned on their own, flicking swiftly and purposefully through chapters on kings and queens, Jacks and Jills, lords and knights, squires and serfs, until each copy displayed the same page.

The music continued. The desperate, tinny song played over the sleeping heads and drifted out across the camp.

Ten cents a dance
that's what they pay me

In the end hut Jangler was still awake, sitting in a comfortable armchair, his stubby fingers laced across his stomach, and ankle-deep in a bowl of warm, soapy water. When he heard the bittersweet melody keening outside, he wiggled his toes and reached for a towel.

Fighters and sailors and bow-legged tailors
can pay for a ticket and rent me!

The nightmares of every young person intensified. Jody found herself shrunk in size and wandering the battlements of the castle model. Lead figures barred her way and the immense face of the Ismus came leering between the towers towards her, his gaunt features obliterating the sky. Across the room, Charm uttered an unhappy cry and turned her shiny face into the pillow. Above them, the dial of the Bakelite device shone more brightly and the grinding tune played on.

In Alasdair's cabin a blue spark spat from the brass grill, followed by a whisker of electrical fire that leaped and jumped about the surrounding wall. The laces on every pair of trainers and shoes began to lash from side to side until they quivered upright, pointing to the ceiling. Then each copy of the open book lifted into the air and formed a revolving circle.

Clothes and bags followed. Finally the children were plucked from their beds. Legs and arms were hoisted by invisible force. Young backs arched and heads lolled down as their bodies floated higher.

I'm there till closing time.
Dance and be merry, it's only a dime.

Now there was another voice in the song. A snarling, bestial noise that grew louder with each passing moment.

Suspended in mid-air, the children spun round helplessly. Their nightmares raged and the dial on the Bakelite bridging device shone brighter and brighter. Even the beds began to judder and lift from the floor. Sparks came shooting from the grill and the hideous voice within the song crowed with thin, pinched laughter.

> *All that you need is a ticket.*
> *Come on, big boy, ten cents a dance.*

Within each hut, at the centre of the spinning books, the darkness was shaking, becoming denser, taking on a shape.

Pulling on his slippers, Jangler started when a series of deafening cracks resounded over the camp. As he fumbled to tie the belt of his dressing gown, he hurried outside.

Fierce gales were blasting through each cabin and their doors were banging. Jangler rushed to the nearest and peered inside. The boys here were pinned to the walls, their possessions thrashing around in a maelstrom before them. Then his eyes beheld the form solidifying in the air and he clapped his hands together appreciatively.

"Bravo!" he called. "Bravo!"

The ugly voice had left the radio. Now it came grunting from the throat of the creature that had crossed over, snapping a foul greeting in response. There was a flash of blue fire. The Bakelite device squawked one last time that night and the creaky old song from the thirties died. The unnatural storm dwindled inside every cabin. Beds, bags, books, shoes, clothes and Alasdair's guitar dropped to the ground. The still sleeping children slid down the walls. Their nightmares were waning, but they remained motionless where they fell.

Jangler waved a hand at them. "Put them back in their beds," he instructed. "And tidy up a bit. It's a pigsty."

The steaming creature's large feet alighted on the carpet and its red-rimmed eyes glared at him.

"At once," Jangler commanded, turning his attention to the other cabins.

"*Myahmyahmyah*," the phlegm-gargling voice answered.

Christina winced. Her right arm hurt where she had landed on it. The suffocating sleep was lifting and her head swam. She felt sick and dizzy. Rough hands hoisted her from the floor and cast her on to the bed. The duvet was thrown over her. An unpleasant, nasal muttering echoed through her stirring thoughts and around the cabin.

"Hurry," she heard someone say.

The girl's eyelids lifted momentarily and she saw that funny, fat old man looking in at the door. She wondered who he was speaking to.

"There isn't much time," he continued tetchily. "They'll be coming out of it soon. They mustn't see any of you. Get a move on – stir your stumps."

Christina thought she saw strange figures passing by behind him. Her eyes closed once more and she rolled her groggy head aside.

"Pretty," an unnatural, tight voice gloated. "Skin smooth…"

The girl's eyes opened again. Was she still dreaming? Still locked in a nightmare? It seemed that something was in the room, something horrific and misshapen. It was across the way from her, leaning over Charm's bed, pawing at the occupant with large, gnarled hands.

"Me want," the voice gurgled. "She mine. She for Bezuel. Oh, yes."

"Leave her alone," Jangler demanded. "Stop the touching. It's too soon. Besides, you'd only break her."

Christina tried to lift her head. She was so tired. Her limbs were like stone. It took every scrap of strength she had.

A small, hunchbacked shape was lifting Charm's baby-doll nightie and peering beneath. A thick finger prodded the pink jewel that pierced her navel.

"Twinkle twinkle," it chuckled throatily. "Me have."

Christina opened her mouth to scream. The creature was naked. Its repulsive, deformed body was mottled with angry blotches, wart clusters and scarlet rashes. She tried to yell, but no sound emerged and her head flopped back against the pillow.

"That one's waking up!" Jangler remarked. "Quickly! Go join the others."

Christina heard a rebellious snort. Then she felt a weight clamber on to her own bed. It came prowling closer, creeping up until it pressed down on her chest.

Despite her terror, her eyes snapped open. The creature was crouching on top of her and she looked straight into the most repugnant face she had ever seen.

"Sleeeeeep!" a hot, stinking whisper breathed. "No wakey... no wakey."

Darkness closed in again and the seven-year-old passed out.

"Obey me!" Jangler barked. "Get off there at once!"

The creature lurched away and the door slammed shut.

When Jody finally awoke, it was still dark outside. Her joints ached as if they had been wrenched at. She gazed, bleary-eyed, around the cabin. In the gloom she could just make out another girl sitting up in bed, rubbing her shoulder and sucking the air through her teeth.

"Someone punched me," the girl complained. "Which of you cows did that?"

"Ow!" another yelped as she turned over. "My ribs. I've been thumped in my ribs."

Then Christina came to. Her shrill screams woke everyone in that hut and most of the boys next door.

Jody leaped out of bed. Forgetting her cruel words the previous afternoon, she put her arms round the little girl and tried to calm her.

"Just a bad dream," she said soothingly. "Don't fret, it's all OK. Hush, hush."

Christina shook her head violently and shoved the teenager away.

"A monster!" she shrieked. "A monster was here!"

"Shut her row, can't you?" Charm moaned. "Some of us is trying to sleep in here – know what I mean?"

But Christina would not be quiet. She pushed herself back along the bed, pressed against the wall and covered herself with the duvet.

"It was here!" she screeched. "It was!"

One of the other girls opened the bathroom door and the light within came flooding out. It was then they saw the state of the cabin. Clothes were strewn everywhere, chairs in the TV area were upturned, pictures were askew and bags had been emptied.

"My make-up!" Charm bawled when she saw her scattered bottles and brushes. She pointed an accusing, painted fingernail at Jody. "You did this! You sour-faced, jealous munter!" she cried.

"Oh, go do one, you thick airhead," Jody snapped back. "I wouldn't touch your animal-tested warpaint. It repulses me. Doesn't it disgust you to know you're not the first dog to have worn that muck?"

Charm jumped up and switched the main lights on. The others groaned at her, but she ignored them and began gathering up her precious belongings.

Then they heard the yells and din of a scuffle next door. Marcus had awoken with a cut on his forehead and found his clothes slung into corners. He instantly accused Lee and the fight that had been brewing all day finally erupted. It was fuelled by the anger that had simmered impotently within each of them during recent months. They brawled their way down the stairs, barging and dragging one another between the beds and outside, on to the grass. Other lads came whooping after them, cheering and calling for blood.

Most of the girls in Jody's cabin ran to see and the other three huts emptied quickly to watch the pair kick and punch the sense out of one another. Marcus charged into Lee with teeth bared like a pit bull. He managed to land one good thump in the other lad's solid gut, but that was all.

Lee was naturally stronger and, back in the old days, before *Dancing Jax*, while Marcus was spinning girls like plates and preening himself, he had been surviving on a Peckham estate. He was versed in every trick of the street. Seizing hold of the other boy's arm, he swung him round then elbowed him powerfully in the stomach. As Marcus doubled over, Lee smashed the back of his fist up into the boy's mouth. Marcus recoiled. Lee's foot hooked round his ankles and felled him. Lee stamped on the hand that had thumped him then dropped heavily on to Marcus's chest and started to rearrange his face.

The goading cheers of the other boys ceased. This was too violent for them. Some girls cried for it to stop.

"Enough!" a young voice yelled suddenly. Jim Parker's slender frame sprang forward and tried to intervene. "I will not stand by and permit this! Stand back! Let him go."

Lee didn't even hear him so Jim made a grab at his right arm. The twelve-year-old was flung aside and went sprawling on the grass in an undignified tangle. Lee raised his fist again, preparing to deliver Marcus a cheekbone-crunching blow.

"That *is* enough!" Alasdair shouted, pushing through the kids at the front. "You'll kill him."

He crooked his arms round Lee's neck and, on the fourth attempt, managed to drag him clear. Marcus's lip was pouring with blood and one eye was already swelling.

"Had it comin'!" Lee spat. "He got no respect!"

"Leave it!" Alasdair told him. "Back off and calm down!"

Marcus lay gasping and winded. His tongue dabbed tentatively at his lip. Then he raised his head and hurled a torrent of ignorant hate abuse.

Lee lunged at him again and Alasdair struggled to pull him away once more.

"You're gonna be crapping your teeth out when I'm done!" Lee promised. "You is lucky I ain't got my blade on me – I'd stick you!"

"Come on, ladies!" Alasdair scolded, trying to douse their fury with humour. "Put your handbags doon. You're scaring the wee ones."

Marcus sat up and winced.

"He started it," he said accusingly, glaring at Lee with one eye. "He cut

140

me when I was asleep and chucked my stuff about."

Alasdair jumped in before Lee could yell back.

"We've all had our stuff thrown about," he told them. "And some of my lads woke wi' bruises. Something crazy's gone on. It's no just you!"

One of the girls spoke up and said it had happened in their cabin too. Someone from Jody's hut said the same.

"Can this circus get any more insane?" Alasdair wondered aloud. He turned back to Lee and Marcus. "You two big jessies need to apologise to one another then maybe we can all go back to bed. God knows what mad hoops we'll be made to jump through in the morning so we need proper shut-eye. No, I'm no making fun of your eye, Marcus. Go clean that up. Put a cold flannel on it."

Marcus got to his feet. He glowered at Lee for a moment then stormed past and headed back to their cabin. Lee hissed through his teeth at him.

"I know he's a choob," Alasdair agreed, "but do you no think we've got enough on our plate without dumping even more? What do you reckon old Mainwaring'll say when he sees you've Picasso'd yon himbo's face? And then there's the Ismus guy – they'll no be happy. It's no exactly the cuddly photo op they was planning."

Lee scowled. He knew the Scot was right. "Yeah," he said.

Alasdair nodded. "Just chill and go easy on the moron," he suggested. "OK?"

He raised his hands and told everyone the show was over and they should return to their cabins. The children began to disperse.

"That Jangler guy must sleep with plugs in his ears," Lee said. "How come he ain't out here by now?"

Alasdair had begun to puzzle about that too.

"His light's still off," he observed, glancing at the end cabin.

Lee frowned. "But check out that empty one next door," he whispered.

Alasdair shook his head. "What about it? That's dark too."

"Yeah, but them curtains, when we all turned in before – they was open. Now they's shut."

He pondered on that a moment then shrugged it off. He stared awkwardly at the ground.

"Thanks," he mumbled.

"What for?"

"Stopping me getting all Moulinex on that prototard's face back then."

"Yon skirt-chasing poser isnae the problem here."

"No, but you tell me how I can beat the life out of that damn book and I'll do it."

"If it was that easy, I'd have done it myself, pal – and don't think I didnae try at the beginning! I was out there on the streets, fighting against the Jax mobs that were marching through Edinburgh, reading it through loudhailers, convertin' as they went. I've had the people I was fightin' with get turned as I was stood right next to them and then been chased like a mad dog by both lots. So don't think you're the only one who's had it bad – it didnae all just go on doon in London you know. "

Lee grinned and introduced himself, clasping Alasdair's hand firmly and shaking it.

"You got any spare bunks in your place?" he asked with a laugh. "I'm done sleeping next to that Lynxstain. His aftershave is cutting through my nicotine and making my eyes water."

"Just two more days," Alasdair chuckled. "Then you'll never see or smell him again."

"Amen to that!"

Lee clicked his fingers and clapped the other boy's shoulder. "Catch you later," he said, heading back to the cabin.

Alasdair smiled faintly. He understood that somehow he had passed a test of acceptance and felt quietly pleased with himself. Lee probably hadn't shaken hands with anyone for a long time.

He was about to return to his own dorm when he saw Jim Parker lingering on the grass. The boy was gazing up at the stars. Here in the middle of nowhere, away from the light pollution of towns and cities, they were fiercely bright.

"Hey!" Alasdair said. "That was real brave what you tried to do. Brave but daft – he's a big lad that one, could've smacked you into next week."

Jim turned a solemn face to him.

"A coward can't fight injustice," he said gravely.

The Scot almost laughed, but he saw the boy was deadly earnest.

"Well, pick which fights to break up a wee bit more wisely next time," he advised.

"A hero never chooses his battles," Jim said. "They choose him."

"Er… aye…"

Jim smiled. "You don't understand," he said cryptically. "It doesn't matter. Why should you?"

"No… I'm just dog-tired. I'm away to grab a couple of hours before the panto kicks off again. You should too."

Jim caught his wrist.

"I won't let anything happen to the rest of us while we're here," he promised, placing a hand on his chest as though making a vow. "You don't need to worry. I'll protect you."

Alasdair managed an uncertain grin and went back to his own cabin.

"Two days is too many," he muttered under his breath.

Throughout the fight Jody had remained inside with Christina. Lads belting one another didn't interest or impress her. She was more concerned with what had happened in here while they were sleeping.

"It's well nuts," she said. "What the bugger's going on? Who's been flinging our gear about and thumping us – and why didn't none of us wake up?"

"Poultrygeists, innit?" Charm declared, zipping up one of her beauty bags as she strode to the bathroom to check herself out in the mirror. "I seen all them celeb ghost fings on the telly. They lob stuff at you, it's a proven fact is what it is. It's your actual science, cos they use special info-red cameras – what make your face green. So it's totally true. It's not fake nor nofink."

"Shut it," Jody warned her. "This little'un's scared enough without you making it worse. There's no such things as ghosts."

Christina was still shaking with terror.

"I know who did it," she whispered. "It wasn't ghosts. I saw him. You was wrong. He *is* real. He was right here! Him from the book."

"Who? Who did you see?"

"Mr Big Nose."

9

JUST TWO HOURS later, in the first grey light of morning, those who had managed to get back to sleep were awakened by a police siren wailing up the long road to the camp. The vehicle pulled up outside the cabins and was greeted by Jangler, already fully dressed in his gaoler's outfit.

Jody hadn't slept. She had stayed by Christina's side the whole time, even after the little girl had drifted into a fitful sleep. Drawn to the din, Jody went to the door and looked out, sunken-eyed.

Two officers had got out of the car, but she couldn't hear what they said to Jangler. The old man was nodding and ticking something on his clipboard. Then he waved his pen at the vehicle and called, "Margaret Blessing?"

One of the officers opened a rear door and the passenger Jody had hitherto overlooked, emerged.

"Blimey," Jody said in surprise.

With her hair turbaned in a towel, Charm looked out over her shoulder and grimaced.

"I'm not being funny nor nofink," she said. "But I hope she's not going to be in here wiv us. I don't want that using our bog, know what I mean?"

"Maggie," the new arrival corrected the old man. "Just Maggie. Don't like 'Margaret' and 'Mags' sounds like top-shelf newsagent smut. Bet you know all about that, don'tya? You look the grubby type."

"A fine dance you've led us, young lady," he scolded, ignoring her. "Get a move on – you've missed one day already."

In the cabin next door, Marcus had been tending to his bruises in the bathroom when he heard the approaching siren. His eye was a mess, puffed-up and purple and a throbbing weight on his face. He had a fat lip too. At least the nose wasn't broken. He scrutinised himself from every angle. When the swelling and bruises had faded, he'd still look good, he decided. The humiliating defeat by Lee hurt much more than his injuries. He wouldn't be able to live that down here. The weekend couldn't be over soon enough for him now.

Marcus regarded his reflection anew and removed his shirt. He raised his fists and twisted from side to side. Then he struck some poses, pretending he was Robert De Niro in *Raging Bull*.

"You talking to me?" he grunted, completely confusing two different films. "You talking to me?"

It was then he heard the siren, shortly followed by Jangler's words summoning the passenger out of the police car. Marcus recalled what Spencer had said the previous evening. One of the girls wasn't accounted for yet. This had to be her – she'd finally arrived!

Still shirtless, he hurried from the bathroom and ran between the beds, where the siren-jolted boys were rubbing their eyes grumpily. He'd been right about one thing – it did stink of sweaty socks and BO down here.

"Please, please, please be a babe," he prayed. "Please be blonde, please have monumental, flawless boobs and a peachy bum that was born to wear a thong."

Pushing open the door, he stood on the step and stretched – as though inhaling nature's invigorating splendour was something he did every morning. Puffing out his chest, he nonchalantly stroked his abs and let his gaze wander from the dawn sky to the group standing by the police car.

"Bloody hell!" he spluttered.

Squeezing herself out of the vehicle was the fattest girl he'd ever seen. He almost didn't believe it at first and thought she was wearing one of those comedy sumo suits. If her bum was a peach, then it was one dreamed up by Roald Dahl. Her head was a round pink ball with a face in the middle of it and her hair was dyed a shocking fuchsia. She was wearing a home-made, but pretty good outsized copy of a Mooncaster gown and pinned to her bodice was a Jill of Hearts playing card.

Disgust and disappointment crept on to Marcus's face. From the next cabin, he heard Jody snickering at him. He was about to dart back inside when the new arrival glanced over.

"*Phwoar!*" Maggie shouted, eyeing him up and down. "Hello, sexy! Now that's what I call perfect – amazing bod and a face that looks like a pepperoni pizza! You're just begging to be eaten, aren't you? Bit cold for you out here, is it? I could hang my coat on them nips!"

Marcus was so taken aback he couldn't think of anything to say in return but, when she whistled at him, he covered his bare chest with his hands and fled.

"If you're going in there to bring out cake," she called, "I'll just have to marry you!"

Laughing, she turned back to Jangler who was trying to tell her which was her chalet.

"All right, all right," she said. "So, any fit lads in there?"

"Certainly not!" the old man said indignantly. "There will be no mingling in the dormitories."

"OK, babes, keep your dinky beard on. A mucky weekend away was too much to hope for."

Jangler escorted her to the third cabin along.

"In there," he said. "You've plenty of time to unpack and settle in. The kitchen staff haven't arrived yet. Breakfast will be served in the main block when they do and then the tiring women will be here to supply everyone with appropriate clothing for today."

"What's wrong with what I'm wearing?" she asked. "It's copied straight from the pictures in the book – and copied pretty well! The only difference is I added pockets. Where's a girl to keep her Curly Wurlys?"

The old man snorted through his nose as he viewed her costume. Then he snatched the playing card from her bodice and ripped it up.

"You are not a Jill of Hearts!" he said crossly. "You've been masquerading as that noble princess for far too long. You'll be given an outfit far less grand and more suited to your aberrant status, young lady. Shame on you for what you've been doing… making people believe you had embraced the hallowed text all this time. Outrageous mendacity!"

"Yeah, yeah, heard all that a hundred times already, from everyone I know and more that I don't. So, you think the new frock'll fit, do you? If I bend down and split something, showing all my tumpsy, it'll be your fault – you dirty old Lockpick. I said you was grubby."

"All measurements were submitted to the Holy Enchanter's personal tailor and team of seamstresses over two weeks ago. We have costumes waiting for everyone – even you."

"Whoopydoo," she answered flatly. Pushing open the cabin door, she plunged inside.

"Hiya, girls," she greeted them, jiggling both hands in the air enthusiastically. "I'm Maggie and yes, I'm a big fatty so get over it and let's have a riot this weekend – yeah? Who's got some music? Turn it on and crank it up to eleven!"

Outside, Jangler made a note on his clipboard. "Finally all the rabbits are in their hutches," he murmured with satisfaction.

Sometime later, after the first communal reading of the day had taken place, breakfast was livelier than any of them had expected. This was solely due to Maggie. In the dining hall, her brash, hearty voice seemed everywhere. She laughed when she saw the great model of the castle, she laughed at the solemn faces of the other teenagers and she whooped and cheered when the serving maids emerged from the kitchen bearing tray after tray of food. She made a point of trying to speak to everyone, even the youngest, and explained why she had only arrived that morning.

"I've been on the run," she told them, tucking into a bowl of porridge, liberally drizzled with honey and topped with flaked almonds. "For the past few months I've been pretending I was one of the blessed be crowd, that the book had worked on me. But two weeks ago I got rumbled."

She paused a moment to push the bowl away and reach for some buttery oatcakes, whilst eyeing the dishes piled high with scrambled eggs and fried mushrooms.

"I tried to make a break for it over to France," she continued. "Not a hope in hell. All the ports are locked down tight and last night I got caught at Dover. I totally suck at inconspicuous. Still, this stuff's better than croissants and I'll have some of that gorgeous-looking ham when you're ready, babes!"

The last request was directed at one of the wenches carrying a tray of cooked meats, which was considerably lighter once Maggie had sent her away again.

Jody marvelled at the girl's confidence. Lee was more wary and kept his responses to a mumble and a shrug. Alasdair doubted how anyone could pretend that the book had worked on them and get away with it for so long. Surely no one nowadays was genuinely this brash and tirelessly jolly? Charm was relieved the cameras hadn't arrived yet. This ebullient girl was going to be competition. If Charm understood anything, it was the fame game and how reality television worked. Outgoing, oversized people like this were instant smashes with audiences. Anyone who lived up to basic stereotypes always did well. There was a car-crash sort of fascination for grotesques. Charm realised she would have to up her own game to vie for coverage with this one.

Marcus, on the other hand, was completely intimidated and sank back behind the castle model, hoping Lardzilla, as he had named her, would forget about him. This made her flirt and heckle him even more.

"Want me to get some raw bacon from the kitchen for you, gawjus?" she called over the miniature battlements. "You could put it on that eye. Real shiner that is. You been fighting over some lucky girl? You'll make me jealous!"

Marcus shook his head and reached for a goblet of ale.

"Booze for breakfast!" Maggie exclaimed. "This place is bloody fabulous! If I'd known it was going to be this good, I wouldn't have tried to do a bunk."

She turned to Charm, who was sitting diagonally across from her on the adjoining table, and pointed a podgy finger in her direction. "I bet he was scrapping over you, wasn't he?" she declared, her round face beaming.

"You're beautiful you are. You should have blokes beating each other up over you all the time!"

Her good-natured sincerity was so disarming that Charm's schemes to grab every scrap of media attention came to a startled halt and she hadn't a clue how to respond.

Not touching any of the food put before her, Christina sat, subdued and resentful. No one believed she had seen a Punchinello monster. Jody had reassured her it was just a bad dream. She knew it wasn't. She wanted to get far away from here.

During breakfast, a van painted in the livery of the four Mooncaster Under Kings drove into the camp. A scrolling sign bore the name *Busy Needles – we'll have you in stitches*. Two women dressed as seamstresses of the Court unloaded three rails of brand-new costumes and wheeled them into the lecture room. Each outfit had a name tag attached and, when everyone had finished eating, Jangler directed the children through to collect them.

Maggie hung back to pick at the plates that had barely been touched, while the serving girls began clearing away.

"You got a doggy bag?" she asked. "You're not going to chuck this stuff in the bin, are you? What a waste!"

One of the wenches dipped into a curtsy before answering. "Bless you, no, Mistress," she said. "There's a pig farm just a few leagues from here. This will go help feed them."

Jody had waited to go into the lecture room with the new girl. Hearing this, she cried, "That's disgusting! Are those pigs going to be eating ham and bacon? Aren't there laws against that? Whatever happened to Defra? Aren't there rules no more?"

"'Tis too good to just throw away," the wench answered with a look of confusion. "Even in this here dream world that would be sheer folly."

"But turning animals into cannibals isn't?" Jody demanded, sickened.

Maggie flicked a ham frill that had strayed on to her sleeve back to the table and led Jody away. "Save your breath," she said. "There's no point arguing. You should know that by now. This place isn't real to them so why should they care? Let's go play dress-up with the rest."

In the lecture room Jangler was reading out names and the mercers were doling out the new costumes. There were no velvets, sumptuous golden cloths or jewel-coloured silks among them. The apparel was the sort that the ordinary peasant folk of Mooncaster would wear: brown leather jerkins, surcoats and doublets, woollen hose, rough, homespun kirtles and coarse linen shirts. There were also cloaks, which the younger children received eagerly and tried on before anything else.

Lee was examining the outfit he had been given, his lip curling with contempt.

"I ain't wearing no tights, man," he declared. "No way I'm putting them on – or them pointy pixie boots."

"You must," Jangler instructed. "How can you fully enter into the spirit of this weekend and seize this opportunity to become one with the hallowed text if you can't even be bothered to look the part?"

"See, here's the thing," the boy explained. "And watch my lips cos I ain't gonna keep saying this – I. Ain't. Wearing. No. Tights. My name ain't Billy Elliot. You hearin' me?"

The old man opened his mouth to answer, but checked himself and forced an indulgent smile to his face.

"Very well," he relented. "This is, after all, meant to be a fun weekend. No one is going to compel you to do anything you don't want to."

"Can I get that in writing?" Lee muttered.

"Well, I'll wear them," Marcus said with a casual shrug. "They're just like long johns. They don't threaten my masculinity."

Lee shook his head at that. The fool was trying to wind him up. He tossed the outfit on the floor and walked off.

Jangler watched him go then made some notes on his clipboard.

"Now hurry up, everyone," he addressed the others. "Take them away and get changed quickly. You've an exciting day ahead and lots to cram in. There's a delightful surprise on its way right now."

"I'm not touching leather," Jody protested. "I won't put these here shoes on you've give me. I'll stick to my trainers."

Jangler added a few more notes to his list.

Maggie rolled her eyes. "Brown!" she exclaimed. "They've given me a big brown frock and a big brown cape. I'm going to look like a bloody Christmas pudding!"

Charm was also disappointed in her outfit. She didn't like drab colours. These were muddy reds and mustards and the fabric looked itchy. But she was determined to "sparkle and effervesce" at all times. Maybe she could add some touches of pink from her luggage.

"When's the Ismus gettin' here?" she asked brightly.

Her cheery grin faltered when Jangler informed her that the Holy Enchanter wasn't going to make an appearance today. Neither were the Jacks and Jills.

"What about the paps then?" she asked.

"No, they're not invited," came the bleak reply. "I find them too distracting. We're keeping it simple. No cameras, no reporters. I'm sure we'll be able to focus on the words of Austerly Fellows much better for it."

"Yeah, lovely," Charm said, her smile fading.

Soon the chalets were noisy with children pulling on their new outfits. A tiring woman visited each of the three cabins where the girls were puzzling over where certain articles of underclothing went and how to lace themselves into the outer garments. Every girl under the age of ten had to wear a white cap called a coif, which was tied under the chin. They loved the full skirts and dainty leather shoes. Only Christina refused to get changed. Jody didn't want her to get into trouble so, after much cajoling, managed to persuade her into the new clothes. But the little girl was adamant about retaining her trainers, as Jody had done.

"Better for running," Christina told her. "We should run away. It's not safe here."

Lee lay on his bed, smoking his second cigarette of the morning. He tried to drown out the excited chatter of the boys below by listening to his iPod. But he could still hear their shrieks and shouts as they laughed at one another and flashes of harsh light bounced around the walls as they took photos with their phones.

Spencer wondered if the tailors had got his measurements correct. His hose were extremely baggy and shapeless and, being grey, looked like very wrinkly elephant legs.

Jim had taken his outfit into the toilet to change. No one thought anything of that. He had done the same the previous evening and they assumed he was shy of undressing in front of strangers. That wasn't the reason. He emerged patting the front of his tan jerkin with a secretive smile. Then he donned the dark green cloak, which was part of the outfit, and flapped it experimentally behind him.

"It's a start," he muttered to himself.

Marcus had chosen to change downstairs, to avoid the cloud from Lee's cigarette that fogged the mezzanine. He made loud objections that the codpiece wasn't nearly big enough, then strutted around with his shirt unlaced and the tall, 'sugar-sack' felt hat positioned at a rakish angle on his head.

"Romeo is in da house!" he proclaimed, grabbing his crotch and swaggering between the beds. "Watch out, damsels."

The other lads were glad when a commotion outside gave them an excuse to ignore him and hurry out.

Two cabins along, after helping the younger boys get dressed, Alasdair was only just pulling on his new boots when he too heard the sound. At first it was like distant hail, clattering over rooftops. It grew steadily louder. Jumping up, he rushed out to see.

"Oh, wow," the boy murmured when he saw what was coming down the long approach road. "That's amazing."

The road had become a river of bay and chestnut horses and ponies. At least fifty of them were trotting towards the camp. All of them were saddled up, but most were riderless. Here and there, on the flanks of that oncoming surge, men and women from the stables made sure they kept to the road and guided them through the gates.

There were many riding centres scattered throughout the New Forest. The animals that came flooding into the camp that morning had come from four of the nearest. Leaving the long road behind them, they tossed their heads and broke out of the tight formation, to go cantering over the expansive lawn, flicking their ears and swishing their tails.

By now every child had come out to see them. Even Lee stood in the doorway of the cabin and watched, blowing smoke from the corner of his mouth.

"This is your surprise!" Jangler announced grandly. "Today we are going for a trek through the forest, just as we might if you were in the Realm of the Dawn Prince. Imagine we're questing through the Western Wild Wood or Hunter's Chase. It will bring you closer to the real world than ever."

"Have we got to?" Jody asked.

"I recommend you do," the old man told her. "Most emphatically."

"Did that sound like a threat to you?" the girl whispered to Maggie.

"Babes, since I got found out, everything sounds like a threat. Now I just go where they point me and keep my gob shut… well, mostly."

Charm had accessorised her drab costume. A glittery pink scarf was tied loosely around her waist and a diamanté Alice band secured a plain linen headdress instead of the plaited woollen strap it had come with. Gucci sunglasses completed this unusual look. She was determined to stand out even if there weren't any cameras present.

Tommy Williams stood amazed, yet excited and fearful at the sight of the horses. They seemed enormous to him. Dressed as a page, his pale face was half hidden in a dark blue hood, whose tapering point dangled down past his knees. He looked more like one of Santa's elves that had fallen on hard times than a medieval peasant. Similarly dressed, but in a dark red hood, Rupesh stood next to him. He too was afraid.

"We are to climb up there?" the boy asked.

"It's only like a big donkey!" Tommy said.

"We don't have such things in Upton Park," Rupesh said meekly.

Few of the children had ever ridden before, but the stable staff were there to help. The smaller ones were hoisted on to patient ponies while the teenagers were helped into the stirrups of their mounts. The animals were well accustomed to novice riders and stood stock-still whilst these tricky manoeuvres took place. The girls were horrified to learn they were expected to ride side-saddle and watched a demonstration with open mouths.

"To do otherwise would be unseemly," Jangler told them. "Only menfolk sit astride."

"Stuff it," Jody said. "I can't do that. It don't look safe."

"You'll have to, young lady. The special saddles are already fitted and you cannot remain here alone. Riding is what this day is about."

The finality with which he said that made Jody, and any others who were thinking of refusing to get on their horses, realise they had no choice but to comply.

"You got any nags with stabilisers?" Maggie asked uncertainly. "And with an HGV licence? I'm a wide load."

She was presented with a cob brought specially for her. After much persuasion, pushing and shoving, accompanied by panicky yells, she was heaved on to the saddle.

"Don't we get one of those cute black hard hats?" she asked. "What if we fall off? Cos you know, that's more than likely. I've toppled off a pair of shoes with a one-inch heel before now, so…"

A woman from the stables beamed up at her. "There's none of that health and safety nonsense any more," she said. "We couldn't let your friend there ride wearing her trainers if there was. So no, no need for hats."

"Oh, brilliant," Maggie mumbled. "So I just go 'timberrrr' and get concussion or brain damage?"

"Only here," the woman said breezily. "And it might be the very thing to wake you up in our true world. Perhaps you should all fall off and see?"

"You should do stand-up – you're a scream, you are."

Marcus got on to his horse without assistance and gripped the beast with his knees. His good eye gave Charm a wink charged with meaning.

Spencer hesitated before mounting. A glorious idea popped into his head and he nipped back into the cabin for a moment. Alasdair wandered over to Lee.

"You doing this?" he asked.

Lee took one final drag and grunted. "Don't think there's an option B," he said. "The old guy seems set. You ever see them dogs made to dance on talent shows? That's us today. We is required to perform – but at least I won't look like a prize dick while I'm doing it."

He eyed the green woollen cowl Alasdair was wearing. "You look like a refugee from a straight-to-DVD Robin Hood flick," he scoffed.

"That would be infinitely preferable," the Scot replied. "At least then I'd be merry."

Eventually every young person was securely in the saddle. Even Jangler was perched on a grey pony. With the stables' staff leading them in groups, the children filed through the gate.

It was another warm, sunny day – far too warm for those woollen clothes and ludicrous hats and hoods. Lee was glad he was only in his trackie bottoms and black vest. As the horses passed up the long forest road, he glanced back at the compound. He had the feeling they were being purposely kept away from there today. A dozen possible reasons occurred, but he forgot about them when he saw one of the seamstresses leave the main block and walk to the supposedly empty chalet. With her notebook and tape measure in hand, she knocked on the door and was admitted.

Lee put his earphones in and wondered about that.

With such a large group of novice riders, progress was slow, but there was no hurry and they met no other traffic. The children quickly realised that all they had to do was stay on. The stables' staff and the placid animals themselves did everything for them. Even the reins were just there for show. Once they understood this, the kids who had brought their phones and had already swapped numbers started texting one another. They had discovered first thing that morning the signal had been restored. No one cared where they were headed. It was such a refreshing change from what they were used to and if they had to pretend to be interested in that book, so what? This was great.

If Jangler was irritated by the constant beeping of the mobiles, he didn't show it. He was engrossed in his copy of *Dancing Jax* and, even in the saddle, was rocking backwards and forwards.

They hadn't gone far when Spencer brought out the item he had been hiding under his cloak. He took a nervous breath then put it on his head.

"Ha! Herr Spenzer!" Marcus hooted. "Who do you think you are? Clint Eastwood?"

"Nope," the boy answered with a drawl as he tilted the Stetson back with one finger. "I'm Yul Brynner."

Wearing his cowboy hat with pride and a great big grin, Spencer inserted his earphones and the rousing theme to *The Magnificent Seven* began. The sun was beating down, he was on a horse and, when he closed his eyes, everyone else disappeared and he was transported into another life – one a thousand miles away from Mooncaster and the misery that book had brought. The only thing that would have put this into 'beyond perfect' territory would have been a gun slung round his hips.

Marcus was more than happy to be riding almost parallel to Charm and spent most of the morning trying to chat her up. He may as well have been talking to an iceberg in sunglasses.

"How about kissing my bruises better?" he eventually asked in desperation.

For everyone else the hours passed pleasantly. They left the main road far behind and rode through woodland and over heaths. The only blights on that picturesque landscape were the choking thickets of minchet that had taken hold in places, strangling trees and fouling the air with the stink of decay.

After a while, it seemed as if they really had magically crossed into the medieval countryside of *Dancing Jax*. The only other creatures they saw were wild ponies and once a small herd of fallow deer ran shyly into distant trees.

The hours slipped by. After several unscheduled stops for toilet breaks behind bushes, midday had come and gone. Grumbling requests for drinks and general complaints about numb bottoms had already started. And then, finally, they saw a thread of smoke rising into the clean blue sky beyond the next range of trees. Drawing closer, they heard a flute playing and the path led to a sunlit clearing, crowded with pavilion tents striped in scarlet and black. Many people dressed as serfs were bustling about. Two large fires were burning and over each was a spit where a pig and a lamb were being roasted.

"Gross," Jody uttered.

"Welcome, welcome!" a woman cried. "Gracious me, we thought you'd never get here. All is prepared and awaiting your pleasure."

Jangler dismounted, rather stiffly.

"Here is our picnic," he declared. "I'm sure you've worked up a keen appetite. Let us see what Mistress Slab has cooked up for us."

With legs ever so slightly bowed, he ambled over to the first of three trestle tables that were laden with appetising dishes.

Maggie gazed at the spread appreciatively. "All you guys do is eat!" she laughed. "I think I've died and gone to heaven. Get me down off this thing. My stomach's making Jurassic Park noises."

Everyone was glad to get out of the saddle and stretch their legs, especially the girls. Their backs and shoulders were aching badly from hunching sideways for so long. Nobody realised just how hungry they were and they swarmed round the tables like flies. The roast pork and lamb were cooked to perfection but, before the greedy carnivores could tuck in, they had to endure yet another communal reading.

A short while later Lee and Alasdair were eating their lunch on the grass beside one of the tents.

"You really knock that stuff back, huh?" Lee observed as the Scot embarked on his second goblet of wine.

"Thirsty work, being on a horse. S'all right for you in your vest. I've sweated pints in these clothes."

"And there was me blaming them animals for that smell."

"Did you clock that lad in the cowboy hat? I dinnae think old Mainwaring was impressed."

"The kid's got style. Anything that gives them the finger gets a thumbs-up from me."

Alasdair wiped his mouth and looked over at the others. "What do you make of the new lass?" he asked. "Does she no seem a bit fake to you?"

"I don't trust no one who buys into that damn book," Lee said. "Or even pretends to."

A shadow fell across their faces and they looked up to see Charm almost upon them, the hem of her skirt held daintily in one hand, grapes and a pear in the other.

"Can I sit 'ere wiv you?" she asked. "That Marcus is doing my nut in. He won't leave me alone. I ain't interested. Is he fick or summink? My Uncle Frank had a Yorkie like him – that's a dog not a bar of chocolate. Always yapping and, whenever it saw me, it'd hump my Uggs. That lad's just the same. If I'm near you, he might leave me alone for five minutes. You don't mind, do you?"

She knelt on the ground before they could answer and launched into her usual introduction.

"… an' I fizz and sparkle, like space dust," she concluded with a flash of perfect teeth.

Alasdair took another gulp.

"What part of London you from?" Lee asked. "Or is it Essex?"

The girl gave a squawk of delight and clapped her hands. "Is that what you fink? Oh, that is well wicked. I ain't from down south at all. No, I'm from Bolton, Lancashire, innit."

"Say what?"

"But the accent?" Alasdair said.

"Voice coachin' from since I were nine and a half!" she declared proudly. "My idea that was, not Uncle Frank's – he's my manager, not my real uncle, but he's me ma's bloke so I call him that. So, the accent, I'm media savvy, see – even when I was a little kid I knew. The Americans, bless 'em, can't understand a northern accent. Look at whasserface, poor cow. I wasn't going to have that happen to me. I'll be over there some day wiv my own show and stuff. That was The Plan anyway, before this Mooncaster fing started."

"Is you for real?"

"Oh, yes – I've not had Botox nor nofink yet. Only me tan's fake – how did people manage before you could spray it on? You an' me should talk more. I could learn a lot from a proper London geezer. If you fink any of what comes out my mouth don't sound right, you tell me, yeah?"

Whilst Lee searched for a reply, Alasdair turned aside to hide his smirk.

"So, why ain't you dressed up like the rest of us?" she asked Lee. "You're spoiling the ensembleness. What if there was cameras here? You'd stand out and look well wrong."

"You think?"

The way he said that made Alasdair glance at him curiously. There was a barely veiled, growling anger in those two simple words. The Scottish boy wondered why.

"Nothing more important than the look," she blundered on. "It's all about the brand, innit? You're ruining the… what's the word? Intergritty of the brand, you are."

A crease appeared on Lee's forehead and he clamped his lips tight shut.

"Is anyone else's bum sore?" a voice interrupted. "My cheeks are raging like I've got toothache down there! I've got pains in muscles I thought had packed up and moved out years ago."

It was Maggie. She and Jody were wandering over. Christina remained at the trestles, making up for her lack of breakfast. Jangler was gathering the younger children about him and trying to explain the rules of a peasants' game to them.

"Ooh – that's the trouble with your rear end," Maggie said, easing herself on to the stool she had dragged with her. "Even when it's giving you gyp, you've still got to sit on it." She burped and banged her chest. "I pity that horse on the way back. What I ate just now you could make a whole new lambpig creature out of. Bloody lovely it was though."

Jody gave a shudder of revulsion. The smell of the roasted meat and hot, dripping fat sputtering and smoking in the flames made her feel sick. She hadn't even been able to stomach the fruit on offer. Tired after too little sleep and too long a ride, she was ready for a quarrel. She was glad Charm was here. She couldn't think of a more suitable target.

"The younger kids are going to play games in a bit," Maggie said.

"It's too hot to be running about," Alasdair muttered, lying back in the grass.

"What sorta games?" Charm asked, wondering if she should involve herself.

"I dunno," Maggie answered. "Something from the book. l heard one of them servants say they've got all sorts of Jax-type things lined up. Rather them than me, it's boiling in this frock – not that I'd ever run about anyway. The chafing is chronic."

"They ain't real servants," Lee blurted, talking over her. "They's just more fool zombies. Don't you start calling them servants or maids or none of that! Five months back, they was probably collecting trolleys outside Sainsbury's or working in a bank or some crap."

Charm looked at him, confused. "Don't you want to get to the castle?" she asked.

"Girl, when you gonna wake up and see what's happenin'?" he shouted back at her. "You can't be that dumb!"

"I wouldn't put money on it," Jody chipped in.

"But, like, it's true!" Charm protested. "Everyone knows it!"

"True?" Jody cried. "You really are thick as you look! Mass delusion and hysteria, that's what it is. You don't seriously believe there's another world, separate from this, and the only way to it is via that badly written book? You're a single-tasking mouth-breather in lipgloss!"

"Just cos you look like a librarian don't mean you're clever nor nofink," Charm retorted. "Course it's true. Mooncaster's a real, proper place – me ma wouldn't lie to me. We're just a bit slow gettin' there, that's all. What else you lot doing 'ere then? I can't wait for it to happen to me! It's gonna be well awesome!"

Lee pressed his lips together even tighter and tore a clump of grass from the ground. His anger was rising.

"Now I don't believe it's real," Maggie put in. "I'm not that daft. But I will say this – that book's the best thing that ever happened to me."

The others stared at her.

"What do you mean?" Jody demanded.

Maggie gave a guilty sort of grin.

"There's a lad at my school, see," she began a little sheepishly. "Drop-dead gorgeous he is, one of them special blokes that can't be the same species as the rest of us, cos everything about him is so amazing. Well, he reads the book and thinks he's a knight who's madly in love with that Jill of Hearts…"

"Dinnae tell me that's why you pretended to be her?" Alasdair groaned.

"Too right I did! I couldn't believe it. Soon as I pinned that card on, he were all over me."

"That's no very honest."

"Eww, tacky," Charm added.

"It's twisted is what it is."

Maggie cast her face down. "Yeah, well," she mumbled. "It was the best few months I'd had for a long time. *Dancing Jax* isn't all bad."

"I can't believe you said that!" Jody gasped. "How can you sit there and defend that evil, sodding book? Just look what it's done to us – to everything!"

"But if this is just a dream to begin wiv…" Charm persisted.

Jody gave a shout of frustration. There was no getting through to her.

"And if it makes people happy," Maggie ventured. "What's so wrong about that? Wish I was as happy and certain as the blessed be mob."

"But you are happy! And confident!"

Maggie shook her head. "When you're this big, you have to have an even bigger front to hide behind," she said. "Can't slip into the background. There's always some nasty mouth to sling insults cos they think your brain's made of Yorkshire pudding. Best defence is to get in with the fat jokes first, make them laugh with you, not at you. What's so great is *Dancing Jax* got rid of that. Size, money, or what the neighbours think, don't matter no more to them that's read it. That's got to be a good thing."

"Course it is," Charm agreed. "Life is brilliant in the castle. Me ma says it's more fairer than here."

This was too much for Lee. He leaped up and exploded at them.

"Oh, yeah, it's fair!" he snapped. "I'll tell you just how fair!"

He held up his hand. "See this skin?" he demanded. "Take a good, long look. That colour don't exist in your cosy fairy tale, written by a minted white guy almost a hundred years ago. You ever stop and think about it? How many black people are in them pages? None! But what do you think happens when a black person reads it and gets sucked in there? I'll tell you, cos it happened to everyone I know. My family, my brothers…"

He paused to take a steadying breath.

"They read that book and they think they is *white*! White peasants, white lords and ladies, white servants. But that ain't the worst – oh, no. When they snap out of it and they's back here…" He ground his teeth, impassioned beyond speech, and kicked the tent behind him.

The others were too shocked to say anything.

"I never thought," Maggie whispered eventually.

Lee rounded on her. "Course you didn't!" he cried. "You was too busy playing at being a fat-ass princess and tricking some poor guy into slobbering over you! No one thought. No one did nuthin'!"

He spun around to storm off, but there was still more he had to say and he turned back.

"My mother," he continued fiercely. "She's a strong woman, strong and proud. Everyone on my estate got a lot of time and respect for her. She brought up three kids on her own, doing all kinds of stuff to keep us fed and clothed and out of trouble, best she can. You know what she does now? I'll tell you so you can chew on it. When my mother looks in the mirror, she can't understand why her dreams have painted her this colour. She sees her reflection and... she laughs. She laughs at her black face. All my friends laugh at their black faces. That's what *Dancing Jax* has done and that's why I won't wear no dressy-up clothes!"

10

IT WAS AFTER seven when they returned to the holiday compound. The smaller children were nodding in their saddles. They had played old-fashioned games all afternoon: running races, throwing horseshoes, climbing and swinging on ropes – even the boisterous Mooncot sport of Wumpenruff, which added to everyone's bruises. Marcus couldn't resist competing, although the smaller boys were no match for him. He won every game until Jangler banned him from taking part.

On the way back, Christina withdrew even further into herself. She would rather be at home with her uncaring parents than heading to the cabin, where monsters prowled around at night. Plodding up the long forest road to the camp, the boys in Spencer's cabin were looking forward to a long session on the Xbox. Spencer and Jim were thinking about two totally different things. One of them had experienced a fantastic day and had grown to love the saddle. The other was wondering when his great moment would come. Surely it had to be soon?

Lee hadn't said a word since his outburst and those who had witnessed it didn't dare approach him. What could they possibly say? Luckily Marcus was placed too far down the column of horses to make any ignorant comments and Alasdair wondered if he should have a quiet word with him. Would Marcus be sympathetic enough to care? Alasdair was doubtful. He took a swig of wine from the leather bottle he had brought back from the picnic.

"What's been going on here?" Jody asked in surprise.

She was staring ahead at the camp. The wooden gates were now sandwiched between two five-metre-high posts, as wide as telegraph poles. Garlands of spring flowers and small lanterns were strung across to soften their imposing presence. As they rode in, the children saw more posts, cemented into the ground, standing ten metres apart. They formed a wide perimeter around the chalets and the main block. Swags of flowers and glimmering lanterns connected each one.

"Awwww… that's well pretty," Charm cooed. "Like a fairyland."

Now Lee understood why they had been kept away for the entire day. He sucked the air through his teeth and hated the fact he was right about what was going on.

"For the grand closing festivities tomorrow!" Jangler declared, waving his arms at the decorated posts. "A truly spectacular conclusion to your weekend has been arranged. You won't believe your eyes!"

"I just want to fast-forward the whole bloody day and get out of here," Jody grumbled, although she had no desire to go back to Bristol either. The only thing she really wanted at that precise moment was a shower.

The children dismounted and the horses and ponies were led away. Out of the main block serving wenches appeared, bearing trays of fruit punch, which they called "The Queen of Hearts' May Cup", to refresh them after their long ride. The drinks were received gladly and glugged back in no time. Alasdair poured his away when no one was looking and refilled the goblet with wine. Lee sniffed the punch with suspicion and tipped it on the ground in disgust. All he wanted was a glass of water, fresh from the bathroom tap. He headed towards the cabin, but Jangler called him back.

"The fun is not quite over yet," he announced.

"I'm still waiting for it to begin," Jody mumbled.

"Before you disperse," the old man continued. "And before you head to the dining hall, where a delicious cold supper awaits – there is yet one more game left to play."

"Can we no play it tomorrow?" Alasdair spoke up.

"Oh, no," Jangler told him. "It must be played tonight. There'll be no time tomorrow and it really must be played as darkness falls."

"The kids are a wee bit shattered after all the running about today. I dinnae think they'll be up to much."

Jangler gave a broad smile, showing his babylike teeth. "They will when they hear what this game is," he said. "The peasant children of Mooncot take immense delight in it. It is their most favourite game of all. They call it 'Bite of the Werewolf'."

A murmur of excitement spread through the younger ones who were suddenly fully awake.

"How do you play?" Tommy asked, his eyes round and wider than normal.

Jangler peered over the rim of his spectacles at everyone.

"Only one of you here is a werewolf," he informed them gravely. "I will choose who. The rest of you must run and hide in the woodland behind the chalets. The werewolf will count up to a hundred… then come hunting. When he catches you, he must bite. Then you too are savage and snarling as he and must turn your skin inside out to reveal the beast within when the moon is full and high. The two of you continue the hunt. Seek out the cowering, cringing humans. They are your meat and drink this night. You are driven to swell the ranks of your woebegotten pack. And so the terrible infection spreads. Whoever is the last one to remain unbitten, wins."

"Wicked," Tommy breathed.

The others thought the same and couldn't wait to get started. Alasdair was astonished by how quickly they had recovered from their long day. They seemed bursting with energy again.

Jody put a hand to her head. She felt weird, almost giddy. The same tingling thrill of anticipation that the under-tens were feeling was making the hairs on the back of her neck rise. She wanted to run headlong into the trees and never stop.

"What's wrong with me?" she murmured. "I can hardly breathe."

Standing close by, Maggie began to giggle. "I feel really… silly," she said. "Really… ha ha ha!"

Christina looked up at them, worried and bewildered. She too felt strange. Without warning, she let out a high, unnatural laugh and spun around, stamping her feet.

Marcus's head was swimming. He desperately wanted to be the

werewolf. He wanted to be the focus of everyone's attention. To be taken seriously for a change. Charm couldn't ignore him then. He'd hunt her down and give her the biggest love bite she'd ever had. He threw back his head and let out a howl.

Charm didn't hear him. She was gazing at the lanterns strung between the posts. She had never seen such bright, beautiful colours. It was spellbinding. The lights seemed to play over her drab woollen costume and transform it into an enchanting gown of pink tulle and chiffon.

"I'm a princess!" she cried, twirling around in a slow, stumbling waltz.

Alasdair stared at them with mounting concern. His senses were pleasantly numbed by the combination of wine and the day's sun, but he could see something was seriously wrong here.

"What've you done?" he yelled at Jangler. "What was that May Cup stuff?"

The old man chuckled, but didn't answer. The effects of the drink were most satisfactory. It had worked far faster than he had expected. The children were energised, agitated, receptive and anxious to play the game.

"Someone's been busy mixing cocktails," Lee said to Alasdair. "Could be all kinds of chemistry in that fruit punch. It's gonna get messy here. I hope to hell he knew what he was doing or he'll croak someone."

"What?" the Scot cried, aghast. "Actual drugs? He spiked it? I thought it was strong Red Bull or something. They wouldn't do that to us!"

"Boy, you gotta get wise. Look at them kids. They's half out their domes. They is crunk. There ain't nuthin' the blessed be psychos won't do. We's only lab rats to them."

"But that's… just evil!"

"Why is that news?"

"We've got to stop it!"

"I don't get involved no more."

Alasdair glared at him. "You are involved!" he shouted. "You're here – you're in this with the rest of us. Whatever you've been through doesnae give you a free pass from responsibility. We've all suffered. We've all got reasons to feel sorry for ourselves. This isnae just about you – it's no about race. It's about being a human being and caring what happens to each other – to these wee lads an' lasses! Otherwise you may as well pin a playing card on and join the zombie brigade."

Lee was about to shrug, but thought better of it. The boy's angry words had hit home.

"Too late to stop it," he said. "Kids already downed the junk. Best we can do is make sure they don't do nuthin' stupid."

"Like what? What'll happen?"

"Oh, just cos I'm the only black person left in the country, I'm an expert on drugs – is that what you're sayin'?"

"No! You live on a rough estate in South London. You must have more of a clue than me."

"Well, OK. Maybe I have. Depends what that old fool medicined them with and how they react. If they freak, we could be lookin' at anything. Like pullin' their own teeth out, eating their hands, climbin' a roof to jump off, thinking they can fly or just the simple stuff like killing each other."

"Be serious!"

"I am."

"And the werewolf is…" Jangler finally called out.

"Me! Me!" Marcus begged. "Please, please, please!"

Jangler took no notice and pointed straight at Spencer.

"The boy with the cowboy hat!" he declared.

Marcus cursed and Spencer punched the air, shouting a triumphant, "Yee-haw!"

"I won't be a werewolf though!" he said. "I'm going to be a werecoyote!"

He snarled at the small kids closest to him and they squealed in mock horror.

"Once the hallucinations kick in," Lee muttered, "they won't enjoy this dumb-ass game so much."

Jangler clapped his hands. "What are you waiting for?" he asked. "The moon is rising and the skin of the werewolf is itching. Soon he will shed his human guise and be a beast of fur and sinew, sniffing out the blood of the weak. You must flee, run to the trees – go hide, whilst you can! Run for your lives – hurry! Hurry!"

Spencer began counting. The children screamed and raced off between the chalets towards the woods. Jody ran with them. Under the May Cup's influence, she was completely swept along by the urgency of the game. At that moment, it was the most important thing in the world. She had to run and hide and not be bitten.

With the hem of her kirtle in her hands, as though running from a palace ball at midnight, Charm hurried over the lawn to the woodland. Marcus kept alongside her, encouraging her onward. Huffing and blowing, but still laughing, Maggie lumbered after.

Lee and Alasdair watched them hare away and disappear into the settling darkness.

"This is a nightmare!" the Scot exclaimed. "How are we going to keep an eye on all of them?"

"That's not the worst thing," Lee said. "I wasn't gonna say, but there's something out there, in them woods. Something not right, something to scare the soul right out your bones. I saw it last night. I don't know what it was – just saw a shape and I don't know if there's more than one, but playing hide-and-seek in them trees is like taking a stroll through some lions, wearing a necklace made of burgers."

Alasdair stared at him in disbelief.

"And what's even extra bad," Lee added grimly, "I am clean out of cigarettes."

Alasdair was already running after the squealing children. He threw a vicious glance at Jangler as he dashed by and shouted, "If anything happens to a single one of them, you're dead!"

The old man pulled at his pointed beard and smiled. Lee pointed warningly at him as he ran by.

"Happy hunting, my Lord," he murmured, thinking of what was waiting in those trees.

"Fifty-seven, fifty-eight, fifty-nine…" Spencer counted.

Jangler turned and looked over at the cabin next to his own. In the window, a corner of the curtain lifted and he nodded at it.

The wood was filled with the sound of children shrieking and laughing, searching for hiding places, but too excited and nervous to stay concealed. They raced round trees, ducked under low branches and crawled into caves of bracken. When they encountered one another, they screamed and wheeled around, tearing back the way they had come. But gradually the fun turned to fear as the drink took total control and the happy sounds became shrieks of terror and panic.

High overhead the leaves rustled. A darkness moved from tree to tree. The frothing mould of Austerly Fellows kept a hungry watch. It had been patient, but now it was time.

Breathless and anxious, Jody collapsed against an oak and slid to the ground. Somewhere out there she heard Christina calling for her. Jody trembled and hugged herself. Fear hit her in waves, freezing the blood that pumped through her pounding heart. She looked down at the roots spread out below the tree. Were they twisting and writhing in the soil?

"No," she told herself. "It isn't real."

Craning her head back, she stared at the dimming sky through the leaf canopy and beads of icy sweat dotted her forehead. The branches started to move. They rippled like tentacles and she could feel the bark pushing against her back as the oak tree breathed.

Squeezing her eyes shut, she put her head between her knees and covered her ears.

Marcus had pursued Charm deep into the wood.

"This is far enough!" he called, taking hold of her hand and pulling her to a stop. "No one'll find us here, Beautiful."

"I don't wanna get bit," she answered. "I'm royalty I am. Royalty can't get bit. In the book a unicorn saves the Jill of Whatsit from the werewolf. I need to find meself a unicorn. Here, uni uni… here, uni uni…"

Marcus pulled her closer. She staggered into him.

"If you're looking for a horny animal," he began crassly.

"'Ere!" she sniggered, blinking at him. "Your face. It's a proper mess, innit? You look like a mashed purple spud!"

"You like playing hard to get, don't you? I used to enjoy that before *DJ*, but not now, not when we've got so little time. Two days wasted and tomorrow's the last one."

"The sun'll come out, tomorrow!" she sang. "I love that film, I do. An' I like *Legally Blonde*! Oh, doubly love that, I do. No one else spotted the dodgy syrup on her near the end after she wins the case. I did. I'm not fick, see."

"God, you're so sexy," Marcus breathed. "You and me deserve each other. Come here!"

He put his arms round her and leaned in for the kiss.

"What you doing?" she screeched, pushing him away. "You got the wrong princess. I'm not kissin' no frogs!"

She thrust him back so forcefully he lost his balance and went crashing into a patch of nettles.

"Here, uni uni," she called, tottering off into the distance. "Here, uni uni…"

Back at the camp, Spencer had counted up to eighty.

Alasdair ran into the trees. He could hear a babble of young voices and the noise of many children crashing through the undergrowth some way ahead. He saw nothing.

Lee came jogging up behind. He was out of breath, but with a clearer idea of what to do.

"You go left, I go right," he directed. "Pull them kids outta there. Drag 'em if you have to. We gotta stop this stupid game."

Alasdair agreed and plunged into the wood. Lee stared at the gloomy, shadow-wrapped trees and tried not to think of his terror the previous night. The food he had stashed was somewhere over there – the place where he had seen that horror rear up in front of him.

"Lee Jules Sherlon Charles," he addressed himself sternly. "You better man-up. Get your scared ass in there and do this."

With a fierce look on his face, he ran in.

Alasdair pressed deeper into the woodland. Cupping his hands round his mouth, he called the names of the boys in his hut, then shouted for Jody, Maggie, Charm and Marcus.

Suddenly a voice cried down to him from above.

"Run!" it warned. "You must hide. A werewolf is coming!"

Alasdair started and took a step back. "Who's that?" he asked.

A movement high up the nearest tree caught his eye. He glimpsed a cloaked figure clambering among the boughs.

"Come doon from there!" he shouted. "Get doon here – right noo."

"I'm keeping a lookout!" the young voice answered. "When I see the ferocious beast, I'm going to fight it and save everyone."

"We're no playing that game no more. Come doon!"

There was a flurry of leaves and the sound of boots slipping against bark. A boy blur swung into view. Then it dropped down. He landed on one knee, with a fist touching the ground and his head lowered. Alasdair had seen that exact same pose in a dozen superhero movies. He thought it looked stupid and phoney in those, but here it was downright barmy. He wondered if the lad had hurt his knee doing that.

The boy raised his face. It was set and serious. Alasdair recognised him as the one who had tried to break up the fight between Lee and Marcus.

"Oh, it's you," he said. "Dinnae go climbing anything. Just go back to where the trees start and wait. I'll be sending everyone else that way, soon as I find them."

"I will aid you in your search," Jim Parker declared, rising and putting his hands on his sides.

"Nay, thanks. I reckon I can manage."

"Ha!" Jim laughed. "You don't think I'll be much use, just a kid – yes?"

"I dinnae want a debate. Can you no just do as I'm askin'?"

Jim folded his arms and came closer.

"You're wrong, you know," he said, lowering his voice to a whisper. "I'm not just any normal person. I'm more than that."

Alasdair didn't have time for this crazy, drug-induced nonsense. He shook his head and tried continuing on his way. Jim jumped in front of him.

"It's true!" he said. "I've got a secret. No one must know. I shouldn't tell anyone, but I think I can trust you."

"I'm no interested," the Scot replied crossly. "Just shift yourself out of here and wait."

Jim grabbed his shoulders. "I'm not like everyone else! I've suspected it for a while, but now I know. This weekend it's going to happen to me. I'm going to change. I feel stronger already. I think it's started."

"Oh, hell," Alasdair uttered, shrugging him off. "No more *Jax* rubbish."

"No, not that! The book can't work on me – I'm special."

"You an' me both, laddie."

"I wouldn't have believed it either before," Jim continued. "But it's the only thing that makes sense. Don't you see? If that book can have such power then other things must do as well. Other astounding things are possible – they can happen. Look, I'll show you, but you mustn't breathe a word!"

Before Alasdair could answer, the boy had pulled his shirt open and bared his chest.

"Oh, God!" Alasdair cried in horror. "Who did that to ye?"

Even in the failing light he could see an ugly pale scar forming a large 'J' on Jim's skin.

"Did your folks do it? Did they? Because the book hadn't worked on you, they thought burning the mark of a Jack into you would help it along? They branded you! The sadistic lunatics!"

The younger boy laughed.

"They didn't do it!" he boasted. "I did – with my father's soldering iron. It did hurt but I had to. It was part of the change, you see. Part of the ordeal you have to go through. And it doesn't stand for 'Jack', it stands for 'Jim'. That's my name, Jim Parker. But when I get my powers, I'm going to be known as 'Jim Credible'."

"Your powers?"

"Yes. I'm turning into a superhero, like the mutants in the X-Men. It's going to happen this weekend. I'm absolutely certain. The need is dire, the hour is dark and someone has to step forward. That's how these things work. It's so I can protect everyone. I told you last night I would. I'm going to stand against the Ismus and fight for what he's destroying. A hero for Britain, and everything that makes this country great: King Arthur, Nelson, Henry the Eighth, Francis Drake, Stonehenge, football, chips, Shakespeare, Merlin – Nessie!"

Alasdair recoiled, but was consumed with pity. Whatever Jim had been through in the last five months, it had tipped him over the edge. His way of coping with the insanity of *Dancing Jax* had been to retreat from reality and go quietly insane himself. It was a wonder more of them hadn't gone the same way. Maybe they had and he just hadn't noticed.

"OK," the Scot said gently. "You come help find the others with me, eh?"

"Remember," Jim cautioned, fastening up his shirt. "Not a word. I don't even know what my powers are going to be yet."

"I promise," Alasdair said sadly.

Deep in the wood Marcus was blowing on his hands. They were burning and bumpy with stings. He was glad now of his costume's long sleeves and woollen hose.

"I'm done with her," he fumed, thinking about Charm. "It's her loss. I've had better."

He stumbled forward, not caring where he was going. When he finally looked up from his hands, he saw a familiar figure crouched at the base of an oak tree ahead.

"Ooo-arr," he greeted. "It be Velma from Scooby Doo – though in your case it's more like Scooby Don't."

Jody lifted her face. She was shivering.

"You want my jacket thing?" Marcus offered, removing his jerkin and putting it over her shoulders.

She stared at him, wild-eyed. Her lips moved to speak, but she said nothing.

Marcus glanced around quickly. They were alone. He knelt next to her.

"I know you an' me got off on the wrong foot," he said. "How about we start over? Do you er… you know, fancy a quick one? Might as well while we're here, eh? Silly not to. We won't get another chance and we'll be bussed back first thing Monday."

The girl looked confused. To her, Marcus was a wobbling shape in the midst of a shimmering, undulating world and his voice seemed to be emanating from the tree behind her.

"I won't tell nobody," he said coaxingly.

At that moment, Spencer came charging into the wood, yipping and howling like a coyote.

Jody heard that. To her, it was coming from everywhere. The surrounding trees were screaming.

"Make it stop!" she shrieked. "Make it stop! Make it stop!"

Marcus pulled away and swore. "You're such a buzzkill!" he ranted. "You're like anti-Viagra! Know what, I was only offering out of charity. I wouldn't touch you with someone else's."

He staggered off.

Still terrified, Jody cradled her head in her heads, sobbing.

Spencer's howls carried through the twilight.

"I gotta tell Kid Coyote to shut it," Lee muttered. "He's making it even worse."

All he'd seen since entering the wood were the backs of fleeing children and he wasn't fast enough to catch them.

Entering a glade, he followed one of the many new trails criss-crossing the bracken and stopped abruptly. Two pairs of frightened eyes were peering up from beneath the fern fronds. Rupesh and Tommy were hunched together on the ground, hoping he'd walk by.

"Hey, babes in the wood," he said. "Get out here."

"The werewolf!" Tommy whimpered. "He'll eat us!"

Rupesh began scuttling away.

"Get back here!" Lee ordered. "I'm a good guy. Don't make me haul you out. It'll put me in a real bad mood."

The boys whispered to one another, then crept out shyly.

Another howl went coursing through the trees. The boys shrank back and would have run off if Lee hadn't snatched hold of them.

"I have really got to have harsh words with that cowboy," he grumbled.

Maggie was sitting on a fallen tree, mopping her brow with her sleeve.

"That werewolf'll just have to bite me," she said breathlessly. "This chassis isn't built for chasing about."

Her large frame shook as she laughed at nothing. Then she hitched up the medieval skirts she had twice tripped over and squinted at her grazed shins. The light was failing fast now, but her fuchsia hair almost glowed in the gloom. Looking at her bare legs, she tittered and swished the skirt about, kicking her feet in the air as she hummed the cancan. Then she toppled over and fell back, off the tree trunk.

Marcus found her howling with laughter, legs flailing helplessly above her head.

"What's so funny?" he asked.

Maggie twisted her head about to see who this upside-down person was.

"Hello, gawjus!" she said. "I'm stuck! That's what's funny. Everything's funny – ha ha ha ha! You're hilarious."

"Don't you laugh at me!" he snapped. "I'm sick of being laughed at. Everyone laughs at me here. You're idiots the lot of you!"

"Oh, poor luv," she said sympathetically. "I won't do it again, Brownie's honour… ooh – now I'm thinking of chocolate brownies – ha ha ha ha!"

"You want a hand getting up?"

"You got a forklift on standby there?" she spluttered.

"Your body is disgusting," Marcus said. "You know that, don't you? How does anyone get so immense?"

"Perseverance," she laughed. "It's not easy you know. Anyone can be skinny and ponce about in Lycra. Takes serious hard work and dedication to get this big."

"Why is everything a joke to you? Aren't you ashamed to be so obese?"

"No, but my far from delightful stepmother is – or was – and that's what mattered. Anyway I like to think of myself as Rubenesque and voluptuous."

"Vomitous, more like."

She raised her hand and twirled it about.

"Give me a pull up then," she said.

Marcus reached out and clasped her hand in both of his. He pulled and strained, digging his heels in the ground. Maggie lifted momentarily then slumped back again, yanking him down on top of her. She burst out laughing once more.

Her body quaked with mirth and the boy slid off. But he didn't jump up straight away or make vicious jibes about bouncy castles. He felt her breath rising and falling next to him and could feel her heat through the linen of his shirt. All expression drained from Marcus's face as he realised he hadn't been this close to anyone in a long time. The swaggering front he had hidden behind collapsed like a castle of sand beneath a cold, crashing wave and he suddenly felt totally alone. The shock of it forced a painful cry from deep in his chest and tears fell from his eyes.

Maggie's laughter ceased and she turned to him.

"What's the matter?" she asked. "I was only messing. Not making fun of you."

Marcus rolled over and hid his face.

"I'm so bloody lonely," he wept desperately. "I've got no one, no friends, my family don't want to know. I've got nothing. I can't stand it."

"Oh, babes," she said tenderly. "Come here."

She pulled him closer, moved the nettled hand from his face and kissed him. Marcus kissed back.

Christina had wandered fearfully through the trees, searching for Jody. Finally she found her, still huddled under the oak, still locked in the May Cup nightmare. The seven-year-old ran over and threw her arms round her.

"It's OK," Christina whispered, stroking her hair. "We'll be OK. Don't be scared."

Jody couldn't hear her.

Spencer was bounding through the undergrowth. He had read countless books on the Old West and the knowledge inflamed the effects of the drugs. Now he was convinced he was the coyote from Native American mythology. He was Akba Atatdia, Old Man Coyote, he without family, the First Scolder, the Spying Moon, the trickster god who created the Milky Way.

Spencer truly believed that's who he was. When he caught any of the others, he wasn't going to bite them. The boy removed his spectacles. Akba Atatdia was a tremendous show-off – his party trick was to juggle his own eyeballs. That's what he was going to do.

High above, the real predator had viewed the young people running through the woodland in various states of fear, panic, elation, lust and paranoia. At last the dark cloud of frothing mould made its selection. The foaming black mass flowed through the branches and poured down on to the head of the one it had chosen.

A scream more shrill, more horrific than any so far that night rang out under the trees. In the chaos and confusion, nobody recognised it for what it was. In that moment, one of those young people died and the splinter of Austerly Fellows' mind seized control of the body.

In his cabin, Jangler was wondering if he should remove his bothersome shoes when a jaunty little tune announced the ringing of his phone.

"Hello?" he said, holding it to his face, bending one waxed end of his moustache as he did so.

"My dear Lockpick," the voice of the Ismus spoke into his ear. "It is done."

The old man beamed and tapped his desk with his free hand.

"Splendid, my Lord!" he cried. "I promise I shan't try to guess which one you're hiding inside."

"You'd better go out there and call them in before they damage themselves. They're bumbling about like the hopeless dullards they are. Put them to bed for the night. They need to be bright-eyed for tomorrow."

"Of course. So shall I switch off the bridging devices?"

"Whatever for? Don't get soft on me, Jangler. Let's not forget what function the dirty aberrants are serving there. The Queen of Hearts' May Cup is the perfect fuel to inspire their darkest dreams."

"Of course, my Lord. Is everything prepared for the morrow?"

"Don't you worry about that. Today I returned to the house in Felixstowe and made a certain arrangement. Tomorrow will be... spectacular."

"Ho ho! I'm sure it will."

"And what of our new friends? Are they settling in?"

"They're getting a bit restless. They don't like being cooped up in their chalet."

The Ismus chuckled. "They'll have the run of the place soon enough," he said. "What's one more day?"

"What indeed?"

"A transport will be there at five o'clock this morning to pick up tonight's arrivals."

"I shall attend to it."

"Faithful Jangler."

"Your humble servant."

The Ismus hung up. The old man attended to the waxed tip of his moustache, then he lit a lantern, took up a brass handbell and went outside. He paused a moment at the cabin next to his and tapped lightly at the window.

"Not long now, Captain," he said.

Nasal growls and snarls answered from within.

11

JODY AWOKE WITH a ferocious thirst. Her tongue felt furry and glued to the roof of her mouth. She stared at the cabin ceiling for several minutes, wondering where she was.

It was Charm's outraged voice that reminded her.

"My stuff's all over the floor again! This ain't funny."

Jody propped herself up. The inside of the chalet was just as untidy as the previous morning. Christina was sitting up in bed looking at her.

"You better?" the little girl asked. "You wasn't well last night."

"What's gone on?" Jody muttered in a rasping voice.

None of the girls could remember much. They recalled running into the wood, but not much after that. Little by little they pieced together scraps of what had happened. But it was vague and uncertain. They wondered if they had imagined half of it. The only memory that they did seem sure about was the sight of Jangler striding through the darkness, holding a lantern in one hand and clanging a bell with the other. Not one of them knew a thing about what happened later. Hours after they had collapsed into their beds, the Bakelite device had started playing another old song from the 1930s. Before sunrise a transit van had taken the creatures that had crossed over this time out of the camp.

"I dunno how I got to bed," Charm said. "Me mind's a blank."

If Jody had felt better, she would have made a sarcastic comment, but she was scratching her head and yawning.

"How'd I get so wasted?" she murmured. "I didn't drink much – hardly anything."

"Can't believe I was fall-down drunk and there weren't no paps to take a photo," Charm said indignantly. "That would of made the Sundays that would, 'Teenage model in booze shame' – would of been awesome publicity. Could of got a sofa spot on breakfast telly out of it – or a cosy chat about my problem on *This Morning*. Me ma would love that."

Jody grimaced. "Do you ever stop?" she complained. "Why do you even care about that twaddle if you think none of this is real and just a dream?"

"Cos the harder you try in your dream, the better time you have in Mooncaster. You don't know nofink, you, do you? When I get there, it's gonna be mind-blowing."

"That'd only take an asthmatic wasp with a straw, for you," Jody said. "Who says you're gonna get there anyway? It's our last day in this dump and it's done no good to no one. Nobody's been taken over by the book yet. Don't seem likely it's gonna work now, does it? You're stuck in this dream like the rest of us."

A worried look passed over Charm's face and she took herself to the bathroom.

"Don't be hours in there!" Jody shouted. "You're not the only one here, you know!"

"Our last day," Christina repeated sorrowfully.

Alasdair was already washed and dressed. He hurried outside and found Lee standing on the step of his cabin, staring at the cars that were pulling into the camp because there was no more parking room on the approach road. Colourful bunting had been added to the flower garlands between the wooden posts, a maypole was being erected in the centre of the lawn, swing boats were being unloaded from a lorry and, to the left of the stage, an old-fashioned helter-skelter was rising.

"More fun and frolics," the Scot observed dourly. "So how's the bonny wee world with you today?"

"You don't wanna know. I'm in a real nasty mood. Woke up with a bruised right arm, no cigarettes and another day of this BS to get through."

"Everyone else OK? My lads seem fine, a few headaches and our hut were a mess again. After last night though, I'm just relieved they're in one piece."

"Did you see cowboy kid? I had to drag him outta there. He was far gone – howled all the way back here."

"What about Jim, is he OK?"

"That the quiet, serious guy? Yeah, he's cool, don't say much, why?"

"Just keep an eye out today. I dinnae think he's too well."

"Only today?"

"Well, we're getting out of here tomorrow."

"Ya think?"

Alasdair took a phone from his pocket. "Charged it up at last," he said. "You can have my number."

Lee shook his head. "Don't think it'll be necessary," he answered, looking away.

Alasdair concealed his disappointment and changed the subject hastily.

"I fired off some emails last night, when we got back in. Told the news sites in America about them drugging us."

"Won't make no difference, too late for anyone to stop this now."

"It might!"

"Even if they believed you, ain't no one can stop this thing. It's a cancer and it's only gonna get bigger."

"Did ye know there's actually a protein called JAK that helps cancer cells spread through the body?"

"Not a bit surprised."

Marcus was slow getting ready that morning. Unlike a lot of the others, his recollection of the night before was all too clear and it made him cringe. If he hadn't been so hungry, he would have skipped breakfast completely. With the enthusiasm of a condemned man walking to the gallows, he made his way to the dining hall.

"Here he is!" Maggie's voice called when he entered. "Mornin', babes! I saved a seat next to me."

Marcus looked at her coldly and gave the slightest acknowledging nod. Then he walked straight past and took his usual place on the other side of the model castle.

Maggie lowered her eyes and pushed her plate away. She understood.

By now everyone had heard they had been drugged and were hesitant about drinking the ale. Jody was furious and when Jangler appeared, she leaped up to yell at him.

"What's all this?" he asked, beaming the most innocent of smiles. "Such fanciful notions! Dear me, as if I would sanction such a terrible thing. No tincture or potion was administered, I assure you. You were a trifle overwrought after the excitement of the day. That is all. Youthful high spirits – such exuberance is to be expected in this merry month. The wild woses of the woods will not be denied their rowdy play."

Lee hissed through his teeth. Alasdair slammed the table.

"That's a lie!" he said. "Everyone 'cept me an' Lee was out their boxes last night. You was lucky no one got hurt."

"Life is littered with mischance and stumbled steps," Jangler replied icily. "We must daily thank our guiding fortune we do not fall prey to harm and hazard."

"You threatening me?"

One half of Jangler's moustache gave a twitch. "What a lurid imagination you possess," he said. "So much the better for today. I guarantee that many of you, maybe even all, will finally be welcomed into the Realm of the Dawn Prince. The Holy Enchanter has decreed it will be so and, as the media will be present to record the wondrous event, may I suggest you don the agreeable costumes you were wearing yesterday."

Only Charm responded with any enthusiasm.

"Do be careful out there," he added solemnly. "That jackanapes, the Jockey, has decided to show his tricksy face here, so be wary. Who knows what mischief and mayhem that marplot may cause?"

Leaving the dining hall to return to his organising duties, he paused a moment and looked back at his young charges. Inside one of them a fragment of his Lord was hiding. Jangler couldn't resist wondering which one.

"No, I must not," he told himself strictly. "I must treat each of them the same, bury my curiosity, file it away for now. At the appropriate hour, the Holy Enchanter will tell me, when he learns the identity of the Castle Creeper."

Two hours later, the day was in full swing and rich in pageantry. There was a fairground atmosphere, with falconry displays, demonstrations of swordsmanship, jugglers and fire-eaters. There were double the amount of stalls and entertainments as Friday and even more people dressed as characters from the book; some were even rigged out in full armour. The Jacks and Jills were present once again and occupied four thrones on the raised stage. The Harlequin Priests and the three Black Face Dames stood silent and impassive behind them. Paparazzi and news crews swarmed everywhere.

Kate Kryzewski and Sam, her cameraman, were there. Above the waist, the reporter was dressed smartly in a navy jacket and pale blue blouse but below, just out of frame, she wore a ragged skirt sewn from patches of grubby cloth and she was barefoot. A tambourine with the image of a human ear printed on the skin hung from her belt. Every now and then she tapped it to make sure it was still there. If the Jockey made a nuisance of himself, she would shake it in his face and send him running. So far he had kept out of her way, and she had only glimpsed him skipping in and out of the crowd, dancing around the maypole, tangling the ribbons and causing chaos. That was pretty paltry mischief for him.

Kate and Sam had got a trove of footage yesterday at Great Ormond Street where sick children told how they were healthy and well in Mooncaster. A small boy in a wheelchair tearfully explained that he could run and play there and didn't understand why he had to keep coming back to this painful dream.

Today Kate wanted to interview the aberrants and find out how their weekend was going. But the ones she encountered weren't cooperative and their contributions would never get used in her report.

"It's a total dead loss," Jody muttered into the microphone. "Just like you are now. How much of a fight did you put up before they got you? So much for them promises you made in the coach the first day. Epic fail there, love. You look a right wazzock in that get-up. What's it supposed to be – Cinderella meets the Apprentice?"

"Get that outta my face!" Lee snarled, pushing the camera away.

"Do ye know the old guy spiked our drinks last night?" Alasdair shouted into the lens. "I dinnae even trust the food here noo. God knows what else he's been doing, but we keep wakin' up wi' bruises. What does that tell ye? What you gonna do about it?"

"I just want to get out of this hole," Marcus said sulkily.

Kate and Sam moved on. They pushed through dancers and mummers, stilt-walkers and three people in a dragon costume blowing butane flames over everyone's heads.

In spite of Jangler's appeal, most of the children hadn't bothered with their costumes today and those that did wore them mixed with their ordinary clothes. Spencer had replaced the baggy grey hose with jeans, but he retained the doublet. Topping it off was his Stetson. It made for an unusual combination.

"Er… I had a cool time yesterday," he mumbled timidly. "Finally got to ride a horse. Made the whole weekend worthwhile. I'm going to see if I can have a go on some of those here today. I'd love to go to America. It's my dream."

Tommy and Rupesh came into focus next. The two of them had become firm friends over the past couple of days.

"We were scared of the werewolf," Rupesh said hesitantly whilst Tommy whispered something into his ear. "But the other games we played yesterday were very nice. We don't like that dragon over there."

"The food here's good," Maggie said, forcing herself to be jolly when she felt the polar opposite. "And there's tons of it. I could live here full time.

Well, if a certain someone wasn't around I would."

Finally Kate and Sam found Charm. The Bolton-born model had taken extra care with her appearance that day. Her make-up was immaculate and the accents of pink ornamenting her medieval costume matched the handbag hanging from the crook of her arm. She had been practising what to say all morning, determined to outshine the others and get maximum airtime. The fifteen-year-old delivered the perfect interview. It was just the sort of upbeat filler Kate's report needed.

"I am so, so grateful for the diamond opportunity I've been given," the girl gushed like a contestant on a talent show final. "I've been on such a magical journey this weekend. It's been a proper roller coaster of emotions, it really has, no word of a lie, no messin'. I've still got no idea how new this forest is though – looks dead old to me. I wish the Ismus fella was here. I'd fank him personally. He's lovely, ain't he? I feel dead safe when he's about, cos he watches over us, don't he? Like my Uncle Frank did, only more… bigger and magic, like one of them wizards, but dishy wiv it. Where is he anyway? His three bruisers are over there, but he ain't here. They don't go nowhere wivout him, do they? That's well weird."

As she spoke, they became aware of a remote whirring. Everyone looked to the sky. A helicopter was in the distance, bearing straight for the camp. The older children had grown to hate and fear that sound. There had been widespread use of helicopters by the police to hunt down anyone who resisted *Dancing Jax*. Passages from the book had been broadcast from on-board loudspeakers as searchlights scoured the streets below. There had been no escaping them.

As it drew closer, the crowd realised something was dangling beneath, on a long cable. It was a figure, clad in black.

"Ohhhh… Myyyyy… God!" Charm squealed. "It's him, innit!"

Strapped into a safety harness, swooping over the forest with outstretched arms, the Holy Enchanter came flying. The tails of his short leather jacket flapped madly behind him and his shoulder-length hair streamed in the wind. The downdraught of the rotor blades flattened the treetops as he approached. It was as if even nature bowed down before him.

On the ground the crowd went wild. They cheered themselves hoarse. Hats and headdresses were hurled into the air. Old Scorch the dragon let rip with a fountain of flame and Jangler dropped his clipboard in astonishment. He hadn't expected so dramatic and spectacular an entrance.

Sam's camera was trained skyward. This was better than the arrival of any rock star at a stadium. The helicopter circled the campsite three times. When it positioned itself above the stage, the winch began to feed out the cable. The Ismus descended, to a triumphant blaring of trumpets, and he viewed his subjects with a benevolent smile. It was like the advent of a god among mortals.

"Crazy-assed psycho," Lee muttered, almost in admiration.

Jody was too jaded and stubborn to let herself be impressed by this over-the-top, messianic spectacle.

"Macho poser," she said bitterly. "His ego's so massive it'd influence tides."

At her side Christina could only gape as the man floated down from the sky, like an elegant spider on a thread.

"Little Miss Muffet," she breathed softly.

"They'd never get me doing that!" Maggie exclaimed. "It wouldn't get off the ground for one thing."

Somewhere in the crowd Jim Parker was transfixed and his eyes were filled with envy. He was certain his own superpower would be immense strength, but he hoped and longed for the ability to fly. How else could he get to where he was needed in time? It was only reasonable for the two to go together. He watched the Ismus's descent with the professional and critical interest of a rival. The boy's right hand moved unconsciously to his chest and he pressed it against the self-inflicted scar, while his left sought the reassuring touch of the cape he had donned over his T-shirt that morning.

Throughout his downward progress, the Ismus remained locked in a cruciform. It was supremely stylish and a strikingly potent image. He landed on the stage with such balletic grace Jim made up his mind that was how he would always land. No more thudding down on one knee for him; that had hurt like mad and it was still swollen. Perhaps the invulnerability aspect of his powers was the slowest to develop.

The crowd was going mental. They would have stampeded the stage if the Black Face Dames hadn't stepped forward and blocked them. The Jacks and Jills almost leaped up to greet him, but the Harlequin Priests shook their heads and they remained seated. As the people roared and applauded, the Priests unfastened the harness and signalled to the pilot. The helicopter moved off. Once the noise of the blades had faded, the Holy Enchanter addressed his devoted flock.

"Blessed be to all who dwell within the thirteen hills!" he proclaimed.

This prompted more extended cheering.

"To all who faithfully await the return of the Dawn Prince from exile. To all who are gathered here today, to celebrate and rejoice in the hallowed text of Austerly Fellows – the visionary who opened the way to Mooncaster!"

Tommy and Rupesh covered their ears. The ovation was louder than the helicopter had been.

The Ismus raised his hands for silence and suddenly every voice was stilled. Only the sound of birdsong could be heard around the camp. He looked pleased as he surveyed the expectant, adoring faces. There were over six hundred people there.

During this suspenseful hush, Alasdair downed a goblet of wine, casting aside his suspicions about what else it may contain. He couldn't begin to guess what that Russell Brand clone was about to do on the stage and quite frankly he'd had enough of this tiresome charade to care.

"The time to unlock the gates of Mooncaster for these poor, outcast children has come at last," the Ismus announced with absolute authority. "Today they shall be admitted into the halls of the White Castle and look upon the worshipful Empty Throne in the Great Hall. It is my sacred duty and privilege to be the bearer of this most blessed invitation – from the Dawn Prince Himself!"

The crowd gasped as one. This was a staggering revelation and the

Harlequin Priests dropped to their knees. Jangler removed his spectacles and bowed his head in reverence.

"I bring unto ye the Word," the Ismus cried. "And the Word is – *Enter*."

He gestured to those at the front of the stage to clear a space and they parted like the Red Sea.

"Bring the suffering little children unto me," he commanded.

Jody, Christina, Lee, Maggie and the others were impelled by firm but gentle pressure towards the stage. When all thirty-one of them had been guided and herded into place, the Ismus addressed them like a kindly father.

"Too long you have endured your grievous isolation alone, shut in the purgatory of this grey dream. Now you shall know the bliss and acceptance you have always yearned for. Wake up to your true life and give praise to He who must return! Even now He is reaching out to gather you home. Hearken to His call."

Lowering his outstretched arms, he closed his eyes and uttered strange words under his breath. His hands closed into fists and a tremor shook his frame. A spasm of pain contorted his face and he clenched his teeth.

Alasdair stared at him curiously. What was the nutcase doing?

The Black Face Dames appeared uneasy. The Harlequin Priests clasped their hands in prayer. The crowd held its breath. Something momentous was about to occur.

"Commence the reading!" the Ismus ordered in a strangled voice.

At the back of the stage, choristers took up their copies of *Dancing Jax* and began reciting the chapter as they had been instructed.

"*'Twas the Night of All Dark, the Witching Eve, when unclean powers are at their height and malice stirs sleeping bones.*"

Jody looked back at the crowd. They were already nodding and under the book's spell, back in the fantasy existence they were addicted to. She glanced up at the Ismus and was shocked to see the transformation that had come over him. His face was deathly pale and he was shuddering uncontrollably. His eyes were hidden beneath crunched-down brows and sweat poured through his hair. He was exerting all his strength, straining and marshalling some tremendous force.

The girl put her arm round Christina and drew her close. She didn't like this.

"Thirteen lamps must be lit at the boundary stones," the choristers chanted as they too rocked backwards and forwards. *"The fiends that prowl abroad must be kept at bay on this, the most treacherous night of the year. Ne'er let the lamps fail. Bar the unknown shapes that creep about the village. Ware, Mooncot, ware!"*

The warm spring sunlight grew dim. Colour and brightness drained from the world. The blue of the sky sickened to a sombre slate and shadows deepened. A wintry chill crept into the camp.

Tommy and Rupesh held on to one another. Marcus couldn't understand what was happening. This wasn't right. It was eerie. He shivered, partly from the sudden, unnatural cold, mostly from fear. Dread stole into every heart but one.

Charm could hardly contain her excitement. She could feel the hairs on her neck prickling and gooseflesh bumped through her spray tan. This was going to be it! She was going to wake up in the White Castle and be a princess or a noblewoman of high birth. She was about to close her eyes so that she could open them in Mooncaster when she saw a thread of black smoke rising from the Ismus's collar.

"Oi!" she cried in panic. "He's on fire! He's burning!"

The children watched, dumbfounded, as oily clouds poured from the back of his jacket. Then tips of ragged flame went licking up the nape of his neck.

"Do summink!" Charm shouted to the Black Face Dames.

They did not hear her. They saw nothing. They were oblivious to everything here. They were worlds away, in Mooncaster.

"Someone!" Charm yelled.

But the Priests had prostrated themselves on the floor. The Jacks and Jills were rocking in their seats and the choristers continued reading.

Charm snatched the nearest goblet of ale. She rushed at the stage to douse the flames, but Lee pulled her back.

"Let it be," he told her. "Don't you mess with what's going down with that sick trash. The show's only just started."

The Ismus let out an agonised scream. His knees buckled, but he remained standing. Then his entire jacket burst into flames. The leather burned like paper, turning to ash in moments. He thrashed his arms wildly, tearing it from his body, flinging the glowing tatters away.

The fires raging over the Ismus's back dwindled and his shrieks of anguish became a triumphant, crowing yell.

His eyes snapped open and he grinned at the stupefied, frightened young faces staring up at him. Spinning on one heel, he executed a perfect revolution and the children drew their breath.

The man's naked back blazed with a pattern of fierce, angry light that swirled through his skin like paths of lava. Mystical symbols and words from an ancient language covered his shoulders. They flowed down his spine and snaked along his arms. It was the living contract he had made months ago in Felixstowe when he had endured the Great Ordeal, sitting upon an iron throne filled with red-hot coals.

"The way is opened!" he exulted.

He raised his arms and fire spat into life along them once more. Then, to the children's disbelief, he rose from the stage. This time there was no harness, no cable – no helicopter high above. The Ismus ascended into the air unaided. He floated up over the heads of his bodyguards and sailed out over the upturned young faces.

"Sweet Jesus," Lee uttered.

"That's impossible!" Marcus spluttered. "It's a trick – can't be real!"

"No way," Alasdair whispered. "No bloody way!"

"I told you it were true!" Charm squealed, clapping her hands. "Me ma wouldn't lie to me! This is so wicked – it's awesomeness on a plate! Yes! Yes! Yes!"

"That is so cool," Tommy breathed.

"Yes," Rupesh said, marvelling at the levitating man. "And also it is scary."

"Flame on," Jim murmured, his wonderment mixed with jealousy.

The Ismus drifted directly above them. Then, hanging in mid-air, he joined in the reading. He needed no copy of the book. He knew every word.

"And on the Night of All Dark," he declaimed, *"the peasant children made neepjack lanterns and paraded them around the boundary stones…"*

His voice was different. It was rough and loud. It came rumbling from his throat as though rising from some deep region beneath the earth. It boomed out over the campsite and the day grew even darker. Soon there was no other sound but the words bellowing from his mouth.

Charm stopped jumping up and down with glee and covered her ears. Jody held Christina more tightly than ever and tears streamed down her face. The voice was thundering inside her head. It hammered and squalled inside the children's minds. The youngest screamed. Then the teenagers did the same.

All around them, the crowd uttered cries of pain. The horses stamped and reared. The Jacks and Jills slumped on their thrones. The choristers dropped their books and cradled their heads in their hands. The Black Face Dames collapsed and the Harlequin Priests writhed in torment on the stage. Kate Kryzewski fainted and Sam fell on his camera. Jangler sank to the ground, emitting a pitiful wail.

"My Lord!" he whimpered as he passed out. "Too much! Too strong!"

Over six hundred devotees of *Dancing Jax* sagged and sprawled on their faces. Only the thirty-one aberrant children remained standing.

The forces channelling through the Ismus intensified. He arched his back and the patterns seared in his skin burned more fiercely than ever, spitting flames and shining with white and violet light. The throbbing glare beat down upon the stricken youngsters.

"It hurts!" Jim bawled, clawing his scalp.

Marcus doubled over. Lee thought his temples were going to explode. Rupesh hugged Tommy. Spencer covered his face with his Stetson and sobbed into it. Alasdair was yelling abuse at the Ismus, calling him every obscene name he had ever heard. Maggie was shrieking and Jody clung desperately to Christina.

It was then she felt something warm and wet in the little girl's hair. Lifting her shaking hand, she saw her fingers were stained crimson. Then she felt a trickle down her own neck.

Bright ribbons of blood were streaking from the back of every child's head. There was a flare of white flames from above and the blast overwhelmed them. The children were hurled to the ground. Their cries ended and they lost consciousness. Tommy's hand was still clasped in Rupesh's.

"Get a move on, Tully!" an exasperated voice came echoing inside his head. "We'll be late!"

Whinnying in terror, the horses bolted from the camp.

12

IT WAS THE Night of All Dark in the Realm of the Dawn Prince.

The last lump of flesh was scraped out of the head.

Tully looked up from the turnip he had been hollowing. Finally it was done! It had been tough work. The creamy orange flesh was as difficult to dig into as frozen ground and he hoped he hadn't ruined one of his mother's precious spoons in the gouging. He had chosen this turnip from the pile especially. It was almost as large as his own head. The greater part of its fine, fat globe was as rich a purple as he had seen on any of the nobles riding through the village and the rest was a warm buttery colour, like the rind on a cheese. This specimen also boasted a cluster of fibrous roots at the bottom, which made for an excellent beard. Using his own sharp little knife, he busied himself cutting a fearsome face into what he had decided should be the front.

Across the table his brother, Rufus, watched him impatiently. He had finished his turnip some time ago.

"Make haste!" the older boy told him. "We'll miss the bonfire and everything!"

"Don't you leave those chunks and shavings on the table," their mother cautioned as she bustled into the small kitchen bearing stick bundles for the fire. "Be sure to put them in the pot for the stew tomorrow and, when you've done later, put what's left of your lanterns in the pail for the pig. Don't go throwing it away and wasting it."

Rufus promised, but Tully made no answer. Cutting out the mouth was a tricky procedure. He gave the turnip a wide, peggy grin and sat back to appreciate his handiwork.

"Where's its nose?" Rufus laughed. "You can't have a neepjack with no nose."

"I don't want it to have one," Tully replied.

"Just two triangles for eyes," their mother tutted. "Whatever next?"

"Should have a nose," a sleepy voice piped up from the settle near the fire.

"There now!" Rufus said. "Grandfather says it should have one! And he's nigh on seventy and the oldest person in Mooncot so he should know – seen more neepjacks on Ween Night than either you or I have."

"Or me," their mother added.

"Pog's more fearsome without a nose," Tully stated decisively.

"His name's Pog, is it?" the old man by the fire chuckled. "There's fanciful." He rummaged in the pockets of his jerkin and held out the nubs of two candles. "Here – take this for him and whatever your brother's is called."

"Wet the Bed Walter," Rufus declared with a giggle.

"Pog thanks you," Tully said, taking the candle stumps from his grandfather.

"Got them from Malinda herself," the old man said, with a wink to his daughter. "Must be mighty special I'm thinking."

Tully gasped and took the stumps gingerly. He held one over the rushlight he had been working by, dripped a puddle of hot wax into the empty turnip and pushed it in place.

"Here, wrap up well," the woman chided, tying the children's hooded woollen cloaks about their young shoulders and placing a felt hat on her head over her coif. "There's a mist rising off the pond. Now make haste – you'll miss the flame dance if you dally so."

Tully was almost done. He threaded a string through the sides of Pog's head and up through the sliced-off top that served as the lid. Then he took the rushlight from the iron holder and pushed the flame in through one of the triangular eyes.

"Come, Pog," he whispered an expectant incantation. "Come wake, come alive. Be my guard on the road this night. Keep me safe from foes and witches, as long as you're alight."

The candle within spluttered and burned with a bright yellow tongue. It shone through the lantern's eyes and mouth, through the slot in the lid Tully had made as a chimney and glowed softly through the flesh.

"Hail, Pog!" he cooed. "Welcome to our hearth and home. This is my mother. That is my brother, he is nine, and yonder is my grandfather – he's seen sixty-eight Witching Evens so you've probably noticed him before. I am Tully. I will be eight next spring."

A whisker of smoke curled upwards.

"Look!" he told his family. "He's very happy to meet us."

"You're a mooncalf," Rufus snorted, lighting Wet the Bed Walter.

"Foolish child," his mother chortled. "Leave magick spells to the likes of fairy godmothers, Court magicians and wicked witches. We don't want none of that in our little cottage. Now let us be gone and join your father up by the mound."

The boys picked their turnip lanterns up by the string handles, ran over to kiss their grandfather then hurried out of the kitchen.

"Just you mind to bar this door," the woman told the old man. "With most of the village up at the fire, any roaming footpad or villain could make himself right at home and help himself to our supper."

"Not tonight they won't," her father answered, easing himself back into the settle and closing his eyes. "The boundary stones each have their lamp. No evil thing will dare tread past our doors. I'll have myself a nice quiet doze by the hearth while you're gone."

Pulling on a shawl, the woman bustled out into the night.

A chill was in the air. The first fingers of the approaching winter had crept over the northern hills. No moon hung in the night sky and autumn's stars appeared colder and more remote than ever.

Mooncot was a small village. The humble thatched dwellings huddled either side of the single road that led from the White Castle. A half-timbered tavern, The Silver Penny, was at one end and the stone mill house was at the other, beside the pond.

With their lanterns swinging in their hands, Tully and Rufus ran diagonally across the empty street. They did not wait for their mother. Holding their noses, they hurried through the gap between Mistress Sarah's two-room cottage which, throughout the summer, was always bedecked with fragrant flowers – and the rickety, stinking hovel of Dung-Breathed Billy the Midden-Man. Once clear of the pong, and the angry honking of Mistress Sarah's geese, they charged up the gentle rise into the turnip field and beyond that, over the freshly ploughed strips that were waiting for next year's sowing.

Pog and Wet the Bed Walter lit their way with slivers and wedges of orange light. The brothers called out to each other in scary, growling voices until a glow appeared on the horizon. A river of golden sparks and glowing embers was flowing up into the night.

"They lit the bonfire already!" Rufus cried. "Hurry!"

They raced to the hedgerow that fenced the strips in and jumped over the low stile. A grassy hill climbed steeply beyond and crowning that was a ring of ancient stones.

Every Ween the villagers lit a bonfire within that circle. Many years ago, wise men had calculated it to be the exact centre of the Kingdom and so bonfires were lit there and fed with herbs of virtue and protection. Invocations to the good spirits of the land would be sung and then the menfolk would dance clockwise round the stones as close as they dared, as their hats scorched and eyebrows and whiskers smoked and singed. The women would dance a little further away, widdershins, and then the children would dance in a third outer ring.

When Tully and Rufus reached the summit, the dancing had already started. Aiken Woodside the Ploughman, or 'Aiken Fingers' as he was commonly called, was playing a hearty tune on his fiddle.

The boys deposited their neepjacks on the ground, amongst a crowd of other ferocious-looking lanterns, and joined their young friends in the outer circle.

It was a glorious, happy time, filled with light, laughter, music and crackling flames. When the boys' mother caught up with them, the fire was still blazing tall and the enthusiasm for the dancing had not abated. In the distance, behind them, the gleaming, milky walls and towers of Mooncaster Castle reared against the starry heavens. The Under Kings and nobles were having their own celebration that night.

Tully had an idea. He wanted to take Pog round the bounds of the village, to show him each of the thirteen marker stones and the enchanted lanterns that kept them safe that night. Rufus wanted to do it too. So did their friends Clover Ditchy, Benwick, Neddy, Muddy Legs Woodside, Peasy Meadow and Lynnet.

None of them would dare venture over the fields at night normally, but tonight was special. What harm could befall them?

Excited, they assured their parents they would return as soon as they had visited the thirteenth marker and swore not to step beyond the village bounds.

"I want to go too!" Clover's six-year-old sister, Gunnhild, demanded.

"You're too small," he told her. "Maybe next year if you grow bigger."

The little girl scowled and pouted.

The others took up their neepjacks, admiring one another's handiwork, and pulled frightful faces to match those carved in the turnips. Then they raced down the hill and back to the village.

The first marker was at the edge of the millpond. Muddy Legs reached it first because he didn't mind splashing across the corners. The boundary stone was a roughly hewn, diamond-shaped, weathered block of granite. In the side facing away from the village a deep niche had been cut and, placed inside that, was the first of the warding lamps. This was a tall cylinder, made of silver and set with coloured glass. It and the other twelve were a gift from the Holy Enchanter whose own hand had engraved words of power in the metal. A stout candle within was lit at sundown and would still be burning well after dawn when the danger was past.

"Look, Pog," Tully said, holding his neepjack high. "That's keeping the evil fiends of the wild away. Ramptana the Court Magician, from the castle, lights these himself, every year."

The other children laughed at him for talking to his turnip.

"Let me see your lanterns!" a soft, sad voice called.

The children turned back to the pond and saw a grey figure rising from the water, wrapped in mist, with long dark hair streaming upwards. It was the ghost of Brynwin, the miller's daughter, who drowned whilst reaching too far picking water lilies on her tenth birthday.

"Hello, Brynwin!" they shouted, gathering on the bank. They all knew the drowned girl and weren't afraid. She wasn't wicked or frightening, she was just sad and moped a lot – but then she had good cause to. She couldn't even leave the confines of the pond and spent most midnights skulking in the reeds, feeling sorry for herself.

"So many scary faces!" she said, her cold blue lips almost managing a smile. "I wish I had a turnip lantern. It might frighten off the family of toads that have moved in. Terrible noisy they are and they've got no manners."

"We'd lend you ours," Rufus offered. "But we're on our way round the boundary and have to go straight home after."

The drowned girl's spectral face turned towards the village.

"You should go back now," she warned them. "The Night of All Dark is not a time to play games. Evil is mustering about Mooncot. Dark shapes are slinking from the woods and creeping along the ditches. I can sense them. And there are other dangers…"

"Not tonight!" Tully said confidently. "The thirteen lamps will guard us."

They bade her farewell and hurried on their way. The ghost of Brynwin retreated to the centre of the pond, shaking her head as she sank into the dark water.

If only they had hearkened to her words.

The eight children ran to the far corner of the next field, where the second marker stone was beneath a towering elm tree. It cast a glimmering radiance up into the lofty branches. Tully lifted Pog to see and, sniggering, the others mimicked him – even Rufus. Gently teasing him, everyone had given their turnips names now. There was Flameburp, Muckyroots, Sprouty Top, Burny, Candlebrains and Purple Fatty.

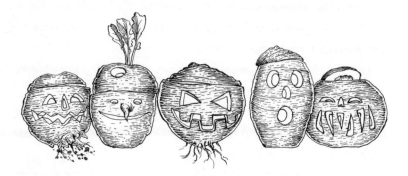

Relishing being out on this night-time adventure, they set off for the next marker, which stood in front of the long barrow where the bones of long-dead chieftains were interred. The village was left further and further behind.

"What's that yonder?" Rufus called, pointing to a dark shape at the side of the path ahead, beyond the reach of their lanterns' light.

The children halted a moment.

"Is it a bear?" Muddy Legs asked hopefully.

"That's never big enough to be a bear!" Peasy chided, lifting Burny, her lantern, higher. "Besides, the Cinnamon Bear don't never leave his cave up Hunter's Chase and he's the only bear in these parts."

"A dead horse then?"

Lynnet scowled at him. "'Tis some old sacks dropped there by a wandering rogue, most like," she said decisively.

"Ill-gotten gains, that's what they'll be," Muddy Legs speculated. "Spoils and such. The hidey place of robbers and footpads."

"Not a very good hidey place," Rufus remarked. "Just at the side of the path, not even under the hedge. Why didn't they put them in the barrow? It's only across the next field and no one ever goes in there."

"It's too scary, that's why!" Benwick muttered.

"No doubt they'll be back soon," Neddy said. "Their haul was prob'ly too much for one carting."

"It might be stolen treasure!" Tully suggested.

"More like flour, stole from the mill," Lynnet commented with her usual disregard for the fanciful.

"Or," Muddy Legs said with relish, "it might be chopped-up bodies. Some arms and a head or two – murderers do that."

The children didn't like that idea. Even though they knew nothing could harm them that night, they were uneasy as to what those sacks might contain.

Holding their neepjacks out before them, they crept further along the path, trepidatious and fearful.

Suddenly Tully let out a cry, which made everyone jump.

"Why, those aren't sacks at all! 'Tis a person!"

"A dead one?" asked the bloodthirsty Muddy Legs. "Is it murdered? Are there bits hacked off? Is there gore? Does it look like jam?"

Tully and Rufus ran forward and knelt beside the stricken figure. It was an old man. Much to Muddy Legs' disappointment, he was not chopped up. He was still alive, but out cold.

"Quick, your lanterns!" Rufus told the others urgently. The children brought them closer and they stared at the person prostrate on the ground.

"He's not a serf," Lynnet observed. "That's velvet he's wearing."

"Turn him over," Benwick said. "Let's see who he is."

"Look at the moons and stars on his gown," Peasy said admiringly.

"And what a beard! It's long as my dad's arm, that is."

"And white as milk!"

"That's a nasty lump on his head. Seen smaller duck eggs."

Tully rocked back on his heels. "You know who this is!" he breathed in disbelief. "It's Ramptana the Court Magician!"

"No!" every child gasped.

"Why, so it is!" Neddy confirmed. "What's he doing here?"

"And who clobbered him?"

"Robbers and murderers," Muddy Legs whispered in mock terror.

Ever practical, Lynnet removed her cloak, rolled it up and placed it under the old gentleman's head. She patted his face to try and bring him round, but he remained unconscious.

"We have to get help," she said. "He must have been here for hours. He might've catched his death. Take off your cloaks and cover him, he's icy."

The other children obeyed then Rufus waved Wet the Bed Walter over the path and inspected the ground. "Look here," he observed, "Footprints… well, paw prints!"

"Is it a dog?" Tully asked. "Did one of the hounds get out and attack him?"

"That's no dog," Clover said, who knew about these things because Bertolf the dog boy was his best friend. "It's a…"

"A fox, I think you'll find," a new, strange voice interrupted.

The children started. Rufus and Muddy Legs leaped up. Everyone looked around anxiously.

"Who's there?" Rufus demanded, peering into the surrounding darkness.

"You can't chop us all," Muddy Legs said defiantly, even though his voice wobbled.

"My dear grubby fellow," the suave, cultivated voice replied, "I've no intention of carving you into kiddie collops. I did have a date planned with a few delectable chickens tonight, but alack, it appears I'm fated to miss out on a good clucking. I'm too tender-hearted, that's my trouble. I've been sitting here wondering what to do for an interminably long time. That old clod is such a dunderhead, he's only got himself to blame."

The children could tell the speaker was close by, in the field bordered by the path, but he was concealed in the gloom. They held their neepjacks out and the radiating slices of orange light struck a reflected glint in two golden eyes.

It was a large dog fox, who stared back at them with an insolent grin on his face.

"What curious gimcracks," the animal remarked. "Root vegetables with candles inside! You people really are most extraordinarily eccentric. Whatever next, fish slippers?"

"The fox with human speech!" Rufus exclaimed.

"The talking fox!" The others chimed in.

The fox rolled his eyes. "One day, one of you humans will surprise me with an original 'hello'," he sighed.

"Don't listen to it!" Benwick told the others. "It's an enemy of the Realm! The Ismus decreed it so. Look what it did to Ramptana."

"I sit before you, blameless in this!" the fox objected. "There I was, minding my own vulpine business, walking along, looking forward to some feathery jawplay in the henhouse, when I chanced upon this senile old charlatan doddering down the path towards me. He shied a stone in my direction so I directed some pointed backchat at him, larded with home truths. He didn't like them so he ran at me – at his age too, the silly old conjuror! Anyway, the laces on the hapless booby's shoe were undone. He tripped over them and hit his head on the very stone he propelled at me. Wasn't that a poetic coincidence? I do so adore symmetry in life, don't you?"

Tully and his brother marvelled at the urbane fox. They wanted to take him home and introduce him to their grandfather.

"Don't believe it!" Benwick insisted. "Twisty as a snake, that's what it is. It's in league with the witch, everyone knows that."

The animal flicked its brush and stretched.

"If you insist on defaming me with crude and clumsy clichés, and repeating groundless slander," he said, "I shall bid you goodnight. I only tarried because of the foulness gathering around your village. Beardy here may be as useful as a sugar shield, but he doesn't deserve to be tormented by the evil horrors massing out there. Now you small people are here to take care of it, I can depart. There may yet be time for some fowlness of my own – ho ho!"

"Wait!" Tully cried. "What's this?"

He had been examining the large satchel Ramptana had been carrying and drew from it a silver cylinder studded with coloured glass. There were more inside.

"The warding lamps!" Rufus uttered in dismay.

"He didn't light them all!" Peasy exclaimed as Muddy Legs began to wail.

The fox flicked his ears. "What's amiss?" he asked.

"The village is undefended!" they said in horror. "On Witching Eve!"

"Our parents!" Clover cried. "My little sister – they're up on the hill. They do not know."

"And you," the fox told them. "You little cubs are out here, alone... with the hungry terrors of the woods closing in."

"What will we do?" Benwick asked in a panic.

"Muddy Legs is the fastest runner," Lynnet said. "He must run to the hilltop and warn them. We'll hurry back to the village."

"But what about Ramptana?" Tully cried. "We can't leave him here to get chewed or worse."

"He'll slow us down," Benwick said.

"He's right," the fox intervened. "If a mere four-legged animal, with a trifle more innate cunning and a keener sense of self-preservation than any of you possess, may proffer a suggestion? Warning your kin won't be enough. They cannot stand against the forces gathering around your village and none of you will make it back there if you attempt to carry that bearded burden with you."

"What then?" Rufus asked.

"I shall run," the fox volunteered, "fleet and silent, to the White Castle and call for aid. Cover the wrinkly old nuisance's face with your cloaks and hope he is passed over by the things that are approaching. Flee for your hearths as fast as you can. Don't look back, don't pause to challenge unfamiliar shadows and do not think to dart across the empty fields to call your parents home. You will never make it to that hill alive."

"I don't trust it," Benwick said uncertainly. "Who in the castle is going to listen to the talking fox? It's Haxxentrot's familiar!"

The fox looked affronted, but there wasn't time to argue. "Why are you still stood there like Widow Tallowax's washing on a line?" he barked. "The Bad Shepherd is abroad this night!"

That was enough. The children turned pale and took flight back down the path, their turnip lanterns swinging wildly in their hands, throwing abstract shapes around them.

The fox watched them sprint into the dark and took a deep breath as he flexed his legs, preparing for the long, desperate race to Mooncaster.

"Now," he said grimly. "I've a favour owing from the son of an Under King and it's time to collect."

There was a creamy flash of the tip of his tail, a scrape of soil was kicked into the air – *and he was gone.*

Back at the bonfire a sudden screech cut through the merrymaking. It was a hideous, malice-filled voice and went echoing across the sky.

Aiken Fingers stopped playing and the villagers looked around in consternation. Where had it come from?

It was little Gunnhild who saw it first. The weaver's six-year-old daughter cried out and pointed high above the fields.

"Witch!" she shrieked. "Witch!"

Mothers clutched their children and oak-hearted men blanched. For in the night sky, the figure of Haxxentrot, the malevolent crone, was riding her hayfork – flying through the darkness.

A Bogey Boy sat behind her. His stunted legs swung from side to side and his white, wobbly head was grinning at the sight of the horrified villagers down on the hill. Haxxentrot cackled and croaked an order. Jub opened his sack and a ghastly green light illuminated his ugly face. He delved his long fingers into the bag and fished out a glowing glass phial. Haxxentrot leaned to one side and the hayfork veered towards the hilltop.

"How can this be?" the villagers cried. "What of the warding lamps?

How have they failed? Run!"

"My sons!" Rufus and Tully's mother wept. "They are out there!"

Fleeing from the stone circle, they rushed down the hill, stumbling and tripping in their haste to escape the hag from the Forbidden Tower.

Haxxentrot zoomed through the flurrying embers that soared into the night. The twinkling ash eddied and swarmed about her. Then she circled around and Jub flung the glowing phial.

Like a sickly falling star it burned a trail of green fire through the air. When it struck the ground, there was a flash of olive-coloured flame and a sulphurous cloud belched forth. Jub threw another and another and another until the lower slopes were completely encircled by a curtain of thick, choking, yellow vapour.

The villagers halted. They were too afraid to pass through that barrier of unnatural smoke. It did not disperse. It curdled and churned, clinging firmly to the ground. They were trapped on the hillside.

Wulfhand the stonemason stepped forward. He was the broadest man in Mooncot, and the strongest person in the village since the disappearance of Dora the blacksmith's daughter. He could plough a furrow faster than two oxen and shook acorns down from trees.

"Smoke holds no terror for me," he declared.

Rhoswen, his tiny sapling of a wife, flung her arms about him. "'Tis witchery!" she cried. "Go not into that foulness. Stay – I beseech you!"

Her husband cupped her tearful face in his big palms and stooped to kiss her brow. Then he straightened his mighty back and strode towards the twisting fog bank. The cloying vapour wrapped round him and he was lost from sight.

The villagers waited anxiously and Rhoswen wrung her hands. Suddenly a man's terror-filled scream sounded from the smoke and an instant later, Wulfhand came blundering back out.

High above, Haxxentrot cackled shrilly.

The village folk crowded round the stonemason. He was shivering and sweating.

"Don't go in there!" he cried. "Don't…"

"What did you see?" his wife implored.

Wulfhand glanced back and shuddered. "There are… things growing and moving," he uttered. "Creatures with baleful eyes."

"Look!" Aiken shouted. "There are shapes in the smoke!"

Shadowy silhouettes were prowling within the sulphurous fumes. The horrified villagers counted nine of them. They were the size of bulls. Each possessed two long, serpentine tails and their eyes shone like rushlights. Skulking in the smoke, they paced around the hill and began to yowl and mewl.

"What are they?" the villagers cried, backing fearfully away, up the slope.

Haxxentrot came swooping down. The prongs of her hayfork raked through the vapour and she called out to her newly grown creatures.

"Go, my Tibbs!" she cackled. "The mice are there for the hunting. Torment and devour them! Kill them all!"

A paw as large as a hoof emerged from the yellow fog. Then another. Then a monstrous head came after. It was a hideous giant cat – covered in coarse, dark green fur. Spitting ferociously, it slinked out on to the grass, its two tails flicking behind. More of the nightmares came from every side.

The villagers uttered cries of despair. They were only peasants, without swords or spears to defend themselves. Their longbows had been left in their homes. All they had were short knives, but those would be useless against such horrors as these.

"To the fire!" Aiken called. "Pull out burning sticks! Arm yourselves with flame. 'Tis our only hope."

Screaming, they ran back up the hill.

Padding the ground with their paws, their claws extending and retracting, ripping through the turf in anticipation of a substance much more tender and succulent, the green cats lowered their great heads and hunched down. The blades of their shoulders pushed up into twin points. Their sinister, hungry purring was harrowing to hear. They allowed their scurrying quarry enough distance to make the sport more amusing. Then they flattened their ears and sprang after them.

Haxxentrot shrieked with evil laughter. From her lofty perch in the sky, she stared down at the terrified people racing towards the bonfire. Behind her, the Bogey Boy sniggered gleefully. Then Jub's eyes grew rounder than ever and he pointed across the land, over the thatched rooftops, towards the high white walls of the castle. Horses were galloping out, over the drawbridge. He saw the bright glitter of swords held high and the gleam of knights in armour, with the Jack of Clubs riding at their head. The talking fox had succeeded!

Jub tugged at his mistress's cloak and she shook a bony fist at the unwelcome sight, spitting with displeasure. Then her annoyance turned to consternation as Jub let out a squeak of alarm. Flying above the knights, a silver-tipped wand in his right hand, the fabled Moonshield in the other, was the Ismus.

On the hill the villagers had reached the bonfire and were wielding flaming brands. Pushing their children behind them, they waited for the huge cats to strike. The nine creatures pounced. A bitter battle began. Claws lashed out, cloth and flesh were torn, fire swung round in blazing arcs, fur was scorched and children screamed.

Then, high overhead, as he flew over the hilltop, the voice of the Ismus called out words of hope.

"Hold fast, my gentle lambs! Despair ye not! Deliverance is nigh!"

Thudding vibrations shook the hill. The monstrous felines wavered and cast their almond eyes down the slope. With a fearless shout, the Jack of Clubs, riding on Ironheart, last of the untameable steeds, came charging through the encircling wall of sulphurous smoke. After him rode a host of knights from every Royal House. Soon the hill rang with screeching yowls of pain as the horses plunged into the fray and the cats felt the keen edges of Mooncaster steel. Ironheart reared and pounded one of their heads into the grass with his hooves, mashing it like an overripe damson. Swords carved deep into tough green sinew. Double tails were sliced through and left wriggling on the ground like furry snakes. The cats hissed and roared, but could not escape. One leaped into the bonfire rather than face the terrible wrath of the Jack of Clubs and the villagers drove the rest into the path of the sweeping blades with their flaming torches.

In the sky the Ismus glared at Haxxentrot in the distance. The witch was flying away. With wand and shield in hand, the Holy Enchanter pursued her through the air.

Bursts of emerald fire and bolts of purple lightning flashed and flared between the stars as a mighty contest of magick commenced.

Down in the village, Tully and the others came running up the street, breathless and frightened. They had imagined all types of terrors chasing them through the fields.

"Come to ours!" Rufus urged. "There's nobody in your cottages. Our grandfather is home. It'll be safer there!"

Hurrying through the deep shadows, their only welcome was the din of Mistress Sarah's geese. Echoing and reverberating down the narrow thoroughfare, even their honking sounded shrill and strange. The village had never appeared so sinister and threatening before. A hostile pulse threaded the night and every corner seemed crowded with unfriendly eyes. The children wished the small windows were aglow with cheery firelight to unburden their hearts and spur them on their way, but every dwelling was shuttered and deserted. They were gladder than ever to have their neepjacks with them.

They were so anxious and afraid they barely noticed the smell that hung about Dung-Breathed Billy's hovel, but when they passed Mistress Sarah's cottage, they suddenly realised the geese had ceased honking.

The children's footsteps faltered. Those birds were better than guard dogs. They made a frightful racket whenever they heard footsteps on the road. Why were they now silent?

Tully looked at his brother nervously. Something was very, very wrong.

"Everyone, into ours, quick!" Rufus whispered, pushing them towards their cottage.

"But the geese," Tully said. "We must go see!"

"No!" Rufus ordered. "This way now!"

Tully's curiosity outweighed his fear. "I'll be but a moment," he promised. "Besides, Pog will protect me."

Before his brother could grab him, Tully darted into the alley between the hovel and the cottage.

Mistress Sarah's six geese were penned in the garden around the back. A fence of wicker hurdles, twined about with fading nasturtiums, prevented them waddling into the village to peck and hiss at passers-by.

Tully ran to the fence. Holding Pog aloft, he peered over. The turnip lantern's candlelight flooded down into the garden. The horror of what he saw there made the boy choke with shock.

The six geese were dead. Their white corpses were strewn wantonly about the ground. It had been a frenzied attack. A bloody hole had been punched into each of their snowy breasts.

And the killer was still there.

A tall figure, dressed in a shabby, tattered robe and soil-clogged sandals, was crouching over the last limp bird – ripping out its heart. Seeing Pog's light and hearing Tully's strangled cry, the figure sprang up.

It was a man – but a savage, brutal distortion of a man. His black hair was long, dirty and matted and his haggard face was ingrained with filth. His straggly beard was greasy and knotted and his red, blood-wet lips parted in a repugnant, feral snarl, baring stained and broken teeth. Thick brows growing halfway down a thin, hooked nose sheltered two brown, glaring eyes that bulged outward.

It was the nightmare apparition everyone in the Kingdom feared most, even more than Haxxentrot. It was the Bad Shepherd.

Tully was rooted to the spot. His own heart thumped violently. He stared open-mouthed at the tall, ragged man, unable to move.

The Bad Shepherd's repulsive snarl widened to a leer and the deranged malignance in those eyes burned even more fiercely. The goose's heart fell from his fingers. Letting loose an insane shriek, he lunged forward.

His bloody fingers caught Tully by the throat and he kicked the wicker fence down. Crowing, he shook the boy wildly, squeezing the breath from him. Then he dragged him out of the alley. Pog went rolling over the ground.

The Bad Shepherd burst, berserking, into the street and the other children screamed. Rufus darted forward, but the fiend hoisted Tully above his head like a bag of apples and prepared to hurl him against the nearest wall, to dash out his brains.

"Please!" Rufus pleaded, backing away. "Don't hurt him. Please! We'll give you anything you want. Just don't hurt him!"

The Bad Shepherd bawled unintelligible words in reply.

"We… we don't have any coin," Rufus stammered. "But we have food. You want food? Please put my brother down!"

The man growled and his awful face contorted as he gave vent to a horrendous screech. Then he swung Tully around, seized him by the ankles and ran at the wall, whooping.

"Noooo!" Rufus howled. "Help us! Someone help us!"

One of the countless shadows filling that benighted street suddenly rushed out. It slammed into the Bad Shepherd's side. The madman crumpled before the unexpected force and went crashing to the floor. Tully was knocked from his grasp and lay on his back, gasping.

For a moment, Rufus and the others were too astonished to react. They stared at the Bad Shepherd. He was crawling on his knees, as bewildered and amazed as they were. Standing over him was a three-dimensional patch of darkness, roughly human in shape, but blurred and indistinct. It kicked out and landed a heavy blow in the fiend's stomach.

The Bad Shepherd shrieked and tried to scrabble to his feet. Another kick sent him sprawling. Then the uncanny, living shadow ran to a woodpile and snatched up a heavy log. Armed with this, it charged. But the nightmare of Mooncaster was already back on his feet and ready. His strong hands caught hold of the weapon, spun the shadow round and shoved it viciously against a door. The wood creaked under the blow and the shadow grunted with pain. Then it rallied, wrested the log from those bloody fingers and used it to beat him across the street.

It was a desperate fight. The Bad Shepherd fell back from those hammering blows until finally the mysterious shadow had him trapped in a corner.

Rufus darted over to his brother and hastily made sure he was all right. Tully was dazed and frightened. There were tears in his eyes and ugly bruises were already forming on his neck. But he was alive. Rufus dragged him to the step of their cottage where the others were banging on the door.

"Let us in! Let us in!" they shouted.

"Grandfather must have barred it after all!" Rufus cried. "Wake up in there!"

Tully clutched at his throat and stared down the street, to where the shadow had raised the log above its head to deal a death blow. The Bad Shepherd raged and spat defiantly, daring the strange phantom to strike.

"Do it," Tully breathed. "Kill the mad dog!"

The shadow tensed and the weapon trembled. Then the dark shape relaxed and stepped away. With a wave of its arm, it signalled the Bad Shepherd to leave, and turned to come walking back.

But the Bad Shepherd would not depart. Incensed, he ran to that woodpile and took up a more deadly weapon. Screeching wildly, he leaped at the shadow, whirling an axe about his head.

"Look out!" Tully tried to yell, but his voice had been crushed. He could not be heard above the frantic clamouring of the other children trying to wake his grandfather.

The axe blade came rushing through the air. At the very last instant, the shadow was aware of it and dodged aside. The axe rang against a stone wall, striking a shower of sparks. The Bad Shepherd ranted in fury and whirled around, shouldering the shadow to the ground. The axe was raised again. There was no escaping now.

The children could barely watch. Whatever, or whoever, that shadow-shape may be, it could not survive pitted against such untempered cruelty and madness. Behind the Bad Shepherd's stark, bulging eyes there was no reason, no compassion, just an unquenchable, deranged compulsion to butcher and destroy.

"He's going to chop it up," Muddy Legs uttered, feeling faint. "What does shadow-blood look like?"

Peasy and Benwick covered their eyes.

And then a most incredible thing happened. A torrent of orange flame blasted into the street. It came squalling from the alley between Mistress Sarah's cottage and the hovel. For a moment, it lit up the night and everyone felt the heat beating on their faces. The Bad Shepherd hesitated, his maniacal expression consumed with doubt.

Another spout of flame roared across the street. What new, perilous creature was this?

"Is it a dragon?" Lynnet murmured, ready to believe anything now.

A third scorching spout streaked out, and then the fire-breather emerged from the alley.

Tully could not believe his eyes. He rubbed them swiftly and looked again. To his unending astonishment and wonder, Pog, the turnip lantern, came scampering into view. The fibrous roots sprouting from its chin had grown into twiggy legs and carried it along like a spider. Flames licked from the peg-toothed mouth and dripped out of the triangular eyes. The lantern scuttered into the street, and turned to face the Bad Shepherd.

It bobbed slowly up and down and a funnel of black smoke pumped up from the hole in its lid as a warning.

The man began to lower the axe. Then, emitting a hideous, bawling cry, he shook his head defiantly. Screaming insanely, he lifted the weapon high again, to hack and hew the fallen shadow-figure.

Pog roared with flame and charged forward. When it passed the children, their lanterns also burst into life and tore their strings from their hands to go chasing after.

Eight enchanted neepjacks went bouncing and hopping up the street, spitting jets of angry flame at the Bad Shepherd. The man's tattered robe caught light and his beard burned. He screeched wilder than ever, threw the axe down and fled from the village with the turnip lanterns hot on his heels.

Tully and the others gaped as the figure disappeared into the night, pursued by their neepjacks. But how?

"Once that villain is beyond your boundaries," a new voice said, "your charming lanterns will take the place of the warding lamps tonight and keep this village safe from harm. Henceforth on Ween Night, if you carve the same faces and call them by their names, those guardians will awaken and protect you."

The children wrenched their eyes from the fiery neepjacks in the distance and looked down the street. A kindly-looking, elderly woman, with apple cheeks and twinkling blue eyes, was stepping lightly towards them. She wore a dress of dusty pink, picked out with gold stars, and a shawl of golden lace covered her shoulders. In her hand was a long but crooked silver wand tipped with an amber star, which she leaned on like a walking cane.

"Malinda!" the children gasped.

"Will we ever be rid of that scourge?" she remarked crossly. "He is the bane of the Kingdom. We've all suffered so much at his brutish hands."

The mutilated stumps of her wings trembled slightly. The retired Fairy Godmother pulled the shawl a little tighter and gave the youngsters a benevolent smile.

"I came as swiftly as I could," she said. "Thank Fortune I was in the castle when the alarm was raised."

She lowered her eyes and the children saw the talking fox was trotting along beside her. A plump dead hen was in his jaws so he said nothing but gave them a lusty wink then darted off.

"We would have been killed if it wasn't for the shadow-shape!" Rufus told her. "It saved us."

Malinda peered along the street.

"Where is it now?" she asked urgently.

"Over there," Lynnet said, pointing to where the shadow-figure had fallen.

"It's gone!" Benwick exclaimed.

Tully ran over to the place where the Bad Shepherd had stood over the shadow. The ground was bare.

"Whoever you are!" Malinda's silvery voice called out to the empty night air. "I can help you. Do not be afraid! Do not run away."

There was no response. Malinda sighed sorrowfully.

"What was it?" Clover asked. "I never heard of nothing like that before."

The Fairy Godmother gave a sad, far-off smile.

"It is the Castle Creeper," she said. "The poor thing must be terribly frightened. It is almost solid and visible here now."

The children did not understand her words, but Tully came running back, greatly excited, with something in his hands.

"I found a thing! I found a thing!" he rasped with his injured voice. "A funny sort of cord, divided at one end and with two tiny hooves. The shadow must've dropped it in the struggle."

Malinda held out her hand and he passed the unfamiliar find over.

"Most curious," she said, inspecting it by a soft radiance from her wand's amber star and blinking in perplexity. "Whatever can it be?"

No one in Mooncaster had ever seen a pair of earphones before.

"We must show the Ismus," she said, popping them into the small purse hanging from her girdle. "He will know."

At that moment, the door of the cottage opened and Tully's grandfather stood there – yawning and staring out in sleepy bewilderment.

"What's been going on here?" he asked. "Why, there's the good lady Malinda herself and who's this a-lying on our step?"

It was Muddy Legs. He had fainted.

Tommy Williams regained consciousness with a weak smile on his face. "Poor Muddy Legs," he murmured groggily.

The sun was shining over the holiday camp once more and the stricken crowd was coming to, whimpering and uttering groans. Rolling over in the sunshine, Tommy reached for his throat and winced when he touched the bruising there. "I am Tully," he whispered hoarsely. "I am a Two of Clubs."

Beside him Rupesh opened his eyes and grinned. "I am Rufus!" he declared, elated. "I am a Two of Clubs also, and you – you are my brother!"

"Blessed be!" Tommy cried.

"Blessed be!" six other young voices repeated around them.

13

THE THREE BLACK Face Dames awoke and immediately rushed from the stage. The Ismus was lying face down on the ground. The scars on his back were no longer burning, but were charred and scabbed and black. The bodyguards lifted him gently and his eyes flickered open.

"Never let me do that again," he said, exhausted but with a wry twist to his mouth.

They carried their Lord to Jangler's cabin and laid him on the bed, on his stomach.

All across the camp, people were reviving and staggering to their feet. Marcus picked himself up, clutching the back of his head. His vision was bleary and he gazed around at the others.

Charm was swaying unsteadily, rubbing her forehead. Alasdair was doubled over, trying not to heave. Lee's eyes were closed and he took deep gulping breaths. Jody was making sure Christina was all right and Jim was staring at his trembling hands. Spencer's face was ashen. Maggie was still on the ground, too weak to rise.

"We blacked out!" she exclaimed, staring at the mass of people slowly recovering in the compound. "Every last one of us. That's damn freaky!"

"Did I imagine it?" Spencer muttered. "Or did that man fly over our heads – on fire?"

"What were in the drinks this time?" Alasdair asked.

"It really happened," Jody told them angrily. "It did! Don't pretend it didn't!"

"That's crazy!" Marcus snapped. "Just crazy!"

"Eww! Ewww!" Charm squealed when she discovered the blood in her hair and down her neck. "What's goin' on?"

They touched the backs of their heads then looked at the blood on their fingers. Most of them shuddered in shock and revulsion. Eight of them laughed.

Shaken and pale, Jangler dusted himself down and retrieved his clipboard. That made him feel better. Clambering on to the stage, he called for quiet and viewed the children sternly.

"Which of you have awakened to your true lives?" he demanded in a businesslike tone. "Who now can be accounted amongst the blessed?"

Tommy and Rupesh jumped up and down eagerly. Six more children did the same.

"Patrick Hunter, Daniel Foster, Beth McCormack, Oliver Gaskin, Diane Haywood, Mason Stuart," Jangler said, jotting down their names. "Only eight of you? Most disappointing. So much effort for so very little. What a senseless risk."

The eight new converts to the world of *Dancing Jax* were led away from the others by the Harlequin Priests, who took them to a sunny and peaceful corner of the camp, away from the stumbling confusion of the crowd. It was there that Kate Kryzewski interviewed them and got the "afters" her report desperately needed safely in the can.

"Wait!" Charm called to Jangler. "That's not it, is it? Nofink happened to me. Why didn't I wake up in the castle? I can't remember nofink. How come?"

The old man regarded her through his spectacles.

"You may well ask, young woman," he said tersely. "I don't know why you and the rest are not deemed fit to join us at Court, but there you are. Now I suggest you enjoy what remains of the festivities today. Tomorrow's an early start; the transport will be here first thing."

He made some ticks on his clipboard then walked off the stage.

"Oi!" Charm cried out. "This ain't the end, is it? It can't be! That ain't fair! All I got were this bleedin' headache. There's no one more wanting to go there than me! Please, gimme more time, another go! I'll do whatever!"

But Jangler wasn't listening. He headed for his cabin and entered with a respectful bowing of the head.

"My Lord?" he addressed the figure lying on his bed. "It is done."

"How many?"

"Only eight, I fear."

The Ismus reared his head. "Is that all?" he growled.

"Young people are so very stubborn," Jangler said apologetically. "And this group appear more so than most. But I shall whip that out of them, you'll see. And at least, this way, enough remain to power the bridging devices."

The Ismus rested his head on the pillow. "Yes," he sighed. "That is certainly important; until more centres are established in other countries, the transfers must continue here."

Jangler nodded then wondered why the Holy Enchanter was laughing softly.

"My Lord?" he asked.

"The manifestation of the Castle Creeper is nearly wholly complete now," the Ismus said. "Even as I battled Haxxentrot, I felt that trespass more sharply than ever."

"We must discover the identity of that person with all speed!"

"There may be a way of deducing that more quickly than you think, dear Lockpick," the Ismus told him. He reached out his hand, which, up till then, had been clenched in a fist, and opened it. A pair of earphones fell out.

"From Mooncaster," he said. "The Creeper was careless and left those behind. Organise a rigorous search and see which of those remaining aberrants is missing such a pair."

Jangler rubbed his hands together and chuckled.

"At once!" he promised. He pulled the door open, but was startled to find a burly man in a tight costume of caramel-coloured leather blocking the way. Jangler took a nervous but irritated step back.

"Haw haw haw!" the Jockey sniggered, tiptoeing inside. "What a game you have played this day, Most Holy One. How you set every head to thunder and thump as if the very castle walls were tumbling down about our ears. I was having such a merry time with a serving maid before you did that! How unthinkably boorish of you to spoil the Jockey's sport."

"Why are you here today?" the Ismus asked suspiciously "I did not request or desire it."

The Jockey looked surprised. "I would be failing my obligations if I were not close by, to sprinkle your hours with discord and levity in equal measure," he replied. "Besides, it was the height of bad manners on your part not to invite me to this pet project of yours. You know how I hate being left out of things – however squalid. Naughty of you!"

Jangler tried to get past him, but the Jockey caught his hands and danced him around the room.

"Your feet are so leaden!" he mocked. "Do you wear iron socks?"

The old man wrenched himself free and pushed the Jockey away. He had no time for his nonsense.

"Let me be about my Lord's business!" he demanded.

"Oh, take your grisly visage away," the Jockey dismissed him. "'Tis true – your scowls turn milk to cheese in the udder. But first I want you to see the gift I've brought our dear Ismus, to cheer him and his poor, crispy back."

Chortling, he reached into his pocket.

"I've just skipped through each one of these beastly shacks," he bragged. "And weaved in and out of those witless children out there, dipping with such dexterous, nimble fingers and brought you these. I know they'll amuse you – hoo hoo hoo!"

With a flourish, he presented a bundle of wires. Every pair of earphones in the camp was there. Jangler uttered a cry of frustration and the Ismus stared at them angrily, which made the Jockey titter all the more.

"You can't have it too easy," he snickered, wagging a stout finger at them as he swept out of the cabin. "Haw haw haw – I hampered you, I thwarted you, I spoiled it, I puzzled it. Keep the dance a-twirling, keep the pieces spinning, keep the Lord a-guessing."

Jangler pulled at his neat little beard. "What shall I do, my Lord?" he asked.

"Send them home!" the Ismus snarled in a temper. "Send everyone home, the mummers, the choristers, the cooks, the stilt-walkers, the Jacks and Jills. Empty this camp of everyone but those children. Do it!"

Jangler hurried out and the Ismus called to his bodyguards to bring his car. "Get me away from this place!" he commanded. "I've other pressing matters to attend to. And see that the Jockey climbs aboard no vehicle. He may ride us at Court, but he won't be riding with us today. Let him tittup all the way back to London in that squeaky costume."

The Black Face Dames bowed and hastened to obey. The Ismus glared at the tangled ball of earphones in his hands and threw it against the wall.

Within an hour, the camp was deserted. Jangler had shooed everyone away. The place looked a wreck. Bunting and ribbons had come loose from the poles and were straggling over the ground and snagged on forsaken stalls. Discarded goblets, pewter plates covered in crumbs and chicken bones littered the lawn. Here and there were odd articles of clothing, a shoe, a headdress, a forgotten cloak. A desolate sense of abandonment and profound disappointment sat heavy over the place.

Jody and Maggie sat on the deserted stage, gazing at the untidy camp. They and the others were still trying to come to terms with everything they had experienced that day. It seemed so unreal, so impossible.

"So that's that then," Maggie muttered with a morose air of finality. "All a bit of a waste of time, wasn't it?"

The other girl pulled her hands inside the sleeves of her cardigan and nodded.

"What were it for?" she asked. "What were any of it for? I can't get my head round it. What happened today, the way he just burst into flames and lifted up, that was mental, mad – it just can't happen… but it did. And then the way everyone passed out – it don't make sense, none of it."

"It's what the Ismus does in the book though," Maggie said. "He flies."

"But that's only a book! People, real people, can't fly."

"There's nothing 'only' about it. You should know that by now, babes."

Jody shook her head. If she allowed herself to believe in the smallest aspect of the world of *Dancing Jax* then that door might swing wide open and she was too afraid to let that happen. She had to keep a tight grip on what little reality she was still able to understand. Taking a sobering breath, she looked over at the chalets. Christina and most of the others were lying down inside, with pounding headaches. A bitterly unhappy, disillusioned Charm was packing her suitcases in readiness for the journey back the next morning.

"What are you going home to?" Jody asked Maggie.

"Don't call it home no more, but then it's not been good there since Janice the stepmother from hell moved in, back when I was twelve. Wasn't no love lost there, manipulative cow she is – or was before all this."

"My mum and dad were great."

"So was my dad till she got her hooks in him. I hated the way she treated him, but he couldn't see it, starting rows just cos she was bored, turning on the waterworks to get her way, criticising everything I ever did, like it were a competition between us for his attention."

"She sounds… choice."

"She was. That's why I got so big."

"Eh?"

"A martyr in Marigolds she was. Loved having her snotty friends round and whining to them about how hard done to she were; by me, by my dad – by not having new scatter cushions, or by whatever small thing happened to her that week. Suffering in public is what pushed Janice's buttons. Squeezing out sympathy was an Olympic event to her and she won gold every time – the warped harpy."

"So how did that make you big?"

"Control freak, wasn't she? Thought she was subtle about it, but I knew what she was up to, even if Dad didn't. Kept dropping hints; someone on the telly was a bit full in the face and wasn't it ugly, my school uniform was looking a bit tight, leaving diet magazines around the house, disapproving looks at the dinner table, asking when my puppy fat was going to go. She worked and worked to give me a complex. Oh, she'd have loved a stepdaughter with an eating disorder – she was salivating at the prospect of those pitying looks, being right in the centre of a tragedy like that. 'There goes Mrs Blessing, poor woman, her girl's anorexic you know, just skin and bone, how does she cope? Must be such a worry…'."

Maggie stroked her stomach with a victorious smile.

"I got myself an eating disorder all right," she snorted. "But not the one she wanted. I managed to put on sixty-five kilos in three and a bit years. And I did it just to spite her. There's no pity to be milked having a stepdaughter who's morbidly obese. Shame, blame and ridicule is what she got instead, cos the neighbours, my teachers, the doctors, my poor dad, all believed it was her fault. And you know, seeing her more and more mortified every day was worth every forced mouthful, every painful cramp, every jeer, every snub – even the risk of diabetes."

Jody didn't know what to say. Her life experience hadn't prepared her for anything like that. She couldn't begin to comprehend what would possess someone to do that to themselves. More than ever she realised just how lucky she had been until that book came along.

"So that's me," Maggie said, filling the silence. "That's what I'll be going back to tomorrow, though it's all changed now obviously, but she's still a cow, just a brainwashed one. How about you? Bristol, yeah?"

"I've nowhere else," Jody answered simply.

"None of us has, babes."

Jim Parker was standing at the top of the helter-skelter, looking out over the camp. He could see everything from up there. The late afternoon breeze ruffled through his hair and caused the cloak to flap behind him. He gazed longingly at the encircling trees and imagined himself flying over them. The Ismus had proven such a thing was possible, just as Jim knew it would be. Since coming round that afternoon, the twelve-year-old had felt different. Over the recent months, he had developed a habit of testing himself, pinching or pricking his skin to see if the invulnerability had started to take effect. Since the black-out, his right arm had been numb. When he pushed a fork into it, he had felt nothing.

The boy didn't hear Lee discussing the same lack of sensation with Alasdair. They concluded it was some sort of nerve damage brought on by whatever had made their heads bleed and they hoped it was temporary. Jim, however, was certain his transformation was beginning.

Jumping on to the slide, he rushed down and around the helter-skelter, cheering and jubilant.

"He's got the right idea," Maggie remarked, watching him come scooting off at the bottom then go running round the camp, waving his arms in the air. "We should have a last-night party, really go for it big style."

Jody considered her a moment. "You know," she murmured, "you're bloody right."

"Let's rock this dump!" Maggie shouted.

Later that evening, the children Maggie had managed to enthuse with her idea, and who were feeling up to it, took over the lecture room in the main block. Drew and Nicholas, two of the video-gamers from Spencer's cabin, worked out how to connect an MP3 player through the AV equipment there. Music thumped through the camp. Maggie threw herself into the dancing, dragging Jody and Christina on to the floor.

Marcus stayed well clear. He remained in his cabin, sitting quietly on his bed. 'Hiding' was too strong a word. 'Avoiding' was more accurate. He didn't want any embarrassing scenes with Lardzilla. She might throw herself at him in a desperate attempt for one final snog. He shuddered at the thought and continued folding his clothes and packing them away.

"Not going out?" a voice asked.

Marcus looked up. He had thought he was quite alone. Jim's head appeared on the stairs.

"Nah," Marcus said. "I'm too old to dance with kids. I'm more of a stand at the bar, eyeing up the totty type anyway – and this well is bone dry."

"Can I come up?" Jim asked.

"Sure, I'm just putting my gear away. Never got to wear these Hollister shorts. And the Ralph Lauren shirts never saw the light of day. Why aren't you over there jigging about?"

"Not my thing," Jim said. "I wanted to race instead."

"Race?"

"Yes, I asked the other lads, but they weren't interested."

"Funny time to want to race."

Jim started running on the spot. "I'm full of energy!" he said. "Like I'm about to burst."

"Why don't you jog round the camp then? Take your cloak off first though – you'd look like Batman running for a bus."

Jim smiled to himself and touched the centre of his T-shirt. Was it really so obvious? Could people tell he was changing?

"Aren't you going to do your exercises?" he asked. "I saw you the other night. We could train together."

Marcus shook his head. "Nah," he said flatly. "Not with that racket going on out there. Early to bed for me, then straight on that coach first thing. Be glad to leave this hole. Been a waste of my time; can't wait to get back to Manc."

"You must still have lots of friends there then?"

Marcus looked away. "Course I have," he bluffed. "Even *DJ* can't stop the Marcus magnetism. Got loads of mates, me. Loads!"

Jim viewed the older boy's bruised and beaten face.

"I tried to stop him you know," he said. "Tried to stop that fight."

Marcus put the last of his clothes away.

"I wasn't strong enough then," Jim continued. "I'm sorry. I know I'm stronger now."

Marcus said nothing. He regretted he hadn't made an effort to be nicer to this kid. He regretted a lot of things.

"Know what," he said, "pull that bedside table out and I'll give you an arm-wrestle."

Jim obeyed hurriedly and Marcus proceeded to let him win every contest. His defeats were loud and convincing. He thought he was being kind, but it was the worst thing he had ever done. It was the final proof Jim needed. He believed his powers had arrived.

Lee was outside on the step, wishing for the hundredth time he'd brought more cigarettes with him. It was really getting to him now and he'd resorted to chewing a pencil end. He had no intention of joining that lame party – he was ready to snap. Besides, there was nothing to celebrate. Wrapped in thought, he stared at the camp gates.

"Not in the mood neither?" Charm asked as she sat beside him. "I can't even listen to my own tunes now to get away from that din. Why'd they go and rob our headphones? I had a lovely baby pink pair."

Lee said nothing. She straightened her back, correcting her posture, always conscious of how she looked. The music continued to pound.

"I'm surprised old whassisface hasn't put the kybosh on that already," she said, looking past Lee to the end chalet. "Not seen him since tea. Thought he'd be in there the minute they turned it right up. Funny little fussy bloke, ain't he? Proper rude to me he was earlier, totally ignored me when I tried to ask him stuff."

She paused to allow the boy to respond. He didn't. Charm returned her attention to the main block.

"I dunno how they can," she complained. "I'm gutted, totally gutted. I was so sure it were gonna happen for me this weekend, so was me ma. It ain't fair. I want it more than they do, know what I mean? Them lucky kids, the ones who got there, all they've been doin' since is read togevver. They got all the cameras on 'em before. I couldn't get a look-in. Makes you sick it does."

Lee made no answer. The girl carried on.

"It were goin' so well," she said, clasping her hands round one knee and leaning back. "The Plan were all worked out. I was goin' to be dead famous, get meself papped outside clubs, be seen wiv footballers or pop stars, though they don't last long nowadays, so a footballer's the best bet, providin' he don't get injured nor regulated nor nofink. You got to be so careful see; the public can turn on you in a minute. If summink like that happened, I was gonna get tropical ill, like Foreign Legion disease, cos malaria's been done, to get them back on side. Then I'd have my own product ranges and I'd go to America and then…"

She gave a sad, wistful sigh. "I worked so 'ard. Now what am I gonna do? No one's interested in this country no more, if you ain't part of the book fing. *Heat* magazine's full of knights and queens, but they're just nobodies, ordinary nobodies wiv bad hair and faces like old chip pans. What sort of a future I got now wiv that going on? There's nofink at home, 'cept me ma – an' Uncle Frank."

"You got a hell of a lot more than the rest of us," Lee grunted.

Charm thought for a moment. "S'pose," she said. "But I've not been able to get through to me ma all weekend. I've rang but no answer, sent her texts but had nofink back. That ain't like her. Maybe she was told it was part of the fing here. That we shouldn't have no contact, like in *Big Bruvver*. That'd make sense. We used to luurve *BB*, me an' her."

She brightened. "Yeah," she said, the smile returning to her face. "That'd be it. An' there's always a chance I really could wake up in the castle tomorrow – or the day after."

Lee shook his head and spat on the ground. The girl bit her lip.

"About what you said yesterday," she began carefully. "Wiv your family and mates and stuff. I didn't know none of that kind of fing were 'appening. I'm sorry. That's like well wrong. My mouth runs off sometimes wivout finkin', but I got me a good heart, honest. I really wouldn't want to go that place if it is all white. That's just wicked – and not wicked in the good way. That little Indian lad… well, I says he's Indian, he might not be – I dunno,

I didn't speak to him before it worked on him, and it's too late now. I saw him and them other turned kids, laughing at his colour during tea. That's plain evil, ain't it?"

Still staring into the distance, Lee nodded.

Charm wondered what else to say. "Shall I tell you what flavour you is?" she asked. "I always do this, it's one of my gimmicks; you need a gimmick if you're gonna catch on wiv the public. This is what it is, right – I tell people what their flavour is. So, for example…"

"Girl, if you say 'dark chocolate', one of us is going to have to get up and leave, to avoid necessary violence."

"I wasn't gonna say that!" she cried. "I was gonna say you're a Brazil nut, hard to crack but soft and sweet in the middle. Now though, I reckon you're one of them tiny round chillies, not much to look at, but one bite'll blow your head off."

Lee rose and walked away, but he was laughing. Charm noticed he had an empty holdall with him.

"What you doing?" she called.

"Looting me some life insurance," he answered.

Alasdair wasn't in the mood for dancing and they weren't playing his sort of music, but it was good to see the others enjoying themselves on their last night. Leaving the lecture room, he went into the dining hall where the remains of their final tea still covered the tables. It had hardly been touched because most of them had felt too shaken to eat. He was glad it hadn't been cleared away and filled a goblet with wine, downing it in two gulps. He poured himself another and flexed his hand. His arm was still numb. A number of the children had complained of pins and needles or loss of feeling in their limbs since passing out that afternoon. Old Captain Mainwaring hadn't shown the slightest interest when informed and told them not to waste his time with their 'infantile bleating'.

The door swung open again and Maggie came stomping in, clapping her hands and jerking her head from side to side.

"Brilliant!" she shouted above the din. "Dancing always gives me the munchies. I could murder a kebab, but this'll do just fine. You back to bonnie Scotty land in the morning then?"

"Dinnae have a choice!" he yelled back.

"You know what we should do," she told him, waving a half-eaten chicken leg. "We should email that website and see if we can get out of this barmy country completely."

"What website's that?"

"The one by that maths teacher. The bloke everybody thought was a loony before all this happened, the one the papers had a field day with. What was his name? I tried Googling him before I did my flit to Dover, but couldn't find anything."

"Baxter," Alasdair said. "It were Martin Baxter. I've tried his site. Talk about paranoia – the guy's a nutcase. Says there's a big conspiracy to get him off the Web and track him down."

"How is that nuttier than what's going on here?"

The boy began his third goblet. "Aye, mebbe not."

"We should all stay in touch though," she persisted, making short work of a piece of ham and mushroom pie. "'Cos being stuck in York with Janice and my dad will drive me totally round the twist. And if one of us does manage to get in touch with that Baxter bloke, p'raps he could help get us all away."

Alasdair agreed and they decided to swap numbers with everyone tomorrow morning. Then Maggie eyed the untouched syllabubs, fruit tarts and savouries piped with soft cheese. A devilish grin spread over her face.

"You know what we really, really need to do in this place before we go?" she asked.

"What?"

"FOOD FIGHT!" she shrieked, squashing a savoury in the boy's face then hurrying back into the lecture room with the plate.

That was it. Total, sticky, in your face or wherever hadn't been splodged chaos reigned for the next half-hour. Food and ale went everywhere. Everybody got completely covered. It was caked in their hair, over their clothes, in their ears, across the faux stone walls and on the floor. Alasdair tried to save a jug of wine, but Jody tipped it down his front and Christina tucked a slice of beef in his trousers. Then, when the tables were bare and the children's appetite for mayhem still boiled, they tore down the priceless tapestries and dragged them through the slops and swills. Even that was not enough. Their resentment and anger were ripe and ready to explode. They wanted to smash something, to really demonstrate how furious and despairing they were.

Slowly everyone turned to stare at the great model of the White Castle. Could they? Did they dare?

"What are you waiting for?" Jody shouted.

In the lecture room, an old track by the Arctic Monkeys started blaring. Dragging the nearest table out of the way, Jody lunged at the model with a meat skewer. The attack was as fast and ferocious as the music. She stabbed the castle with all the hate and anguish *Dancing Jax* had brought her. The others stared fearfully for a moment then they too seized knives, forks, cleavers and joined in, swept along by the blind need to destroy or hurt some aspect of that foul book – accompanied by the ballistic guitars of 'Brianstorm'.

Returning from the woods to refill his holdall, Lee stopped. The noise coming from the main block was different to before. Now there were furious screams and yells amid the music. There was a wild, manic quality he didn't like.

"This place is out of control," he muttered. "Why ain't that old guy stopping it?"

Charm had gone back inside the cabin. Hunched over the bathroom sink, with a towel over her head, she was steaming her pores before removing her make-up. She did not hear the door opening behind her. When she stood up and looked in the mirror, she got the fright of her life and screamed. Jody and Christina were standing directly behind her. At first she didn't recognise them. They were plastered with food and filth and their eyes were alight with menace. They looked like unholy creatures from a horror film.

Before Charm could speak, they pelted her with raw eggs, raided from the kitchen fridge. They rubbed yolks into her hair and crushed the shells against her face, scratching her skin.

"How's that then, Barbie?" Jody bawled. "Girls like you make me puke. You make animal-testing big business. Without all that muck on your face, you're nothing. Your name shouldn't be Charm, it should be Chum, like the dog food!"

Christina thought that was hysterical and laughed like a small hyena.

Charm stood frozen with shock. Angered by the very sight of her and spurred on by Christina's laughter, Jody pulled her hair then punched her in the stomach. Suddenly two strong hands caught hold of Jody's arms and dragged her away. With Christina hurrying behind, shrieking in protest, the girl was hauled out of the cabin.

Standing on the step, Lee glared at her.

"What is wrong with you?" he snapped.

"Hypocrite!" Jody shouted back. "It were all right for you to lay into Marcus the other night!"

"That was different and you don't know what you're talking about. What's that girl in there done to you? She is not the enemy here! Don't you know that by now? Or is it just cos you're jealous? Look at you, you're a freakin' mess. You're disgusting. But before you clean yourself up, you best go put a stop to the riot goin' down in that dinner hall. You think you're goin' back home tomorrow? You is seriously foolin' yourself!"

Jody's eyes flashed at him. But the night air was cooling her anger rapidly and her sopping, ale-soaked clothes suddenly felt worse than any Glastonbury mud. The last traces of fury drained out of her. She looked at Christina. The seven-year-old was in a wretched state and Jody felt ashamed for what she had done. Then she became aware of the sound of smashing and destruction coming from the main block. Without saying another word, she ran off to try and stop it.

Christina lingered to glower at Lee, but he hissed through his teeth and went back inside.

"You OK?" he asked Charm who was now sitting on her bed, dabbing her face with the towel.

The girl nodded but she really wasn't.

"Where do Tweedledum and Tweedledumber sleep?" he asked.

She pointed across the room. Lee grabbed handfuls of Jody and Christina's belongings then threw them out of the door until there was nothing left.

"They ain't sleeping in here no more," he said. "They can bunk in with their horizontally challenged friend."

Charm tried to thank him, but she was shaking too much and was close to breaking down. More than ever she wanted her mother. She missed her so much it hurt far more than Jody's punch.

"Hey!" Lee told her sternly. "You stop that. If you got tears, you'd best save them for another time. Cos there's goin' to be worse than this, this ain't nuthin'. You gotta be strong. Now you go wash that crap off and I'll go tell Absolutely Drabulous they've been evicted."

Charm managed a wobbly smile.

Lee left her to it and went back outside.

"Brazil nut," he told himself.

The music had stopped. He looked around the camp and wondered what the morning would bring.

In Alasdair's chalet, Tommy Williams, Rupesh and the six other children who had entered the world of *Dancing Jax* that day continued to read, rocking backwards and forwards, their eyes dark and glassy.

Just before dawn, a truck drove out of the camp. Inside were five new arrivals, brought into this world by the Bakelite bridging devices. Within the cabins, the children lay where they had fallen. This time they were not returned to their beds. Eight of them, however, had slept peacefully. As the truck rumbled up the forest road, it passed a van coming the other way.

The *Busy Needles* vehicle parked in front of Jangler's chalet, where the old man was waiting to meet it. Two seamstresses got out and took the new costumes they had made into the cabin next to his.

Jangler gazed around at the state of the camp and added to the copious notes he had already made.

Maggie was one of the first up. She awoke hungry and, when she went outside, could smell sausages frying.

"Oh, fantastic!" she said.

Jody and Christina had been compelled to sleep on the floor in her cabin. Lee was adamant they stay away from Charm and no one dared oppose him in the mood he was in. They had spent their energies wrecking the dining hall and the memory of what they had done caused Jody to draw a shameful breath. She couldn't understand why she had gone so far. It seemed to make sense at the time, but now… She wondered if they would have to pay for the damage. She didn't have any money and there was no way her parents would cough up.

Then she thought of Charm and couldn't believe how vindictive and unpleasant she had been. That wasn't like her. Calling the vapid airhead names was one thing, but physical violence? Jody ran her fingers through her mousey hair. What sort of mindless thug was she turning into?

"Let's go help tidy that mess up," she suggested. "It's the least we can do and might show in our favour if we get prosecuted."

Maggie raised her eyebrows. "That won't happen, will it?" she asked. "Was only a food fight."

"And the model, and those tapestries, they were ancient. We could be in serious lumber."

They hurried to the main block and were appalled by what they saw in the dining hall. It looked even worse in broad daylight, like the aftermath of a hurricane. No one had started clearing it up yet. There were noises coming from the kitchen and the two girls popped their heads round the door.

"Morning," Jody greeted three women dressed as medieval cooks. "Just wondered if we could lend a hand clearing up and getting the hall ready for breakfast?"

The women stared back at them. They looked totally out of place in that brushed steel kitchen.

"No breakfast," one of them said curtly.

Maggie looked at the wide serving dish piled high with sausages and at the large frying pan in which even more were squeaking as they cooked.

"Them's not for the likes of you," the woman told her severely.

"I'll be happy with just cereal," Jody said. "I don't eat death tubes."

"No breakfast," the woman repeated.

"Who are all those bangers for then?" Maggie asked. "There's mushrooms there as well."

There was no answer. The women carried on with what they were doing. Jody realised one of them was removing everything from the fridge and another was doing the same to the storeroom.

"If you've got a mop and a brush," she said, "we'll make a start."

Again no reply. It was as if they didn't exist.

The two girls came away, puzzled.

"I'm starved," Maggie complained. "That smell is driving me mental. My buds are literally squirting."

Outside, more children were surfacing. Charm appeared, in her sunglasses, her hair tucked under a pink camouflage BAPE baseball cap. She trawled her fake Louis Vuitton cases across to the gates and perched on one. She didn't want to have anything to do with the others. She just wanted to go home. Fixing her eyes on the long forest road, she waited.

When Lee came out, he saw her. He took a step forward then stopped himself.

"Why don't you go over?" Alasdair asked.

"What for?"

The Scottish lad laughed. "I'm no blind," he said. "Get over there and give the lassie your number at least."

Lee shook his head. "No point," he replied. "She ain't goin' no place."

Alasdair didn't understand what he meant, but at that moment, their attention was diverted by Jangler, who called out the names of the eight children from yesterday. Tommy, Rupesh and the others went into his cabin clasping their copies of the book and soon the cooks entered, bearing the steaming food.

"Private brekky club for the chosen ones," Alasdair observed bitterly.

Lee hardly heard him. One of the cooks had taken a large plate of sausages into the chalet next to the old man's.

"Who the hell is in there?" he murmured.

The smell of the breakfast passing by drew comments from everyone. Where was theirs? They went to the dining hall, but returned disappointed and famished. The cooks had left and taken every morsel of food with them. The shelves were completely bare. There wasn't even a stock cube left. An hour dragged by. Phone numbers and addresses were exchanged. An emotional Jody crossed her heart and promised she would be in touch with Christina every single day and that the seven-year-old could come and visit. Maggie gave everybody, excluding Marcus, a big hug. At half past nine almost all cases, rucksacks and bags were on the lawn. Lee's was still upstairs on his bed. He hadn't even packed.

The sound of a coach came rumbling up the road. Charm jumped up, excited to greet her mother. She glanced back to where Lee was sitting outside his cabin and decided that before she left, she should say goodbye to him. The coach pulled into the camp and Kate Kryzewski got out, followed by Sam. They wanted the happy reunion footage.

Jangler emerged from his chalet, flicking his moustache and smacking his lips after a hearty meal. Rupesh and the rest followed him; each of them now wore a playing card, and he guided them to the coach.

"Don't we get any breakfast then?" Marcus asked as he marched by.

The question went unanswered. Tommy Williams' parents were next off the coach and the little boy raced over to them.

"I am Tully!" he shouted. "A Two of Clubs!"

Their faces lit up and Sam captured a heart-warming embrace. The other seven new converts experienced the same loving reception from their families. The remaining youngsters looked for their parents on the coach, but there was no one else aboard.

"Couldn't be bothered then?" Jody remarked. "Typical."

"I came down on my own anyway," Marcus said to anyone who was listening. "Fine by me."

"My folks dinnae even know or care where I am," Alasdair muttered flatly.

Charm went up to Jangler and asked when the other coach would arrive. He stared at her in surprise.

"Other coach?" he said. "There is no other coach. This is it. Now, Patrick, Beth, Oliver, Mason, Daniel, Tommy and Rupesh, climb inside and have a safe journey. Blessed be to you all."

The reunited families thanked him effusively and Kate and Sam got back on to conduct closing interviews. No one else was permitted on-board. The doors closed.

"What do you mean there's no other coach?" Charm demanded. "That can't be it. Where's me ma? Is she driving down with Uncle Frank or what? Has she said?"

Around her the other confused children wanted answers too. Where were their parents? Why hadn't they been allowed on that coach? What time would their transport get here? Why hadn't there been any breakfast that morning?

The coach's engine started. Children had to hurry out of the way as it turned around and departed back through the gates.

"What's goin' on?" Charm cried.

On the step of his cabin Lee watched the scene unfold pretty much exactly as he had expected. Jangler was surrounded by hungry, impatient and bad-tempered young people. They wanted answers, but he wasn't giving them.

"This is where it gets ugly," Lee said.

The noise of a second engine drew their attention back to the forest road. This had to be the second coach.

"This'll be me ma!" Charm said confidently. But the smile on her face faded and she removed her Gucci sunglasses for a better look.

Lorries were coming towards the camp: four ordinary builder's trucks, carrying great bales of wire fencing. One van brought up the rear. The vehicles came in and Jangler went over to have words with the foreman. Ten men jumped out of the van.

"What's going on?" Maggie asked.

The men immediately began unloading the trucks.

"Hey," Alasdair asked one of them. "What are ye doin'?"

A disgusted expression appeared on the man's face and he averted his eyes from this aberrant scum. Ladders were carried to the tall wooden posts nearest the gate. Bunting, lanterns and flowers were ripped down and the first bale of fencing was rolled across.

Jody took hold of Christina's hand. Power tools began to whirr, followed by hammering as the high fences went up. The children watched in confusion, but a horrible suspicion was forming in the older ones.

"You can't be serious," Alasdair shouted, rounding on Jangler.

"I don't… I don't get it," Spencer muttered, clutching his Stetson nervously.

"What's happening?" Charm insisted. "Why ain't me ma here? What them blokes doin'? What's them fences for? Can I get a bleedin' answer?"

Tucking his clipboard under his arm, Jangler made his way back to his chalet. The children followed, some out of anger, the rest because they didn't know what else to do and weren't quite sure what this meant. Lee rose from the step and stood among them. As the noise of the workmen continued, Jangler cleared his throat and mimed the removal of invisible gloves.

"Firstly," he began with even more pompous self-importance than usual, "let me make this perfectly clear. There will be no further transport. You will not be returning to your previous homes. You will no longer be indulged and tolerated out there. There is no place in society for abominations such as yourselves."

His audience murmured in disbelief at what they were hearing. The hate in the old man's voice was unmistakable.

"The tomfoolery of the past few days is now at an end," he continued. "From this day forward, you are internees. This camp is your only home. You will remain here until the age of sixteen, when you will be relocated to an adult camp. You will not go beyond the boundaries that are being erected right now unless supervised by guards under my strict orders. If you do, there will be punishments."

"What the hell are you saying?" Jody shouted. "You can't do this. You can't make us prisoners."

"Too right he can't!" Alasdair supported her.

"He's gone nuts," Marcus declared.

"What guards?" Lee demanded.

"I have the full blessing of the Ismus in this," Jangler told them. "I am the Lockpick, gaoler of Mooncaster. My word is now law here. You will obey me or suffer the consequences. You have no rights except the ones I deem fit to grant. And do not think you can continue idling your days away as you have been doing. You will be made to work, to earn your bed and board. This is not a holiday camp."

"Could've fooled me!" Maggie jeered.

"I repeat. This is not a holiday camp. If you do not work, you will not eat. I have made a list and divided you into groups; these will be your work parties. I will pin the schedule and rota in the dining hall. I suggest you familiarise yourselves with both because ignorance will not be accepted as an excuse for shirking your duties. If you try to avoid the work, you will be punished."

"Blimey," Charm exclaimed. "He's serious. He means it!"

"Indeed I do. And the sooner you recognise that, the better."

"Up yours!" Maggie called, finishing off with a raspberry.

"I suggest you calm down so we can get on with the business of the day," he said. "There is a tremendous amount to get through. Firstly, the condition of this internment camp is an absolute disgrace. That must be attended to immediately. Then there is the very grave matter concerning the wanton destruction of the beautiful model of the White Castle, plus the sheer vandalism and criminality which occurred last night. That will not go unpunished. The ringleader will be made an example of."

"He's so getting off on that word 'punish'," Maggie commented.

"Why are we even listening to him?" Alasdair cried. "Dinnae give him the oxygen of attention. I am going oot that gate right noo and that jumped-up wee man isnae gonna stop me."

"Don't do anything stupid, man," Lee warned.

"Och, what's he gonna do? Hit me wi' his pathetic clipboard? I'll lamp him if he tries anything."

The Scot turned to the others. "I'm away," he told them. "Who else is wi' me?"

Just about everyone agreed and they headed for the gates. Lee hung back. He knew it couldn't be that easy. He was right, again.

"Captain!" Jangler called. "It's time!"

The door of the supposedly empty chalet was yanked open. A hideous, humpbacked creature came running out. Lee jumped in shock. He hadn't expected this, not this.

"What the actual hell is that?" he breathed.

Charm screamed, just as she predicted she would if she ever saw one of those things. Other children joined her. Nobody could believe what they were seeing. Jody shook her head in denial and squeezed Christina's hand.

"No way," she murmured incredulously. "Can't be!"

"Mr Big Nose," the little girl said hollowly. "I told you he was here."

It was a Punchinello Guard from the book – right there in front of their eyes, in the sunlight and completely real. This wasn't a dwarf actor in a clever costume with a special-effects head, this was genuine – a living, snarling creature of ugly flesh and gristle. It was dressed in an exact copy of the outfits worn by the guards in the book: a yellow frilled tunic with scarlet and blue buttons. There was a ruff around the join where the hideous chin jutted from the barrel chest and a yellow, Napoleonic-style hat was pulled down on its head. It should have looked preposterous and absurd, but the clownish costume only made that grotesque face appear even more terrifying.

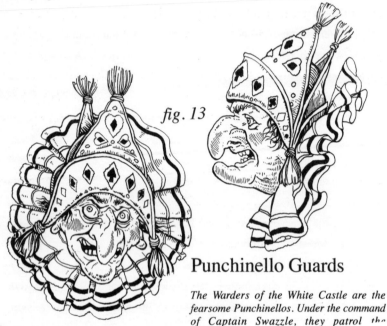

fig. 13

Punchinello Guards

The Warders of the White Castle are the fearsome Punchinellos. Under the command of Captain Swazzle, they patrol the battlements of Moo

Alasdair and the others started backing away. The Punchinello shouted an order and four more of the hideous creatures sprang from the cabin, clutching medieval-looking spears and wearing different curved hats. The children screamed louder and fled towards the road. The day had suddenly turned into a nightmare.

Squawking in strange, pinched voices, the guards leaped after them. Moving swiftly on their short, bowed legs, they overtook the terrified children and stood before the gates. They jabbed their spears forward, taunting and goading, forcing the youngsters back. One of them leered at Charm and licked its lips with a grey tongue.

Marcus couldn't take it in. This was insane. It was happening so fast the world seemed to be spinning around him. He tried to remain rational, be calm. Be a man.

"Whatever those are," he voiced sceptically, "they wouldn't dare lay a finger on us. Besides, there's only five of them. What's stopping the rest of you? I'm going."

He picked up his bag and marched forward defiantly.

The nearest guard ran at him. It struck the boy across the face with a powerful fist and he fell to the ground. The creature stood on his chest and grinned, prodding the spear tip against his neck.

"Oh, yes, oh, yes," the guard gloated. "Let me kill. Me want to kill."

Marcus had never been so frightened in his life. He looked up into those cruel, squinting eyes and knew he was a nudge away from death.

"No! Please! Please!" he begged.

"Get off him!" Alasdair shouted.

Maggie looked desperately at the workmen and cried for help, but they calmly carried on putting the fences up. To them it was only natural seeing Punchinellos and the aberrants deserved what was coming to them.

"I can't believe you people!" Maggie yelled at them. "How can you just stand there?"

"All right, Captain!" Jangler commanded. "That will do. Call your fellow off. The point has been well made."

Captain Swazzle complied reluctantly. The guard took his foot from Marcus's chest and drove the spear into the turf close to the boy's ear.

"Next time," he growled threateningly, "Yikker not wait for order. Yikker will set your blood free. Yikker no like your smell. It make Yikker angry. You stink."

Marcus spluttered an apology. The guard waddled away, wiping his great nose. The boy needed Alasdair and Lee to help him to his feet.

"Get some smarts," Lee told him. "Don't do nuthin' like that again.

Those things ain't foolin'."

"Captain Swazzle and his fine guards have been brought into this world to guarantee your obedience." Jangler addressed the children with a dark chuckle. "Don't antagonise them. They really are as vicious as they appear. There is nothing they would like more than to butcher the lot of you. You may be rejects but you have at least read the sacred text numerous times: you know what the Punchinellos are capable of. There are no creatures more aggressive and violent in all the land. They are the bloodiest fighters in my Lord's service, so beware. Now where was I? Oh, yes, the despicable destruction of the castle model. Unless the instigator of that hateful crime steps forward to be made an example of, you shall go without food for the rest of the day."

He looked at them expectantly. "Well, own up. Who did it?"

The children stirred unhappily. They were all hungry but they said nothing. Jody felt her cheeks burn. She was the one who had attacked the model first, but she wasn't going to confess to that and nobody blamed her.

"Very well," Jangler said. "I can see it's pointless trying to appeal to any sense of decency or honour. You filth have none. I do, in point of fact, know precisely who it was." He snapped his fingers at one of the guards then pointed at Jody. "Take her!" he said.

"Stop!" Alasdair yelled as the creature elbowed its way through the horrified children. "It wasnae her. It were me! I smashed your crappy toy fort to bits. It were me! Not her! She had nothing to do wi' it! And I'd do it again! Leave her be!"

"You don't want to do this!" Lee warned the old man.

"I rather think I do," came the remorseless reply.

It was no use protesting. The Punchinello seized Jody by the hair and dragged her out. The girl shrieked and struggled, but he was too strong and she was hauled backwards over the lawn, kicking and crying.

"Jody!" Christina howled, running after until another guard charged round to bar the way.

"Let her go!" Alasdair demanded. "You're a maniac! Who do ye think you are?"

"I am Jangler!" the old man laughed. "Your gaoler."

The guard pushed the girl against the maypole and tore the cardigan from her. Then he tied her hands and hitched her so high her feet could hardly reach the floor. He sniggered gleefully and unhooked a lash from his belt.

"Jody Jody Jody Jody," he taunted, taking a practice swing.

"No!" Maggie screeched.

"What's it doin'?" Charm muttered.

Alasdair tried to dash forward, but Captain Swazzle swung the spear shaft under the boy's legs and threw him backwards.

Jim Parker had watched everything with a mounting awareness that his moment was drawing very close. The excitement he felt was electric. It took his breath away. This would be the first public demonstration of his new powers. It was precisely the sort of perilous situation the heroes in his comic books encountered. The Punchinellos were worthy adversaries for the debut of Jim Credible.

His right hand pressed against his chest and his face assumed a steely determination. He had pledged to protect the other kids here and that's what he was going to do. This was it. This would be his first battle. In his troubled imagination he heard the galvanising brassy introduction of a John Williams theme, heralding the appearance of a new champion in the pantheon of fantastic superheroes.

The twelve-year-old stepped forward.

"Untie her!" he demanded as the guard raised the lash to strike. "Or you will be sorry. You only get one warning."

The Punchinellos stared at him and crowed with laughter.

Alasdair lifted his head. "Oh, God, no," he uttered when he realised what was in the boy's mind. "No, Jim! Stop! Get back here!"

"I am Jim Credible," the young hero declared boldly. "Leave this place now, while you still can. I will not allow you to hurt any of these people."

Marcus looked on, mystified and fearful. He couldn't understand. What did the boy think he was doing? "Don't!" he cried. "Are you crazy?" He wanted to run and get him, but was far too scared.

"What you up to, kid?" Lee called. "This ain't no game!"

But Jim was beyond reason now. In his mind the 'J' on his chest shone out through his T-shirt with a blue light and superhuman strength pumped through his veins, inflating his physique. He thought the horrified gasps and calls of the others were cries of amazement now that they saw him for who he really was. He would have to swear them to secrecy when he was done here. His true identity must always remain an enigma.

The guards were still laughing when he rushed at the one with the lash and launched himself at him. He caught the astonished creature by the head and the two of them went rolling on the ground. Jim's juvenile fists pounded the Punchinello's misshapen face, but the blows did not send the monster careering through the air as he expected. Instead the guard roared with rage, lurched to his feet and reached for the spear he had set aside. Jim leaped up to charge again. The Punchinello gave a bestial snarl and rammed the weapon into the boy's chest – straight through the middle of his self-inflicted scar.

There was a ghastly, stretched silence. The others watched him stumble. As Jim fell, his eyes were filled with confusion and surprise.

Then Maggie screamed. Charm covered her face and Marcus sank to his knees.

"What have you done?" Alasdair gasped in stunned disbelief. "Get an ambulance! My God! My God!"

He would have raced to Jim's side if Lee hadn't caught his arm and spun him around.

"You want to end up the same? The kid's gone! Look at him. There's nothing you, nor no one, can do. He's dead! Don't give those things an excuse to do that to you."

"They k… killed him!" Maggie stuttered, staggering backwards. "They killed him!" She turned to the workmen again. One of them had started eating his packed lunch. "Damn you!" she cursed.

By Jim's behaviour, Jangler knew the splinter of Austerly Fellows had not been hiding inside him. He consulted his clipboard with mild annoyance. "Now I shall have to rearrange the work parties," he tutted. "Let me see, that makes only twenty-two of you now. Ho, two little ducks – as they say in Bingo."

He peered over at the guards and instructed them to get on with the flogging. The lash began its work and the five Punchinellos hopped and danced as Jody cried out.

"That's the way to do it!" their odious, nasal voices rejoiced. "That's the way to do it!"

"And so, with these heart-warming family reunions continuing behind me," Kate Kryzewski said to camera on the coach, "I am more than happy to admit I was wrong. My initial reaction to *Dancing Jax* was prejudicial and deeply flawed. There is no 'Jaxis of evil' here. It's merely a different and new way of looking at the world but, as you can see, children and families are very much front and centre of that, something we in America can fully appreciate and applaud. All I've witnessed this weekend is the joy this book has given to the people of the UK. It has transformed the lives of the sick and disabled and I've seen, first hand, the astonishing rehabilitation of convicted felons. What I say to you, America, is do not be afraid of this truly incredible work. Its wisdom and philosophy should be embraced. The benefits it could bring our society are only to be guessed at. This is Kate Kryzewski ending her special report for NBC Nightly News."

14

MARCUS SHOVELLED THE last spadeful of soil on to the grave and patted it down respectfully. It was getting dark. Had all this happened in just one day? How had a handful of hours taken this already upside-down world and ripped it inside out so violently?

Jangler had made the teenagers dig the hole themselves. He refused to allow the body out of the camp. Besides, he had said, no one out there cared what happened to them any more. The sooner they understood that, the easier it would be for them. He generously allowed the use of a spade, but first things first: there was important work to do. The camp had to be cleared of litter and he wanted the dining hall "sparkling like a new pin" before anything else was to be done.

No one dared object. They were numb with shock and traumatised by what they had seen. Their lives had shifted into an even higher gear of insanity and they were straining to adjust and take it in. Jim's body lay in the sun for most of the day. Close by, Jody remained tied to the maypole. Her back was striped with blood and her head lolled to one side. Alasdair's pleas to send her to hospital or even just fetch a doctor fell on deaf ears.

A Punchinello stood guard, keeping everyone back.

"Is she dead too?" Christina asked Maggie.

"No," Maggie answered, trying to sound positive for the little girl's sake. "She'll be fine, just you wait and see. Soon as we get these jobs done, we'll bring her inside and make her better."

Before they could begin, however, Jangler had them line up in three rows, alphabetically, telling them they must always assemble this way in future. Then he had the guards confiscate every mobile phone, tablet, media player and relevant chargers. They emptied the luggage on the ground, hunting through everything, tearing bags apart if they thought there was a hidden pouch or compartment. One of the creatures pawed through Charm's clothes with a disgusting grin, his great bristled nose twitching and sampling. They took their finds over to the old man who then instructed them to search the children's pockets.

Fourteen more phones were found. The leering guard patted Charm down thoroughly with his large gnarled hands, taking much longer than necessary.

"You already found me phone in me handbag!" she said, cringing at his clammy touch. "I ain't got another one!"

"Bezuel like," he whispered covetously in her ear. "Pretty."

The girl shut her eyes and pretended it wasn't happening. She wanted to retch when she felt his warty fingers on her. If she hadn't been so frightened of what he might do, she would have slapped that foul face.

Jangler surveyed the haul with satisfaction. "No more beeps or raucous ringtones," he said happily. "No more inane chatter or moronic texting. Just perfect peace – and no one will be tempted to email foreign news sites."

Alasdair looked up sharply. Did Mainwaring know about the messages he had sent yesterday? The old man was not looking in his direction; maybe it was just coincidence. He looked over to the maypole. If the rest of the world could see that, it wouldn't waste another moment in taking military action against this mad, barbaric country.

"Now," Jangler said. "Before you get down to work, let's begin with a chapter – something humorous about Lumpstick, the droll rat catcher and mole choker. The night he chased those blue rodents through the Queen of Hearts' boudoir…"

No one could believe their ears. Just metres away, Jim's blood was soaking into the ground, Jody's back was in urgent need of medical attention and here he was giving a reading from that book as if nothing had happened. Alasdair wondered if the old man had been insane even before *Dancing Jax*. The boy glanced around at the Punchinellos. They weren't taking any notice of Jangler's pompous preaching either. What were they? Where did they come from? How did they get here?

When the reading was over, Jangler sighed dreamily and the children were finally permitted to commence work. They set to it with vigour and determination. The sooner they finished, the sooner they could get to Jody. They scrubbed and swept, mopped and polished until the main block looked better than when they first arrived. Then they hurried about the camp with bin bags, picking up streamers and garlands, anything that made it look untidy. It was past two o'clock before Jangler was content with what they had done and allowed them to attend to Jody and the dead boy.

Jody was their immediate concern. There was nothing anyone could do for Jim now, but Marcus covered him with a cloak as Alasdair cut her down. She groaned as the wounds on her back opened again. Anxiously the Scot and Maggie carried her into the cabin and put her on the nearest bed.

Christina looked on, staring with wide eyes at the raw flesh.

"Got to clean that," Maggie said, trying to be practical and stop herself thinking about the dead boy still outside. She wanted to stop thinking about everything. She wished she could run on autopilot and do what had to be done without wanting to scream every few seconds. Taking a steadying breath, she forced herself to inspect the wounds.

"It won't look so bad once that dried blood is washed off," she said for Christina's benefit.

"Yes, it will," the little girl uttered.

"'Ere," a voice said. "Use this."

A large natural sponge was pushed under Maggie's nose. She looked up and there was Charm. The animosity of the past had been forgotten.

"Thanks," Maggie said, "but it's no good, it's not sterile. We've got to be real careful. If this gets infected…"

"I'll go boil it," the model suggested. "That'll be all right, won't it?"

Maggie wasn't sure. "I think so. I don't know. I'm not a doctor! I hate biology."

Charm held out her hand to Christina. "Why don't you come wiv me to the kitchen?" she said. "You can help."

"I want to stay," the seven-year-old said stubbornly.

Maggie stroked the little girl's hair. "Don't you worry," she promised. "Jody's not going anywhere. You'd be helping make her better if you went."

"Yeah," Charm said. "Cos I am hopeless, can't switch a kettle on, me – and fink toast is just bread wiv a spray tan. Come on."

She led Christina outside and Maggie mouthed a "Thank you".

It was then Marcus came running in, carrying a green plastic case.

"Every canteen's got a first-aid kit!" he announced, opening it up. "Knew there'd be one. Found it right at the back of a cupboard – how mad is that?"

"You're a bloody miracle!" Maggie cried. She almost said she could kiss him, but stopped just in time in case he took it the wrong way. Then she realised how stupid she was being. Their recent history was so insignificant right now.

"What's it got in there?" she asked.

"Bandages, wipes, lots of little blue plasters, not very useful... tons of other good stuff."

She reached for a dressing then thought better of it. "I'd better wash my hands first," she said, running to the bathroom.

Alasdair had been hovering nearby. "If I had a phone," he said trying to control his anger, "every news agency in the world would see this – and poor Jim out there."

"Are we really going to bury him?" Marcus asked. "That's…"

"There's no right word for what this is," Alasdair snapped. "But the old lunatic is correct about one thing. Nobody out there in this country gives a monkey's what happens to us. The police are all Jaxed up. We're on our own here. This is it. This is our normal from now on. They could skewer us all and no one would do a thing."

"How… how do you bury someone?"

"We start by digging a very big hole and take it from there."

They were about to leave the cabin when Maggie emerged from the bathroom.

"Did I hear you wanted a mobile?" she asked.

"Aye," he said. "But what's the use of…" He stopped when she handed him her iPhone.

"How did you manage that?" Marcus asked. "Those monsters looked everywhere."

Maggie coughed and looked at the ceiling. "Not quite everywhere," she said. "It pays having a quick brain and a bum the size of Wales."

In spite of everything Alasdair managed a grim laugh. Picking up the phone, he took photos of Jody's back.

"That won't prove a thing though," Marcus said. "We should've done them when she was still tied up. Who'd believe it anyway?"

Alasdair knew he was right. Only a photo of Jim would do. That irrefutable evidence would convince everyone. But how would they be able to get a photo of him out there, under the fierce scrutiny of those guards?

Presently Alasdair, Lee, Marcus and the boys who had shared the cabin with Jim gathered about his body. A coffin was out of the question, Jangler had said, with an indignant snort. So they had decided to wrap him tightly in his duvet, together with his beloved comic books and whatever mementoes from home he had brought with him. It wasn't much to show for twelve years of life. They didn't even know what his family was like, or if he had any brothers or sisters. Until the night of the drugged May Cup, he hadn't really said much to anyone.

They stared down at the cloak that still covered him, unsure how they were going to do this. Two Punchinellos were leaning on their spears, watching and snickering at their ashen faces. The sound of splintering wood filled the air as the stage was pulled apart and Jangler was giving instructions to the foreman about the helter-skelter.

"Someone needs to lift that cloak off," Lee said gently.

Marcus volunteered. He felt he owed the dead boy. If he hadn't been so cowardly earlier, he might have been able to stop him attacking the guard. Crouching down, he held his breath and drew the cloak aside.

"Don't you call me a fat cow!" Maggie's voice hollered suddenly.

"You're right!" Charm yelled back at her. "Cows ain't nowhere near as big as you. You're a giant munter, you are! You don't need one gastric band – you need a whole bleedin' music festival."

"Shut it, you tangerine-faced twig!"

"Yeah, well, at least I didn't fall out of the minger tree – and then ate it!"

"Come here, you scrawny bitch!"

The two girls started fighting. They pulled each other's hair and Charm shrieked shrilly.

The Punchinellos turned to view them and cackled. Moments later, Alasdair ran over and pulled the girls apart.

"What is the matter with you?" he cried, leading Maggie back to the cabin and sending Charm off to her own. "Are you both mental? We dinnae need this!"

Once they were back inside, he let out a sigh of relief and brandished the phone. "We got one," he said. "But you really dinnae wanna see. I could hardly bear to look."

Maggie shook her head in agreement and returned to nursing Jody.

"The minger tree?" the wounded girl muttered.

"I had to tell her that one," Maggie chuckled, relieved to see Jody awake. "That poor girl's a bit too nice and couldn't think of anything nasty enough. I've heard all the fat insults there are."

"Nice? Don't you believe it."

Alasdair tapped away at the phone.

"Och, there's only ten per cent of juice left!" he said with irritation. "How'd you let it get so low?"

"I was looking at YouTube in bed first thing," Maggie explained sheepishly. "And taking pictures always drains it real fast."

He composed a hasty follow-up email to the one he had sent out the other night, attaching the shocking, macabre photograph taken during the girls' diversion. Then he did a rapid search for the news sites, adding them to the address list. Abruptly the screen went blank.

"No!" he cried in exasperation. "I was just about to send. Quick! Where's the charger?"

Maggie's face fell. "They've got it," she said apologetically. "I couldn't hide that as well."

Alasdair stared at her a moment, then he covered his eyes in defeat.

"Plugs have prongs," she added dismally.

The boy lifted his face and stared out of the door as a fresh, dangerous idea took hold. "There's only one thing to do then," he said decisively. "We're going to have to steal the charger back from old Mainwaring's hut."

Lee and Marcus took it in turns to dig the grave.

They chose a spot furthest away from the chalets, close to the newly completed fence. One of the Punchinellos oversaw them as they toiled. It was the one called Yikker and he delighted in kicking earth back into the grave when Marcus was trying to dig it out.

Spencer scrounged a wide piece of wood from the dismantled stage. Nicholas, one of the Xbox boys, turned out to be good at drawing and he printed Jim's name and age on it in felt pen. It was a pitiable memorial.

Apart from Jody, every other young person gathered at the graveside to pay their respects, as the duvet bundle was lowered reverently into the ground.

"Shouldn't we say something?" Maggie asked. "Something religious about dust and that kind of thing? A prayer maybe?"

"Do you even know if he was a Christian?" Lee asked.

"No, but it doesn't seem right, just putting him down there without special words."

Charm agreed with her. "Got to do it proper," she said. "We ain't animals."

But nobody knew the right words to say and Google was no longer an option.

"Hell," Lee said. "I'll do it. I heard me enough sermons, something must've stuck."

He did his best, and the other children took solace in what he said, but he felt a fraud. He never did have much of a faith before that book took over and certainly none after. Seeing how easily his grandmother had removed her favourite painting of Jesus from the wall and replaced it with a print of Mooncaster had killed that. Where was God when Jim had needed him? Where was he for them right now?

"We should sing something too," Maggie suggested when Lee finished speaking. "What hymns do we know?"

Only a few of them knew any by heart. They were going to give up on it when Charm began to sing, in a faint, wavering voice.

Silent night, holy night.

At first they thought she was making a sick joke or was too stupid to know it was only a Christmas carol. But, as she sang, they found meaning in those familiar, moving words and, one by one, joined in.

> *Holy infant so tender and mild.*
> *Sleep in heavenly peace.*
> *Sleep in heavenly peace.*

One verse was enough. They couldn't make it through another. They cast handfuls of soil into the grave and said goodbye to the boy they had hardly known, but who had died trying to protect them. Marcus and Lee remained to fill in the hole.

Because Jangler had ordered the removal of all the "frivolous and blousy" hanging baskets and planters from the camp, the only floral tributes were small bunches of daisies the younger children had collected from the rear lawn.

And so, when Marcus patted the last shovel-load down, and the light began to fail, he tried to get his head around this awful, devastating day.

Everything was in place now. The workmen had left in their trucks hours ago. They had laboured long to get it completed in time. The camp was surrounded by a high fence, topped with vicious barbed wire, and the low wooden gates had been replaced with a tall barrier of meshed steel. The stage was gone and the helter-skelter's slide had been removed, together with its cheery fairground covering.

Marcus stared up at what remained. A forbidding, skeletal tower reared into the evening sky. Stationed at the top, a Punchinello paced round the platform, glaring down over the camp, keeping vigilant watch. Two others patrolled the perimeter.

An eight o'clock curfew had been announced earlier. When Jangler came to reclaim the spade, he reminded them that hour was approaching.

"If any of you are discovered outside your chalets after then," he warned, "Captain Swazzle and his chaps have been instructed to show no mercy, not that they would anyway, so you had best hurry along. An early night will do you the world of good anyhow. You'll need your strength tomorrow. I think I was far too lenient today. Lumpstick's comical escapades always sweeten my nature. Oh, and boys… pleasant dreams."

The lads went to their cabin. Marcus paused before entering.

"So this is it," he said, too exhausted and hungry to be outraged. "This is our life from now on. Locked up and forgotten, with monsters for warders."

"You better get used to it," Lee told him.

Marcus stared into the dorm. The flat-screen television had been torn from the wall and taken away, and so had the Xbox. His eyes roamed over the beds, resting finally on the empty one. He drew a hand across his bruised face.

"No chance," he muttered. "They're not keeping me here. I'm not ending up on the wrong end of one of them spears. That Yikker swine has already got it in for me. No, I'm going to get out of here – or die trying."

Throughout the camp, the children were tearful with hunger. Their growling stomachs ached and they dreaded what new terrors the following day would bring.

In Alasdair's hut, the Scottish lad was completely alone. The six other boys had gone home on the coach that morning and so much had happened in the meantime he had forgotten to move his belongings into the other cabin till it was too late. He strummed his guitar softly, playing a melancholy tune. He wanted to talk to Lee, but there hadn't been a chance. He needed to sound him out about schemes to sneak into Jangler's cabin without getting caught. He had to get that phone charger and soon.

"I cannae hack being stuck in here till I'm sixteen!" he told the walls.

The girls had been more organised. Two from Maggie's cabin had gone in with Charm to allow Jody to stay where she was and Christina to be at her side. Jody's wounds had been cleaned and dressed as well as Maggie could manage. Her back felt as though it was scored with flame-filled trenches. But her mind was concentrated on the Punchinello Guards.

"There's nothing like them on this world," she ranted. "Nothing! But that can only mean… Mooncaster is real, an actual other place, in another dimension, parallel universe or something. Does that mean everything else in the book exists out there somewhere?"

Christina nodded sombrely.

"Hurts your brain, doesn't it?" Maggie said. "I can't think about it. I'm doing my teeth then turning in."

She took her toiletry bag into the bathroom and closed the door behind her. A guilty, furtive look was on her round face. Unzipping the bag, she brought out two Mars bars and a Twix, handling them like sacred relics. She had taken them as snacks for the ferry ride to France before she was captured, but there had been so much food here she hadn't touched them since. Now the overweight girl unwrapped one of the Mars bars and the smell of the warm chocolate sent her into raptures. She hadn't eaten a thing all day and was ravenous. She knew she should share it with the others, at least with Jody and Christina, but she couldn't stop herself and gobbled it down in moments.

"Whoever invented chocolate," she whispered, "I hope you had a bloody long and lovely life."

She looked at the inviting second bar and made short work of that too. It brought instant comfort and for several delicious moments blanked out what had happened.

"Must save the Twix," she told herself sternly. "Give one each to Jody and Christina."

A few minutes later, Maggie hated herself and stuffed three empty wrappers into her pocket.

Two cabins along, Charm was moisturising mechanically. She could cope with the hunger. She pretended it was one of her detox days, except without the fruit smoothies. Many unbelievable and harrowing things had occurred today, but she kept returning to the most painful, and the one which caused her the most grief. Why hadn't her mother turned up? She had promised she would be there. Charm's hatred for *Dancing Jax* finally blossomed.

Next door, Lee lay on his bed, staring at the ceiling. Something had been bugging him and now he realised what it was. How did Jangler know Jody had instigated the attack on the castle model? Someone had to have grassed her up. There was no other explanation. But who? The only people who had seen it happen were the other children.

"This place blows worse than I thought," he muttered in disgust.

"What's that?" Marcus asked, coming up the stairs after showering, towelling his hair. "Didn't hear you."

Lee kept his realisation to himself. He knew the other boy hadn't been in the dining hall last night, but someone else could have told him. The past five months had taught Lee to trust nobody. Even Alasdair was a suspect.

"Just sayin' it's been a tough, brainsick day," he lied. "I need to get me some sleep."

"In your trainers?" Marcus observed.

"From now on I am going to be ready for anything, at any time."

Even as he said it, the lights went off. It was the same in every cabin. They were plunged into total darkness. Some of the younger girls screamed in panic, their voices carrying through the camp.

"Eight o'clock," Marcus said. "Lights out."

"Another thing we're going to have to get used to," Lee commented, turning on his side.

"Not me," Marcus promised himself.

"You did good today, Ladies' Man. Did that kid proud. Maybe you ain't such an asshole after all."

Marcus snorted. "Is that really what it takes for us to be mates?" he said. "Digging some poor lad's grave together?"

"I never said we was mates," Lee corrected him. "Goodnight, pussy face."

Marcus couldn't tell if he was serious, but at that moment, he didn't care. He was mentally, emotionally and physically drained. He found his bed in the dark and crawled into it. Within minutes, he was sound asleep.

Lee remained wide awake. There was something he had to do. He closed his eyes and focused. In a soft, barely audible whisper, he began reciting the opening lines of *Dancing Jax*. He felt the same sharp cramp in his heart he had experienced those previous times and his skin began to crawl. Then that icy, rushing sensation took hold, followed by the roaring in his ears, the lurching of his stomach and the burning at the back of his throat.

It was a mild autumn afternoon in the Realm of the Dawn Prince. A sweet rain shower was still glistening on the hedgerows, sparkling over ripe clusters of fat, juicy brambles. The Kingdom was washed clean and the larks were singing in a forget-me-not sky.

Lee looked up. A lonely country road stretched before him. In the hazy distance, beyond the thatched roofs and smoking chimneys of Mooncot, the towers and battlements of the White Castle rose gleaming in the sunlight. He took a step back. It was always a jolt, finding himself here, but he was gradually getting used to it.

His heel splashed in a puddle and he glanced down at his muddy Nike. With a startled cry on his lips, he scanned up the length of his trackie bottoms, to his T-shirt. He could actually see them! This time he was visible, not a shadow-shape, not an ethereal presence. He was properly here! His mind was his own, he wasn't dressed as one of those lame fairy-tale characters and he knew precisely who he was. Apprehensive, he raised his hands before his eyes. Then he leaped in the air, giving a euphoric shout. His skin was black.

"Who goes there?" a wheezing voice called from above.

Lee wheeled about. He didn't want to be discovered. When he saw who spoke, he relaxed and laughed.

At the side of the road was a tall gibbet. Within the iron cage suspended beneath was a withered, cadaverous figure, more bones than papery flesh. Threadbare rags, grey with age, still covered the emaciated corpse. Hanks of grizzled hair clung to the wormy skull, but in the dark sockets there were no eyes. Gorcrows sent by Haxxentrot had dined on them long ago.

"How dare you ridicule me so?" the chattering jaw demanded. "No one mocks Oak-Chested Jacky Samson – brawny cut-throat and baron turned brigand, Bane of the Northern Marches – and lives!"

Two skeleton hands gripped the iron cage to shake it fiercely, but it was the fragile bones that rattled.

"How long you been up there, my man?" Lee asked. "Cos you ain't the buffed roid monkey you think you is."

The skull gnashed its teeth and one of them fell out. The skeleton sagged and gave a miserable groan.

"Nine winters have seen me dangling in this rusty surcoat," it said. "How was I to know the old beldame my horse kicked into a stream as I rode by was a witch? Famous I was, in my prime. Big, burly Jacky Samson, the high-born robber and sometime pirate. When the Constable caught me carousing at The Silver Penny, I didn't grudge the shackles, nor the fate that awaited. Jacky's sword had lopped many a head, my lad, and he'd enjoyed the full merry of a fast burned life. So I knew the reckoning was squarely earned. What I didn't bargain for was the malice and might of the crone in the Forbidden Tower. Afflicted me with one of her spells she did, so poor Jacky can't ever die proper, just keeps lingering. There's a thrush's nest in his ribs, spiders in his brainpan and this winter may see the ligaments finally crumble and Jacky will be a pile of loose, unconnected bones up here. Not much of an unlife – and awful lonesome too."

"Sounds hardcore, friend."

"You have a curious form of speech," the corpse said, angling the hole where its left ear had been in his direction. "You don't sound like a knight or a serf. Who are you, stranger?"

Lee grinned widely.

"I believe in this here neighbourhood they call me the Castle Creeper."

15

AT FIVE IN the morning the usual transit van left the camp, fully laden. Jangler saw it depart and peered into one of the cabins. As he anticipated, the nightmares had been particularly vivid and powerful that night. This time some of the beds had been overturned. The children were still locked in the bridging devices' unnatural sleep.

He consulted his watch and his moustache gave a sideways twitch. "They've got one hour," he said.

At six he rang his bell outside on the lawn. The children came to, uttering pained groans. Jody had fallen on her back and cried out.

"What goes on here at night?" Maggie asked angrily as she helped her on to the bed. "You don't think them hunchback things come in and slap us about, do you? But how could they without waking us up? We can't have been drugged yesterday. It just don't make sense."

"Remind me the last time anything did," Jody said.

Maggie glanced at the time and swore. According to the work roster she was due in the kitchen in five minutes and didn't dare be late. She pulled on some clothes and hurried out.

A Punchinello was waiting for her. He was perched on one of the steel surfaces, a spear across his knees. A thirteen-year-old girl called Esther, from another cabin, had also been assigned cooking duties. When Maggie arrived, she was already there, afraid to be alone in the room with that creature. She was cracking her knuckles nervously.

"Are we supposed to make the breakfast for everyone?" Maggie asked. "It's sexist is what it is."

The Punchinello licked his teeth. "Yes, you cook," he said. "You make."

"But there's nothing in the storeroom," Maggie said.

The guard pointed at the door with his spear. "Food, yes, in there."

The girls went to see. There had been a delivery of eight large plastic containers.

"Plenty for week," the creature said.

"Dunno why I've been put in the kitchen." Maggie grumbled. "Just cos I enjoy my grub doesn't mean I'm Gordon flippin' Ramsay. I can fry an egg and use a microwave, but that's about it."

"We can sort out twenty two-breakfasts OK," Esther said optimistically, acutely aware that the guard's eyes had narrowed and his mouth was downturned. "And if there's cornflakes and bread for toast, it'll be dead easy. We'll worry about lunch and dinner after. We can do it."

They opened the nearest container.

"Must be a mistake," Maggie said.

They opened another and another. She hurried back into the kitchen. The Punchinello was laughing now.

"What's going on?" Maggie asked. "Where's the food? Them boxes are just filled with garbage, old peelings and cabbage leaves."

"Is good, yes?"

"We can't eat that!"

"Came from good eaty places!" the guard replied. "Good food, yes? Yum yum."

Maggie tried to make sense of what it was saying. "Do you mean those boxes came from restaurants? That we're expected to eat their scraps and leavings? Basically what we've got in there came from their bins? You wouldn't feed those leftovers to animals."

"Piggy wiggy farm no want," the Punchinello told her with a shrug.

"So it's not even fit for pigs?"

Esther hugged herself and wept silently. She was so unbelievably hungry. Maggie opened the large fridge. It was crammed with trays of raw sausages. Her mouth watered, but she knew they weren't for her and the others. That was why the guard was in here, to make sure none of them were stolen.

"Squassages!" he sniggered, kicking his feet against the cupboards with childish glee.

"I'm going to speak to the Jangler bloke," Maggie said angrily. "We can't seriously be expected to eat that muck. This can't be right."

But it was right. Jangler informed her that was the only food they were going to get this week and if she didn't get a move on cooking something, the work parties were going to have to begin the day with empty stomachs.

After the first reading of the day, conducted outside on the lawn, the others gathered in the dining hall, desperate for something to eat; they smelled the sausages cooking and their hopes soared. Maggie had to break the bad news and began slopping out a thin soup. It was the only thing she could think to do with the rubbish provided.

"I can't eat this," Marcus protested in disgust. "It's swill."

"I know," she agreed. "But it's all there is. I can't cook what isn't there."

"Are ye serious?" Alasdair asked. "Is this really what we're getting from noo on?"

"Looks like it."

The children stared at their bowls in dismay. Christina wrinkled her nose. Maggie told the seven-year-old to eat up then she could take a bowl to Jody who had remained in the cabin, unable to move.

"Are we just going to accept this?" Alasdair challenged everyone.

"You want to go argue it out?" Marcus asked. "You'll be keeping Jim company, out there in the ground, if you do. You can dig your own grave though; there's no way I want to do that again."

The rest of them knew he was right. Charm was the first to tuck in.

"It's full of vitamins, innit?" she said, with a fixed smile. "See, it's got... green bits and no carbs. Better for you than a fry-up. Brilliant for the complexion."

She didn't convince them, but they were so famished they lifted the spoons to their trembling lips.

"If you don't eat nofink," she continued more seriously, "you ain't gonna make it. So get it down your necks."

"Least it might clear up your zits, Herr Spenzer," Marcus said, grimacing as he sniffed it.

Lee stirred his spoon through the unappetising contents of his bowl. He glanced out of the window at the fence behind the main block. Out there, in the woods, were the provisions he had stashed. He had guessed it would come to this. He had known they were never getting out of here after the weekend was over. All he had to do was figure out how to get through that wire and bring the food in, bit by bit. How was he going to manage that? And there was something else.

At that moment, under his pillow, was an apple he had brought back from Mooncaster last night. He had pulled it from a tree as an experiment to see what would happen. He didn't want to eat anything there in case, on his return, it turned to slime or was riddled with maggots. When he had examined it, first thing, it looked just as edible here as it did there. That gave him plenty to think about. What else could he bring back from that place?

"We have to talk." Alasdair's earnest whisper broke into his thoughts. "I've got to figure a way to get into Mainwaring's cabin."

Lee looked around the table before answering. "You're crazy," he muttered back. "And there's too many ears here."

Before they could continue, Captain Swazzle came stomping in. Breakfast was over. Nineteen frightened children were quickly split into the two groups written on the roster. Christina tried to run out of the dining hall, calling for Jody. The creature called Yikker snatched her back and pushed her roughly into the others. Marcus caught her and stopped her darting off again.

"Don't make them angry," he urged, trying to calm her down. "You saw what they can do."

"No speak!" Yikker snarled, glaring at him and pinching his long, curved nose. "You stink big!"

Four guards then shunted everyone out, herding them towards the gates, pushing and shoving the stragglers with ungentle hands.

"Where they being taken?" a worried Maggie asked the Captain.

"You curtsy to Captain!" he screamed at her, stamping one foot.

"Abrants always bow and curtsy to Captain! You are scum – you are dirty, under-boot wormdung!"

Maggie obeyed hastily. "Sorry," she said. "I didn't know we had to. If… if you don't mind me asking, where are my friends going?"

The Punchinello twirled one of his whiskery eyebrows with a long finger. "Heigh ho," he sang with a sardonic grin. "Off to work they go."

"Outside the camp? What work are they doing out there?"

Swazzle coughed up a ball of phlegm at her feet, licked his teeth and swaggered away.

"A simple 'mind your own business' would have done," the girl muttered.

Alasdair was asking the same questions of the guard closest to him.

"Where we going?" he demanded.

"No talk," he growled. "Or Anchu spike!"

Jangler unlocked the gates and swung them open.

"Remember," he cautioned the children sternly, "the Captain's bonny boys are just waiting for an excuse to wet their spears again. Don't antagonise them. Do precisely what they say. You may be leaving the confines of the camp, but one false step out there will be fatal. Two deaths in as many days really would be so very careless of you."

The Punchinellos laughed raucously and drove their young prisoners up the forest road. Jangler closed the gates behind them and turned one of his many keys in the lock.

Lee looked back at the sealed camp then up the long road. Where were they headed?

Jody sucked the air through her teeth as she tried to raise herself to eat the soup Maggie had brought. Her wounds had opened in the night and she could barely move. Even Jangler could see that, otherwise she would have joined the work parties.

"Why outside?" she asked. "What's out there?"

Maggie had no answer. "P'raps to help out at a stables or do the dirty work in a big house or hotel?"

"They don't send kids up chimneys no more."

"There's a lot of things they never used to do any more, but it don't stop them now!"

Jody slurped the soup thoughtfully. She didn't think it was that bad. Then a sickening thought struck her.

"What if," she began. "What if they've been taken out… to be murdered? That's what always happens. Those monsters could be filling in a mass grave right now."

"Don't say that!" Maggie cried. "It's horrible!"

"We've got to expect it. It's inevitable. You do realise, as soon as they want rid of us, we're done for in this place. It's a concentration camp, for heaven's sake! Look what they're still doing in countries where that book *hasn't* brainwashed everyone; human beings do terrible things to other human beings – *hello, Guantanamo Bay*. And those guards out there aren't even human. They see us as a lower form of life. Frankly I don't know why they've bothered keeping us alive. What's the point? What's in it for them?"

"You shouldn't talk like that, it's morbid."

"No, it's realistic. Honestly – we're on borrowed time here and the clock's ticking."

The day passed slowly and no sign was seen of the others. Maggie and Esther sorted through more of the peelings, washed the usable elements, sorted them into piles and made a thicker, more substantial soup for lunch. But no one returned to eat it. Jangler fitted a padlock on the fridge then retired to his cabin and Captain Swazzle disappeared into the one next to it, reappearing on the hour to patrol the fence.

It was getting on for six o'clock. Maggie was standing on the step of her chalet, staring anxiously through the gates, when at last she spotted them.

"They're here!" she called back to Jody, as she and Esther ran forward.

They hurried to the gates and their faces fell. The other children were stumbling and staggering along the road. They looked dirty and exhausted; some of the younger ones were being helped by the teenagers. Their clothes were torn and, when they drew closer, Maggie saw that their arms and faces were covered in scratches, many of them bleeding. Their hands were stained a livid greyish-yellow colour and then the smell hit her nostrils.

Maggie and Esther shrank back and choked. A fetid stench of decay and corruption flowed before the returning group. It was unbearable. By this time Jangler had emerged from his cabin and came to unlock the gate.

Christina was on Marcus's shoulders. Her head drooped forward. She was worn out. It had been a shattering day for all of them.

They shambled into the camp, where some of them collapsed immediately on to the grass, unable to take another step. Jangler closed and locked the gates behind them.

"What happened?" Maggie asked.

Alasdair turned his weary eyes towards her as Charm tottered past, heading for her cabin. Jody would have paid money to see her in that wretched state. The teen model looked a wreck. Cuts covered her bare arms, not one of her fingernails had survived the day's labour intact and her hair was wild and stuck with twigs and dried lumps of minchet.

"Soon as we reached the road, they split the two groups," Alasdair explained to Maggie. "We only just met up again half an hour ago. They marched us miles this morning and again just noo. I dinnae know about the others, but we went to a spot where them plants have taken over. Gone mad they have, really choking the trees, strangling everything. There was a truck waiting. We had to fill it wi' that reekin' fruit. Been pickin' it all day wi'out a break. It's no easy and there's clouds of flies everywhere. You cannae breathe or speak wi'out swallowing a dozen at a time – an' that's all we've eaten. Ye cannae eat that minchet slop. Apart from it tasting like cat sick, It doesnae fill you an' makes the hunger even worse wi' gut ache after."

Lee wiped the sweat from his face. He'd been in the other work party.

"Same here," he said. "We were taken miles the other way – there was a truck waiting for us to fill too."

"It's a jungle in some places," Alasdair continued. "You cannae get through them vines and they're covered wi' sharp spines and needles. We've all been cut to ribbons. The wee ones had to crawl deep into thickets cos the biggest fruits are right inside the shady bits. Then, when we'd done, those vicious beggars marched us back, 'lickety-split, lickety-split' they said, no dawdling allowed, like we're marines on a training run. We're dead on oor feet. I just wanna crash oot."

"I've got some more soup ready," Maggie said gently. "It's better this time, more filling and I used a handblender thing so it's nice and thick."

"I got to wash this clarty muck off first," Alasdair said in revulsion. "I'd puke if I tried to eat right noo."

It was long after seven o'clock by the time they had all showered and eaten. They were glad of the soup and no longer cared it was made from kitchen waste. At that moment in time, it was the most welcome, most delicious meal they'd ever tasted.

Charm had scrubbed her hands almost raw, but couldn't get the ugly juice stains out.

"I spend me a fortune on manicures," she moaned despondently. "They're ruined now. I'll never get no work being a hand model again. If we ever get out of 'ere, I'll have to wear gloves. If we get out… like that's ever gonna happen. Is it gonna be same as this every day? I don't fink I can do it – an' that Bez monster's been leching at me the whole time. Ugh, his beady eyes were on stalks."

"You can do it," Lee told her. "You're stronger than you think."

Alasdair tried to move his stuff into the other boys' cabin, but Jangler wouldn't permit it and ordered Nicholas and Drew to move across to join him instead. It wouldn't do for one of the bridging devices to be left without any young minds to tune into.

Irritated, the Scottish lad went to have a quiet word with Lee. Marcus was spark out on the other bed.

"What we talked about this morning," Alasdair began in a low whisper. "I meant it. We need to get a charger back from that old guy's cabin."

"Ain't interested," Lee answered with a shake of his head.

"How can you no be interested? It'll get us oot of here!"

Lee rubbed his eyes and yawned. "You're foolin' yourself," he told him. "There won't never be no cavalry coming to rescue us. We's stuck here. You're just going to get yourself stuck on one of them Mr Punch's cocktail spears."

"So that's it, you're giving up? You're just going to lie back and take this? Soup and slavery, how long do you think we'll last on that? I'd give it a month at the most. Look at the state of us after just one day of it!"

"I ain't risking my neck for no dumb scheme to swipe a phone charger."

"Is this you no getting involved again? I thought you was just being selfish last time, but that's no it. You've been saying all along we weren't ever going to get out of here. You guessed there'd be fences and guards."

"No, those guards were a surprise to me too."

"But you knew about the fences. Why the hell did you no tell anyone? We could've done something about it if we'd known."

"Real question you should ask yourself is, why didn't you expect the fences? Did you really think you was only here for a happy weekend? They was a foregone bit of obvious to me."

"If I'd known, I'd have run. I wouldn't have sat back and waited for it to happen. You took that choice away from me – and everyone else here."

"Oh, be real. How far do you think you'd have got if you'd run away? They'd have caught you and brought you right back. I saved you a lot of wasted hope and energy."

Alasdair moved away from him.

"For a minute there I almost thought you was chicken, but that's no it. The problem wi' you is, you've given up. Och, you're full of the big man, sassy talk and attitude, but you've really caved in and surrendered inside, haven't ye?"

Lee checked his watch. "Almost eight," he said dryly. "You'd best get back to your own place before lights out."

"I'm goin' all right," Alasdair said. "I cannae stand the smell of defeat and self-loathing in here; it honks worse than what we were picking all day long."

He stomped down the stairs and returned to his own cabin. Lee put a pen in his mouth and wished he could light it. On the next bed Marcus stirred.

"Now who's got their handbags out?" the Manchester lad asked with a mocking grin.

"Shut up, Lynxstain."

"You're both right though," Marcus said, turning over. "And both wrong too. Trying to nick something from that Jangler's cabin is a moronic idea. Trying to get out of here isn't. I'm going to escape, first chance I get."

"Then you'll wind up dead."

"Not if I'm clever about it."

"Then you'll definitely wind up dead."

Spencer was sitting on the step when the lights went out. Jumping up, he opened the door hurriedly then glanced over at the wooden skelter tower. One of the Punchinellos was stationed at the top. He was sniggering and humming to himself, his ugly face illuminated by a flickering glow. The boy heard faint but familiar sounds and realised the creature was holding his own media player in its large hands, watching one of his Western movies.

"Cat Ballou..." the guard gargled along to the title music. "Cat Ballooowooowooo."

Spencer had seen that film dozens of times. It was one of the few comedy Westerns he enjoyed, with two terrific performances from Lee Marvin in dual roles: one an over-the-hill, drunken gunslinger, the other a sinister hired gun with a false silver nose. Spencer hated that the revolting guard was going through his collection and didn't understand why it would even be interested. It was incomprehensible and sort of creepy. Perhaps it

271

and the others were also going through their phones, reading the texts and poring over the photographs.

"You!" a sharp voice screamed at him from the darkness nearby. "Go – in hut!"

Another of the sentries came scampering towards him, out of the night, spear in hand. Spencer obeyed quickly and kicked the door shut behind him.

In the blackness of their cabin, Maggie and Jody were speaking softly so as not to disturb Christina who was sleeping in the bed between them.

"What you were on about before," Maggie said. "You don't really believe that, do you?"

"You've seen the way they treat us. How can you believe otherwise?"

"It won't ever come to that."

"I bet that's what everyone else it ever happened to thought, before they got murdered. Let them eat cake, yeah?"

"Don't say that word!"

"Murdered?"

"No, cake."

There was a short silence, filled only by the soft sleeping breaths of the others around them.

"What I want to know," Jody murmured eventually, "is what were those two trucks for? Who, or what, wants all that filthy minchet fruit?"

Maggie remained silent and Jody realised she had fallen asleep. Jody stayed awake, thinking, for several hours.

At midnight, the Bakelite devices began to hum and another old song from the 1930s crackled through the camp...

In the morning the cabins were in disarray once more. When Jangler rang his bell, the children picked themselves up from the floor, aching and bruised again.

Maggie went to the main block. There was a plastic carrier bag beside the doors. Curious, she picked it up and looked inside. It was full of apples, almost two dozen fresh, rosy apples – rounder and redder and shinier than any she had ever seen. Their fragrance was strong, sweet and delicious.

The girl gave a cry of surprise then looked around sharply. The guard in the tower was glaring down at her. Hugging the bag close, she pushed open the doors and hurried to the kitchen, hiding her precious find under a chair in the dining hall on the way. She had no idea where the apples had come from, but she was sure they were forbidden.

The same Punchinello as yesterday was waiting for her, impatient for his "squassages".

As work began on the morning soup, in the first cabin Charm had managed to monopolise the bathroom yet again. Gazing at her scratched and weary face in the mirror, she hardly recognised herself and indulged in tears of self-pity.

"Hurry up in there!" the other girls called outside the door.

Charm recalled what Lee had told her and realised he was right. Yes, she was strong. You didn't get far in the modelling world by being a pushover. You bounce back no matter how many knocks you get. Ambition equalled ruthlessness. She'd elbowed her way into many situations and junkets by sheer force of personality and determination. Her mother had always joked she had a steel core. The girl's face hardened and she pulled her frayed nerves and self-confidence together. Yes, she was tough enough.

"If you can blag your way past Security at the TV Choice Awards and don't never flinch at a home bikini wax, this ain't nofink, doll," she scolded herself.

Reaching into the shower, she turned it on and when it ran warm, stepped inside. The water beat against her upturned face. Standing there, motionless, she imagined herself somewhere glamorous: beneath a tropical waterfall – on a photo shoot for swimwear or even her own calendar. These were the dreams that had always sustained and inspired her.

"Forget that," she said, squeezing shampoo on her palm and massaging it into her scalp. "You've got to get yourself a new Plan."

Soon the foamy water was swirling down the drain between her feet. With her eyes shut tightly against the soap, she heard the others start tapping on the door again.

"Gimme a bleedin' chance!" she called out.

The tapping continued. With water in her ears, the noise sounded strange, not like knocking at all any more. In fact, not even like knuckles on wood, more like pliers snipping at a plate.

"Hold your horses!" she shouted.

The tapping became more urgent and was joined by frantic scratching.

"Cross your legs!" she said, really getting annoyed now. "I'm almost done."

Then something scraped across her foot. Charm wiped her eyes and glanced down.

There was a jagged, CD-sized hole in the shower tray, beside the drain. The ceramic had been bitten and chewed by powerful jaws. A bent and broken stick was poking out of it. That's what had touched her foot. Suddenly the stick moved. It jerked and scrabbled around the hole. Even under the warm shower, the shock of realisation froze the girl's blood. It wasn't a stick. It was a long segmented leg, like that of an insect, magnified many times.

The curved claw at the end tapped and groped the glazed surface, blindly exploring this splashing world. Then a second leg pushed up from the darkness below, rapidly followed by another and another. Four spindly jointed legs, spiky with coarse hairs, clattered and slithered on the shower tray, trying to get a grip. Two black, glittering eyes, surrounded by dark, wiry fur, squeezed up out of the hole. Then, twisting and distorting with strain, came a fleshy mouth, crowded with fangs and razor-sharp teeth.

Charm screamed and threw the shampoo bottle at it.

It bounced off. The eyes fixed on her and the jaws snapped the air greedily. The hideous face lunged to bite her, but the hole it had made was too small. The rest of its body couldn't pass through. It screamed back at her, then wriggled down in a frenzy and immediately began crunching more of the ceramic away with its teeth.

Still shrieking, Charm leaped clear. She snatched up her robe and wrenched at the door, forgetting she had bolted it.

"Let me out!" she screeched in terror.

The noise of the snapping ceramic ceased abruptly. Trembling, she turned and saw the legs reappear. The savage face came after, its eyes riveted on her. This time the rest of its body was pulled out with ease and, with it, four more insect-like legs.

Charm didn't know what it was. Its kind had never sullied this world before. It was the size of a large terrier. There was no head, just those protruding eyes and the vicious mouth, which slashed across the front of the body.

For a moment, it stood in the shower, tensing and shaking itself in the warm water. Then, with jaws gaping as wide as they could, it sprang forward.

Charm never stopped screaming, but she hurled everything she could lay her hands on at it: soap, perfume, toothpaste tube, toilet roll, glass tumbler, hair brush and can of hairspray. It ducked and dodged the missiles, but didn't falter and came running for her. As it jumped up, she flung a towel. It was a lucky throw. The towel covered the creature completely. It let out a muffled yowl as it fell, then wheeled around, demented, trying to get out from under, but only became even more tangled and wrapped.

The maddened bundle lurched from side to side. It banged into the sink pedestal and snarled furiously. Charm searched for something she could smash down on top of that reeling shape, to splatter the thing beneath it, but there was nothing. Then her terror doubled. Four more legs were rising from the hole in the shower tray. Another of those nightmares surfaced into the bathroom, jaws snapping.

She spun back to the door. This time she remembered the bolt, dragged it back, rescued her make-up bag and flew out.

"What you been doing in there?" an irate twelve-year-old girl, at the front of the queue, demanded. "Was you singing death metal? You suck."

Charm stared at her dumbly. Before she could answer, a thud rammed into the door and feverish clawing of the wood began.

"What's in there?" a younger girl asked. "Is it a dog? Can I stroke it?"

"Let me in," the first girl insisted. "I'm busting."

Charm wouldn't let go of the handle. "You can't!" she cried. "Everyone clear out! Go get one of them guard fings. Get the old bloke! Hurry! Move it!"

The girls didn't understand. Then one of them squealed. A jointed leg was thrashing under the door and the unmistakable sound of ripping and splintering wood began.

"Get out!" Charm yelled again. "All of you!"

Still clutching their toothbrushes, the girls fled from the chalet. Charm took one last horrified look at the bottom of the door. The teeth that had bitten through a ceramic shower tray would make very short work of a flimsy bit of wood.

Shutting the outer door behind her, she ran out on to the lawn where the panicking girls were scattering in all directions. Jangler was over by the skelter tower, discussing the day's schedule with Captain Swazzle. The two of them regarded the screaming girls with sneering derision.

"Female hysterics," the old man commented. "They're obviously feeding too well if they have so much spare energy to burn."

Christina left Jody's side to see what the disturbance was. Lee was sitting on his step, turning a chewed-up pen over in his fingers. When Charm came racing from the cabin, he rose and ran after her.

"Whassup?" he asked.

The girl couldn't stop to explain. She rushed across to Jangler and the Captain.

"There's fings!" she jabbered wildly. "Back there! Revulsive fings – comin' up out the plughole. Big, hairy spidery fings wiv a gob full of teeth!"

Jangler scowled irascibly at her over the top of his spectacles, but Captain Swazzle sniffed the air and tightened his grip on the spear.

"Me smell witchy pets," he announced. "Doggy-Long-Legs."

Jangler's expression changed at once. "The Gangles?" he cried in dismay. "Here? How did… where are they?"

"In our bathroom!" Charm answered. "But they won't be in there long, not wiv them choppers."

Jangler wasn't listening; he was already darting up the tower steps to escape them and Captain Swazzle was bawling orders to the other guards as he scampered towards the invaded cabin.

By now the other children had been lured outside by the noise.

"What's happenin'?" Alasdair asked Christina.

The little girl shook her head. Marcus folded his arms and looked on with the same attitude Jangler first displayed. Spencer leaned out, wearing his Stetson.

"Still playing John Wayne, Herr Spenzer?" Marcus asked. "It only makes you look twice the dork you already are, you know. Look at this palaver; there's a big spider in the shower or something."

Captain Swazzle reached Charm's cabin. The Punchinello's hand made a grab for the door handle but, with a splitting and rending of wood, the first of the ferocious spider creatures burst out and scuttled between the Captain's legs.

The watching children screamed in horror as the thing zigzagged swiftly over the lawn, veering from one side to the other as it chased them, nipping at their heels.

Marcus started and barged past Spencer, running into the cabin. Christina wailed but was too afraid to move. Lee and Charm were pursued round the tower. Then one of the other guards hurried over, yelling an attack cry. The Punchinello's spear came stabbing down, each blow narrowly missing the scurrying, eight-legged target.

Squawking in frustration, the guard dived forward. The spear drove clean through the furry body, and into the ground beneath. The long legs flailed and the fanged mouth gurgled in pain as bile-coloured blood came bubbling up. Then the legs became still and went limp.

"Bezuel kill!" the guard crowed in triumph, pulling the spear from the ground with the thing still impaled on it. "Doggy-Long-Legs deaded. Oh, yes, oh, yes…"

At the top of the tower, Jangler applauded and started to come down, mopping his face with a handkerchief in relief. The other Punchinellos gave nasal congratulations to Bezuel, who danced in a circle, twirling the grisly trophy above its scarlet hat.

"What the hell was it?" Lee breathed.

Charm hugged herself and rubbed her arms. "I dunno," she said. "But … there was more than one."

At that moment, the door to her cabin burst apart and a mass of snapping Doggy-Long-Legs came spilling out on to the lawn. Captain Swazzle gave a shrill howl and hopped out of their path as they swarmed into the camp. There were hundreds of them. The children who were still outside stared in disbelief. Then they had to run to save themselves from ravaging jaws.

fig. 37

Jangler retreated back up to the sentry platform and looked down at the dark, furry tide spreading out below.

"This should not be happening!" he protested anxiously as some of them came galloping towards the base of the tower. "Make it stop! Captain, do something!"

Seven of the spidery creatures leaped up on to the wooden framework and began crawling upwards. The rest of them went hunting for the youngest, easiest prey. When she saw part of the surging horde swerve aside and come sprinting straight for her on their gangling legs, instead of running back into her cabin, Christina panicked and fled away from it.

In the kitchen of the main block, Maggie and Esther heard the shrieks and unnatural noises outside. The Punchinello that was supervising had dashed off to answer his Captain's call. A moment later, Lee and Charm came tearing through the dining hall, pursued by dozens of nightmarish creatures. Lee threw his weight against the kitchen door, smashing it shut, crunching and squashing the legs and fierce faces that were almost inside. One of the spindly limbs snapped off and dropped to the floor, twitching.

Maggie and Esther gawped then cried out when more legs and teeth appeared beneath the door, seeking a way in.

"What are they?" Maggie asked.

"Hungry!" Lee hollered back. "That's all you need to know. Now break out the blades – or whatever you got in here!"

Seizing large catering knives from the magnetic rack, they hacked whatever came scrabbling under the door. But they forgot about the other exit and did not close the window. Doggy-Long-Legs were furiously chewing their way in behind them and more came creeping silently over the sill.

Out in the camp the five Punchinellos fought like nothing Marcus had ever seen. Watching from the safety of his cabin, he saw them go trampling into the midst of those spidery things with a burning fervour and an unquenchable relish for slaughter. Bloodshed and carnage was what they lived for.

"What chance have we got getting past just one of them?" he murmured. "Just look, they're loving this."

The guards' spears skewered countless eight-legged horrors and the heels of their boots crushed just as many furry bodies till the bones cracked and eyes popped out. When one of the things leaped up to rip out Captain Swazzle's throat, the Punchinello caught it in one hand and squeezed out its life. Another guard gave a piercing yowl when one of them sprang high, clamped its jaws around the great hooked nose and chomped its way forward.

Marcus pressed his own nose against the glass. He couldn't take in what he saw. Suddenly one of those things launched itself at his stunned face and smacked into the pane. The boy fell back. The Doggy-Long-Legs dropped on to the step, legs in the air, then righted itself and instantly started attacking the door.

"It's getting in!" Spencer cried, stumbling away between the beds.

"Where you going?" Marcus shouted angrily. "Get something to block this with!"

Spencer ran into the bathroom then out again and up the stairs to the mezzanine.

"There's nothing up there!" Marcus yelled at him.

Lumps of wet wood spat into the cabin as the fangs made a fist-sized hole in the door. A jet-black eye bulged behind it then the four front legs thrust inward, followed by the teeth. Marcus yanked off one of his trainers and battered the snarling intruder with it. The jaws frothed and jerked around, snapping until they bit through the sole, ripped the trainer from his hand and shredded it. Marcus jumped up and searched frantically for some other weapon. He snatched up a chair and whirled about, just as the thing came flying at him. He belted it away and it went spinning sideways, struck the wall and slid down behind one of the beds.

"Fifteen love to the Marcusmeister!" he yelled before edging away, scanning the floor, waiting for it to come scuttling out.

"Come on, you little leggy beggar," he muttered. "Come out where I can see you."

There was a rustle under the bed. Then suddenly it was under the next. Then it was beneath the furthest one. Marcus couldn't keep track. He turned and then it was on the other side of the room, racing under the beds there. Then there was silence.

Marcus looked right and left. He had no idea where it was hiding. He stepped further down the aisle, his eyes darting around. Nervously he put the chair down and stooped to peer under the beds.

Shooting from the shadows, the creature came screaming for his face. Marcus's reflexes saved him. He rolled sharply to the left and the Doggy-Long-Legs sailed over his head. It landed on the bed behind him, then came rampaging back for another attack. Galloping over the duvet, it bounded into the air. Marcus reached out, caught hold of three long legs then swung it around and bashed the body against the floor, again and again until the five other legs stopped scratching and clawing at him.

"Game, set and match," he shouted. "Who's the daddy? Who's the daddy?"

Spencer came tiptoeing down the stairs.

"Is it dead?" he asked fearfully.

"Come kiss it and find out," Marcus replied. "Fine cowboy you are, Sheriff Yellowboots."

Spencer looked beyond him to the door, where another pair of eyes was peering through the ragged hole.

Out in the camp, Jangler was swatting the Doggy-Long-Legs that clambered on to the tower platform with his clipboard and sending them crashing to the ground.

"The trouble with cat flaps," he told himself, out of breath with the exertion, "is they don't just let your own pets in, but anything else too! Mr Fellows really should have thought of this. Whatever next? Take that, you foul Gangle Hound!"

Many of the children had found refuge in the cabins, but some were still running about in terror. Christina was one of them. Six spider things pursued her, driving the seven-year-old towards the fence. The girl could go no further. She tried to climb the wire, but couldn't. She felt a thump in her back and a segmented leg hooked round her throat. The sound of grinding fangs drew close to her ear and she squeezed her eyes shut.

"Jabby jabby jabby!" a Punchinello squawked merrily as the Doggy-Long-Legs was harpooned from her shoulders. The guard spiked the others that surrounded her, like a murderous park keeper collecting gruesome litter, then hurried back into the main battle.

Christina gripped the wire mesh grimly, but she wasn't out of danger yet. There were still many more of those things marauding through the camp.

In the kitchen, Charm, Lee, Maggie and Esther had been pinned against the central table, fending the creatures off from every side. Armed with a masher and a cordless handblender, Maggie was a formidable force to be reckoned with. Churned-up corpses were piled in an oozing heap in front of her. Lee was the most deadly. He wielded a large knife with skill and precision and more than made up for Charm and Esther's weaker defence.

The creatures scurried around them warily. One of them got too close to Esther and Maggie's blender came swooping down, splattering the ghastly face around the room. That was enough. The others barked and yapped in defeat then went hurrying through the window and back out of the half-chewed doors.

"We beat them!" Maggie cried in amazement. "They've… er… legged it!"

"Not funny," Charm said.

Brandishing the knife, Lee moved to the exit.

"This ain't over yet," he said. "We have to get every one of those things or we won't never know what's gonna jump out at us."

"I'm not going out there," Esther refused.

"Fine," Lee told her. "You stay in here on your own. If they come back, let us know."

Esther went with them.

Outside, the Punchinellos were winning. Even the one with the half-eaten nose was still vigorously combating the insect-like vermin. The lawn was littered with speared bodies. Christina stepped through them as though in a dream. Her young eyes stared at the unreal spectacle and her ears were filled with the guards' bloodthirsty war cries. She saw Lee and the others come running from the main block, waving weapons in the air, and witnessed them joining the fight. The spider things were no longer attacking. They were in retreat.

One darted by, right in front of her, but she was no longer of any interest to them. Only escape mattered now. It headed for the fence and was up the mesh like lightning. It squeezed through the barbed wire at the top – then dropped down the other side. Others were doing the same. The Doggy-Long-Legs were leaving the camp and disappearing into the surrounding woods.

By the time Christina reached her cabin and returned to Jody, not a single one remained inside the perimeter.

"Are you all right?" a frantic Jody asked. "I couldn't do anything to help. I'm so sorry."

The little girl gazed distractedly out of the door, at the Punchinellos who were dancing a victory jig round the maypole.

"I'm OK," she answered in a voice devoid of emotion. "I don't have any scared left."

Out there Lee spat on the ground. "Damn," he cursed. "Too many got away. They can come back here any time."

Charm shuddered and he put his arm round her.

Jangler descended from the skelter tower. By the time he reached the ground, he was out of breath and his fright had turned to irritation. He saw Lee with the knife and ordered Captain Swazzle to deal with it. The Punchinello brought his spear to bear and the teenagers threw their weapons down.

"I will not have this!" Jangler berated them. "I will not have you bearing arms. These utensils must never leave the kitchen. If it happens again, there will be the severest punishments. From now on every item of cutlery will be accounted for at the end of each work shift and every meal."

"Oi!" Charm objected. "We was only stoppin' them 'orrible fings from makin' a meal of us!"

"You should be grateful!" Maggie added.

Jangler blustered and wiped his spectacles. Then he sighed and nodded. "Your assistance is appreciated," he said. "Although I'm sure the Captain and his stout lads would have managed quite well on their own. I shall permit one sausage for each aberrant this morning. Go see to it."

Maggie and Esther hurried back to the kitchen before he changed his mind.

"What were them fings?" Charm asked.

"They were the Gangle Hounds," he told her. "A pack of Haxxentrot's dangerous pets that dwell in and around the Forbidden Tower. Most disagreeable. They never normally leave the vicinity of her dreadful abode."

"How'd they get under my flamin' shower?"

The old man fidgeted and looked away. "I don't know," he replied, but Charm and Lee could tell he was lying. "A witch's trick perhaps? That would be so like her. At least they're gone."

"For now," Lee said. "What if they come back, in the night?"

"Oh, most unlikely," Jangler assured them. "The Doggy-Long-Legs crave minchet fruit most of all, even more than the Punchinellos do. That's why they were chasing you. They could smell it on your hands from yesterday. They'll be scampering through the forest right now, headed for the nearest crop and spinning nests in them. They won't be back, oh, no."

"But what if more come up that plughole?" Charm cried.

"Yes, that is unfortunate. I shall have that bathroom boarded up at once and made secure. Every damaged door must also be attended to. By the time you return from your work this evening, it shall be done. You females in that chalet will have to use other facilities from now on."

"I ain't stoppin' in that place!" she exclaimed. "I ain't fick!"

"You must," he told her. "And that is an end to it."

"But what about when we wanna go the bog after the lights go off? What we s'posed to do then?"

"I believe there are some buckets in the kitchen. I suggest you avail yourself of one of them."

"Eewwww! Mingin'!"

"Wait," Lee began slowly. "Did you say you're sending us outside, out there – to pick that muck again?"

"Of course. How else are you to earn your keep?"

"Even though you've just said those piranha spider mongrels are going to be hiding in them stinking bushes?"

Jangler smiled. "You will have to take especial care," he advised. "Watch where you put your hands; you'll be no use without fingers."

He turned his attention to the innumerable corpses covering the lawn, with the mini forest of jointed legs, bent at every angle. He frowned. This would never do. It would have to be dealt with forthwith. Calling Captain Swazzle over, he started giving instructions.

Lee and Charm walked back to the cabins. Alasdair was standing on the step of his, looking very pleased with himself. Whilst everyone else had been occupied, he had kept his head and made full use of the unexpected diversion by slipping unnoticed into Jangler's cabin. Maggie's phone was already being charged and the emails had been sent. It wouldn't be long now. The world would see what was really going on here.

Gazing across the camp, Alasdair's eyes rested on Jangler and Captain Swazzle. They appeared to be quarrelling.

"Spear too slow," Captain Swazzle was growling at the old man. "Not enough quick."

"But that's all you use in Mooncaster!" Jangler objected. "Why would you want to change? It's *the* Punchinello weapon."

The Captain gave a thin laugh. "We not in castle now," he said. "We here – in dream. We say spear no good for dream."

"Oh, maybe. Perhaps you're right. This grey place can be confusing. Sometimes I…" He checked himself and wrote on his clipboard. "So I'll order you and your valiant crew some new weapons. What alternatives would you prefer? Swords? Axes? Crossbows even? How about a mace or two?"

The Punchinello shook his ugly head and his nasal voice demanded, "We want guns. Plenty guns. *Bang bang* – yes."

16

IT WAS ALMOST midday by the time the children were sent out of the camp to work. The Punchinellos had massed the Doggy-Long-Legs bodies in a great pile, including the ones from the kitchen, where Maggie and Esther scrubbed every surface clean. The ration of sausages was received gladly by everyone – except Jody. She let Christina have hers and Maggie gave her two of the mysterious apples to make up for it. They were careful not to let Jangler or the guards know about them, but where had the delicious apples come from? Only Lee knew the answer to that and he pretended to be as ignorant as the rest.

Later that evening, after an exhausting afternoon picking minchet, fearful of what might be lurking within every shadowy thicket, the work parties returned. In their absence, workmen had visited the camp once more and the chewed doors had been crudely boarded over. The entrance to the bathroom in Charm's cabin had been nailed shut and stout planks had been fixed across the frame.

"Them spider fings could bite through that faster than it takes me to put me lipgloss on," Charm commented. "This place ain't safe. I won't get a wink of sleep now."

With one bathroom out of commission, the queues for showers in the other chalets were longer than usual. Whilst the children tried to cleanse themselves of the day's stink and ate their soup, the Punchinellos built a small bonfire, using the workmen's leftover wood. At first the young internees thought it was to burn the bodies on, but they were wrong. They soon realised the five Punchinellos were *cooking* the Doggy-Long-Legs.

Using their spears as toasting forks, they turned the corpses over in the flames. The spindly legs frazzled and curled up around the charring bodies. A pungent reek of black smoke rose high above the camp. Taking swigs from jars of wine, the guards sang dirty songs. It was customary for the castle guards to celebrate and carouse after winning a skirmish and they intended to play their parts to the nth degree. The one with the half-eaten nose now wore a tight bandage and looked strangely deformed in the company of the others.

Fresh from the shower, Marcus stared out at them.

"Tonight would have been the perfect time to get out of this place," he said. "They're getting paralytic. We could escape dead easy."

"Then where would you go?" Lee asked.

"Nearest village. There's one a couple of miles that way. We get there, nick a car and burn rubber."

"And every police force and zombie vigilante in the country will be after you."

Outside, by the fire, the Punchinello called Yikker put the wine down, sniffed the air and a snarl rippled along his top lip. He turned towards the cabin, where Marcus was standing in the doorway, and clenched his large fists.

"Got to be better than being stuck here with them," the teenager said, moving out of sight when he saw Yikker glowering at him. "There'll be another night like this and they'll get rat-faced again. I'll have something more definite worked out by then. You coming with me?"

Lee shook his head. "You gotta get a better plan than that!" he said. "Even if you could get over the fence, you wouldn't last three hours out there."

Marcus said nothing. He walked back, between the beds, then examined the open area beneath the stairs. Crouching down, he pulled the edge of the beige carpet and peeled it back. There was a sheet of plywood underneath. The chalets were merely wooden boxes, raised off the ground by concrete blocks. Under this floor there was nothing, just a void and then the soil. An idea began to form in Marcus's mind.

Alasdair had taken his guitar to Jody's cabin and was playing it softly, singing 'Fields of Gold'. He really was very good.

Resting her head on the pillow, eyes lightly closed, Jody imagined being free and walking "among the fields of barley". Close by, Christina curled up on her bed, entranced. Gradually the other girls in there broke off their conversations and turned to listen. The two on the mezzanine crept down to sit on the stairs. The sandy-haired Scot held them spellbound. There was a sadness and a yearning, in the song and in his voice, that reached deep inside and made them remember how life had been, before one book had changed it all. At that moment, they felt the contrast and the pain of what they had lost more keenly than ever.

Watching the Punchinellos from the door, Maggie gagged as she saw them crunch their teeth into the roasted Doggy-Long-Legs.

"Barfarama!" she uttered in revulsion. And the spell of the song was broken. "I can't believe they're eating those things! In fact, they're not just eating, they're bingeing on them."

"Can ye no?" Alasdair asked. "Two days ago would ye have believed you'd be eating kitchen rubbish?"

"That's different," the girl said.

"No, it's not," Jody joined in, nettled that the music had been interrupted. "It's just a shift in what you see as normal. We don't even question what those guards are now – or where they come from. We've accepted them as part of our life here. This time next week, or the week after, you might be glad of some roasted spider-mouth monsters to eat."

Maggie shivered. "Not ruddy likely," she said.

"We're going to see a lot of changes," Jody told them gravely. "I've been thinking about it – not much else I can do at the minute. It's going to get awful worse here. Think about the absolute basic stuff, like when the soap runs out – or the toothpaste, or the loo roll. What happens then?"

"I hadn't thought about that," Maggie confessed. "Don't you think the old guy will replace it?"

Jody laughed. "You kidding?" she said. "Take a look at my back if you want to see what he thinks of us. And how about malnutrition? We can't live on just soup or expect phantom apples to appear from nowhere. We're going to start getting weak and sick. You look thinner in the face already."

"I'm non-stop starving. It's driving me mental. My body isn't used to this."

"It will be. And how about this one – what sort of germs or diseases do those guards carry? Could be as strange and as alien as they are. As for the spider things, don't tell me they weren't crawling with fleas or lice or God knows what else. You think we're going to be immune to that?"

"Aliens?" Maggie muttered. "Sooner you're up and about again the better. You're driving yourself crackers lying there all day. Oh, I could kill for some cheese and crackers… a great big lump of cheddar would be awesome. Why does everything relate back to food?"

Alasdair played a loud chord to cut through their misery.

"We willnae be here much longer," he promised. "I bet you we'll be oot of this hellhole this time next week."

"Dream on!" Jody mocked, rolling her eyes.

Alasdair produced the phone from his pocket and handed it to Maggie.

"Fully charged and the emails went oot this morning," he boasted. "All we got to do noo is wait. I hoped there might be something on the news sites by noo, but no. Probably keeping it hush-hush till they send the troops in."

"You're amazing!" Maggie declared. "How'd you manage it?"

"The name's Bond," the boy replied, raising one eyebrow. "Alasdair Bond."

"You said your name was Alasdair Mackenzie," Christina disputed.

"It were a joke."

Maggie was so excited by the news she stood up and waved the phone in the air. If Alasdair hadn't been distracted, he would have stopped her.

"Hey, girls!" she called to the others in the cabin. "We're getting out of here!"

They stared back at her sceptically.

"Heard that one before," a girl called Sally said.

"I'll wait till the coach is here before I start packing," another added with weary cynicism.

Maggie folded her arms, disappointed by the unimpressed reaction. "It's true," she insisted. "Alasdair's positive about it. You're a jaded lot. I'm going to tell everyone else."

She turned to leave but Alasdair pulled her back.

"What do ye think you're doing?" he asked.

"Popping next door. Why?"

"The fewer folk that know the better!" he said. "I cannae believe you just blabbed to everyone in here. I dinnae want old Mainwaring to overhear someone gassing about it."

Maggie huffed. "No one'd be that stupid," she said, dismissing his concern with a shrug.

Alasdair could see she wasn't going to listen to reason. She was too hungry to spread the news. He wished he'd kept his own mouth shut.

"Well, dinnae take the phone wi' you," he said firmly.

Maggie dearly wanted to show it to everyone else, but perhaps he had a point.

"Hide it in your case for now," Jody suggested.

"Oh, all right," she agreed.

Maggie tucked the phone in among her clothes then hurried out to spread the happy tidings.

"She's a liability," Alasdair said. "Keep an eye on her. Dinnae let her use it after it gets dark. Every guard in the camp'd see the light. She'd only be wasting the battery on YouTube or Angry Birds or something equally useless. I've a mind to take the phone back to my cabin."

"It's not yours," Christina told him. "That's stealing."

"I dinnae care. It's our only contact wi' the outside world. We cannae afford to let that big-mouth risk losing it."

"Put it under my mattress," Jody said. "Then she can't accuse you of taking it. I'll have a word. I'll say we thought it best to hide it somewhere

safer. It's best if she doesnae know where it is. She knows what she's like
– the slightest bit of temptation and she gives in."

"Putting her in charge of the kitchen were a bad idea then," Alasdair
said, making sure no one was looking as he removed the phone from
Maggie's case and slid it under the bed.

"She wouldn't eat more than her share," Jody told him. "She's all right
she is."

Alasdair picked up his guitar. "I'm just in a cranky mood," he sighed.
"Impatient to get oot of here, I suppose. I'll leave you fair lassies and see
ye in the morning."

Returning to his own cabin, the Scot glanced over at the fire where
the Punchinellos were glugging down the wine. He moistened his lips.
He so wanted a drink. Just then Maggie emerged from one of the other
cabins and hurried into another. To his surprise, he felt a twinge of envy.
He wished he could be the one to tell Lee everything had worked out fine
without his help.

"Dinnae be so petty," he admonished himself. He entered his cabin and
lay on his bed, wondering how soon they would be liberated.

The night closed in. Long after lights out the guards continued to sit
around the fire, hooting and snorting, squawking to one another in a
filthy-sounding, quacking language of their own. Eventually four of them
staggered and waddled back to their own chalet whilst the other tried to
climb the steps of the skelter tower, but fell asleep halfway up.

In the darkness of the cabin, Lee stared blindly at the pitched ceiling
above his bed. Marcus was already fast asleep in the one nearby. Lee's
nose wrinkled. There was a peculiar smell coming from the other end of
the mezzanine. Why didn't Marcus spray his trainers as well as the rest of
him?

Lee closed his eyes and started murmuring the words of *Dancing
Jax*. Tonight would be a perfect time to return with something a bit more

ambitious and substantial than apples. He had taken an enormous risk slipping out with them first thing that morning. He was surprised the sentry in the tower hadn't spotted him. He didn't know it was glued to Spencer's media player at the time, having watched five Westerns through the night.

Lee felt the usual pain in his heart and the rush of blasting cold. His eardrums thumped and the pit of his stomach dropped as though he was falling…

It was a frosty winter's night. The moon was in a waxing crescent and the diamond dust of floating ice in the sharp air ringed it around with a halo.

Lee looked up and shivered. He wasn't dressed for this sort of weather. His breath blew out in clouds of grey vapour and he rubbed his pimpling forearms as he swayed unsteadily. The disorientation he always felt when first arriving here never lasted long. He gazed about him, hoping to see the by now familiar landmarks. He appeared to be in a meadow. Dark shapes of twisted, naked trees and looming pines grew far off on his left and bare, craggy rocks climbed over to his right. There was no sign of the White Castle, or the village. He still hadn't learned how to command the wheres and whens of his entrances here. There had to be a way of influencing them, but that control was eluding him.

"You gotta hone your technique," he told himself. "You is plain wack at this."

He took a step forward and jumped back instantly. His trainer had cracked through a layer of ice and freezing water engulfed his foot.

"Every damn time!" he grumbled.

Kicking the dead grasses and reeds that surrounded him aside, he discovered he was on a narrow strip of spongy ground. Everywhere else was swampy water. The boy's swearing formed stuttering, foggy shapes in the air. He had absolutely no idea whereabouts in the world of *Dancing Jax* he was. For all he knew he might even be beyond one of the thirteen hills. He tried to visualise the map at the front of the book. Was there anywhere like this bog drawn there? He couldn't remember.

Twisting about, he tested the ground carefully before taking another step. It seemed firm behind him so he progressed slowly that way, creeping bit by bit through the marsh. He didn't know where he was headed, but as long as this soggy, ice-crackling path led to solid, dry earth that was good enough. If he could make it to those trees and beyond, there might be a view he would recognise. He had been hoping to reach the village tonight and steal some loaves from the miller. That would make Maggie's eyes pop out in the morning.

The moon rose higher. It was so bright it cast a ghostly sheen over the landscape. The only sounds were the dry rustle of the dead grasses and the occasional plop or gurgle when a bubble rose to the surface beyond the frozen edges, so when Lee heard high-pitched squeaking overhead, he almost toppled over in shock. Glancing up, he saw black, winged shapes flapping through the dark.

"Bats," he said. "Like this place isn't goth enough already?"

He tracked their course for some moments then sucked the bitter air between his teeth when he saw where they were headed. He hadn't noticed it before. It was partly hidden by the shrouding pines. But there, in the middle distance, was a solitary tower.

Silhouetted against the wintry sky, it stood bleak and threatening. The frosty moonlight gleamed dimly on its rough stonework and curved round the tiled pinnacle in the centre of the crenellated crown. Fearsome spikes jutted from the tapering sides and the faintest greenish glow near the top betrayed an arched, open window.

"*Okaaaay*," Lee murmured uneasily. "Wild guess – that ain't the Fairy Godmother's penthouse crib."

It was time to go. The miller's bread could wait for another day. He wasn't going to stop here another minute more. He turned around to retrace his squelching, splintering steps, then halted.

A soft pink light was drifting behind the grasses. A glimmering rosy flame was floating over the water.

"Oh, don't you be a will-o'-the-wisp!" he hissed. "You guys is always bad news!"

Uncertain what to do, he waited and the glow sailed nearer until he finally got a proper look. It wasn't a will-o'-the-*wisp.*

The flame was inside a small, jewel-like lantern, no bigger than his cigarette lighter. The lantern was swinging from an ornate hook above a shapely, miniature boat with delicate, filigree dragonfly wings at the stern. It was all made from gleaming, glinting gold but only the size of a shoebox. Sitting upon silken cushions within was a doll, with a beautiful, cherubic face and long, golden hair that tumbled over her shoulders. Live butterflies, drowsy with the cold, were sewn into those cascading tresses and she wore a gossamer gown, embroidered with silver flowers and tiny crystals. Just as Lee was wondering what on earth a doll in a blingy boat was doing out here on a night like this, she moved. With a jolt, he realised she was real.

The boat continued to sail slowly by on the marsh's sluggish current. The girl turned to look at him and her pale face dimpled in surprise.

"By the good earth's blood!" she declared. "What are you? You are tall as a tree and your visage is as the very night. Are you a giant emissary sent by the King?"

Lee overcame his own shock and grinned at her. This sick place was full of mad surprises.

"No," he said. "I don't have nuthin' to do with the castle guys if I can help it."

"Not those kings, silly," she laughed sweetly. "There are many monarchs above and below this land. I myself am Telein – daughter to the king 'neath the stone hill."

"Well, hello, Princess," he answered, smirking as he made a clumsy bow.

"You are not of the Marsh King's court? Strange, there ought to be someone here to greet me. 'Tis most discourteous."

"I'm just passin' through," he replied. "Don't know no Marsh King."

Telein sat forward in the boat and cupped a hand round her mouth. "Then you are indeed fortunate," she whispered. "'Tis rumoured he is uncommon ugly."

Lee chuckled. He liked this dainty princess.

"Mind if I aks a personal question?" he ventured.

"I do not see how I could prevent it," she replied pertly. "But I may choose to withhold my answer."

"Don't mean no disrespect, nor nuthin', so don't take this the wrong way, but – is you a fairy or a gnome or elf or what?"

Telein rocked back on her cushions and clapped her hands in amusement.

"Verily you are an untutored fellow!" she laughed. "I am of the tribe of Danu. In truth, could you not tell? Are we so forgotten?"

"I'm a real newbie round these parts."

Her bright green eyes stared off into the gloom. "We were here long before the Dawn Prince raised the walls of Mooncaster," she said. "And before the Lamia fouled the sky. But we forsook this upper world, ages past, and made our abode deep below – in the golden caves."

Lee wasn't any wiser but he let it pass and crouched down to be level with her. She really did have the prettiest, cutest face. The soft lantern light danced in the boat's burnished timbers and reflected up into her eyes – making them sparkle with brilliant, emerald fires.

He wished he still had his phone to take a photo. He didn't know enough fancy words to ever describe her. A Victorian romantic painter like Millais could have conveyed the intangible bloom in her cheek, the lustre of her curls and the hint of a smile that pulled and played at the corners of her lips. And a poet would have expressed the exquisite, otherworldly nature of this vision far more eloquently than Lee could ever hope to articulate.

"So why's you out in your iddy-biddy, pimped-up dinghy tonight?" he asked.

"I journey to see the Marsh King," she explained. "From the rock mouth I have travelled, whence I joined the poisoned stream and passed through the empty, sleeping land. Now my voyage is ending. Each midwinter a maiden of the Danu must come pay tribute to the ruler of this kingdom. This year the honour is mine."

"Tribute? What, sing and dance and tell him he's the greatest – crap like that?"

She gurgled with laughter. "I am no nightingale," she said. "The king's ears shall be sorely grieved if he commands me to sing. Lilts and refrains trickle ever through my fingers."

"Ha, you an' me both. I can't hold a tune either! Don't stop me though."

Telein smoothed the folds of her gown. "Would that singing were my only duty this night," she said with a heartfelt sigh.

"Whassup?" Lee asked gently.

She clasped her tiny hands beneath her chin to keep it from trembling. "This is my bride night," she pronounced. "And this vessel is my dowry."

"No way! You're marrying that uglord? What the hell for?"

"The Marsh King takes a new wife every midwinter," she explained solemnly. "It is the bargain 'twixt our peoples. A meagre price to pay for peace, else he will send his army to assail our golden chambers. It has been thus for many years."

"It's extortion is what it is."

"You speak a puzzling tongue, my night-faced giant."

"Right now I'm fluent in the language of Angrymad. You can't get wed to no serial sleazebag gangster you never seen! What happened to all them other wives? How many does he want?"

Telein shook her head. "No one knows," she answered with a worried frown. "Once the stream bears the brides from our hill, neither word nor token ever comes back to us."

"Girl – your Royal Highness – you gotta get outta that tacky ride! Right now!"

"I cannot. I shall do my duty. The bargain must be kept. The wary peace will hold."

A sudden surge in the current took hold of the glittering craft and it was whisked further out over the marsh. Lee jumped up and ran along the boggy causeway to keep pace with it, but the boat whirled unerringly closer to the centre of the freezing waters.

"Honey!" he shouted. "Trust me, get outta there."

"I am confounded as to why there is no retinue to greet me," she murmured, peering into the empty darkness beyond the reach of the lantern's rosy light. "Where are his halls and mansions?"

"Princess!" Lee yelled. "You listen to me! Get back here – fast as you can."

She looked around her, distracted. This wasn't how it was supposed to be. Where was the music? The feasting? The cheering subjects? Her unease turned to fear. This evil, desolate place was heavy with menace and danger. She had to get away.

"My giant!" she hailed across the marsh. "Save me. I beg you. I cannot swim!"

Lee was already kicking off his trainers and wading into the icy swamp. He had only advanced two paces when the sucking mud pulled him down and closed about his waist. He had to fight to dredge himself back to the bank and lay there, gasping and steaming from the effort. He couldn't reach her. There was nothing he could do. He had to think, quickly.

"Use your hands as paddles!" he shouted desperately. "It's the only way!"

Nodding, she knelt forward into the prow and put out her arms.

And then it happened. The boat pitched alarmingly as huge bubbles erupted beneath it. The lantern swung off its hook and splashed into the foaming water. It glimmered like a pink star as it journeyed down into the murk and Telein shrieked in horror and despair. The dwindling glow had disclosed a vast, dark shape rising from the miry deep.

The boat tipped and capsized. The golden timbers sank instantly. The princess was flung clear and she thrashed her tiny hands, trying to keep afloat.

An immense island of slime and sludge lifted up behind her and founts of black mud squirted from crusted nostrils. Then two great speckled eyes blinked open. It was an immense and ancient frog, grown bloated and huge over countless years. The Marsh King was here.

Lee roared at the princess to kick with her legs and waved his arms to show how to pull herself through the frothing waves.

"Don't look back!" he bawled at her, his own legs shaking at the sight and stench of that monster. "Keep looking straight at me; don't you turn round. Come on! Swim to me. You can do this! Come on!"

She struggled and spluttered, bobbing up and down on violent, scummy swells as Lee looked on helplessly.

The Marsh King's tawny eyes roved over the foaming surface of its watery realm and fixed on Telein's terrified floundering. The glistening ridges of its head slid forward silently and a cavernous mouth opened, revealing a row of needle-like teeth. It bit down hard.

Lee fell back and covered his face. The princess's agonised screams did not last long. The Marsh King champed and chewed and swallowed her down. Then it swung around and its hungry stare fell on Lee.

The horror-stricken boy was on his hands and knees. He felt sick. He had to get out of this psychotic train wreck of a place. He couldn't take any more.

Lee slithered to his feet. Then fell down again. His foot was caught. He turned to look and yelled. The end of a pallid, mottled tongue was wrapped about his ankle. The rest stretched across the marsh, down into the enormous frog's mouth. Then it began to drag him from the bank.

The teenager kicked at the tongue with his other foot, but it was no use. It was hard as iron. He lashed out with his fists and tore at it with his fingers, but it was hopeless and he was towed back into the water.

Frantic, he reached into the pocket of his trackie bottoms and took out a penknife. Then he stabbed and slashed like a maniac. Black blood gushed out and the Marsh King bellowed. The tongue whipped back into the awful mouth and the eyes enlarged with wrath. The swamp boiled as the monster reared up and plunged forward.

Lee hauled himself from the mud and ran over the quaking path, snatching his Nikes as he lurched by. The Marsh King's gargantuan bulk came lumbering after. The boy heard the splayed, webbed feet slapping over the bank at horrible speed and clouds of angry breath came billowing around him. He slammed his fears to the back of his mind and focused on getting back – to that other place, what he knew as the real world. He summoned the memory of the cabin; the feathery duvet beneath him, even the overpowering smells of Marcus's shower gel and body spray… He leaped into the air and the Marsh King bore down.

Lee's legs kicked and he hit out with his fists. Then he fell off the bed.

It was dark but warm and dry and Marcus was snoring. Lee almost wept in relief. He was back and he was covered in mud. Exhausted and distraught at what he had seen, he stumbled downstairs and hit the shower, still fully dressed.

"That were too close," he told himself. "Last time – that were the last time."

Ten minutes later, his wrung-out clothes were hanging over the mezzanine banister. He threw off the muddy duvet and collapsed on to the bed. He prayed he wouldn't be haunted by images of Telein, but knew he would never forget that last glimpse of her, disappearing down the monster's throat.

Sleep claimed him.

It was after midnight when the Bakelite devices began to hum and unconsciousness stole over the children. Above their heads the dials glowed and static crackled. Another creaky song from the 1930s came winding from the brass grill.

> Roll up the carpet,
> push back the chairs,
> get some music on the radio.

From one of the cabins a figure crept out into the night. It made its way stealthily in front of the others. Reaching the far end, it stooped at the gaoler's door.

> *When you're feeling tired of dancing,*
> *try and find a place to park.*
> *Go to any cosy corner,*
> *take advantage of the dark.*

Jangler was dozing in his armchair with a handkerchief over his face, so he didn't notice when one of the camp's postcards, present in every bedside drawer, slipped in over the carpet. On the back, written in Austerly Fellows' unmistakable, forthright hand, a simple message read:

My dear Lockpick,
I thought you should know - there is a mobile phone
hidden in this camp.

17

IT WASN'T QUITE light when the handbell rang outside the chalets. Jangler swung it vigorously. The postcard was stuffed into his pocket. He had just overseen the departure of the latest transit van of new arrivals from the camp and was fairly confident nothing else had come through. Now it was time to act on this information from Mr Fellows.

Captain Swazzle and three of his guards came staggering from their hut, clasping their pounding heads. Their beady eyes were redder than usual.

"Get the aberrants out here!" the old man ordered brusquely. "Without delay!"

The Captain squawked at the other Punchinellos and they went barging into the cabins, where the children were slowly coming round, aching and bruised as usual.

Still blinking, and before they had a chance to get dressed, they were lined up in rows outside. Captain Swazzle made them bow and curtsy. Even Jody was hauled out and forced to stand with them. The girl gritted her teeth. Her back was healing slowly, but it stung like mad. At her side, Christina slipped her hand into hers.

"Why's he so cross?" the seven-year-old whispered.

Jody shook her head. No one knew. They hadn't seen the old man possessed by this cold rage before.

"It's loads earlier than normal," Maggie murmured. "What's going on?"

"I've not put me face on yet," Charm grumbled.

Lee stared at the ground. He didn't want to catch anyone's eye. He hadn't recovered from his harrowing experience in the Frog Marsh. He didn't know if he ever would.

Jangler's face was grave and severe.

"A despicable attempt has been made to thwart my Lord's great design," he began. "Bleating emails were dispatched from this camp to certain news desks in the United States. Complaints were made about your treatment here, accompanied by a photograph of the dead boy."

Alasdair's heart jumped. How did he know that? The other children stirred uncomfortably. Spencer fidgeted with his hands. He wished he had brought his Stetson out here with him. He was beginning to feel anxious whenever he was parted from it.

"There are those among you who believe they deserve better," the old man continued scornfully. "To do so questions the wisdom of the Holy Enchanter. For the final time I will say this: you are the lowest form of unwelcome parasite to crawl upon the surface of this dream world. You are tolerated purely because of my Lord's grace and compassion. Were it my choice, you would be slaughtered where you stand right now. But I am a good and loyal servant, so I must keep you alive. But know this, from here on there will be no more leniency. If rules continue to be flouted, the punishments will make you wish the sordid fumblings of your parents had never taken place."

Alasdair's jaw muscles tightened. Soon that overinflated little oaf would stand trial for crimes against humanity and he couldn't wait to give evidence.

Jangler had a quick, inaudible conversation with Captain Swazzle, who then shouted at the Punchinellos in their own language and called the one down from the skelter tower. The guards went back into the cabins and started searching, turning over beds and ransacking cases.

"Och, no," Alasdair breathed. It was obvious what they were hunting for.

Maggie saw Marcus biting the inside of his cheek. He looked sick with worry. What was he hiding? Before she could begin to speculate, Yikker came striding out of her cabin with the phone and Anchu swaggered from Alasdair's, twirling the charger. Jangler made them show him where the items had been found then returned to his step.

"So," he said coldly. "Once again you demonstrate I have been too tender-hearted. A whipping was not lesson enough. I was too mild. This time it must be more memorable, more lasting. Take her away!"

Captain Swazzle strode towards the children. "Jody Jody Jody…" he snickered, wagging a finger.

The girl sagged and shook her head. "Please, no!" she pleaded. "Not again!"

"You'll have the skin off her back!" Maggie cried.

"It wasnae her!" Alasdair yelled. "It were me. I sent them emails! She had nothing to do wi' it. I hid the phone under her mattress. She didnae know anything about it. Leave her alone. Get your filthy hands off her!"

Not thinking of his own safety, he ran at the Captain. With one effortless smack, Swazzle sent him flying. Then he caught hold of Jody and dragged her from the line. Christina clutched at her, but the Punchinello thrust the little girl aside.

"Jody Jody Jody…" he taunted, marching her away.

Alasdair would have sprung back up, but Yikker was ready with a spear and eager for him to do something reckless. The other guards levelled their weapons at the rest of them.

"Stay down!" Marcus's voice called.

The young prisoners stared helplessly after Swazzle and the girl. Where was she being taken? The Captain skipped a little dance. Her fear was glorious to see. Jody thought she was going to be tied to the maypole but, when they passed it, she became even more afraid.

"Where we going?" she cried.

"To special place," Swazzle cackled. "Just for Jody. Lucky Jody. It nice – it snug."

He pushed and pulled her past the cabins, towards the main block where he hauled her down the side and out of sight. Presently the others heard a confused clangorous din of metal objects being slung to the ground, quickly followed by the girl's muffled screams and frenzied hammering.

"What's happening?" Maggie cried. The other guards sniggered.

"You're stark raving mad!" Alasdair yelled at Jangler. "The UN are gonna crucify you!"

"The UN?" Jangler repeated, with a mystified lift of his eyebrows. "Oh, you think your puling missives achieved something, do you?"

"You'll find oot soon enough!"

The old man clasped his hands in front of him and gave a cruel smile. "Dear Miss Kryzewski and Sam have been so frightfully busy," he said proudly. "Ever since their return to America they have been exceedingly liberal with the contents of several crates that have been sitting patiently in the docks for a month or more. They were especially generous in the major newsrooms. I'm afraid, within moments of your tattling emails arriving, they were deleted."

Alasdair's face fell. "That's no true!" he said.

"Aberrants are not worth lying to," came the contemptuous response.

The boy's hopes were utterly crushed. He was devastated. It felt worse than if the Punchinello's spear had pierced him.

A quacking laugh sounded over by the main block and Captain Swazzle waddled back into view. The urgent hammering continued, together with Jody's stifled screams to be let out.

"Where is she?" Maggie demanded. "What's he done with her?"

Jangler was only too delighted to explain. "You may not have observed a small, padlocked door around the back of that building," he said. "It's a poky little cupboard of a thing, used to store tools and suchlike. The shovel I loaned you the other day is kept there. Or rather it was. I do believe our gallant Captain has just divested it of those handy sundries and deposited the interfering Jody Barnes within. And there she will remain, for three days and three nights. During which time she will be given no food and no water and, it is to be hoped, learn the error of her ways. During the period of her confinement, if any of you are caught trying to communicate with her, she shall remain an extra three days and nights and you will first be whipped and then thrown in there the moment she is let out. Do I make myself clear?"

The children were too shocked and aghast to react.

"Three days?" Alasdair eventually said. "That's inhuman! It's torture!"

"And now," the old man addressed him, "what of you? So much to say for yourself, so self-righteous, so indignant, so exceedingly tiresome. This phone cable was discovered in your belongings. Whatever shall we do with you?"

"I dinnae care!" the boy shouted in defiance.

Jangler considered a moment then muttered something to Captain Swazzle who gave a raucous laugh and disappeared into the Scot's cabin. When the Punchinello returned, it was carrying the boy's guitar.

"I've heard you trying to play this," Jangler declared with a disdainful sniff. "There are few things worse than amateurs inflicting their lamentable efforts on others. Thankfully the hallowed text has consigned those dismal television talent contests to the past. I view what is about to happen as a benevolent act in the interests of the public ear. Captain, if you please."

Swazzle grinned and proceeded to smash the guitar against the corner of the cabin. Then he threw the splintered body down and trampled the ragged remnants into even smaller fragments.

"Most gratifying," Jangler remarked. "That was the most tuneful sound the deplorable instrument has made in the whole time it's been here. Now for the other part of the punishment. Captain, if you would be so kind – break one of his hands."

Still clutching the stump of the fretboard, its severed strings waving in the air, the Punchinello came striding over to Alasdair. The other children flinched and looked away. Jangler blinked up at the brightening sky.

"I think we're in for a spot of rain later," he observed.

No one knew how Alasdair got through the rest of that day. After Swazzle had gloatingly obeyed the order, the boy writhed on the ground, howling. Jangler took no notice and forbade any of the children to go to him until the first reading from *Dancing Jax* was over. Once that was done, to ensure they all realised the futility of rebellion, he announced they too would do without food for the next twenty-four hours.

As soon as permission was granted, Marcus raced to the main block where the medical kit had been returned to the kitchen. On his way back he halted. Jody had stopped thumping against the door of the tool cupboard, but he could hear her sobbing in there. The tools were still strewn over the grass. The boy glanced warily around. He wasn't in sight of any guard. It was the work of a moment to pick up a trowel and tuck the blade into the waistband of his joggers and cover the handle with his shirt. Then he ran back to the others.

Charm watched Lee helping Alasdair to his feet.

"Can I help?" she offered.

Lee glanced at her, but all he saw was the face of the tiny princess in the golden boat. He shook his head quickly and turned away.

"You all right?" she asked.

"What do you see about this situation that could possibly be all right?" he snapped back.

Charm took a step back. "Sorry," she said hesitantly. "I was only…"

"Well, don't!"

She moved away, not understanding what she had done to upset him. Standing nearby, Bezuel the guard had seen what had happened and came prowling over.

"No be sad," the Punchinello wheezed in her ear. "You pretty. Me want."

His voice made her jump and she was unnerved to find him leaning in so close. She hated the way those eyes ogled her and his breath was rank. Making a hurried excuse, she dodged aside and got away.

"Bezuel want eat you," the guard called after her.

The girl didn't know how literally he meant that. The guard's attention made her feel ill and she needed to have a hot shower.

Lee had helped Alasdair into his cabin where Maggie tried to inspect the injuries to his hand.

307

"Don't you touch me!" the Scot snarled.

"I know it hurts, babes," she said soothingly. "But I've got to look at it. It needs bandaging."

"Fine! But no by you. Get oot!"

Maggie drew away in surprise. "Why? What've I done?"

"What have you done?" Alasdair snapped vehemently. "This is all your fault. You and that fat mouth o' yours! I told you not to go shootin' your gob off to everyone last night aboot the phone, but you wouldnae listen! That old bumwipe musta heard you."

The girl uttered a dismal cry. "I didn't know!" she spluttered. "I didn't think…"

"You never think!" he shouted. "Get oot!"

"Best if you go," Lee advised her.

Maggie ran out in tears, blundering into Marcus as he came in with the medical kit.

"What's up with you?" he asked.

"Out of my way!" she said, pushing past. She returned to her own cabin, where Christina was tidying Jody's bed.

"He thinks it's my fault," she wept.

The seven-year-old straightened the pillow, pulling out the corners, making it perfect. Then she sat on her own bed.

"It is," she said matter-of-factly, hurting Maggie even more. "You can't keep secrets. My Jody would be here if it weren't for you. You're why she's been locked up and I can't see her."

Marcus, meanwhile, was wondering how to bind Alasdair's hand and put his arm in a sling.

"Why don't you get one of the girls to do this?" he asked. "Maggie's been doing great so far, changing dressings and seeing to cuts and bites."

"Just do the best you can," Lee urged.

"I'm no first-aider," Marcus confessed. "Mind you – I never used to miss an episode of *Casualty* – oh, those sexy nurses!"

"Does your libido no ever stop?" the Scot asked through gritted teeth.

His face was bleached of colour and pouring with sweat.

"Sorry there's no painkillers, dude," Marcus said. "You'll just have to bite on a bullet like they do in films."

"I would if I had one!"

Lee looked around the cabin and grunted. He passed Alasdair a copy of *Dancing Jax* that was lying on the floor; strange how these were always scattered about the carpet first thing in the morning.

"Chew on that," he said.

"As long as it doesnae poison me," the Scot replied, taking it with his good hand and clamping the spine between his teeth.

"Why should you be any different?" Lee remarked.

Marcus started bandaging the broken hand. Even though the circumstances were appalling, he was secretly pleased that he had finally managed to be accepted by these two. As nightmarish as life in this camp was, he no longer felt so alone. He tried to be as gentle as possible and slung Alasdair's arm up to the opposite shoulder.

"I've no idea if it's the right thing to do or what," he said. "That hand's a mess. You won't be playing the banjo again for a while, amigo."

Alasdair leaned gingerly against the headboard. "Dinnae call me that, ya posing ponce," he said.

They were both making light of it because they knew the hand would never mend properly, if at all. Even if it had been attended to by a surgeon, it probably wouldn't be the same again. Captain Swazzle had been too thorough.

"But it's no my hand I'm worried aboot," Alasdair said. "Can a person survive three days wi'out water?"

Marcus chewed his bottom lip. "I remember reading an article in a fitness magazine," he began. "It was all about hydration. It said three to four days is the max the human body can manage."

"So she could die in there?"

"It won't come to that; the old guy will come round. He blows hot and cold he does."

"But if he doesnae?"

"Then she'll be in a real bad way when she gets out. But he'll change his mind."

Marcus closed the medical kit. Before he sealed it, a glint from the scissors it contained flashed across his eyes. It was like a light going on in his head. They would be incredibly useful. He would have to appropriate them later.

"So," he said, changing the subject. "What was the matter with Big Mags just now?"

Alasdair sneered. "I told her she's to blame for this," he said. "Useless fat lump that she is."

"Woah, bit strong for you, that. Thought I was the crude and crass one here?"

"She's lost us our only link to the outside world," the Scot said bitterly. "Our one chance of getting oot o' here. I dinnae have no sympathy for her, the great thick munter."

"She's overweight, not stupid. I'm sure she didn't do it on purpose."

Lee wasn't so certain. "This is the second time the old guy's been tipped off," he said. "First he knew who wrecked that model of the castle, now this."

"That adds up noo," Alasdair muttered, thinking it over. "I didnae trust her from the start. I knew there was something fishy aboot the way she turned up. She's never been one of us."

"Wait," Marcus spoke up. "You know what you're saying? That's a serious accusation. She's not a spy."

"Is she no? Remember her that first day, all chummy wi' everyone? Trying to be best pals an' asking questions? And look at the jammy work she's got in the kitchen; there's no hard slog outside this place, no 'lickety-split' for miles for her. Who's to say they dinnae slip her proper food while we're no here? She could be stuffing her fat face wi' chips and chocolate for all we know."

"That's crazy," Marcus told him. "For one thing, that Esther girl's with her the whole day; for another… well, she wouldn't do that. She's not nasty. There's a few others I'd believe it of before her."

"What you defending her for?"

Marcus shrugged. "Just think you're wrong."

"Lynxstain is right about one thing, for a change," Lee butted in. "We can't be one hundred per cent sure it was her. Suspicious behaviour ain't proof and this ain't *CSI* so we can't get none. Best say nuthin' to no one, but keep our eyes wide open."

"Och, I'll be watching her all right," Alasdair promised.

When Spencer returned to his cabin, he was horrified to find the Punchinello with the half-eaten nose standing by his bed, wearing his Stetson. The guard spun round like a gunslinger when the boy entered and gave a rasping cackle.

"Th… that's my hat," Spencer said. "Could I have it back, please?"

The guard grimaced at him and ground his teeth.

"Me hat," he growled. "Garrugaska want."

Spencer tried to stay calm. "You can't have it," he said nervously. "It's mine and I want it. Please, it's important to me."

"Important to me!" the guard mimicked him unpleasantly. "Me hat now! Garrugaska like."

"Look, I… I'm sorry about your nose," the boy persisted. "But that doesn't mean you can take my stuff."

He moved forward and reached out a trembling hand to grab the Stetson from the creature's head. The Punchinello glared at him.

"You do that, and I'll kill ya!" it threatened in a bizarre parody of John Wayne's drawl. "Step down, pilgrim."

Spencer started and jerked his hand back. He suddenly realised this was the guard that had been watching his media player the other night. Just how many of his Westerns had it seen and how many times, if it was already memorising them?

"I need it," he tried again. "Please, er… Sir."

"If you want to call me that, smile," the Punchinello said, and Spencer recognised the classic Gary Cooper line from *The Virginian*.

The Punchinello grinned then swaggered forward as if wearing spurs. When he drew close to Spencer, he cleared his throat and spat on the floor. Then he pushed his bandaged nose into the boy's face and said, "It's a hell of a thing killing a man. You take away all he's got and all he's ever gonna have." It was word-perfect. The guard was obviously better at repeating lines from movies than actually speaking English properly.

"Clint Eastwood." Spencer identified the quote with a miserable murmur, unable to see through his breathed-on glasses. "Er… *Unforgiven* – one of the best."

The guard blew imaginary cigar smoke in his face then left the cabin as though he was leaving a saloon.

Thoroughly cowed, Spencer stared after him. What was he going to do now? The Stetson was more than a hat to him. It was the symbol of his escape, how he shut out the horror and insanity. It was the only way he could deny the reality of it all. He wasn't sure if he could cope or even survive without it. The Stetson had become a vital part of him and he was bereft.

A second clanging of the bell interrupted his despondency. Jangler had decided that, as they weren't having any breakfast, they should begin work straight away and so everyone was summoned to the gates. With no meals to prepare, Maggie and Esther were also assigned to the work parties. Alasdair wasn't allowed to use a broken hand as an excuse to get off work, Jangler pointed out that he could still pick fruit with the other and so he too was brought to the gates.

He turned a key in the lock and the long trek to the minchet thickets began.

"Hey, Herr Spenzer," Marcus said, nudging him in the back. "What's your hat doing on that guard? You two getting married or something? Do you get to wear his old one?"

Spencer wanted to punch him. Instead he pushed his way through the others to get as far away from Marcus as possible.

"Spenzer and a guard, sittin' in a tree…" Marcus teased.

"Lickety-split!" Yikker ordered. "You, Stinkboy. Go, make legs faster."

Conversation between the children ceased as they were driven like cattle along the forest roads. Maggie wasn't used to exercise like this and she soon found it extremely difficult to keep up with the others. When the two parties divided, Alasdair was in her group. It was gruelling and relentless. The Punchinellos didn't allow any breaks and screamed at them if they worked too slowly. Minchet branches scored her and bluebottle swarms crawled over the bloody scratches. And through all that, Alasdair made her feel even more wretched, with snide remarks, condemning looks and whispers behind her back.

Maggie bore it in unhappy silence. Perhaps she deserved it; she didn't really know. Compared to what Jody was going through and what had happened to Alasdair's hand, this was nothing. It made her fully appreciate how much easier her usual kitchen duties were. She was lucky she didn't have to do this every day.

That evening she lay on her bed, aching and sore and relieved it was over. She didn't know how she'd got through it. In the afternoon, one girl had fainted from hunger and exhaustion. Marcus had acted as packhorse once more and carried her back to the camp whilst others staggered along like the walking dead. Yikker had been on the boy's case throughout the day. Whenever the Punchinello drew near, he retched and spat at him, berating the "honk" of his aftershave and shower gel.

"Make Yikker mad," he growled at him. "Yikker want spill your giblets. Yikker do soon. Lockpick no stop. Lockpick no in charge. Swazzle laugh at he. Yes, Yikker want cut off your skin and throw in stream. Wash stink off. That Yikker plan."

Marcus knew the threats were genuine. As soon as that guard saw an opportunity, he was going to butcher him. The boy took meagre comfort in the knowledge that he had a little scheme of his own – one that would drive that creature crazy. By the time Marcus was done, Yikker would be tearing his lank hair out.

On their return, Alasdair had gone straight to Jangler, to plead for Jody's early release. The old man refused and said if he asked again, he'd have a broken foot to match his hand.

Jody's empty bed was an unsettling presence in the cabin. Occasionally they heard her crying out and kicking the door of the tool cupboard. It had been another warm day and they wondered how hot it had been in that cramped, airless space. How could she manage in there without water for so long? Christina sat up in bed, listening for every miserable sound, until lights out when the two off-duty guards switched on the TV in their quarters. Judging from the blaring car chases and machine-gun fire, they must have been watching a gangster movie. They cheered and hooted excitably until Jangler knocked on their door to complain about the noise. It was strange, those cruel, repulsive creatures being so absorbed in television. Perhaps they merely relished the violence.

Maggie turned away from the empty bed. She tried not to think about Jody's suffering, and her possible blame in it. Instead she directed her thoughts to Marcus. Before the march back here, she had seen him furtively slip two large minchet fruits into his pockets. Why would he do that? You couldn't eat that foul stuff. Then she recalled his worried look, first thing that morning. He was up to something, but what? They hadn't really spoken since the night of the drugged May Cup – and that seemed so long ago now. She tried to fill her mind with something else, but the only other subject was food. Groaning, she buried her face in the pillow.

Three cabins away, Charm was handing her moisturiser round to the other girls. The sun had left their faces and the backs of necks burnt and sore. Moisturiser was the only treatment they had. It didn't relieve the discomfort of the burn, but it stopped their skin feeling so tight and they were grateful.

Charm had tried to speak to Lee at various points during the day, but he continually cold-shouldered her. She didn't know what she'd done to upset him, but told herself she'd try again tomorrow. Before lights out she had made the girls forget about their hunger for a while by organising an impromptu fashion show. Taking her expensive clothes from her fake Louis Vuittons, she shared them and her precious make-up around, then told everyone to go up to the mezzanine and change. When they were ready, they paraded down the stairs, one by one, heads held high and haughty like supermodels. Charm applauded, giving generous marks out of ten and constructive tips to each of them. The girls laughed and for a while their plight, and that of Jody, was pushed from their thoughts. When they remembered, they fell silent and gave Charm her clothes back.

In the boys' cabin next door, Marcus had called Lee and Spencer to the area beneath the stairs.

"Now listen, lads," he began with great solemnity. "I'm going to tell you something and I'm trusting you to keep it to yourselves. With all this talk of snitches, you can't be too careful. Don't breathe a word to anyone, OK?"

"Did you ever win a bore contest?" Lee asked. "Cos you is damn good at it."

Marcus ignored that and carried on. "I want you both to promise to keep schtum about what I'm going to tell you."

Spencer nodded.

"You have to say it out loud," Marcus insisted. "Do it properly."

"I promise not to tell anyone."

"Now you."

Lee rolled his eyes. "Whatever," he said. "Anything so's I can escape your deodoria."

"Escape!" Marcus whispered excitedly. "That's the exact word. Did you ever see that film, *The Great Escape*?"

"Only every Christmas," Lee said, seeing where this was going and thinking the Manchester lad was an even bigger idiot than he had suspected.

"Straight after the one with the big metal guy and the skeleton fight."

"*Jason and the Argonauts*," Spencer couldn't stop himself saying.

"Yeah, that's the thing. With the snaky monster."

"Seven-headed hydra," Spencer corrected.

Lee stared at him with pity. "Kid," he asked. "Did you ever have a life?"

"Oi!" Marcus interrupted. "Can you let me finish? Thank you. So – *The Great Escape* is the one where the POWs dig a tunnel right out of the prison camp."

"Tell me you is not serious," Lee said.

Marcus crouched to unroll the polo shirt he had placed on the floor. Wrapped inside was a trowel and the scissors from the medical kit.

"I gotcha now," Lee declared with mock enthusiasm. "You're going to plant some window boxes for the thirty guys who are gonna come do this digging, then trim their nails or give them a haircut. Sound plan, can't see no flaws there."

"I'm not pretending it won't take a while," Marcus said defensively. "And no one's asking you to come. I just don't want anyone else knowing. This secret stays in our hut, yeah?"

He peeled back the carpet and began scoring a line in the plywood underneath with the scissors. Lee burst out laughing.

"You is gonna be there like forever!"

"Yeah, well, you won't think it's so funny when I've got away. I'll be the Steve McQueen of this place – racing off on a motorbike."

Spencer joined in the laughter. "He got caught in that film!"

"Oh, get lost," Marcus muttered. "I know what I'm doing."

"Where are you going to get all the wood from?" Spencer asked.

"Wood?"

"To shore up the tunnel and stop it burying you alive."

Marcus concentrated on gouging the scissors through the flooring. He hadn't thought that far ahead.

"I'm working on it," he lied.

Lee headed back upstairs. "Whatever keeps you happy and outta my hair, little man," he scoffed. "And hey, the stink up here... is that your trainers or what? Smells like something's crawled in 'em and died. Hang those reekers out the window."

"You can talk! Try cleaning up all that mud and cack you brought in. Where'd you been anyway? Paddling in a ditch?"

Lee didn't answer. A secretive smile stole across Marcus's face. There was nothing smelly about his trainers; he had too many powders and sprays for that to happen. Something else was causing that pungent odour – but he wasn't prepared to spoil that surprise just yet. He continued scoring the plywood.

The next day the children awoke bruised, and many found themselves on the floor again.

"Maybe we're sleepwalkin', innit?" Charm suggested. "My Uncle Frank were always doin' that."

Maggie and Esther were allowed back in the kitchen. On the way, Maggie heard Jody's weakened voice. She sounded delirious and was half singing, half groaning. Maggie stopped to listen.

"There's... there's something tender in the moonlight... on Honolulu Bay..."

Maggie didn't recognise it, but she thought if she whistled something cheerful back, Jody would know she hadn't been forgotten. She looked around quickly. The only guard in sight was up in the skelter tower and facing the other way. The first tune she could think of was 'Always look on the bright side of life' from *Life of Brian*. Maggie wasn't the world's best whistler, but she made a fair stab at it and hoped Jody could hear her.

"You!" the guard shrieked down. "What you do? No whistle! You go make squassages hot!"

Maggie curtsied obediently and pushed open the door. At the back of the building, Jody's forlorn voice was still warbling through the strange song.

"If you... like Ukulele Lady, Ukulele Lady like a'you. If... If you like... to linger where it's shady, Uku... Ukulele Lady linger too..."

It was heartbreaking: only the beginning of the second day and she was already hallucinating in there. How much more of this could she take? Maggie went to the kitchen, depressed to feel so helpless. Anchu, the Punchinello, was waiting and Esther came in soon after.

The two girls prepared an even thicker soup than usual to make up for not eating yesterday. Esther was uncharacteristically quiet that morning, but there wasn't time to ask why. The kitchen scraps were starting to shrivel and grow mouldy in the May heat and they had to throw a large part of them away. Maggie wasn't sure if they'd last out the week, but it made more sense to her to eat well now and worry about tomorrow later.

Over the past couple of days she'd noticed that whenever Esther was tense or nervous, she cracked her knuckles. That was happening a lot this morning.

As soon as Anchu, the guard, took the large plate of sausages to the Punchinello cabin, Maggie quickly put into action the brainwave that had come to her last night. Taking handfuls of parsnip peelings, she fried them in the sausage fat till they were crisp and sprinkled them on top of the soup.

"Is that fancy or what?" she declared with pride. "Came to me in a flash it did. It'll be dead tasty."

Esther was too distracted to say anything. She was always wary of saying much in front of the guard. But, when they were on their own, Maggie could make her laugh and get her chatting about herself. She was the youngest of three, from a family that had been very close and loving. Maggie liked to think she was making this place a little less frightening for her when she asked about things that were familiar and comforting – about the happy times before the book.

"What's up with you today?" she asked. "Not feeling well? You'll be fine with this soup inside you."

Esther could barely look at her.

"OK," Maggie said. "There's an elephant in the room and it's waving a neon sign with my name on. If you've got a problem with me, spill."

The thirteen-year-old cracked her knuckles again. "It's just what everyone's saying."

"About me?"

Esther nodded. "They say you dobbed Jody in to the old man. That he gives you extra food when no one's looking."

Maggie leaned against the table. "They really think that?" she asked, appalled. "How can they? I'd never dream of... and you're with me all ruddy day. When am I supposed to get this extra food?"

Esther shrugged. "Sometimes you go off, by yourself."

"That was to see to Jody's back! I can't believe you're taking this rubbish seriously!"

"They say you're an informer. You do ask a lot of questions about everyone."

"Only cos I'm interested in them! Oh, for God's sake, I'm not having this!"

She strode into the dining hall where the other children had already sat down, impatient and ravenous for their breakfasts.

Maggie looked at each one. Few of them could meet her eyes. So it was true, they had been saying these things. It knocked her sideways, but she wasn't going to let any of them know it.

"I got something to say," she began in a no-nonsense, angry voice. "And you're going to bloody well listen to it if you want to eat this morning. Cos I'll pour the whole sodding lot down the sink if you don't."

They shifted and squirmed in their seats.

"So who here thinks I grassed up Jody?" she demanded bluntly.

Alasdair raised his good hand. Nicholas and Drew from his cabin did the same. Then three of the girls in Esther's dorm followed suit. Most of the others stared at the table. Finally Christina's hand went up.

Maggie couldn't believe it and her round cheeks blazed. But, before she could lay into them, Marcus jumped from his chair.

"You're round the bend, the lot of you!" he cried. "If she's a spy for the Jaxers then I'm Kermit the Frog's jockstrap! This place is driving you nuts. Don't take it out on her!"

"Sit down," Maggie told him. "I don't need you to speak for me."

She waited till he resumed his seat then said to them, "I was going to say how wrong you are and deny it, but... it's not worth it. *You're* not worth it. If that's what you think of me then stuff you. I've spent years being laughed at and called names for how I look. Do you think I'm going to start caring now if you call me some different ones? Hate is hate and ignorance smells the same whatever label you use. You want to call me a spy, informer –you go ahead. How about collaborator? That's a good one. Yeah, shout that at me next time. But you know what, I'll be the one having the last laugh. While you're out there, slaving away in the sun or in the rain or in the snow, if you even make it till the winter, I'll be here having it easy and when you get sick cos you're starving, I'll still be standing cos I've got enough padding on me to outlive every one of you. When you're dead and buried, I'll still be here and doing a salsa on your graves – if you get any!"

With that, she stormed back into the kitchen. Marcus glared in disgust at those who had raised their hands. Charm left her seat and strode after her. Lee sucked his teeth and shook his head at Alasdair.

"Not cool," he uttered.

Charm found Maggie sitting at the table where they had fended off the Doggy-Long-Legs, her head in her hands. Esther was standing by the cooker, looking awkward and slightly ashamed.

"Go feed them toxic scumbags in there," Charm instructed the thirteen-year-old. "Might shut 'em up for five minutes. Hope it blisters their tongues – shame it won't choke 'em!"

She turned to Maggie and put her arms round her.

"Don't," Maggie said, her voice thick with emotion.

"Then don't you dare cry," Charm ordered. "Cos you'll set me off and me mascara will run. What I brought wiv me ain't gonna last forever and I don't wanna waste it."

"How could they?" Maggie uttered.

Charm squeezed her shoulders. "It's cos you're diff'rent," she said. "You're an easy target."

"A big fat one you mean."

"No, you fick mare. You an' me got loads in common."

"Me and you? But you're stunning."

"Like that matters in here!" Charm cried, too honest to bother with false modesty. "I'll let you into a secret…"

"Don't do that. I'm the camp narc, remember – and don't give me that balls about being beautiful on the inside, cos I'm not. If there were ten Wispas on this table, I'd eat all of them."

"Shut your neck and lemme get a word in edgeways. What I were gonna say was when you first got here, I was ragin' jealous, couldn't believe my crappy luck."

"Eh?"

"You was me only competition. I thought you was gonna rob airtime off me, didn't I! Oh, them reality shows would just love you. You're made for telly. You was brilliant, funny, in-your-face and a real lens-hogger. To make it worse, you was nice! I could've clawed your eyes out, you cow!"

She examined her fingernails morosely. "Not that I got claws no more."

"Is that really what you thought?" Maggie asked.

"Too right! Had it sewn up here before you came to stick your neb in. Scared me rotten you did."

"I just wanted to make friends with everyone."

Charm shook her head. "Me ma always says… hang on, how do it go? You can fill your life wiv quaint nancies but you'll only ever have a handful of proper mates."

"I think you mean 'acquaintances'."

"Yeah, summink like that. Fing is, it's a waste of time trying to make everyone like you. I should know – you don't make no mates in the modellin' game. It's smiles to your face and knives at your back. Some evil cats out there."

"Was the modelling thing really so bad?"

"Bad? It were bloody fantastic!"

They both laughed. Then Maggie felt dreadful for finding anything funny.

"This'll be Jody's second day without any water," she said. "She's going to die in that stifling cupboard. Honest to God, I never told Jangler nothing."

"I didn't fink you did."

"But one of the guards might've heard me telling someone else about that phone. So it is my fault. I can't live with that – if she dies cos of me. I'm all knotted up inside. When I think of it, I can't get my breath."

"There's nofink you can do."

Maggie had already made up her mind. "Yes, there is," she said decisively. "Tonight, when it's dark and the camp's gone quiet, I'm going to sneak out and take her water."

Charm gripped her arm. "They'll catch you!" she hissed. "Then *you'll* get whipped and thrown in there – if they don't just kill you on the spot!"

"I don't care," Maggie said. "I'm doing it and no one's going to stop me."

"Please, Miss," a squeaky voice sounded suddenly from the doorway. "I want some more."

It was Marcus, doing a terrible Oliver Twist impression, although he actually thought he was being the Artful Dodger.

"There's more in the pan," Maggie told him. "We've not had any yet."

"I'll have it here with you if you don't mind," he said. "I'm fussy about who I eat with."

"Sure… and listen – thanks for what you said in there. It was appreciated, even if it didn't sound like it."

"No worries. They're well out of order. Next time one of them flops down outside, I'm not lugging them back. One of the guards can drag them by the hair."

"It was Christina what got to me," Maggie said dismally.

Marcus lowered his voice. "I heard what you two were talking about just now," he whispered. "Charm's right – those guard monsters'll kill you. They're spear-happy."

"Don't you say nothing to no one!" Maggie warned him. "And don't try talking me out of it."

"Wasn't going to. But what you need is a diversion, something to keep the guards busy – well away from that cupboard."

"Like what?"

Marcus lifted his bowl and drained the last of his breakfast.

"Finish yours quick and I'll show you," he told her, being mysterious.

A few minutes later, he was leading Maggie up the stairs in his cabin. Charm had been left reluctantly on watch outside.

"Got to say," he said, "I've been a total dick about that night, you know – when we were all spiked. I shouldn't have blanked you after. That was cold – and low."

"Forget it."

"Well, I'm saying sorry now. Thanks for not telling everyone – about what we did. That's how I know you're not a snitch."

Maggie halted.

"You thought I did that for your benefit?" she blurted. "I did that for me! Soon as I knew what a knob you were, I didn't want anyone knowing how stupid I'd been. That's the last thing I want people to know. I might be big but I've got my pride. You're a jerk, Marcus! No one will ever fancy you more than you do yourself."

The boy winced.

"Well… it's good we've cleared that up then," he mumbled in embarrassment.

"More than you have in here – it's filthy. Look at the state of it."

"That's Lee, he's a pig. Traipses mud in and leaves it. Too cool to clean; well, I'm not doing it for him."

"So where's this diversion?"

He led her on to the mezzanine, towards the far end.

"Ugh," she said, covering her nose. "What's that sickly smell? Do all lads' rooms pong like this?"

"It's not usually this bad," he explained. "What you're experiencing is diversion by product – come see."

"You're not making sense. Is it something to do with stink bombs? You serious?"

"Hush," he said, moving his bag from in front of the bedside cupboard. "He might be asleep."

"He?"

Marcus opened the small door, slowly. Maggie bent down to peer in then reared back in shock.

Inside, trussed up tightly with trainer laces, very much awake and frighteningly alert, the black eyes almost popping out of its head and jaws snapping at the air, was a Doggy-Long-Legs.

18

"I CALL HIM Gnasher," Marcus said, beaming proudly like a new father. "Cos he reminds me of that dog in the *Beano*."

"Shut the door!" Maggie squealed.

The boy chuckled at her panic. "Chillax. It's safe. It can't get out. It can't do anything tied up like that. Well, apart from make that smell. I've not had a chance to clean it out in there yet."

"Where'd you get it?"

"He tried to eat my face off the other day – ha! I thought I'd killed it but it was only stunned. I broke three of its legs though and I don't think it's as smart as it was, so it's not factory fresh any more."

"Oh, poor thing… NOT! And you've been hiding it in there since? That's why you were so worried when they were searching for the phone and that's what the minchets were for – you've been feeding it. You're mental!"

"No, I'm a flaming genius – and this is why…"

Once Maggie heard his plan, the day couldn't pass quickly enough. The morning dawdled by and the sun beat down. By the afternoon it was sweltering and the sticky heat lingered into the evening. Jody hadn't made any sound since midday. There was no feeble hitting of the door, no more stilted singing. Maggie fretted they would be too late. When the work parties returned, she joined Marcus and Charm and put the first phase into action.

They had both smuggled plenty of minchet back in their pockets. Dropping one on the ground, just by the step of Marcus's cabin, they took it in turns to discreetly drag it with their feet over the grass.

Standing in the doorway, Lee wondered what was going on. Since when were those three such bosom buds? What did they have to talk about as they wandered about the camp? His eyes lingered on Charm and he wished he could speak to her, but he couldn't get his last visit to the world of Mooncaster out of his head. Maybe tomorrow he'd try, although how he'd explain his recent unpleasant behaviour towards her was something he'd have to sleep on.

To anyone else observing the three of them, it was the same. They looked like they were simply chatting and wandering aimlessly over the lawn. No one could have guessed they were zigzagging a trail of minchet juice and pulp as far from the main block as possible. When there was nothing left of the first sloppy fruit, they surreptitiously dropped another and continued on their seemingly random way. Not even the Punchinellos suspected they were up to something – Charm and Marcus and the other children reeked of minchet anyway. The guards' sensitive nostrils detected nothing out of the ordinary.

Jangler had brought his armchair outside and was sitting in the shade, a battery-operated fan in his hand, trained on his face. Captain Swazzle had presented him with a piece of paper and the old man was reading the scrawled writing with increasing annoyance.

"You're jesting of course," he said gruffly. "I'm afraid I don't see the humour in this."

"No jokey," Swazzle insisted. "Garrugaska not happy – him full woe since nose got bit. He want."

"That ludicrous cowboy hat he's been wearing today has overcooked his brain. These requests are absurd. I'm not sanctioning them. I've already made one concession. I shan't make any more."

"Must!" the Captain growled.

"Moderate your tone when you speak to me, Swazzle! You forget who I am. I'm not one of the prisoners."

The Captain bowed slightly in deference. "Garrugaska need," he wheedled. "Him no good guard unless him get."

Jangler tugged irritably at his small beard. "But the livery of the Punchinellos in the White Castle hasn't changed for hundreds of years," he objected. "There is a wealth of tradition and pageantry to be upheld and respected."

"This no castle," the Captain reminded him a second time. "This dream. Is different."

Jangler sat forward and flicked the paper with exasperation. "Oh, very well," he agreed. "I'll contact the seamstresses, but not about this last item. I absolutely refuse to authorise that. It's too, too much."

"Garrugaska need all," Swazzle said flatly.

Jangler could see the Captain would not let this go. He brought the fan closer to his face. It was so horribly hot and uncomfortable today. He didn't have the energy to argue it out and risk an attack of prickly heat.

"I'll see what I can do," he uttered wearily

The Captain bowed again, then waddled away, snickering.

Jangler considered the badly spelled list once more and went to his cabin to make a phone call. "Utterly asinine," he muttered to himself. "I would never permit this in the castle."

By this time, Marcus and the two girls had reached the far left side of the camp. They scattered what was left of the minchet from their pockets about the ground close to the fence.

"This better work," Maggie said.

"Course it will," Marcus said confidently. "Them spider things can't get enough of the stuff. You should see Gnasher bolt it down."

"OK, if you're sure. I'd better go back to the kitchen and start serving the dinners. Esther prob'ly thinks I'm eating my own bodyweight in crisps and cake in secret someplace right now. You know what you're doing?"

"It was my plan!" he reminded her.

"Yes, course. OK, till half ten then."

"Look, if you're scared, I'll do it."

"Or I will," Charm offered.

Maggie shook her head. "No, it's got to be me. It's my fault Jody's in there. Oh, God, she could be dead already for all we know. I've drunk pints of water today in this heat. What's it been like for her in that sweatbox?"

"Don't fink about it," Charm told her. "Just stick to what we said, yeah?"

Maggie nodded anxiously and headed back to the main block. When she was out of earshot, Charm turned to Marcus.

"You really fink there's a cat in hell's chance of this working?" she asked. "Or was you talkin' a load o' nads?"

The boy honestly didn't know. "If no one tries though," he said, "Velma's definitely going to kark it."

"And if Maggie's caught, she'll go the same way."

"We'll find out in a few hours. Now I'm going to wash this stinking muck off, douse myself in aftershave and body spray and annoy that Yikker swine for a bit. I need to really get up his nose."

The evening crawled by for the three of them. Charm's part in the plan was over but, after lights out, she paced round her cabin, biting what remained of her fingernails.

The hours ticked slowly. Maggie filled them by doing some of her laundry and hanging her washing on the banister. But she kept the bucket she had used close by her bed, half filled with water.

Darkness covered the camp. When it got to ten o'clock, Marcus had to let Spencer and Lee into what was going on. It was impossible to keep it from them any longer.

"You is crazy!" Lee yelled, hurling a pillow at him. "They's both gonna get killed! You end this right now, before it starts!"

Marcus refused. "It's the only chance there is of keeping that girl alive out there!" he hissed back. "So keep the volume down. I don't want the guards looking in this direction."

"You is a dangerous mentalist!" Lee fumed. "I am not a part of this!"

"You never are. It's just you here, isn't it? You never get involved, never help no one. Alasdair's right about one thing – you've given up inside."

"Go to hell."

"Already wearing the T-shirt and matching novelty boxers, thanks."

Spencer was lying in bed, his thoughts thousands of miles away in an imaginary Western town. Since the confiscation of his hat he hadn't said much to anyone. He stirred and scratched his head as he considered Marcus's scheme.

"I think it's brill," he said at length.

"Herr Spenzer!" Marcus whispered, giving him a friendly punch on the arm. "Glad to hear it. Come give me a hand with Gnasher then."

The younger boy hesitated before following him to the mezzanine.

"It won't bite," Marcus promised, before adding, "so long as you keep your hands away from its mouth!"

Switching on a small torch, he opened the door of the bedside cupboard and the Doggy-Long-Legs growled at them.

"Quiet, you!" Marcus told it. "You're getting out of here – you lucky dawg. But first, you're getting a smellover, that's like a makeover but without the lippy and Jimmy Choos."

Reaching in carefully, he hauled it out by the eight tied legs and, to Spencer's surprise and dismay, handed it over.

"Take him for a minute," he said.

"Why?" Spencer squeaked, holding it at arm's length, in fright and revulsion.

"Cos I need my hands free to be creative. This is a job for the maestro."

Marcus rummaged through his toiletry bag and case and brought out his shower gel, aftershave, shampoo, athlete's foot powder, moisturiser, body spray, talc and deodorants. Then, with the lofty, inspired air of a fine artist, he commenced spraying, dusting and squeezing the contents over the creature's coarse black fur.

The Doggy-Long-Legs twisted and wriggled, trying to break loose. It bit at the pungent, squirting mists, then coughed and retched.

Lee covered his nose. "That's worse than its own stink," he said.

When Marcus was satisfied, he took the beast from Spencer, switched off the torch and went downstairs to the entrance. There he waited and stared out at the camp. All was quiet and the night shadows were deep. So much the better. It was half past ten exactly.

Marcus had been studying the guards. Only one Punchinello patrolled the fence at night, while a second surveyed the camp from the tower. The others remained in their cabin, watching television or speaking loudly in their own rough language. The patrol was always clockwise and always took the same amount of time to complete one circuit.

The boy waited until the one on foot came into view. Yes, there he was, swaggering past the gates, headed towards the far right-hand corner. He grinned when he recognised it as Yikker.

"Perfecto!"

Marcus glanced up at the skelter tower. The Punchinello with the bandaged nose was on duty there again. Still wearing Spencer's Stetson, Garrugaska was engrossed in his media player, watching more Westerns.

"Result," Marcus breathed gladly. "That'll make it miles easier."

He lowered his eyes again, just in time to see Yikker turn ninety degrees and begin striding towards the rear of the camp. Soon he was out of sight, behind the main block.

This was it.

Sure enough a large figure, carrying a bucket, hurried in front of his cabin. Maggie was on her way.

"Good luck," he murmured, crossing his fingers. "You've got seven minutes – starting now."

"She's brave," Spencer muttered in admiration behind him. "I couldn't do that."

"Yeah," Marcus agreed with an affectionate smile. "Not bad for a fat bird."

Her heart in her mouth, Maggie hastened to the main building. Luckily everyone in her dorm, even Christina, was sound asleep so she had slipped out with no awkward questions asked.

Pressed against the wall, she sidled along, with a clear view of the back fence in the distance. Swallowing nervously, she saw the guard go by. Then she crept a little closer to the corner of the block. Once there, she waited and leaned out cautiously. It was so dark she could barely see Yikker all the way over there, heading for the far left-hand side of the fence. If it hadn't been for the yellow costume, the guard would have blended into the gloom completely. She held her breath then saw him turn towards the front again and presently he disappeared beyond Jangler's hut at the end.

At once Maggie ran around the back of the building, to the door of the tool cupboard and put her ear to the wood.

"Jody!" she whispered urgently. "Jody – it's me, Maggie. Can you hear me? You awake?"

There was a long, deathly silence. Maggie tapped at the door as quietly as she could.

"Jody," she tried again. "Jody?"

To her immense relief, she heard the faintest of groans inside.

"Where…?" a pitifully frail, parched voice asked groggily. "Who?"

"It's Maggie," she repeated. "I've…"

"Let me out!" the voice begged. "Let me out!"

"*Shhh!*" Maggie hissed. "I'm not supposed to be here. I brought some water for you. Look up."

Throughout the day she had rattled her brains, trying to work out how to get a drink through that locked door. It was only when she had taken a not so casual walk around the camp in the afternoon that she had spotted it wasn't a perfect fit along the top edge of the frame. There was a gap; it wasn't much, but it would be enough.

As well as water, the bucket she carried contained Charm's large sponge, now torn into four smaller pieces. Maggie reached in and made sure they were fully saturated. Then she pushed one carefully into the hole.

"Incoming!" she whispered. The sopping sponge dropped down inside. She heard Jody scramble for it in the darkness then press it to her lips feverishly and leech it dry. Maggie did the same with two more.

"Bless you!" Jody cried gratefully on the other side. "Bless you. You're an angel."

"One more," Maggie said softly. "Then I've got to go."

"No," Jody implored her. "I'll push these back out. More – give me more!"

Maggie looked over her shoulder. Yikker would be approaching the gates again any time now. His sensitive nose would smell her if he got closer. It was time for Marcus to start the diversion so she could get back to her cabin safely.

"I can't stay," she whispered apologetically as she eased the last sponge in. "I've got to get back."

Three almost bone dry sponges came poking through the gap.

"Please!" Jody begged her. "Please! I'm dying – it's killing me… so, so thirsty."

Maggie closed her eyes and nodded. "OK," she said, dunking the sponges back in the bucket.

At that moment, the sound of Yikker's sudden squawking filled the night. The diversion had commenced.

Marcus had given her the seven minutes. That was the average length of time it took the guards to walk a quarter of the way round the camp. When that was up, he opened the cabin door slowly and placed Gnasher on the step.

"Here you go, fella," he said, taking the scissors from his pocket. "Smell that lovely minchet. You must be starved not eating all day."

He waited until the Doggy-Long-Legs' quivering nostrils caught the scent of the trail he and the girls had made earlier. It wasn't long before the creature grew agitated and started slavering.

"Yeah, you like that, don't you? Just follow your snotty nose to the end and you can feed your pugly face with that slimy gloop."

He snipped at the trainer laces and jumped back smartly, closing the door between them.

Gnasher's three crippled legs flopped down uselessly, but the other five stretched then stamped and shakily lifted the hairy body. After being tied up so long, it took a few hesitant, tentative steps. Then it stumbled around and snarled at the door, barking shrilly at Marcus's shadowy figure inside.

"Shut up!" the boy muttered, waving it away. "Get lost, go on – go get your din-dins."

The Doggy-Long-Legs butted its face against the door – hitting the board nailed over the hole it had chewed there the other day.

"It's trying to get back in!" Spencer exclaimed in alarm.

Marcus looked worried but Gnasher quickly gave up. It wasn't as tenacious as it had been. Stumbling backwards, its jaw hanging open, it appeared almost drunk.

"I think you did more damage than you realised," Spencer observed.

"Wait," Marcus whispered.

The Doggy-Long-Legs' wet nostrils quested the air. This time it really had caught the scent. It scratched at the step with its claws and leaped off, on to the grass. With its face buried in the trail, it scampered away, the broken legs dangling behind it.

"Go on, my son!" Marcus enthused. "You beauty."

He and Spencer watched it follow the invisible, zigzagging path across the lawn. Then they heard Yikker shout a challenge.

The Punchinello had almost completed a circuit of the perimeter when his large hooked nose twitched and he smelled the unmistakable, nostril-spiking perfumes of that teenage boy he so wanted to kill.

A foul leer spread across his face. The boy was out after curfew and that meant only one thing. He was at Yikker's mercy, and Yikker wasn't tainted by any such weakness. The guard thrust his spear forward into the dark.

"Stand and disclose!" he squawked.

The sharp, flowery reek grew stronger. Yikker stared at the gloom. Where was the hated boy? He was nowhere to be seen.

"Disclose!" he demanded more fiercely.

Now the stink had changed position. The human was moving fast. Yikker spun around and charged after the smell.

"You no hide!" he shrieked. "You no escape. Yikker kill!"

The guard heard a snuffling noise close to the ground. He let out a bloodthirsty yell and flung the spear. The weapon plunged harmlessly into the soil and Yikker seethed with frustration.

"Where you?" he bawled. "Where you? I catch – I kill!"

In the cabin, the two boys had to clamp their hands over their mouths to prevent their laughter being heard. Watching the Punchinello dart madly from side to side, trying to keep up with the Doggy-Long-Legs, was the funniest sight they'd seen in ages.

Lee descended the stairs behind them.

"Don't tell me that stoopid plan is actually working?" he said.

Marcus was laughing so hard tears were streaming down his face. He nodded and jumped up and down.

Outside, Yikker was haring to the far left-hand side of the camp; in a moment, the guard would be out of sight, beyond Jangler's hut.

"Shouldn't Maggie be coming back now?" Lee asked. "Your pet spider mongrel won't keep that guard busy forever."

Marcus wasn't worried yet. There was still plenty of time. When Yikker realised what he was actually chasing, he was certain to throw a massive tantrum. If Gnasher got caught, then the Punchinello would vent his full fury on it. But if Gnasher managed to escape over the fence, that would drive Yikker insane with rage, thinking it was the boy that had got away.

His laughter ebbed. He wiped his eyes and doubled over to take deep breaths.

"She'll be fine," he said. "There's…"

Suddenly three loud bangs blasted into the night. At first Marcus thought it was fireworks. Lee knew different. He dashed to the door and stared out.

"Jesus!" he cried. "They got guns!"

"What?" Spencer spluttered, backing away.

"Rubbish," Marcus argued.

Two more shots fired and this time there was no mistaking them. Up in the tower, Garrugaska had heard Yikker's shouts of frustration and finally put the media player down. Then he took from his frilled tunic a Colt 1873 Single Action Army revolver, the favoured gun of the Old Wild West, and shot recklessly at the far side of the camp, whooping at the feeling of the lethal power in his hand. White flame spat from the barrel and the Punchinello brayed with excitement.

Beyond Jangler's cabin, Yikker cast the spear away in disgust when Garrugaska started firing. The Punchinello reached into his own tunic and took out a semi-automatic pistol. Every guard had been issued with his preferred gun. Yikker wasted no time in emptying lead into the confusing darkness, where that stinking, perfumed boy was running around unseen. Spent casings came flying out and Yikker danced a jig of joy. This truly was the way to do it.

The gunfire brought the three other Punchinellos from their cabin. They had grabbed their guns and were firing into the air as they ran about, wondering what was happening.

"Oh, God," Marcus breathed as the gunshots thundered over the camp. "Maggie – she's still out there."

Once Yikker had started shouting, Maggie hurried to feed three more dripping sponges through the door.

"That's it!" she told Jody firmly. "I've no more time."

"Don't go!" the imprisoned girl beseeched her.

"I've got to – sorry."

"Come back tomorrow! Please, please!"

"I don't know if I can."

"I'm begging!"

Maggie tore herself away. Bucket in hand she hurried back around the main block, keeping close to the wall and the deeper darkness. Then the shooting began.

Maggie froze with shock. She couldn't believe they had guns. It wasn't possible. Hidden in the night shadows, she gasped shallow breaths – petrified and numb. She didn't know what to do and felt her scalp creep as the full danger and hopelessness of her predicament was brought home.

More gunfire heralded the other guards rampaging from their cabin. How could she ever make it back without being seen and shot dead?

Captain Swazzle, Anchu and Bezuel ran to see Yikker shooting wildly at the fence. Without waiting to ask questions, they raised their guns and joined in, firing at the trees beyond the barbed wire. The Punchinellos loved it. They relished the lethal force of these wondrous new weapons. As befitted his rank, the Captain wielded a sub-machine gun. The brutal discharges illumined their ugly faces in stark flashes, the small explosions reflecting in their red-rimmed, lusty eyes. When the bullets ran out, they reloaded in eager, frenzied haste and continued, rejoicing with every violent recoil.

Carrying a lantern, Jangler came shuffling from his cabin in his dressing gown and slippers. The gunfire had jolted him from a very pleasant doze. At first he thought there was a full-scale attack by enemy forces under way. When he saw the guards were firing indiscriminately at the dark woodland, he scowled and struggled to be heard above the din.

"Captain!" he shouted. "Captain! What is going on?"

The Punchinellos ceased firing and turned to grin at him. Their faces were flushed and they were breathless with the intoxicating thrill of their deadly new toys.

"Guns good," Captain Swazzle said. "We like, very lot. *Blam blam! Bang bang!*"

"So I can see. But what is the meaning of this? Who are you shooting at?"

The Captain looked at him blankly then turned to Yikker for an answer. "What out there?" he asked.

"Abrant scum!" the guard replied. "Stinkboy. He go – over fence – in trees."

"One of the prisoners has escaped?" the old man cried. "How did that happen? How did he get over the barbed wire? Were you sleeping on duty?"

"Stinkboy did magick!" Yikker retorted. "Make Yikker not see. But

Yikker smell he sneak by."

"Magick?" Jangler repeated in disbelief. "Have you been at the wine again?"

"No drink! Yikker smell Stinkboy. Yikker no lie. Stinkboy gone. He out in forest. We go get – quick!"

"Captain," Jangler asked, turning to him for confirmation. "Can you detect anything out here that shouldn't be?"

Swazzle sniffed the air and the others did the same. But the acrid fumes of burned gunpowder masked everything and tickled the sensitive hairs sprouting from their noses. They found that sulphurous smell delicious and savoured it avidly.

Jangler gave a grunt of irritation. "Very well," he said. "We shall have to do a headcount. Get the aberrants out here. We'll see just who is missing and then decide what action to take."

All the children were awake. They stared out through the cabin doors, fearfully wondering what was going on. The noise of the guns terrified them and when the Punchinellos came stomping over to drag them on to the lawn, they were sure they were going to be shot.

Yikker stormed across to Marcus's cabin, just to make certain the boy's bed was empty. When he saw Marcus standing by the door with Lee and Spencer, the guard's mouth fell open.

"Stinkboy!" he shrieked in rage. "What you do here?"

Marcus was still mortally afraid for Maggie, but he tried to act as normal as possible.

"How'd you mean?" he asked. "I was fast asleep till the shooting started. I was having a fantastic dream about juicy ripe melons…"

"Lies!" the guard screamed at him, pulling out the pistol. "Is lies, lies, lies!"

The boys raised their hands instantly.

"Calm down, cuz!" Lee suggested. "You don't want no accidental discharge goin' on with that gat. We ain't gonna be no trouble."

Yikker bared his teeth and waved the gun menacingly in front of

Marcus's eyes. He pressed the barrel to his forehead. It was still hot from firing. The boy cringed as the sadistic guard dragged it across one eyebrow, then down his bruised cheek.

"You make game of Yikker," he hissed. "Big wrong, stinkboy. Yikker no like be fool. Yikker make you wish for bullet in face."

"I... I don't know what you're talking about," Marcus answered. "I've been in bed."

The Punchinello's finger tapped against the trigger. A bead of perspiration ran down the boy's temple.

"Hurry up!" Jangler called impatiently from outside. "Bring them out!"

Yikker sneered, then spat and moved aside.

"Go!" he barked.

The three boys hurried to the door.

"Makin' friends is a life skill you do not have," Lee whispered at Marcus as they ran on to the grass.

The other children were already gathered out there; most were shivering from fear at what they suspected was about to happen. Alasdair was demanding to know what was going on, but Jangler was trying to do a headcount. Christina was wiping the sleep from her eyes and beginning to wonder where Maggie was; she looked around but couldn't see the large girl anywhere. Charm was waiting anxiously for Marcus to emerge and ran to him the instant he appeared.

"I don't know!" he told her, before the girl had time to even ask. "She must still be stuck over there."

"Then she's done for!" Charm gasped. "They'll see she's not 'ere and go lookin'."

Captain Swazzle had seen Yikker come out and shouted at him in their own language. Yikker responded with a sullen shrug of those high, humped shoulders and stared at the ground, mumbling a reply. Swazzle screeched something back, which really didn't need translating. Yikker flinched then glowered at Marcus with fresh hatred.

Jangler was frowning. There did appear to be one person missing. He was about to do a recount when Swazzle came swaggering over.

"Yikker make wrong," the Captain told him. "Boy not gone, boy here."

"What? Then all this commotion was for nothing? You need to have a word with that fellow, Captain. Now wait a moment. I must ascertain there really are twenty-one prisoners here. Get them lined up in rows. It's nigh on impossible when they're higgledy-piggledy like this."

Swazzle shouted at the children and they assembled in their usual lines. Charm looked worriedly at Marcus. This was it. This was when Maggie's absence would be discovered. Charm gazed around desperately. Then she let out a high scream of terror.

"Spider fings!" she cried, pointing towards the fence. "Two of 'em! Aaaaarggh!"

Chaos ensued. The children fled from their rows and the Punchinellos fired their guns into the dark, which made the panic even worse. Charm was squealing in every direction except the main block, seeing Doggy-Long-Legs everywhere. Up in the skelter tower Garrugaska let out a battle cry and came bounding down the stairs to join in the shooting of those nose-eating vermin.

Seizing this chance, Marcus raced to the main building and found Maggie still frozen against the wall. There wasn't time to speak. He knocked the bucket from her tight grasp then grabbed her hand and pulled her back to the front lawn where confusion reigned. Shots fired blindly into the night. The Punchinellos couldn't see any invading Gangles, but they were overjoyed to use their weapons again so soon.

"Stop this!" Jangler commanded once the initial alarm had worn off. "Stop it, I say!"

The guards ceased fire and glared into the surrounding gloom.

"There's nothing there!" the old man shouted angrily. "You're shooting at shadows. You, girl – what did you see?"

Charm was a picture of startled innocence. "I coulda swore I saw them 'orrors!" she exclaimed. "Them guns got my nerves so strung out I'm seein' fings. I'll have awful nightmares tonight, I will."

Jangler grumbled under his breath, but he believed her. He supposed she really was stupid enough. The children were pushed into their rows once more. This time the tally was the right one. The old man dismissed them back to their beds then spoke sternly to Captain Swazzle, threatening to take the guns away if another disruptive incident like this occurred.

"Hey," Lee said to Charm as she made her way back to her cabin.

The girl looked at him questioningly. "You speakin' to me now then?" she asked.

"What you just pulled – that were the smartest thing I seen in a while."

"I dunno what you're on about," she told him with a toss of her head. "Everyone knows I'm fick."

With a crafty smile on her face, she pushed the door open and left him grinning outside.

Maggie didn't have time to thank Marcus. She returned to her cabin and got into bed quickly. She had experienced the narrowest escape and she pulled the duvet over her head to stifle the sobbing that was about to engulf her.

Two beds away Christina was sitting up, staring at her. "Where were you?" the little girl asked. "First you weren't there, and then you was."

"I was on the lav," Maggie answered thickly. "Go to sleep."

Christina continued to stare at her, unable to decide if she was laughing or crying under that quilt.

In Marcus's cabin, he was bouncing around in celebration. "Yes!" he roared. "Yes! Yes!"

"Shut up!" Lee told him. "You want them guards to ask why you's so happy?"

Marcus stretched out his arms and basked in the praise and adoration of an imagined, cheering multitude.

"We won this one!" he said, running up to Spencer and giving him a victory thump. "Damn – it feels good to be a winner again. I hope Gnasher got away – he deserved to. He played a blinder."

Spencer rubbed his arm. "That Yikker's got it in for you now though," he warned. "Like really got it in for you. Worse than ever."

"Ha," Marcus chuckled, unconcerned. "We ran rings round them tonight. Just wait till the tunnel is finished. I'd love to see the look on that monster's face when he knows I've gone for good."

"You're gonna die," Lee told him for the umpteenth time.

Marcus wasn't listening. He felt on top of the world. Tonight, for the first time, they had succeeded in something, gained a small triumph over the insidious, unstoppable evil of *Dancing Jax*. Perhaps it was an omen of better things ahead. That night he slept with a spark of hope in his heart.

Spencer removed his spectacles and placed them on the bedside cabinet. He stared up into the blurred gloom. It wasn't as dark as the thoughts fermenting in his mind. He didn't know how much more of this he could take. Each new, futile day brought some new danger, some new hideous threat. He longed for it to stop, but there was only one way that could happen. Maybe it would have been kinder not to have given Jody any water at all. They had only prolonged her torment. Spencer wished he had the courage to bring an end to his own. His ability to cope with the mounting despair was almost at breaking point.

At the back of the main block, Jody had worn herself out trying to guess what the shooting had meant. Cramped in that airless cupboard, she drifted in and out of sleep.

Many hours later, she heard an old, crackly dance tune play through the camp. She had no idea it was called 'Three O'Clock in the Morning' by Paul Whiteman and his Orchestra. To her, that scratchy piece of music sounded even more sinister than the gunfire because it was so bizarre and incongruous. Jody feared she was hallucinating, especially when unnatural sounds of strange beasts took over once the tune ended. Her head dropped on to her chest and the night passed.

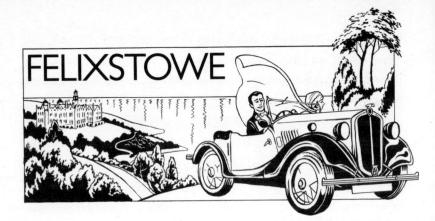

FELIXSTOWE

THURSDAY APRIL 30TH 1936

IT WAS A glorious evening. Estelle Winyard was so enjoying the drive in Simon Beauvoir's darling Morris 8 Tourer with the roof down, she didn't particularly want to attend the party any more.

"Do let's keep driving round and around," she pleaded limply. "The countryside in the spring really is the cat's meow. It's such heaven to be out of stuffy old London. I don't want to go to that beastly party. I shan't know a soul. This is so much more pleasant. Let's cry off and make our excuses tomorrow. You can say I contracted polio, rickets or diphtheria or anything drastic or squalid. I shan't mind, not a jot. We can drive on and on till the petrol runs out and hole up in a barn the entire night."

Simon gave his signature whinnying laugh that was so familiar in Society.

"You do speak the most abject phonus balonus at times!" he scoffed.

He took his eye off the empty country road and looked across at her. She was trailing a swan-white arm out of the car. Her pretty head was swathed in a scarf of ivory chiffon that protected the curls and waves of her glossy brown hair from the streaming wind. Framed by that pale cloud, her face looked more angelic than it deserved.

"You're bally well coming to this shindig," he scolded. "And that's an end to it. We've incurred the wrath of your pater, scooting away for this weekend, so let's make it count... and the look that hotel manager gave us earlier!"

"Felixstowe is an unsophisticated dead end," she said. "I saw a woman sitting in the lobby wearing a cloche hat and another with hair like Mary Pickford! Imagine – in this day and age! I can't see why the Most Evil Man in England would live within a spit of it. Not the right sort of hellhole at all."

"I told you, it's his family seat."

"It's certainly that! I never saw such a back end."

"You'd be surprised who visits him here! All the fraidies who daren't be seen with him in town: archbishops, members of parliament, lords, duchesses, artists, that crashing Simpson woman – she's here quite a bit so you can bet Kingy Boy comes with her. He goes woofing after her heels everywhere."

"Simon, you're the Society oracle. You scribble up all the silly tattlings in Pater's tawdry newspaper: who was at whose dreary dinner, who attended the first night of the opera, who is coming up to town and the rest of that high-hat rot. So tell me, honest injun, is AF really as dangerous as they say? I've only ever seen him once at a distance – at one of the Mitfords' ghastly balls."

"Dear Estelle, you're one of the biggest snobs I know, so don't pretend otherwise. Let those other drippy, dippy debs flirt with fascists or socialism to shock their maiden aunts, but it clangs so hollow when you try, my pretty pirate. You don't give tuppence for the common masses and the unemployed. You simply couldn't live without your daily doses of fizz, frocks and Mayfair salacity."

"You're a beast," she said, pouting. "And you didn't answer the question."

"Yes, I am a beast," he agreed. "But you're about to meet a far greater and more savage one – we're here."

The peacock-blue automobile turned right on to a long track that sloped gently upward and was flanked by trees and an avenue of flaming torches.

Estelle leaned forward, eager to catch her first glimpse of the house she had heard so much about. In the past few years, Fellows End had become notorious. If only half the rumours were true, it would be worth roughing it here in the provinces, for a day or two. As they trundled up the track, a leviathan of a Rolls Royce came roaring towards them. Simon swerved aside to let it thunder past.

"Did you eyeball who that was in there?" he declared. "Only the Nazi fellow, Ribbentrop."

"That German who flits about town, boring everyone about how wonderful Mr Hitler is? Pater says he's a pushy parvenu and, as soon as his novelty value wears off, the grand invitations will dry up. Fancy him being here!"

"I told you AF knows everyone. I wonder why he's not stopping for the bunfight? Don't Nazis waggle their legs, or do they have to keep them rigid for those goose-steps?"

The nineteen-year-old girl at his side wasn't listening. She was staring ahead, open-mouthed. The family home of Austerly Fellows had come into view.

"Oh – it's perfectly monstrous!" she exclaimed with repulsed fascination.

"Yes, rather a trifle Poe-ish, but not everywhere can boast Savoy modernity. I think it has a certain… unique charm."

"It must be a hoot at Hallowe'en."

He drove up to the large, ugly building and Estelle shivered when they passed into its shadow. There were many gleaming cars parked on the gravel in front. Simon found a space and tucked his humble Tourer beside a Bentley. Leaping out, he whistled at the dazzling array of motors on show. It was going to be a very prestigious gathering.

Estelle remained in her seat. She stared up at the forbidding building. Efforts had been made to jolly it up with paper lanterns strung around the porch and around the sides, but they made the rest of the gloomy, misshapen house appear sullen and brooding in contrast.

"I don't like it," she announced. "I want to go back."

Simon tweaked the white bow tie at his throat. "You, my dear, daffy girl," he said, "are capriciousness incarnate. Sitting-room thrill-seekers, such as you, are all the same. You think you crave the frisson of excitement to ginger up your humdrummery, but you're too bound by convention to actually dare do anything about it. A rouged Mrs Grundy I name you. Stay out here if you wish, by all means, but I'm not leaving this place till I've sampled AF's booze. My throat feels like the contents of King Tut's bandages. I'm positively squeaking for a cocktail or four. Besides, I've got my column to think of. I'm agog to find out who's here tonight."

"You're an absolute stinker!" she told him.

He bowed in polite acquiescence and she couldn't help admiring how handsome he was in full evening dress and Brylcreemed hair.

"Well, open the door for me, you cad."

Simon strode around the motor and obeyed. Estelle poured herself out of the passenger seat. Her silver satin gown clung and shimmered about her slender frame and she took several moments to carefully unwind the chiffon from her head and drape it about her bare shoulders. Then they exchanged teasing glances. They both knew the glamour quotient of this party had suddenly rocketed.

"Just don't get ossified on Manhattans!" she cautioned, tapping him with her beaded purse.

The young man crooked his arm and she slid her own into it.

"Let's go meet the great and the bad," he said. "There's no social set more impossible to break into than this. What we have here is the absolute pinnacle of the climber's ladder. Princesses and prime ministers have been snubbed and turned away from awful Austerly's *haut monde* bashes. He doesn't give a fig whom he insults."

"Ladders don't have pinnacles, you ass," she corrected. "And how *did* you wangle an invite? You never told me."

He only tapped the side of his nose in reply and, as they were now standing in front of the open door, she couldn't press the matter.

A thick-set, scowling Arab in a fez salaamed and gestured silently for them to enter. Estelle raised her pencilled brows. Mr Fellows was well known for his love of the exotic and this entrance hall did not disappoint. The skins and heads of animals she had only seen in zoos were hung on the panelled walls and a python was draped down the banister. Her delight when it reared its head, proving itself to be alive, manifested in a nursery type gasp from her lips.

The air was thick with incense, streaming from a large brass burner standing in the centre. A huge Moroccan lantern, studded with hundreds of pieces of coloured glass and now fitted with electric light, hung from the ceiling, zinging the place with brilliant jewel colours. Two small Indian boys, carrying silver trays sparkling with cocktails and flutes of champagne, stepped forward from one corner. They looked so alike they could have been twins. Estelle stared at them intently and stifled a giggle as she took a glass.

Simon led her further into the hall, towards the agreeable sounds of lively chatter and jazz.

"So far it's the bee's knees," she whispered to him. "Is it true he's the head of cults and king of the witches? I do hope so – it would be too Gothically sublime of him. I'd hate for all this to be mere faddery. They say his eyes are the most intense things you'll ever see. Just one stare from them and he was able to deflower the three Rashton sisters and then moved on to their mother – all in the same night. How deliciously degenerate. Of course no one would ever dream of speaking to them again. They were ruined and had to move to Italy. Only Mussolini would take them in!"

They had come to an internal door, where an amply proportioned Chinese woman in a tight black silk dress, decorated with scarlet dragons, welcomed them with a dead-eyed smile. Estelle thought she twisted the door knob as if she was wringing the neck of a chicken and moved past her hastily when she waved them in.

This large, book-lined space was ablaze with light. Two enormous crystal chandeliers shone like captured suns above and were reflected in countless mirrors all around. Cigars and cigarettes in holders formed their own hazy atmosphere above the invited guests and Estelle took several minutes to absorb the sight of these people. Simon was doing the same, with a professional eye.

It was a select gathering. There were only about fifty people there, but the quality of them made up for the low numbers. Estelle recognised several lords and a countess, as well as a handful of Right Honourables and an industrial tycoon. Over by the ostentatious buffet, a leading man from the London stage was helping himself to oysters, while next to him a red-faced foreign ambassador thought it amusing to try and outstare the salmon. The opulent attire of the women made her own elegant gown feel positively dowdy by comparison. Diamonds or emeralds glittered at every throat, dangled from ear lobes like overripe fruit and weighed down wrists and fingers.

"I say," Simon muttered, downing his cocktail with one practised tilt of the head. "We're the poor relations here, old thing. This is the cream of the crop. I could fill a week's worth of columns, just with the letters after their names. Let's meander through and see if we can spot our devilish host."

Taking her by the hand, he escorted her into the throng. Estelle hoped she could eavesdrop on mystical conversations, concerning divination, pagan rituals and forest orgies. But the snatches of dialogue she overheard weren't very promising, just the usual empty chatter one caught at any London function. So-and-so was travelling on the first transatlantic flight of the *Hindenburg Zeppelin* in less than a week, while someone else was boarding the *Queen Mary* for its maiden voyage at the end of the month. How sorry they were to hear of King Fuad of Egypt's death two days ago. Who was going to attend the Berlin Olympics later that summer and how long could the recent Palestinian revolt be expected to continue?

Marinading this talk was the crackling music that streamed from a gramophone. Estelle wondered why real musicians hadn't been engaged. Then she noticed something that took her mind off the dance tunes and she nudged Simon discreetly.

In the crowd, several people were wearing animal masks. She saw a fox, a goat, a stag and a hound. Combined with their formal eveningwear, it looked outlandish, sinister even.

"Did they think it was fancy dress?" she tittered. "Why don't they remove those silly masks?"

"Those are members of the Inner Circle," he whispered reverently. "Extremely powerful people in their own right, but toweringly influential in occult matters. They never let their faces be seen. I think even you would be amazed if you knew who they were. Wouldn't surprise me if there was some very blue blood in that crowd."

"You have done your homework!"

He smiled and grabbed another glass from a passing female servant, who was scantily clad in strips of tiger skin.

"Where is AF?" Estelle asked. "Can you see him?"

"Not yet, but I've spotted his sister over there."

"Sister?"

"Well, half-sister to be pedantic. Haven't you heard about Augusta? She doesn't make it to London often, quite the stop-at-home wallflower. Let's go ingratiate – I do 'ingratiate' terribly well."

He whirled her across the room to where a sallow-faced, nervy-looking middle-aged woman with droopy hair and equally droopy eyelids hovered by the gramophone, sorting through a stack of recordings.

"Miss Augusta?" Simon addressed her boldly. "My name is Simon Beauvoir. May I present Miss Estelle Winyard?"

The woman offered a damp, reticent hand and gave a slight, flinching nod. Estelle had never seen such a wet lettuce. No wonder she avoided London. Nobody would ever take any notice of her there. Her one talent appeared to be the same as those peculiar reptiles that could blend into the background. What a plain Jane for the sister of the most discussed and reviled man in the country.

"Winyard?" Augusta repeated, blinking as she peered at Estelle. "Isn't that the name of the newspaper man who denounced my brother recently?"

"That's Pater," Estelle confessed with a vivacious laugh. "Firmly embedded in the age of Victoria I'm afraid – a perfect fossil. I do apologise. I hope you won't hold it against me?"

"I won't," Augusta answered, returning her morose eyes to the shellac disc in her other hand.

"Do you like Al Bowlly, Miss Winyard?" she inquired.

"He's a bit languid and dreamy for me. I prefer it jumping and wild – like Lil Armstrong and—"

"I almost worship Al Bowlly," Augusta talked over her. "He has an enchanting voice. I wish he hadn't moved to the United States back in thirty-four. No one seems to appreciate him properly here any longer. I sometimes feel I'm his last fan. I like the music of Paul Whiteman and Ray Noble too. I listen to them on the wireless, but prefer playing the recordings myself. That way I can select what I want, when I want. I'd have a gramophone in every room if Austerly would allow it. Wouldn't music wherever you go be simply marvellous? I'm sure they'll make that happen one day. Don't you find these modern devices ingenious? One of my brother's many acquaintances is very high up in the BBC. Apparently they're beginning a high-definition television service later this year. Four hundred and five lines – imagine that."

"I have no idea what that means," Estelle admitted with a fixed grin as she gave Simon a subtle kick to get her away from this freakish bore.

"It means I shall have to get a television set," Augusta said. "I'm sure they will broadcast some lovely music. Perhaps Mr Bowlly will return to perform? I do hope so."

"The few people I know with television sets only bought them to humour their cooks and stop them straying," Estelle told her snootily. "Frankly I think they're the most vulgar gimmick. Television won't last.

In two years' time it'll be forgotten, like every other fad – along with that horrid new board game that goes on forever, Monopoly."

"Miss Fellows is a bit of a boffin," Simon interjected before Estelle became any more insulting. "Wizard clever with the old science, from what I hear."

"I assist my brother with his work, when I can," Augusta answered. "Some of his work, at least – on the technical side. And I do think thermionic valves and glass insulators are quite beautiful."

Estelle was amused to see those sallow cheeks turning a deeper shade of dull. But she'd had more than enough of this monotonous reject and sought refuge in her champagne. Encouraged by the bubbles, she asked, "Where is your brother? I'd so like to meet him."

She had to wait until Augusta had changed a record over before receiving a reply.

"He's attending to business I suppose, if he isn't here."

"And what is his business? Even Pater doesn't know that."

Augusta's long face clouded a moment as she groped for a suitable answer. Then it broke into a gawky smile as she remembered something from Dickens.

"Mankind is his business," she said with a short burst of laughter that sounded more like a bronchial attack in a cat.

While Estelle puzzled on that, Augusta scanned the room.

"There's Irene," she said. "He won't be far from her."

Estelle and Simon turned to see a strikingly handsome woman in a chartreuse gown, weaving through the guests.

Irene Purbright was a statuesque beauty, with large hazel eyes and lustrous, auburn hair. Her proud features had once graced every picture paper. It was as if a Roman goddess had been made flesh. Many suitors from grand families had courted her, but she was too fine and slippery a fish for their clumsy nets and had grown tired of the London seasons. Now she was believed to be one of Austerly Fellows' Five Infernal Muses. Their affair had been yet another shocking episode. The doors of genteel society had been firmly closed against her and her face no longer appeared in *Vogue*. But here she had discovered a grander life, one with ancient fire in its blood and undreamed-of pleasures.

Estelle had heard much about Irene. She had rebelled against conformity and what the world expected of her. Estelle admired that and envied her headstrong independence. As the woman sailed by, Estelle noticed red marks and livid bruises on the alabaster skin of her bare arms and neck. Other women would have covered them up in shame, but not she. Irene displayed them as brazenly as medals.

Leaving Augusta to her recordings, Estelle towed Simon through the room and they followed Irene to the hall. But the woman was nowhere to be seen. Where was she? She couldn't have vanished up the stairs so quickly and she would have had to sprint to the front entrance with a speed equal to Jesse Owens for them not to have seen her leave that way.

They gazed around in bafflement and Simon accepted another cocktail from the two solemn Indian boys. The answer was directly opposite them. Irene had simply crossed the hall and disappeared beyond a door beneath the stairs.

With a bare light bulb illuminating her way, Irene descended the stone steps leading to the cellar. At the bottom she moved through deserted, vaulted chambers until she came to one in which three wide concentric circles had been inscribed in the floor. Five tall black candles were positioned at specific points around the outside. In the centre, standing in front of six large wooden crates, was Austerly Fellows.

The man's back was to her. He did not turn around or acknowledge her straight away; his hands were placed palm down on the top of the nearest crate and his head was bowed as if in prayer. Irene knew him better than that.

"What are you doing skulking down here?" she asked.

"I was discussing certain matters with Hankinson," the man's silken voice said. "I thought it prudent to take out a little insurance against any misadventure tonight. I named him Jangler for the first time. He is so right for that role as Lockpick."

"Hankinson is upstairs being hectored by that Brunhilde of a wife of his, and has been for the past half-hour. You're neglecting your guests, brooding down here. Joachim has stormed out in a Teutonic rage – you might have spared him fifteen minutes."

The Abbot of the Angles straightened and the candlelight glistened around the oiled smoothness of his shaven head. He was tall and dressed in a long, monk-like robe of fine black linen, trimmed and lined with gold silk.

"I don't have time for Ribbentrop's stagnant speeches tonight," he told her as he turned. "You know that."

Irene caught her breath as she always did when his dark eyes pierced her. "I thought…"

"Don't think," he commanded, drawing near and stroking her lily-white throat, closing his fingers round it until they aligned with the freshest bruises. "Your pigeon-brained opinions hold no interest for me. That's not why I keep you."

She lowered her gaze. No one could withstand his penetrating stare for long. He leaned in to lick her face with his thick tongue, dabbling it in the socket of her eye. Then he pulled away.

"Ribbentrop can go hang," he remarked. "His blind allegiance to that ranting Austrian bores me."

"It's not a competition," she said, patting her wet cheek and eyelid dry. "Why do you resent Hitler so much? You've sulked ever since he marched his tin soldiers into the Rhineland last month. Is it really worth supertaxing your spleen over?"

"You comprehend nothing," he said sourly. "We are rivals. We both serve the same master. Did you not know? This *is* a contest, in which we vie for His attention and favour. At the moment, Nazism has the lead. Oh, yes, it's attractive, glamorous and exhilarating, and the early gains and successes will be showily impressive, but it can only ever achieve war –

and wars don't work. My studies guided me down a different path, one that assures a far more lasting and satisfying conclusion. Come, look on this most wonderful sight."

He led her into the circles, to the crates.

"In here," he breathed with barely contained excitement. "Within these wooden boxes lies the true answer, the *only* final solution to the contamination of Peace."

"Your book?" she asked. "After so long, *Dancing Jacks* is completed?"

The thin lips in that strong, fleshy face parted in a repellent smile.

"Nine years I have laboured on this great task. Into those pages I poured all my knowledge, all the ancient wisdoms and teachings I risked everything to learn. Now, finally, it is ready. Ready to do its work. These books are the most powerful artefacts ever to go out into the world. Tonight, after the ceremony, each of our guests will receive twenty copies. The distribution shall begin at once. Within a year, this insipid country will be under my control – and then…"

"May I see it? Can I hold one in my hands?"

Austerly Fellows took a crowbar from the floor, to prise off one of the lids. Then he changed his mind and set it down.

"After the ceremony," he said.

"But am I in it? You said I might be."

"Still searching for immortality?" he observed coldly. "The portraits and Beaton photographs, scandals and newspaper cuttings – they're not enough for you, are they? What an insatiable appetite for commemoration and longevity you do have."

"Am I in it?" she repeated.

He gave a dismissive chuckle. "*Everyone* will be in it. And those few aberrations who slip through will also have their uses. Nothing has been left to chance. Every possibility has been anticipated and accommodated. As for you, my honey-lipped, bunny-hipped paramour, yes – you're in there."

"As your consort, the High Priestess, Labella? Like you told me?"

"No, that role didn't really suit you. I decided upon a much more apposite character, into whom I emptied those parts of you that are now departed. The kind and gentle elements of your nature which were irresistible to a fiend such as I, the essential goodness that I've squeezed out of your bankrupt soul, that's what I put in there."

"If not Labella then… who? A queen?"

His dark eyes glittered at her.

"I made you into a fairy godmother, albeit tragically impaired."

Irene was never sure when he was mocking her.

"Fairy godmother?"

"A very old and tarnished one," he taunted. "Face like a withered apple, with no juice left – a spent anachronism, of no use to anybody. She is retired from Court – living alone and uncared for in the wild wood."

His heartless words stung. Irene had known for some time he was tiring of her. But the thought of life without him was unbearable. She was so totally under his spell and domination.

He gave the crate a last loving caress then strode away. "The ceremony must begin immediately," he instructed. "Has everyone arrived?"

"Yes, *they're* here."

"Then inform the Inner Circle. The time is upon us."

The woman cast a lingering glance at the crates.

"Tonight will go well, won't it?" she asked. "The observance is safe?"

"Nothing I have ever done," he answered gravely, "has ever been more perilous."

Estelle was just about to return to the party with Simon when she was overwhelmed by a breathlessness and creeping dread. She felt the approach of Austerly Fellows like the onset of a fever. Moments before he and Irene emerged from the cellar, his malignant presence flowed out and filled the hall. When he appeared, Estelle drew close to Simon and the shaven-headed man in the monk's robes turned to look on her.

The engines of time and the universe halted as she gazed into the abyss of those pitiless eyes. No brilliant gleam from the Moroccan lamp could ever glint in that darkness. When she was a young girl, Estelle's favourite story had been *The Jungle Book* and now she knew exactly what it was like to be transfixed by Kaa the snake's hypnotic stare.

The predator glided towards her.

"Delicious," he purred. "What wide-eyed innocence in so fragile and pleasing a shell. A startled nymph – crept fresh from a Grecian grove – whom a harsh word might shrivel."

"I'm not that innocent, Mr Fellows," she said, finding her voice and basking in his attention. "Or may I call you AF? I do anyway so I might as well call you that to your face."

The corners of that cruel mouth lifted. "You have the advantage of me, Nymph," he said with amusement. "A most rare occurrence. From whose loins did you spring?"

"This is Miss Estelle Winyard, Sir," Simon spoke up.

Austerly Fellows ignored him and let his eyes drink in every curve of Estelle's figure. Behind him Irene bridled.

"The ceremony," she reminded curtly.

"I told you what to do," he dismissed her, without taking his eyes off Estelle. "Bring the members upstairs."

The woman's handsome face flushed angrily and she threw Estelle a despising glance before swirling past the large Chinese servant and into the party.

"What's upstairs?" Estelle asked, elevating her gaze, knowing how it exposed her young throat. It pleased her to believe she was versed in sin and knew what tricks beguiled men. But she was playing a hazardous, fatal game. She was a minnow, flaunting its silvery tail before the pike.

Her host moved to the staircase and stroked the head of the python that reared to greet him.

"Will you not join us?" he invited her. "The Inner Circle is meeting up there tonight. You might find it… absorbing."

Estelle ran her fingers lightly over the snake's scales. "Nothing would delight me more," she accepted.

Austerly Fellows ascended and she followed, abandoning Simon down in the hall, leaving him holding her champagne.

"Is it true you keep a leopard in the house too?" she asked eagerly.

"I did, but I had to let the animal go. The poor creature's nerves weren't up to a life here. Your tastes would appear to run to the extreme, however. I find that stimulating."

"I was always a wild child," she boasted. "Ran off with the footman when I was seventeen, then ditched him after three days and stowed away on a ship bound for Singapore. Such a lark! Pater doesn't know what to do with me. He despairs, he really does."

"I'm gratified to hear it."

"I don't care what anyone thinks," she continued airily. "It's my life and I refuse to let it go flat and stale. I want to be challenged, to be thrilled and embrace every new scintillating experience and idea. If I want to have a string of lovers, I shall. If I want to take opium and cocaine, so what? I think taboos are there to be broken, don't you? I always sea-bathe naked, no matter where I am – and positively nothing shocks me. A free, bohemian spirit, that's Estelle Winyard."

"And all on your father's wealth," he commented dryly. "How fortunate he can afford your libertinism."

"I don't see what money has to do with anything. I could be freezing in a garret and still feel the same gypsy passion in my veins, probably more fiercely than ever. Pater's cash does blunt reality's raw edge too much sometimes. I've pretended to be poor on oodles of occasions and had such thrillerific japes in soup kitchens and the slums."

They stepped on to a wide landing covered in a long strip of India rubber matting that stole the sound of their footsteps. The half-panelled walls were hung with portraits. Estelle assumed they were of his family: dingy, glazed Victorian faces, staring out of crackled brown varnish. But as they proceeded, the pictures became more up to date. There were arresting images of him in various extravagant costumes, every inch the Eastern mystic or medieval alchemist. She was so taken with one full-length depiction of him as Mephistopheles, dressed from horns to arrowed tail in vermilion, that she didn't realise her host had stopped outside a doorway and was waiting for her.

"You do love your theatrics," she said.

"An indulgence of mine," he replied. "Now if you please, Miss Winyard, let me test just how unshockable you are."

He pushed at the door which, up till then she hadn't given any attention to, but now she stared at it in astonishment. It was unlike every other in the house. It was not panelled, but covered in a bright veneer of burled walnut, streaked across the diagonal with three bands of cherry wood, and the handle was an angular bar of gleaming chrome. It was so out of place in this oppressive mausoleum she couldn't help boggling at it. Then her glance drifted past – into the room beyond.

"Oh, AF!" she exclaimed, momentarily taken aback. "It's the last thing I expected to find."

She went into the large, octagonal, windowless room, twirling around to take it in. It was a perfect match for the ultra-fashionable door. The walls were smooth expanses of lustrous wood, decorated in the Moderne style that, decades later, would be termed art deco. Lalique sconces shone all around. A rayed star design, with radiating lightning flashes, was worked into the ceiling and reproduced on the floor. A row of hooks, the finials of which were shaped like different animal heads, punctuated one wall. They were empty except for one purple robe. But her immediate interest was commanded by the contents of this most unusual room.

Twelve chest-high Bakelite consoles, resembling large, streamlined wirelesses, were arranged in a circle, with the controls and dials facing outward. An even taller thirteenth console stood at the far side.

Estelle's eyes skipped over them, but she couldn't stop looking at the inexplicable, dominating object that stood in the centre. It was a wrought-iron throne that could only have been made for a giant.

Austerly Fellows watched her keenly.

"Whatever can it mean?" she asked. "What is the overblown chair for? It makes me feel like a doll. And these radios – your sister mentioned something about the BBC. Are you going to broadcast your own service to the nation? Or are you an enemy agent, transmitting vital secrets to foreign governments? How outré and splendiferous."

"Time and tide wait for no man – or magus, Miss Winyard. Millennia ago our ceremonies would have been conducted around circles of standing stones. This is my superheterodyne henge."

"You mean these gubbins and thingamabobs are part of your dark arts? How extraordinary! One doesn't stop to think the supernatural and electricity should ever be acquainted."

"What century do you think we're in, Miss Winyard? Progress sweeps all of us along. Did you really believe the Grand Duke of the Inner Circle would still be using scrying glasses and goat entrails? All energy can be utilised. All forces have their positive and negative. I trust you are not disappointed?"

"Well, I was rather hoping naked dancing round a fire at midnight was involved somewhere along the line. Or at least the odd sacrifice."

"Oh, we still do a fair bit of that. We're not iconoclasts – in that sense at least. The old customs and traditions are crucial. Offerings must always be made; only the method of our magick has changed."

Estelle ran a playful finger over the glossy surface of the dappled brown Bakelite, tapped a glass dial and twiddled one of the knobs.

"Why don't you sit on the chair?" the man suggested. "I should like to see you up there."

"You'd have to lift me – I can't reach."

Austerly Fellows stepped between the consoles and guided her in. The floor here formed the centre of the rayed star and was made from a single large sheet of copper. Directly beneath the imposing throne, Estelle noticed a wide brass grill.

"A curious place for a speaker," she said. "The size must make it terrifically loud. Does Augusta clamber up here and blast herself with Al Bowlly? She must be in heaven feeling him trumpeting up her skirts."

Putting his hands round her slim waist, he lifted her on to the iron throne.

"What strong hands you have," she giggled. "Oh! Being up here is divino. It's like having high tea with Nanny. She was a brick. No matter how naughty I was, she never spanked or ratted on me to Pater. And I was so very naughty, practically every day – still am."

Swinging her legs freely, she reached up to place her hands on the arms of the chair. The shapes the ironwork had been fashioned into were exceedingly bizarre. Some of them could almost be the letterforms of an archaic alphabet. Knowing she looked ravishing, she traced her fingers over them for a short while, so that he could admire her. Then she turned back to him and batted her lashes in the most vampish way she could.

"You can have me, you know," she said huskily. "I could be your sixth Infernal Muse. I'm considered rather good at it – fornication, I mean. In certain quarters I've earned the nickname Pirate, because I'm such a jolly roger."

Austerly Fellows retreated between the Bakelite.

"Dear me," she laughed. "I do believe I've shocked the most evil man in England!"

"Quite the contrary, Miss Winyard," he said, flicking a switch on the tallest console and sliding a lever down in a careful, measured movement. "It is I who am about to shock you."

A faint hum emanated from the apparatus and a strange, acrid tang filled the air.

"What are you doing?" she asked impatiently. "I thought you were going to tinker with me, not your exaggerated crystal set."

"I never dine at a trough after the other animals have eaten and fouled it," he said coldly.

The colour rose in her cheeks. "You insufferable prig!" she snapped. "Why else did you invite me up here?"

"He wanted you to come voluntarily, you silly girl," a woman's voice answered her from the door. Irene Purbright was standing there, now clothed in a purple robe. "Far less mess and fuss that way – and it amuses him to toy."

Irene entered and assumed her place at one of the consoles. Behind her, other guests started trailing in. They too were dressed in purple, their faces still hidden behind animal masks. Augusta was among them. The nervy woman went to another console and took up a headset, which she clamped over her ears. She twisted a control and a blissful expression settled on her long face.

Estelle couldn't stomach any more. She was going to leave right away and began easing herself down from the chair.

"I shouldn't do that if I were you," Austerly Fellows advised. "The copper plate in the floor is now live. Three thousand volts are running through it. The jitterbug you'd perform would be highly entertaining, in fact smoking – but it would be a very brief dance."

The girl stared at the copper surrounding the chair. She believed him. Gasping, she slid back on to the seat – as far as she could.

"You can't do this!" she protested angrily. "Let me go or I'll scream this house down!"

"You wouldn't be the first," Irene informed her. "But you're not in Belgravia now. There's no one in this building who will raise an eyebrow and the nearest village is accustomed to our unusual noises. You ought not to have ventured here. Spoilt little rich girls like you always think they're so special, when really they're laughably predictable and the easiest prey."

"If only there were more like you in the world," Austerly Fellows said to Estelle, "*Dancing Jacks* would assert itself so much more rapidly. The vain and shallow, the weak-minded herd with a false sense of entitlement – that's the driest kindling for the hungry fire of my sacred words."

The girl began to despair. Then a familiar face peered in at the doorway.

"Simon!" she yelled. "Oh, thank the Lord!"

"Hullo," he said, striding in. "Look at you, perched up there."

"These people are insane!" she cried. "I can't get down. They've electrified the floor. Help me! Switch it off!"

Simon Beauvoir looked faintly embarrassed. "I shouldn't like to do that, old thing," he said, strolling to the coat hooks to take down the purple robe hanging there. "Why else do you think I brought you? Certainly wasn't for the pleasure of your company. You really are the most tedious, self-centred witch, you know. Oh, no offence, ladies and gents."

Estelle's face dropped. She watched him don the robe, then take his place at the last vacant console. Reaching into the garment's pocket, he brought out a mask in the shape of a wolf's head and put it on.

The girl on the chair stared helplessly at the robed figures around her. Some were wearing headsets, like Augusta. They were all concentrating on the dials and gauges in front of them.

"Daddy will come searching for me!" she warned. "He won't stop until he finds me!"

Her host looked up from the settings and switches.

"Two weeks ago," he explained, "your father denounced me in his rag of a newspaper. I have never sought publicity, but he threatened to expose secrets that are best left in the shadows. I am going to thank him for that by sending you back to him, Miss Winyard. I did have something else in mind but, after your pretty testimonial a few minutes ago, I have decided to deliver unto your father your skull and femurs – wrapped in a black cloth."

Estelle was too horrified to scream.

Unhooking a horn-shaped microphone from his console, he spoke into it and welcomed the Inner Circle to what would undoubtedly be their final meeting. His voice was broadcast throughout the house, so all his followers could hear.

Downstairs the cocktails were set aside and conversations ceased as everyone attended to the Abbot of the Angles – their feared and worshipful leader. A rotund man with a moustache, who could not have looked more like a solicitor from Ipswich if he had tried, put down the black Gladstone bag he had been clutching throughout the evening. The overbearing wife beside him uttered a captivated breath as Austerly Fellows' words reverberated around the room.

"On this blessed Beltane," he addressed them. "At this most auspicious gathering, it is my privilege to announce the completion of my great work. The moment for which we have planned and striven is come at last. The *Dancing Jacks* are ready to make their way in the world."

There was a murmur of astonishment and awe from the guests.

"Tonight you shall each take away first editions. You know what to do with them, where they must be seeded. I bid you, now, to look around and stamp this moment in your memories. This is the night when the world order changed forever and my rule of law began. The hypocrisies of the past will be blasted to oblivion and our Lord in exile will return to us."

There was a ripple of applause. Many of the faithful bowed.

"But no book is truly complete without a dedication," he continued. "And so I, Austerly Fellows, devote this hallowed text unto Him. The *Dancing Jacks* will pave the way for His return among us. Everything we ever dreamed of. Everything we ever wanted. Hail to the Dawn Prince – the Bearer of Light."

The rapturous cheering travelled upstairs. The Grand Duke of the Inner Circle heard them and replaced the microphone on its cradle.

He turned to Estelle. "And now, Miss Winyard, you shall discover what your father could not: the precise nature of my business."

The girl shook her head violently. She didn't want to know. She just wanted to escape.

"I won't tell," she swore.

"I'm well aware of that. I'm anxious for you to see just how my 'exaggerated crystal set' works and to whom I'm transmitting."

"I don't want to!" she cried. "Please!"

"Oh, but you must. In fact, it won't work without you. It operates on a most unique frequency, you see."

She began to wail and weep.

"That's right," he smiled, tuning one of the vernier dials with precision.

There was a snap and a click of static in the room. The lights in the sconces dimmed, until the masked faces of the coven were lit only by the soft amber glow of the instruments below them. Estelle's terror felt as though it would smash out of her chest. The whine of the apparatus wavered in pitch as they tuned in. Then there was a crack of blue light. A bolt of electricity arced from the tall console to the iron chair. Another flashed from Irene's console. Soon every device was spitting jags of energy and the wrought iron sparked about her.

Estelle howled. Strands of blue fire snaked round her slender arms and bolted across her body. The curls on her smouldering scalp lifted and her gown began to char.

Pulling one of the headphones away from her ear, to listen to the screams, Augusta gave her bronchial laugh. Then she returned to the dance band broadcast she had dialled into and closed her eyes dreamily.

Austerly Fellows adjusted a lever and the needle on the illuminated meter travelled steadily along the scale. The way was open and the bridge was forming. Tonight, for the first time, his master's voice would be transmitted to this world. The iron throne was ablaze with electric forces and the girl's figure within could no longer be seen. He wondered how much of her would be left behind afterwards.

Beneath that great chair the brass grill began to quiver and the air above buckled. The power surged. A bass roar came blasting into the room. The Inner Circle gripped the consoles tightly and the Lalique sconces on the walls exploded into white dust.

On the ground floor, the chandeliers began to tinkle and shake. The party guests gazed upward. The ceiling plaster cracked from corner to corner and rained on their heads. A cocktail glass shattered. Then another and another and the mirrors shivered into glittering pieces. The fearsome, deafening roar resounded throughout the building. Books tumbled from the shelves. The servants grovelled on their knees and prayed to their Lord to spare them. Then one chandelier came crashing down, killing two people. A jag of violet fire ripped from the ceiling. It struck one of the

363

men and flung him against the wall. The others saw his skeleton flailing in agony, a pocket watch rattling on the ribs. Then all that was left was a chalky outline on the panelling. More jets of flame came scorching down.

This was beyond anything they had expected. Everyone started screaming and they ran for their lives.

In the octagonal room, the levers on the consoles were moving on their own, feeding more power through the systems. Every needle swung into the red zone and smoke began to stream from the vents. Austerly Fellows clawed at the controls, but could not pull them back. The cone of light around the iron throne was now too intense to look on. It pulsed and flared with multicoloured flames that punched through the walls in searing bursts. X-rays, ultraviolet, gamma rays and infrared discharged in every direction, passing through people and objects, structures and cables – down to the cellars and foundations and deeper still.

A few miles away, the villagers felt a tremor rumble through the earth and windows rattled in their frames. Light bulbs blew and the dogs barked and would not be silenced. In the cowsheds, cattle lowed and tossed their heads, pressing against the walls that were furthest away from Fellows End. Horses reared and kicked their way out of the stables, then went tearing through the fields, leaping fences and hedges and galloped till their hearts burst or their legs broke.

The curious folk who peeped out of their doors saw strange, eerie lights dancing in the distance, in the direction of Fellows End. Crossing themselves, they hurried back indoors and prayed for protection and deliverance.

Then, at last, within the octagonal room, the bridge was fully made. The one to whom *Dancing Jacks* was dedicated, spoke.

At the first sound of that voice, the members of the coven slammed their hands to their ears and fled, their bodies flickering in and out of the bouncing X-rays as they scrambled to escape. Only Austerly Fellows remained. Just the whites of his eyes were showing and his fingernails crunched into the brittle Bakelite of his console as the Dawn Prince addressed him and his ears bled.

The cool April night was soon filled with terrified shrieks. Guests came surging from Fellows End. Some leaped into their automobiles, but most of them stampeded blindly into the surrounding trees. To escape the horrific power was their one instinct. The upper echelons of 1930s society hared through the woods like hunted animals. Silk and satin gowns ripped on twigs and brambles. When they stumbled in the darkness, diamonds dropped into the undergrowth.

Still wearing her headphones, the disconnected flex lashing behind her, Augusta plunged down the track. Her mouth was open in a shrill scream. The voice of the Dawn Prince thundered endlessly in her head. She would never be free of it. Then, above the clamour and tumult, she heard her half-brother's voice bawling. Staggering to a halt, she turned and looked on her family home.

The ugly house was shifting and flitting through the wavelengths and frequencies of the spectrum. For the briefest, crackling instants, sections of brick wall vanished and returned, revealing glimpses of the rooms within. Up there, in the octagonal chamber, in front of that pulsating glare, a human figure was thrashing its arms and crying out in resentful fury.

One final, blinding flash burst outward. Augusta and the fleeing guests were thrown off their feet. The ground quaked and buckled and tree roots splintered. Oaks and elms toppled like dominoes. There was pain and chaos and then darkness.

Sprawled on the gravel, Hankinson struggled for breath. One of the lenses in his spectacles was cracked and his head was reeling. The memory of his wife, crushed beneath the chandelier, shone grimly in his mind, but he thrust it away. There were other, more important, matters to deal with.

Rising, he gazed about him. The night was quiet now. The screams and uproar had been replaced by sobbing. He gazed on the house. It was dead and dark and would remain so for another eighty years.

Then, nearby, he heard a distracted, fitful voice, humming and singing.

"Miss Augusta!" he exclaimed, hurrying to her aid. "Are you injured?"

The woman didn't appear to see or hear him.

"Miss Augusta!" he said again. "Allow me to assist you."

He helped her to stand. Her head lolled to one side. "Thank you, Mr Bowlly," she murmured. "How gallant you are... I always knew you would be..."

"Miss Fellows!" he said, shaking her gently. "Your brother. Where is the Master? Where is the Grand Duke?"

Augusta's demented eyes spun around and she let loose an insane peal of bronchial laughter.

"Austerly is in the house!" she declared, staring at it for the last time. "He is the house! It has soaked him up like blotting paper. My brother is a great inky spot on the walls – ha ha ha ha ha!"

Hankinson stepped away from her, aghast. She had been driven completely mad. He looked about him. The other guests had picked themselves up and were shambling down the track. Their faces would forever bear the leprous mark of this night's horror. He thought he recognised one of them.

"Miss Purbright?" he cried. "Is it you? Madam!"

The once handsome woman turned slowly to stare at him. Her auburn hair was now stark white, her face was pocked with patches of melted skin and the lids of her eyes had evaporated.

"What happened?" he spluttered in shock. "What did He say?"

Irene shook her head and shuffled past.

"The world is unripe," her ragged lips uttered, moving on down the track. "It was too soon. Too soon."

Mr Hankinson staggered back to his bag and clutched it. Breathing hard, he wondered what to do. Then he realised it was up to him now. Austerly Fellows had given him detailed instructions in case of any *force majeure*. The Master left nothing to chance.

"Jangler will do his duty," he vowed. "And so will the future generations of Hankinsons that come after, until the world is ripened. So mote it be."

As Miss Augusta sang 'Goodnight Sweetheart', the solicitor strode purposefully back to the house. The long wait of the faithful had commenced and there was much to be done.

1. Skelter Tower
2. Main Block
3. Gangles Fire
4. Aberrants' Cabins
5. Guards' Cabin
6. Jangler's Cabin
7. Maypole
8. Graves

20

IN THE CAMP, Jody still had one more day of cramped incarceration to endure. Maggie, Charm, Marcus, Lee and Spencer told no one what had been done to take water to her. If there was an informer in the camp, Maggie would face a savage punishment for disobeying Jangler's strict orders. Lee apologised to her as soon as possible for thinking she might be on the old man's side. Then he apologised to Charm for behaving like a jackass. Admitting he was in the wrong was something he wasn't used to. Both girls forgave him, although Charm let him sweat throughout the afternoon before saying as much.

The other children, who suspected Maggie, were still convinced she was a spy and continued treating her with contempt. Nicholas drew a cruel caricature of her on the kitchen door, depicting her as an elephant eating buns, topped with the playing card symbols of the four Royal Houses of Mooncaster. It was grossly unfair and made Marcus furious, but Maggie prevented him from punching the lad's face in. Alasdair seemed to be the main source of this outpouring of spite towards her. Lee tried to tackle him about it, but the Scot wouldn't listen to anything he had to say and what could he say anyway? The only way to prove Maggie's innocence would have been to tell him everything and Lee wasn't sure he could be trusted.

And so the camp was divided, at least until Jody was released. When that happened, she would defend Maggie wholeheartedly and Alasdair would be forced to keep his nasty remarks to himself.

The intervening day was a torment for Alasdair and Christina. As far as they knew, Jody hadn't had any water since the morning she was dragged away. What condition would she be in? Would she even be alive?

Nobody dared do or say anything to provoke the guards. The knowledge that the Punchinellos had guns, and were itching to use them, ensured total obedience during the day's work and in the evening until lights out. The guards greatly enjoyed this craven subservience and bullied them more than ever. Yikker took immense delight in pushing Marcus harder than anyone else and twice fired bullets past the boy's head whilst he was picking the minchet. On the long march back to the camp, Marcus sustained another black eye when Yikker ran up and struck him across the face for no reason.

Finally the morning of Jody's release dawned. It was also the day Garrugaska's new costume arrived. When Spencer saw it, he was sickened and the other children couldn't believe their eyes. The Punchinello had become obsessed with the Westerns on Spencer's media player. Not content with stealing the boy's hat and carrying the right make of revolver, the guard was now dressed as a gunslinger. Gone was the traditional frilled yellow tunic and ruff of Mooncaster. In their place was a black shirt under a black leather waistcoat, with snakeskin boots and spurs that clinked and jingled with every step. A red bandana was tied round the thickly muscled join between head and chest and a fat cheroot was clamped between the mottled teeth. Covering the Punchinello's chewed nose, there was now a highly polished, hooked replacement, made from planished silver. It was a distorted parody of the hired killer Lee Marvin played in *Cat Ballou*.

Garrugaska strutted vainly about the camp, and never was the phrase 'pleased as Punch' more appropriate. Whenever he met one of the young prisoners, he reached for the gun in its holster, then brayed like a donkey at the terror it inspired and chomped on the cheap cigar. Eventually he encountered Spencer and relished blowing real smoke in his face.

"Anything goes wrong," he drawled, quoting John Wayne again. "Anything at all. Your fault, my fault, nobody's fault… I'm gonna blow your head off."

Spencer was too afraid to make any reply. The Punchinello mocked him and the spurs rang as he walked away. He pulled the brim of the Stetson down over those mean, red-ringed eyes and puffed on the stogie. Spencer slumped against the wall. "How much more?" he asked himself.

Presently the children assembled as usual in front of Jangler's cabin. They bowed and curtsied to Captain Swazzle who came striding out, grasping the sub-machine gun in both hands. Armed with just his clipboard and a copy of the book, Jangler followed. The first reading of the day commenced. The children waited impatiently as he read some nonsensical passage about a rabbit made of blue glass. Alasdair could hardly bear it. When were they going to set Jody free? The boy was bursting to demand it, but that vindictive old swine was probably expecting and even wanting him to do just that. Then he would promptly extend her time locked up by another few days. That would finish her off for sure.

"And so," Jangler addressed them, once he had surfaced from the spellbinding words of the hallowed text, "I come to a couple of items of the most exciting news. Just half an hour ago I had a telephone call from the Holy Enchanter, who was delighted to inform me that Germany is now a province of *Dancing Jax*. The resistance to the sacred work has been eradicated there far more quickly than anticipated – the Germans do love to read. And it looks more than likely France, Holland and Italy will follow soon."

The children listened, stony-faced. The older ones wondered how violent that resistance had been and what price the German aberrants had paid. How many had died trying to escape the insidious power of the book? The younger ones could only think about getting their breakfast soup.

"And that is not all!" Jangler continued. "My Lord has announced a most stupendous, ambitious plan!"

He paused to allow them room to gasp in curious wonderment, but none of them did.

"Every broadcaster," he continued crossly, "every channel in the country is agog and aflame with this monumental news! The Holy

371

Enchanter, the Lord Ismus, has unveiled an incredible scheme to recreate the White Castle here – in this grey dream. It will be painstakingly replicated, stone by stone, down to the last detail, from dungeons to battlements. And the village of Mooncot is also going to be built. It is a phenomenal undertaking!

"Fifty square miles of the county of Kent have been requisitioned for this most splendid honour. They will be remodelled. The topography of the land shall be completely reshaped to mirror that of the Dawn Prince's Kingdom. Where there are hills, they shall be flattened to make way for fields and woods. Where there are towns and roads, they shall be buried beneath the thirteen hills. Not once in the history of this miserable nowhere has any work been attempted on such a massive scale. His subjects will never have to be parted from the grand majesty of their home again, not even whilst they sleep. Blessed be to the Ismus!"

The children mumbled a half-hearted response and Jangler dismissed them tetchily. How could anyone not be thrilled to the core with this most amazing news? It took his breath away. But then, he reminded himself, they were only aberrant scum. What more was he expecting?

Consulting his clipboard, he saw the next item requiring his attention. He sniffed brusquely then took up his keys and headed for the main block. It was time to free that irksomely disobedient girl.

Alasdair hurried after him. The old man strode with aggravatingly slow steps and Alasdair guessed it was on purpose. Reaching the door of the tool cupboard, Jangler took longer than necessary to find the correct key. When he unlocked it, the girl within tumbled out. She was barely conscious. Jangler really didn't care if she lived or died. If she was the one his master was hiding inside, he would simply crawl out and take up residence in another of the aberrants.

His hand still in a sling, Alasdair got Nicholas and Drew to carry Jody to bed. Then the Scot put a cup of water to her cracked lips and she drank it gratefully.

"Thank you, Maggie," she uttered in a daze.

"It's no her. It's me, Alasdair – and Christina's here."

Her dry, sunken eyes fluttered open and squinted at the harsh brightness of the cabin.

"Where's Maggie?" her croaking voice asked. "Where is she?"

The boy scowled. "She's in the kitchen," he said. "Prob'ly wi' her greedy face in the trough. I wouldnae let her near ye. Ye dinnae know what's gone on here."

"She… she didn't come back. Why didn't she come back? I begged… she didn't get shot, did she? I heard guns! Was it guns? Or was it… in my head?"

"Aye, well, never mind," the boy said, trying to calm her down. "You just sip at this. There'll be some soup along a wee bit later. Esther said she'll pop round wi' it."

Jody was too frail to continue asking for Maggie and slumped back on the bed. Then she started murmuring a haunting song she had heard in the darkness the previous night.

"Maybe I'm wrong, dreaming of you… dreaming the lonely nights through…"

"Is she going to be OK?" Christina asked.

Alasdair promised she would be back to normal in no time. He hoped he was right about that. Christina knelt by Jody's side and whispered softly to her until she was summoned to join the work parties.

Jody drank a little more then slept fitfully. As the day wore on and her head cleared, she wondered why Maggie had not come to see her. At lunchtime Esther appeared bearing a bowl of thin soup. The restaurant scraps were running low and more weren't due for another two days. After three days of no food at all, soup was all Jody could manage anyway and she couldn't even finish half of that.

"Where's Maggie?" she asked.

Esther became tight-lipped and cracked her knuckles.

"She is OK?" Jody cried. "Those shots I heard. Were they firing at her?"

"Her?" Esther retorted with a sneer. "Why would her friends shoot at her?"

Jody didn't understand.

"Why do you think you were locked up in the first place?" Esther said. "That fat cow told on you, that's why!"

"No."

"It's true! She grassed on you to get more food for herself. I'm sure I've smelled chocolate on her some days. She's in with the Jangler. She's one of the Jax crowd and only pretending to be one of us. Everyone knows it."

Jody shook her head in confusion. "I don't believe it," she said. "Maggie wouldn't. She helped me. She saved me."

"Alasdair saved you," Esther corrected her. "He's been worried sick, he has. He brought you in here, soon as you was let out, and gave you water. The only person that thickopotamus helps is herself. When everyone else is asleep, she creeps into Jangler's hut and they have pizza and fried chicken. Honest to God. There's a girl in my cabin who swears she's heard them laughing and passing round the coleslaw."

"But… but the sponges. That was real. I'm sure it was."

"Sponges?" Esther asked. "Yes, I bet they've got Victoria sponges in there, and éclairs and muffins and brownies. She's never going to lose weight like the rest of us. My clothes are getting baggy on me already and it's only been five days since we started eating leavings."

Jody sank back into the pillow. She needed to rest. This girl had to be mistaken. The things she was saying were crazy.

"No one talks to her no more," she continued. "'Cept that Marcus, the black lad and the speccy one with the zits. Oh, and Charm and the stupid kids in her cabin who do whatever she tells them."

"Charm?"

"Yes. What do you expect? She's just as fake. Always whispering to each other, they are. I think they're all in on it. I bet they get some of the food as well. Chicken nuggets and trifle – whatever's in the old guy's hut."

"Maggie and Charm…" Jody repeated.

Esther returned to the kitchen with a smirk on her face. Maggie was sorting through the last container of peelings, salvaging as much as she could. Anchu was playing with his bullets, lining them up in gleaming rows and talking to them as though they were tiny metal warriors. Maggie had wanted to take the soup to Jody, but the guard had forbidden her and made Esther go instead.

"How is she?" Maggie asked.

Esther shrugged. "As if you care," she answered. "Been scoffing buns like the elephant in the drawing while I've been gone, have you? Yeah, I bet you've crammed at least ten down your fat face."

"Oh, grow up," Maggie told her, exasperated instead of angry. She turned to Anchu and asked permission to visit Jody. The guard refused.

"Pick at garbage," it ordered.

It was only later, when the evening soup was cooked and waiting for the work parties to return, that Maggie was allowed to go and see her friend. Taking a bowl of it with her, she hurried out.

Jody had found the strength to take a long, and much needed, shower late in the afternoon. Maggie found her huddled in bed – a towel wrapped round her shoulders. She looked deep in thought.

"Hello!" Maggie greeted, beaming. "How're you feeling? You had us all anxious this week. You've had a shocking time of it. How's your back now? I bet it needs…"

"Is it true?" Jody interrupted sharply.

"What?"

"That you told about the phone?"

Maggie's heart sank and she guessed how much poison Esther had spouted earlier.

"I gave you water," she said. "Don't you remember?"

"I remember you didn't come back the next night like I begged you to."

"I risked my neck that one time! I couldn't do it again. Those guards have guns now."

"Not much of a risk if they're your pals."

"What, those monsters? You think I'm in with them?"

"Aren't you? And I've been thinking, what about them apples? Where did they come from?"

"I don't know. They was just there."

"Fell out the sky did they? Or maybe Granny Smith brought them, or the Pippin fairy flew in. Come off it. Were they part of your deal? Did you share them out because they weren't deep-fried or smothered in toffee?"

Maggie put the soup on the bedside cabinet and walked to the door.

"I'll come back when you've rested properly, and had a chance to sort your head out. You're looking for someone to blame and just lashing out right now. You're talking mad."

"Am I? Well, you can have a good laugh about it with your best new mate, Barbie, can't you?"

"Eat your soup. That bowl's got more bits in it than anyone else is going to get. And don't tell no one I brought you water. If the old man finds out, we'll both get a whipping."

"Told you that, did he? When you two was having a cosy chat with biscuits? A hobnob with Hobnobs were it?"

"He told everyone," Maggie said as she left.

That evening, before lights out, Alasdair fed the fire of Jody's misplaced anger when she heard what had happened to his hand. She blamed Maggie for that too. The fact it was Maggie's phone in the first place didn't stop them hating her. She had obviously entrapped them with it.

"What are you going to do?" Christina asked.

"First," Jody answered with iron determination, "I'm going to get better. Soon as I'm strong again, I'll make sure she gets what she deserves. She won't ever do anything else like that. She won't be able to."

"Maggie's our enemy, isn't she?"

"I can't believe she had me fooled. That'll learn me."

It was two more days before Jody was deemed fit enough to join the work parties. Then, for the first time, she was sent out with the others. Many hours later, when they returned, she was a walking wreck, having fainted twice and thrown up on the return journey.

That night another postcard was slipped under Jangler's door.

My dear Lockpick,
I think it's time you made life a shade more
intolerable here for us dirty aberrants. My patience
is wearing thin. The Castle Creeper must be flushed
out. Make us suffer, make us howl in anguish, make
us wish we were dead.
AF

21

Maggie had been sleeping poorly. The hostile, toxic atmosphere of her cabin was unbearable and getting worse. They had tried and convicted her and refused to listen to reason. Only the stupefying effect of the Bakelite device gave her troubled mind any respite. The next morning there were rips in the carpet and long scars splintered the wall by the door. Something large and savage had come through in the night.

Maggie didn't have time to notice. She awoke later than usual and dashed straight to the kitchen. When she got there, Anchu was ready to scream at her. Then the guard squawked with laughter and Esther joined in.

Maggie didn't understand until she saw her reflection in the polished steel of the work surfaces. Whilst she had been sleeping, someone had drawn on her face with black felt tip. Maggie now bore an uneven moustache, round spectacles and the rest of her skin was peppered with dots.

Hurt and humiliated, she tried to scrub it off in the sink, but that only made her face red and sore. The ink would not budge and she looked even sillier.

Anchu thought it was hilarious and rolled around laughing, stopping only to take the plate of cooked sausages away for the other Punchinellos. Esther kept sniggering to herself.

"It's a massive improvement, you fat traitor," she said.

Maggie said nothing but made her mind up to change huts. She'd ask Jangler for permission to move into Charm's. She'd had enough. What else might they do to her? She couldn't stand it any more.

When the soup was ready and she could hear the others assembling in the dining hall, she took a deep breath and went in with the bowls.

The surprised silence only lasted a moment. Then everyone from her hut, Alasdair's and Esther's banged the tables and laughed at her.

Charm ran across but Maggie didn't want the proffered hug. She just wanted to get this over with. Marcus and Lee stood up and their fierce expressions quelled every voice.

"Who did it?" Marcus demanded, glaring at Jody.

The girl shrugged, a shadow of a smile on her lips.

"You think the fact you're a girl will stop me belting you?" he said. "Think again, cos it won't. I'll smack that look right off your face."

Alasdair rose from his seat. "Don't you lay a finger on her!" he warned.

"What you going to do about it, Jock?" Marcus snapped back at him. "Not much use with a crippled hand, are you? Plant yourself back down!"

Alasdair kicked the chair away and came around the table. Marcus clenched his fists and was more than ready, but Lee moved in between.

"Do like he said and sit," he told Alasdair.

"You'd really take yon dickhead's side?" the Scot asked.

"You're the dickhead," Lee said. "You're so full of prejudice and spite, you ain't thinking straight. This is not you speaking. You wouldn't have been like this a week ago. Sit down or I'll knock you to the floor and save Marcus the trouble."

"Go on then, try it!"

"You better pray I don't, cos you know what happens when I start and there's no one here strong enough to stop me."

"Oh, please!" Jody interrupted with a contemptuous snort. "Cut the tedious macho stand-off. You don't impress no one. Little boys playing at being hard."

"Keep your gob shut!" Marcus told her. "You're a bitter, ungrateful, butter-faced cow!"

"Dinnae speak to her like that!" Alasdair shouted back at him.

"Why don't you grow a pair? She's got you standing on your head. She's loving it, look at her! Finally getting some attention at last."

They were on the verge of a vicious brawl when a small voice piped up.

"I did it. I drew on her."

They turned. Christina was holding up a felt-tip pen. She stuck out her chin proudly.

"How about belting a seven-year-old girl?" Alasdair goaded Marcus. "Make you a real man that would, eh?"

"No one's belting anybody," Maggie announced. She approached Christina and crouched at her side. "Why did you do it?" she asked gently. "I've not done anything to you. I've not done anything to anyone, cross my heart."

"Jill of Hearts," Jody muttered under her breath.

An unrepentant Christina stared back at Maggie. "I did it cos you're bad," she said simply. "You got my Jody into trouble and got the Big Noses to hurt her."

"No, I didn't. I promise."

"Everyone says so."

"I don't," Charm said. "Cos I know it's not true. You lot are just foul and nasty and picking on someone cos they're different. Bullies is what you are, innit. Didn't you have enough of that outside?"

"Someone grassed us up about the phone," Alasdair said flatly.

"Weren't none of my friends," Lee told him. "I knows that for a fact."

"Oh, yeah?"

"You need to look closer to home. Did they mash your brain when they did your hand? You don't get to judge nobody."

Jody began to chuckle. "It's all gone Lord of the Flies," she said. "And no, Barbie, that didn't have Orlando Bloom in it."

Marcus looked round the tables. "This stops now," he told everyone. "The nastiness, the gossip, the whispering, the cruel drawings…"

"Ooh, aren't you the big moral hero all of a sudden?" Jody remarked. "You gonna bash all of us if we don't behave how you want us to? Setting yourself up as a dictatorship are you?

Lee strode up to her. "You best back down," he warned. "You don't want to be starting no war with me on the other side, because I will win."

"Ooh, I'm dead scared," she said, with a waggle of her head.

"You better be. If there's just one more incident against Maggie, any more abuse or name-calling, no matter who does it, I'll hold you responsible and come looking. I ain't talking no fists. I ain't makin' no empty threat. I'll just set fire to your bed with you in it, or cut you a Peckham facelift and give you a grin you won't never shake. I don't have no preference. You is trash and you best keep outta my way or you'll wish you'd croaked in that cupboard. You hearin' me?"

The insolent smirk slipped off Jody's face. He meant it. She looked at Alasdair – he was too shocked by Lee's words to jump to her defence.

"I aksed if you was hearin' me?" he repeated.

The girl nodded slowly.

Lee pointed to Christina. "Make sure your dumb mini-me there gets the message," he added. "This hate crap ends today – it is over."

Alasdair was bursting to say something, but when Lee was in this mood, he was truly intimidating. The Scottish lad sat down and Jody threw him a disgusted look. She couldn't rely on anyone. Well, that was OK with her. She'd cope with that. She'd bide her time. At least that fat pig was still covered in scribble. That'd take at least a week to get rid of. Until then it'd be a constant reminder of how much people despised her. It was a pity Christina hadn't written the word Spy on her forehead too.

They ate their thin soup in silence and as quickly as possible. They almost longed for the summons to work, so they could get away. The atmosphere in that dining hall was horrible. You could feel the animosity jabbing across the tables.

Charm was acutely aware of how unhappy Maggie was and racked her brains for a way to make her feel better. Normally she would have suggested a makeover, but that was impossible with all the ink on her face. What the girl needed was sisterly support – something stronger than empty-sounding words, which she wasn't very good at anyway. Solidarity, that's what was called for, a meaningful demonstration of friendship. Charm suddenly understood what she had to do.

Reaching for the felt pen, she calmly drew a moustache on her own top lip.

"Don't!" Maggie protested. "It doesn't come off. You don't need to do that!"

Charm smiled at her. "Yes, I do," she said warmly. "Here, will you draw me specs on? I'll only do 'em wrong. And how about a little pointy goatee as well?"

The others watched in astonishment as Maggie took the pen and did what was asked. Charm sat perfectly still and told her not to forget the spots. Esther and her cronies tried to sneer, but they realised nobody would do the same for them – especially no one as attractive as Charm. They fidgeted uncomfortably and stopped looking.

Lee stared over at her. That girl was full of surprises. The scrawl made her the most beautiful person he'd ever seen. On the next table the girls from Charm's cabin whispered to one another and grew excited and giggly. When Maggie had finished, one of them asked for the pen and they immediately set about drawing on each other's faces.

Jody viewed them with disdain. They were mindless sheep. She couldn't believe how stupid they were and it annoyed her that they had taken the enjoyment out of Maggie being the only one covered in graffiti. Some of the girls from her cabin began to look on enviously. Charm had totally turned the situation around and suddenly it seemed like great fun to doodle on your face. Even Christina was scowling to try and mask her interest.

Jody hated Charm more than ever.

It was a grey, cloudy morning. The fine spring weather had broken and rain looked certain. When they gathered on the lawn, ready to leave for the day's work, the Punchinellos stared at them suspiciously. They didn't know what to make of so many drawn-on faces. One was a target for ridicule, but this number looked like some peculiar form of conspiracy. Bezuel went up to Charm and was displeased at what she had done.

"No likey," the guard said.

"Oh, what a bloody shame," the girl replied.

He reached up and grabbed her face, then tried to rub the moustache off her lip with a calloused thumb. Charm cried out and Lee jumped forward. Bezuel bared his teeth and pointed a gun at him.

"It's all right," Charm told Lee. "I'm OK."

Bezuel's beady eyes glowered at the boy and he held the gun at an angle like a gangster rapper. "*Pop pop pop*," he cackled. "Me watchy you."

"I see you too," Lee replied stonily.

Chewing on a cheroot, Garrugaska strutted up and down the rows of prisoners. He spat at the feet of the drawn-on girls. Then his spurs tinkled to a halt when he came to stand beside Spencer. The boy had drawn a long scar down his cheek. The guard with the silver nose looked him up and down and pulled his revolver, twirling it round a fat finger before holding it out to the boy.

"Pick it up, pilgrim," he taunted. "Me know you want. Why don't you try take?"

Spencer was almost tempted. The guard would shoot him dead if he tried. Would that be such a bad thing?

"You's yeller, compadre. Gun good, make you big man."

Garrugaska spun the weapon back into his fist and pushed the barrel against the boy's chest.

"I've killed women and children," he growled, repeating a line from *Unforgiven*. "I've killed everything that walks or crawls at one time or another – and I'm here to kill you."

Spencer felt the barrel bruising the skin through his shirt. He swallowed fearfully, almost wanting the guard to pull the trigger. That would put an end to this.

The Punchinello removed the cheroot and coughed up a glob of brown phlegm that he spat on to the boy's shoe.

"This camp ain't big enough for the two of us," he said, striding away. "One of these days I'm gonna kill ya, tenderfoot."

Spencer shivered. When would this nightmare be over?

Jangler emerged from his cabin with the new postcard tucked into his pocket. He was startled to see the scribbled-on faces and wondered what they meant. There was a palpable tension between the children, however, and that pleased him. It was amusing to observe the two factions at one another's throats. Such heightened emotions and dissent would fuel the Bakelite devices most satisfactorily. The creatures that had transferred last night were the largest yet. They had scarcely fitted in the transit van.

He patted his pocket and made an announcement. Henceforth there would be no more hot water in the bathrooms and cold running water would only be provided for one hour every morning and two hours in the evening. The prisoners groaned with dismay and Jangler congratulated himself. This was only the start. He planned to make other changes they would find even less agreeable. Tomorrow he would turn off the electricity to their cabins and then…

He opened the gates and they filed through, beginning the long march to the minchet thickets. The rain started pattering down and, long before they reached them, the shower had become a drenching downpour that lasted the whole day.

It was still teeming when the children returned in the evening. They were sopping, filthy with mud and shivering. Maggie had thoughtfully put a bucket of boiling water in each bathroom and even Jody was glad to make use of it.

"We're going to catch our deaths in this place," she predicted as she towelled Christina's head.

During the day there had been numerous deliveries coming through the gates. The first was another batch of kitchen waste. Maggie and Esther sorted through it in unfriendly silence. Jangler had refused permission for her to move in with Charm. It suited him to keep the prisoners as wretched as possible. Then a van turned up bearing a large searchlight that was fitted to the sentry platform on the top of the skelter tower. Jangler was determined there would no more night-time panics and confusions in the dark. The other deliveries were solely for the Punchinellos.

Bottles of whisky, rum, tequila, brandy, gin and vodka arrived, together with fifty packets of cigarettes and more cigars. Anchu carried these off to the guards' cabin straight away and came back reeking of gin, with three lit cigarettes in his wide mouth.

That evening the Punchinellos were carousing in their cabin, glugging down the liquor, with the TV blaring. Yikker was on duty in the tower, swigging from a bottle of vodka. Every now and then the searchlight would be switched on and the powerful beam swept over the camp, making the falling rain glitter.

Alasdair stood by the door of his cabin, listening to the drunken guards' filthy talk over the screams of a horror film. They were becoming more like the worst sort of humans every day. His hand was aching and he envied them their whisky. His lips and throat felt dry and he was tired and snappy. He missed the comfort and companionship of his guitar, even though he would never be able to play again. Drew and Nicholas kept their distance. Alasdair considered what Lee had said to him that morning. He really had changed. He was filled with anger the whole time and directing it at the wrong targets. This wasn't the sort of person he wanted to be. Closing his eyes, he played mellow tunes in his mind.

Lee was in Charm's cabin. She was so proud of the girls there, with their felt-tip faces, that she was rewarding them with a night of pampering and everyone was getting their toenails painted. Never having had any close female friends, with the exception of her mother, she revelled in being a big sister to them and did her best at trying to make this awful place bearable and they loved her for it. She had decided on all of their individual flavours and named them cute, sweet things like dandelion and burdock, blueberry muffin and chocolate marshmallow.

Lee declined when she offered to paint his nails, but he greatly enjoyed her company and they chatted easily about their lives before *Dancing Jax*.

"This dorm couldn't be more different to the one I'm stuck in," Maggie declared, wiggling her toes and admiring the hot pink she had just applied. "It's like a morgue in there, but without the sparkling witty banter. I feel like a budgie in a cattery, the way those ratbags stare. That Jangler's a sod for making me stop in with them."

"The guy's a sadist," Lee said.

"You take no notice of them sour mares," Charm told her. "You don't need 'em. They'll realise what a massive mistake they've made, just give it time."

Maggie agreed, but she regretted the loss of Jody's friendship and resented the unjust opinion they had of her. For the moment, things were stuck this way. She tried to take her mind off it. Charm had said her flavour was a crumpet with a big dollop of raspberry jam on top. That made Maggie laugh.

"Do you think Marcus likes hot pink?" she asked.

Lee fell about and Charm grinned.

"Aww, you really like him, don't you?" she said.

Maggie performed a casual shrug. "He's not as bad as he was. He was a total arse at the beginning, but he's stopped trying to be the big I am and his brain's finally climbed out of his pants. The way he sticks up for me is really sweet."

"Go get him, tiger," Charm told her.

Spencer was staring out at the rain. He was keeping watch while Marcus pulled the carpet back beneath the stairs.

"It would be so easy," he muttered to himself. "Be over quick too."

"What's that?" Marcus called, replacing the carpet and stamping on it hastily. "Someone coming?"

"Oh, er… sorry, no. I was just talking to myself."

"Get a grip, dude! How'm I supposed to get anything done if you're chuntering away to yourself?"

"Do you think getting shot hurts?"

"Course it does, you plank."

"But if it's done properly, like lots of bullets in the right places, or just a single one through the head. You wouldn't feel anything, would you? At least not for long."

Marcus was about to rip into him for being mental when he caught the expression on the younger lad's face.

"What you on about?" he asked, wandering over.

Spencer turned away hurriedly. "Nothing," he said.

"Don't sound like nothing. What's the matter with you? You've been moping about with a long face for days."

"I've always got a long face."

"Well, it's even longer than normal. You'll get carpet burns on your chin, mate. That is so not the place for them."

Spencer stared up at the sentry tower. "Doesn't it bother you?" he asked. "This is it for us. We'll never get to be anyone. We've got no life, nothing to look forward to. We'll never get to be good or bad at anything. We're just going to rot here and be forgotten."

"Don't worry, Herr Spenzer," Marcus told him. "You'll be just as mediocre here as you would have been on the outside."

"Is that supposed to help?"

"Oh, come on – so a guard pinched your hat. There's worse going on!"

"It's not just that, but that's all part of it. We're non-people here. We've got no rights, nothing. We're going to die, bit by bit, and nobody out there will know or care."

"I'll kick your backside if you don't stop feeling sorry for yourself. We're all in this. Whining isn't going to solve anything."

"A bullet would."

"What?"

"I can't stand any more," Spencer said emptily. "I really can't. I've had it. I'm thinking, after lights out, all I have to do is open this door and step outside. The guards are desperate to shoot someone – might as well be me. There's a scene in *Cheyenne Autumn*, great movie, when what's left of the Cheyenne Nation are at their lowest. They'd walked over eight hundred miles, through desert and snow, to get home. They were starving and freezing to death and had to seek shelter in an army fort. The army locked them up, without food, water or firewood, and told them they were going to be sent back, to the reservation they had escaped from, in the dead of winter. They wouldn't have survived the journey. They had no hope left and said they would rather kill themselves right there. I never really understood that bit before, but I get it now. I know exactly how they felt. I really don't mind, about being shot – if it's quick."

Marcus stared at him, speechless. Then he spun the lad round and shook him violently.

"Don't you dare think that!" he yelled at him. "Don't you ever, ever dare! You hear me?"

"It's my life!"

"That doesn't mean you can chuck it away! Have you forgotten Jim? That poor mad kid out there in the grave I helped dig? I haven't! He didn't live long enough to get full of self-pity. Those monsters out there butchered him and here you are telling me you're thinking about giving them free target practice. Don't you bloody dare, sunshine!"

"But why would it matter? No one would miss me."

"I would – you stupid apeth!" Marcus shouted. "You're a mate!"

"A mate? You barely tolerate me. That Garrugaska is the only thing who even notices I'm here most of the time."

Marcus let go of him and sat on the nearest bed.

"You're right – I'm sorry," he began, gazing at the floor. "I've said and done lots of things I'm not proud of. I know it sounds lame and namby, but I'm only just starting to understand all sorts of stuff. Before this place, I never really liked myself. Thought I did, but I was a total joke. The mates I had, before *DJ*, wouldn't do for me what Charm did for Maggie today – and they wouldn't have risked their lives to bring water to nobody, like Maggie did the other night. I wouldn't have done it for them neither. They were a shallow crew of jerks and, if everything went back to normal tomorrow, I'd have nothing to do with any of them."

He raised his face. "We are going to get out of here alive," he promised, looking Spencer in the eyes. "We're not going to give up. We owe it to Jim and all the other kids who didn't make it, the ones we'll never hear about. We can't give up, ever. If you've got a problem, anything – you come talk to me about it. Yeah?"

Spencer shifted awkwardly. It was then that Maggie arrived, splashing through the rain, barefoot, to show off her nails.

"What do you think, lads?" she asked. "Does this match my hair or what? You should come next door and let us do yours."

Marcus exchanged glances with the other boy. They'd continue the conversation afterwards and he promised himself he'd make more time for the kid.

Then he jumped up. "No time for girly stuff!" he exclaimed. "We're doing man things in this hut! Grrrr!"

"You what?" she laughed.

"Come here," he said, leading her to the area below the stairs.

"Where's he taking me?" she asked Spencer in mock alarm.

"I'm going to show you something that only me, Herr Spenzer and Lee know about so far," he said, becoming serious for a moment. "This is how much I trust you. Now don't say a word to anyone else."

"As if!" she answered. "Those days are long gone."

Marcus knelt down and peeled the carpet back, revealing a section of the plywood floor that had been scored right through. He lifted it clear and a rush of cold air blew up into their faces. Taking out a torch, he shone it down. Beneath the cabin, a sizeable hole had been dug. The boy lowered himself in. It came up to his chest. Then he grimaced.

"Ugh!" he declared. "It's wet at the bottom!"

"It's been raining all day," she said. "What did you expect? And how are you going to wash that mud off without any water in the taps? You twerp!"

"Er… pay attention to the humungous hole I'm standing in, if you please!"

"All right, so you're digging a tunnel?"

"No, I'm fitting a sunken hot tub! Of course I'm digging a tunnel! I've only been at it a few nights. Not bad progress, eh? These muscles aren't just for show you know."

He shouted to Spencer to begin whistling "the tune". Slouched against the door, the boy half-heartedly gave him a few bars of the theme to *The Great Escape*, while Marcus explained how far he'd go before beginning to dig horizontally and what to do with the excavated soil.

"Up to now I've just chucked it under the cabin, but I can't keep doing that. There'll be too much. I'll have to come up with a better way of getting rid."

He realised Maggie had grown silent.

"What's up?" he asked. "It's stereo long faces in here tonight. Don't you say I'm going to die as well. That's all Lee ever tells me!"

The girl shook her head. "No, I wish you luck. I hope you'll make it."

"*We'll* make it!" he told her. "I'm not going nowhere without you, you daft bugger."

Maggie looked down at herself. "You havin' a laugh? There's no way I can fit in any rabbit hole."

"It's not going to be ready for months!" he said. "And just look at how much you've lost already, at least five kilos I'd say. By the time this tunnel's finished, you'll be skinnier than the finger a supermodel sticks down her throat to upchuck her Ryvitas."

"You think I've lost that much? Really?"

"Could be more. We're on starvation rations here. That's a drastic change to what you were used to."

"I can't believe the amount I had to eat to keep this weight on," she said. "It was a lot! And I used to wash everything down with litres of Coke every day – the full-fat variety. It's a miracle I've got any teeth left. All to spite my stepmother; that's seriously messed up. Makes me feel ill to think about it – what a freak."

"We do weird things when we're not happy. I was a scumbag. I was just telling Herr Spenzer how it's taken this horrible place to open my eyes to what a git I was. Pass me a cup, there's one over there. I need to bail this out, or I really will have made a sunken hot tub, minus the hot bit."

"I'm going to have a load of spare saggy skin," she muttered. "Stretch marks too – very attractive."

"Nah," he said. "You're young – your skin's elastic enough to shrink back. I can show you some exercises for it anyway if you want. As for stretch marks, I've got them on my pec-delt tie-ins. Besides, that sort of thing, it really doesn't matter."

"Yeah, right."

"Seriously, it doesn't."

"Who are you?" she demanded with a baffled stare. "What've you done with the real Marcus?"

The boy winced. "OK, I know, I know. I've been a massive prat. But I'm trying to change. I think you're amazing. You're the bravest person I've ever met. What you did the other night, and the way you put up with the crap that's thrown at you, what you said to Christina this morning instead of whacking her one. I bet Jody put her up to it."

He scooped as much of the muddy water out as he could and reached for the trowel that he stowed at the hole's edge.

"What makes her so twisted anyway? It's not just this place – she was like that when she got here. Face like a squeezed lemon sucking vinegar through a straw, that's her."

"Jody weren't that bad," Maggie told him. "I liked her. But look what she's been through. How would you be after getting whipped and locked up without food or water for three days? No one'd be the same after that."

"See, you're a better person than me – best in this camp."

"Stop it," she said, embarrassed.

"I mean it. If things ever get back to what they were…"

"Like that's ever going to happen!"

"But if they do, I'll ask you on a date and show you Manchester."

"Get lost."

"Honest! Though you'd have to wear a hat over your radioactive hair!"

"That'll grow out," she laughed.

Marcus winked at her and pushed the trowel deep into the soft earth at his feet. The rain had made it strangely squishy and bouncy. It was like standing on an inflated dinghy. He threw a squelchy scoopful under the cabin. Then he dug the blade in again.

"Whay!" he said. "What was that?"

"What?"

"Weird. The hole just gave a little wobble. Not an earthquake, more an earth hiccough. Didn't you feel it up there?"

"No."

He dismissed it and flung the next lump of soil over his shoulder.

"Sick!!" Maggie cried. "What's down there?"

"Why?"

"That mud, look at the colour of it!"

Marcus shone the torch again. The slimy ground beneath his feet was streaked with purple swirls.

"I think I've just dug the world's first Ribena well!" he declared, not sure what to make of it and trying to sound less unnerved than he really was.

"Get out of there," Maggie urged.

The boy crouched down and brought the torch beam closer. He ran the trowel blade through the sludge and more purple fluid came percolating up.

"Marcus!" Maggie shouted. "Get out. Now!"

He pushed the trowel a little deeper. A second tremor juddered the hole around him. This one was stronger. It was time to go. He tried to pull the trowel from the mud, but it wouldn't budge. Then it was torn violently from his hand and disappeared down into the bubbling ground.

For an instant, the boy stared in shock at the empty space where it had been. Then he scrambled to get out. It was too late.

The soft mud exploded. Three fat, boneless tentacles of pallid, pink, worm-like muscle punched up from the bottom of the pit. It was so fast, so sudden. They reared into the air, reaching through the cabin floor, dragging him back. His fingers gouged deep trenches through the mud as he slithered down among them and they whipped about him tightly. Marcus had no chance to yell or struggle. They snatched him down, underground, and he was gone.

There was a brief, stunned silence. Then Maggie screamed. Spencer came running to see what was happening. Before he reached her, the cabin tipped and tilted. The pair of them were flung off their feet and thrown across the bucking floor. Cupboards toppled and the beds slid about the room. The whole chalet lurched as it was lifted off its concrete blocks. The two beds on the mezzanine came crashing through the banister. Maggie and Spencer rolled out of the way just in time. Then Lee and Marcus's belongings came spilling down on top of them.

The cabin continued to heave and pitch. Something was hammering against the floor. Somehow they managed to crawl and stagger between and over the shifting beds and made for the door. As they kicked it open, there was a deafening crunch of splintering wood. Behind them, the floor was punched through. Maggie turned to see the carpet rise to the ceiling. Then it was torn clear and suddenly the room was filled with a forest of writhing, fleshy tentacles, like a gigantic sea anemone.

She screamed again. Spencer dragged her through the door and out into the rain.

"Marcus!" she yelled in horror. "Marcus!"

The beam of the new searchlight dazzled them as it swept over the juddering cabin. The night was filled with noise and voices. Hearing the din, the other children had come running and stared in disbelief at what they saw. Lee and Charm hurried over to Maggie who was now shaking with shock and inconsolable. Jody clasped Christina's hand tightly. How was it possible? How could it be real? Wiping the rain from his eyes, Alasdair stumbled into the crowd and looked on that fearful sight and was struck silent.

The cabin was hoisted to a steep angle and the huge worm-like limbs within were flailing around blindly. They groped and slapped at the walls and dragged against the ceiling. One came smashing through the skylight. Others curled under the beds, lifting and flicking them over. Then one found the door and came snaking out.

The children fled towards the wire fence. Then the Punchinellos came scampering from their hut, followed by Jangler from his.

"What is it?" the old man cried, wiping his glasses. "What is going on? Captain? What is that? What is it?"

The Captain was too busy to answer. Swazzle bawled an order to the other guards and Yikker came haring from the skelter tower to join them. Lining up, side by side, they raised their guns and opened fire. Bullets sprayed into the shuddering building. Peppered with lead, the tentacle that had come wriggling through the door withdrew sharply, drizzling the step with purple blood. The guards jiggled excitedly and hopped closer, their beady eyes brimming with enjoyment and intoxication.

The massive creature within twitched and quivered – stung by every searing bullet. The Punchinellos hooted, revelling in this fabulous new sport. Then the ground rumbled. There was a splitting of wood and plaster and the cabin burst apart. The roof was hurled backwards into the night and the side walls fell against the neighbouring chalets as more tentacles came crashing and spilling up through the shattered floor.

While Garrugaska and Anchu reloaded, Captain Swazzle's machine gun spat a steady, stuttering stream into the centre of that lashing forest. The tentacles rose up, wide as tree trunks at their bases, and towered high above them. Then four of the tallest came swiping down. The Punchinellos leaped away, but Anchu was not nimble enough. One fat, wormy tendril smacked the guard to the ground then grabbed at a wriggling leg. Anchu was plucked, foot first, into the air. The Punchinello screeched and squawked, the gun in his hand firing wildly, until the tentacle curled tightly around, squeezing the guard's squat body and shaking it violently.

The others focused their fire at the root of that glistening pink limb, but their bullets only maddened it. Anchu was slammed against the broken walls then cast, crushed and lifeless, through the air. The guard landed with a heavy, crunching thud by the gate.

Mopping the rain from his bald head with a handkerchief, Jangler gibbered fretfully.

"Your guns are no good, Captain!" he called. "They can't stop it!"

The Punchinellos were not listening. They were darting to and fro beneath the swaying tentacles, shooting into them and jumping out of reach when they came grabbing.

Lee stared up at the monstrous, slippery shapes, wriggling and squirming high into the teeming night. When they passed into the searchlight's fixed beam, the brilliant white glare made them glow fierce and lilac and every threading vein and branching artery stood out starkly.

There wasn't time to even guess what new breed of nightmare this was, but he did wonder how much of it was still beneath the ground. How much was yet unseen?

Leaving Charm to take care of the distraught Maggie, he ran to Jangler and spun the old man around.

"The guards' hut!" he yelled. "Them spears! We need them spears!"

Jangler stared at him a moment, flustered and confused. Then he found himself being dragged towards the Punchinellos' cabin. The door was still open and Lee barged inside. The volume of one of the three large TVs in there was turned up full. A woman was screaming as a rusty hacksaw, wielded by a man in a rubber mask, cut through her neck. Lee didn't look twice at the screen, it was a lame-ass comedy compared to this.

The cabin was an unholy tip and it stank of stale cigars, sweat, urine and vomit. Liquor bottles, cigarette ends and minchet pulp littered the floor and filth was smeared up the walls. MP3 players and magazines were scattered about the dirty beds and half-eaten Doggy-Long-Leg bones festered in the corners, but there, by the stairs, were the spears.

The boy rushed over and snatched them up.

"Yes!" Jangler said behind him. "They might prevail where bullets do not. Hurry!"

Lee dashed out and hurried to the ruins of his cabin, where he threw the weapons down, keeping one for himself. Then he lunged at the nearest rippling column of sinew and drove the spear blade deep inside and twisted it around. The enormous pillar of flesh jerked back and tore the weapon from his grasp. Then it came battering down. Lee dived out of the way and reached for another. When they saw what he was doing, the guards scampered across and seized the remaining three spears. Gunfire continued to rage and sharp blades went stabbing.

Alasdair ran up, half-empty bottles from the Punchinello cabin clamped under his arms. He had got Nicholas and Drew to tear strips from a magazine and tie them around the necks. Using a lighter taken from Swazzle's bedside table, he set one of the strips burning and, with his one good hand, lobbed the whisky bottle into the destroyed building. The bottle smashed but the contents did not catch fire.

Cursing the rain, he set light to the paper tied round a vodka bottle and sent that spinning. This time the glass did not break. Alasdair swore again. He was out of practice.

His mind went back a few months, to a siren-filled night when he and his parents chucked petrol bombs through the windows of the Waterstone's on Princes Street and George Street in Edinburgh and watched them burn. That was the time the loudhailers made their first appearance. Hordes of converted Jaxers roamed the streets, chanting from the book. As Alasdair ran through Princes Street Gardens to escape, the power of Austerly Fellows' words finally overwhelmed his mother and father and they turned on him. They tried to deliver their son to the mob, for it to throw him into the blazing bookshops. He had barely got away with his life. That was the last time he saw his parents.

Alasdair drove the painful memory from his head and looked at the bottle of rum in his hand. Alcohol wasn't as flammable as petrol, but this was ninety-five per cent proof. If this didn't work, nothing else would. He made sure the paper was ablaze with bright yellow flame before hurling the bottle at one of the bed bases. There was a satisfying explosion of glass. Then the alcohol vapour ignited and the spilt rum burned.

"Scotland forever – ya giant bobies!" he yelled, chucking more bottles after it and taking a great swig from the last.

Pale, flickering flames lapped round the threshing forest and deep beneath the ground came a rumbling bellow. Tremors ran through the camp. The Punchinellos ceased shooting and stared about them. For the first time they looked truly afraid. The triumphant grin slid from Alasdair's face. Lee threw his spear down and backed away. Something was coming. The rest of the immense creature was pushing to the surface. Cracks and crevices opened in the shaking lawn, radiating out from the broken cabin. The children cried out and jumped away as the earth bulged and shifted beneath them. The maypole toppled over. Around the camp, the fence posts trembled and the barbed wire rattled. The skelter tower creaked and teetered unsteadily and the searchlight's harsh beam shook through the rain.

Only Jangler stood his ground. He finally knew what to do. Striding up to Yikker, he calmly seized the guard's automatic pistol and took careful aim.

A single shot rang out. On one of the collapsed walls there was a shower of sparks and a fork of blue lightning escaped from the shattered brass grill in the Bakelite device. The static leaped across to the twisting army of tentacles. It flashed and coiled about them. There was a piercing whine and the smashed bridging unit clattered down the wall.

The crackling lights flared. A sound louder than gunfire went booming over the trees. The children covered their ears and blinked – the ruined cabin was empty. The monstrous creature was no longer there. It had snapped out of existence in this world. The debris of the smashed building slid into the open fissure it left behind and across the camp the ground sagged. Huge dips sunk into the lawn. It was over.

"I am heartily sick of uninvited guests," Jangler said with a sniff as he returned the gun to Yikker. "What exactly was that thing? I can't recall anything of that nature in Mooncaster."

Yikker was too slow-witted to think up an answer, but Captain Swazzle was instantly at their side.

"A Marshwyrm," the Captain said with a sideways glance at Yikker.

Jangler pulled at his moustache. "Ah," he said bluffly. "One of those dangerous beasts that sometimes creep in under the hills. I've never seen one; that explains why I didn't recognise it."

"Most nasty," Swazzle declared. "Big trouble."

"Yes, well, it's gone now. Let's get this place back to normal. Such a shame about having to sacrifice the bridging device and a pity about your fallen comrade. He died most courageously. I'll get some of the aberrants to dig a grave. We'll sort the rest of this mess in the morning. It looks like a tornado has struck. Hmm... I suppose the boys from this cabin will have to share with the other three lads. Line everyone up for a quick headcount. Make sure everyone's present and correct."

The guards pushed the stunned, staggering children into their usual rows. Yikker quickly noticed one of them was missing.

"Where Stinkboy?" he demanded. "Where he?"

Maggie raised a tear-stained face.

"He's gone," she said desolately. "That monster dragged him down. Marcus is gone – he's dead."

22

Lee and Spencer were chosen to dig Anchu's grave. It was no use protesting, so they worked as fast as they could. Jangler granted them permission to work past eight o'clock to get the job done. Garrugaska watched, the rain dripping from the Stetson and running down his hooked silver nose as the guard chain-smoked cheroots. When the boys were finished, the dead Punchinello was dropped into the ground, without words or ceremony. The other guards weren't even present. For them there was no grief, no sense of loss, just a corpse to be disposed of and more booze and cigarettes to go round.

Lee wondered what would have happened if Jangler hadn't insisted on the burial. What would they have done? Left the body to rot, or would they have made use of it in the same way they had made use of the dead Doggy-Long-Legs? The boy's skin crawled. He and Spencer filled in the grave as swiftly as they could then handed back the shovels and traipsed into their new cabin.

Lee commandeered the mezzanine for them both. Neither Drew nor Nicholas dared oppose him. Alasdair was standing on a chair examining the Bakelite device fixed to their wall.

"Is it true?" the Scot asked them. "Is Marcus really dead? He's no just escaped under the fence in the confusion?"

Spencer stared at him angrily. "He wouldn't have gone on his own!" he snapped. "He wasn't like that. Marcus was… he was going to take…"

"Oh, he's real dead," Lee interrupted quickly, in case Spencer let slip about the tunnel. He still didn't trust anyone outside their little group. "Maggie says that thing just snatched him clean down. Happened in a click."

"Yeah, but she's no exactly reliable, is she? And him…"

"I was there!" Spencer shouted back. "One second Marcus was talking, the next... he'd disappeared and those massive worms were everywhere! He was my friend, so don't you say anything!"

Alasdair chewed his bottom lip. Spencer's outburst astonished him. That spotty lad was like a ghost usually. He was so quiet and withdrawn you forgot he was there – especially now he no longer had his cowboy hat.

"I didnae like the guy," he admitted. "But I wouldnae have wished that on him."

"Try putting yourself in Maggie's shoes," Lee said. "She did like the guy – a lot."

"What were those things?" Nicholas asked suddenly. "I can't make sense of it. Monsters like that aren't real. What was it? How did it vanish like that?"

"Kid," Lee said impatiently, "you is living in a place where all kinds of crap that shouldn't be real are part of your every day. Why you still aksin' questions from the top of the dork sheet? Somebody smack him awake."

Alasdair tapped the Bakelite unit with his fingers. "It were something to do wi' this," he muttered. "Did ye hear what old Mainwaring said about these jobbies? Called them bridges. How does a knackered old radio bridge anything? What the hell is going on here?"

"You just answered your own question there," Lee replied, trudging up the stairs.

In Maggie's cabin, she was sitting on the edge of her bed, staring blankly into space. Charm had remained with her till lights out when she had to leave. There was nothing she could say, no comfort she could give. Charm asked the other girls in there to look after her, but they made no answer. Most of them were too traumatised by what they had seen. They were terrified something else would rise through the earth to destroy their cabin and kill them too. Jangler had assured them that was not going to happen, but no one believed him.

Jody voiced doubts that no cabin was safe now anyway and they were bound to collapse after all that violent shaking. She pointed to a long crack in the plaster that ran across one wall as evidence the structure was now unsound and dangerous. She demanded they be relocated. The old man merely laughed at the suggestion. Just who did she think they were? If the roofs fell in on them, it wouldn't matter. They weren't important.

And so the girls lay in their beds, wide awake, straining for strange sounds and expecting the floor and walls to tremble and cave in at any moment. How could they possibly get any sleep?

An hour passed and still Maggie did not move. Darkness filled the dorm, but she was unaware of everything around her. Her thoughts were empty and numb. Eventually her face clouded and she uttered a dismal groan.

"I never even saw him without bruises on his face," she declared. "I'll never know what he looked like without those black eyes."

Jody let out a bored grunt. "You didn't miss much," she said unpleasantly. "Marcus were a thick meathead with a mug to match."

Maggie turned, slowly emerging from her frozen daze. "What?" she asked, unable to believe she had heard her correctly.

"Not exactly a tragic loss to the gene pool, were he?" Jody continued. "Least he didn't get to breed. Or maybe he did? Wouldn't surprise me, he were always on the sniff. There's probably half a dozen of his monobrow sprogs dragging their knuckles out of their buggies round Manchester already."

"You'd best shut up," Maggie warned.

"Don't you try bossing me about," Jody told her. "That's what your big-nosed buddies do. I'll say what I think, cos I'm not a hypocrite and I'm being honest. Do you even know what that means?"

"I said, shut up."

Christina sat up in bed and chuckled softly.

"What's it to you anyway?" Jody taunted. "It were plastic satsuma face he had the hots for. Had the horn for her since we got here, he had. Pathetic it were. Us all laughed at him."

That was it. She had pushed too far. Maggie stormed round to her bedside and smacked Jody hard. The girl cried out in surprise and clasped her stinging cheek.

"You know nothing!" Maggie shouted. "Marcus read you right. You are twisted and full of bile and…"

The rest of the sentence was cut short as she was wrenched backwards. Christina had jumped up and caught hold of her hair. Maggie fell back on to the bed. Jody leaped after her, landing on the girl's stomach. She repaid the smack three times over, followed by a punch in the ribs.

"What you goin' to do now, Gutso?" Jody cried. "You only got one macho wazzock left to defend you – and he's too interested in Barbie to do owt about it. With any luck, he'll have caught pneumonia digging that grave out there tonight."

"Hit her again!" Christina urged, tearing at Maggie's hair. "Thump her, scratch her. We hate her, don't we?"

Maggie arched her back and swung her arm round, clouting Jody's head and throwing her off. Then she reached back and shoved Christina roughly with both hands. The seven-year-old squealed and rolled off the bed. Maggie got to her feet in time to confront Jody springing back at her. The two girls fought with their fists. They swiped and flew at each other, but Maggie was the stronger. She landed a punch on Jody's jaw that sent the other girl reeling.

Christina howled and ran at Maggie, with her teeth bared. She clawed and bit her arm till it bled. Maggie picked her up and flung her across the room. Christina landed on one of the other beds and bounced back for another attack.

The other girls were kneeling up, watching the shapes of the combatants vie with each other in the gloom. It took their minds off the horror of before and they started calling out, encouraging Jody to get stuck in and teach the dirty traitor a lesson. Then one of them got out of bed to join in. Another followed. Then another. The dark cabin was alive with violence and anger.

Maggie was surrounded. She couldn't fight them all and she couldn't escape. One foot outside the door would be answered with a hail of bullets.

They had her trapped. The pent-up fears of every girl came boiling to the surface and they lashed out at her. She couldn't defend herself against so many. They tore at her arms and dragged her to the ground. They stood on her hands and pinned her down. A foot pressed heavily on her chest and they sat on her legs. The darkness was thick with their panting breaths and they looked to Jody for instruction.

"Get off me!" Maggie demanded. "Let go!"

Jody leaned over her face, menacingly, then kicked her head. Maggie roared.

"You've had this coming a long time," Jody snarled. "You're filth. You're double-dealing scum. This is payback time."

She spat in her face and ordered the others to do the same. As they obeyed, Jody went searching through the nearest bedside cabinet.

"I know what to do with the likes of her," she said, returning with something in her hand. "If she loves the world of Mooncaster so much, she can eat it."

Then the others realised what she was holding and they murmured uneasily. It was a copy of *Dancing Jax*. Jody laughed at them for being so weak and afraid.

"I'm going to feed her fat face with it," she growled, opening the book and tearing out the first page.

"You're mad!" Maggie shouted. "You can't do this!"

The other girls looked worried. Defacing that book was a serious crime. None of them dared go that far. Jody tore out a second page and crumpled them together.

"Open the whale's mouth," she said.

The girls hesitated and shook their heads.

"Scaredy-cats," Christina called them, pushing through to pinch Maggie's nose tightly and force her chin down.

"Good girl," Jody praised her. "Now let's choke the gormless lardo with Austerly Fellows' evil prose."

She pushed the scrunched-up pages into Maggie's mouth. Then she ripped out more and crammed them in after. The other girls shrank away. The frenzied hysteria had burst and their madness had evaporated. They watched Jody with increasing horror. As Maggie gagged and struggled to breathe, her tormentor began to laugh. It was a horrible, insane sound.

"That's enough," one of them said.

"You'll kill her," another girl cried.

Jody threw them a disgusted glance. "It's what she deserves! We've all suffered in this place. She's a spy for baldy. I hope she does die!"

"Stop!" the girls called. "Stop it!"

"Never! I'm making her eat these lies. This book ruined everything. Don't you want to make her pay? I ruddy do – and if I had a knife, I'd trim some of her ugly blubber off as…"

Suddenly the door was thrown open. The searchlight swept down from the skelter tower and shone directly into the cabin. The girls fell back. Captain Swazzle's grotesque silhouette was standing in the dazzling white glare. The Punchinello barged in, knocked Christina out of the way then seized Jody by the throat.

"Jody Jody Jody," the Captain's nasal voice hissed. "You think you hurt sacred book and we not feel? You very silly. Me punish you big now – oh, yes, oh, yes."

He dragged her, shrieking, from the cabin. Christina tried running out after them, but one of the other girls pulled her back. On the floor, Maggie retched and spat the pages out.

Every guard had sensed the violation of the book. They stationed themselves outside the cabin doors and the children inside peered past them to see what was happening.

Jangler heard the commotion and came trotting out. Captain Swazzle had hauled Jody to the skelter tower and the old man hastened over there.

"A most heinous act!" he exclaimed as soon as he found out what had occurred. "This disgraceful, pig-headed girl refuses to behave. What are we to do with her?"

A wide, leering grin spread over Swazzle's face.

In his cabin, Alasdair was watching helplessly. "What's she s'posed to have done noo?" he demanded, banging on the door glass at the guard standing outside. "Leave her be, ya toaty bawbags!"

Yikker ignored him. The guard was sulking that Marcus was no longer here to torment.

The other prisoners looked on fearfully. Charm put her arms round her girls. She hoped Maggie was all right. What was Jangler going to do to Jody this time? They did not have to wait long for the answer.

Ropes were tied round Jody's wrists and Swazzle darted up the stairs inside the tower. Then the Captain heaved on the ropes and the girl was hoisted halfway up. As she cried and begged for help and mercy, the Punchinello bound her to the timber framework and she hung there, like so much washing on a line.

"You stay," Captain Swazzle called to her. "You stay, you suffer – Jody Jody Jody."

The imp came scampering down the steps again and Jangler nodded his satisfaction.

"Let her dangle there another three days," the old man said. "That should break her. Make sure none of the others get close or speak to her."

Captain Swazzle gave a little skipping dance then narrowed those beady eyes. "We need talk," he said. "We need new clothes."

"If your tunics are dirty, order some of the aberrants to wash them."

"No. Want new different clothes. Not tunics. We no likey tunics. We want change – like Garrugaska."

"You all want to wear cowboy outfits?" Jangler asked in astonishment. "That's ludicrous! This isn't the Alamo or the OK Corral."

"Not cowboy," Swazzle told him. "We want different. Each want different. Must have."

"Very well, I'll see what I can do. But it's most irregular."

"You do. I tell what we want. Must have."

They wandered back to Jangler's cabin to discuss the new clothes, leaving Jody suspended high above the ground, lashed to the skelter tower.

Rising from the floor, Maggie gazed out at her. The other girls stepped away, ashamed of what they had done. Maggie was still aching with grief for the loss of Marcus, but her anger against Jody was spent. Now she felt only pity. Jody's anguished cries mewled into the night and the rain pelted down.

23

THE MORNING REVEALED the full extent of the cabin's destruction. The rain had stopped, but the trees and the barbed wire were still dripping when Lee and Spencer emerged, before anyone else was awake, to sift through the wreckage and salvage as much of their stuff as they could find. They looked up at Jody, hanging on the tower, and shook their heads. She was unconscious. Perhaps that was just as well.

While they foraged, they also collected Marcus's belongings and gave them to Maggie. The girl was numb with grief and shock. Esther had to make the breakfasts alone that day, and she wasn't happy.

As he had done after Jim Parker's death, Jangler generously allowed each internee a sausage. The children ate them in silence. Christina knew Jody would have quoted a list of nauseating ingredients at her if she'd been present, but she ate it anyway. Spencer pushed his plate away, untouched. Did that foul gaoler really think a sausage would somehow make them feel better about Marcus's death? Was he that crazy? It was insulting.

Alasdair tried to speak to Jangler about getting Jody released, but he gave the same harsh warning as last time. Any more appeals would result in her being kept up there even longer and left for the crows to peck at. Her continued disobedience would not be tolerated. Besides, Jangler added with a macabre chuckle, he liked the new addition to the skelter tower – she was like a living decoration on a skeletal Christmas tree.

Alasdair turned away from him, sickened. He didn't think she could survive this one. He wished he'd thrown the old sod to the giant worm monster when he'd had the chance.

And so the day passed. Maggie ate nothing and spent the hours in a mechanical daze. She didn't eat the next day either and it took all Charm's powers of persuasion to get her to sip some of the soup on the third.

Jody's predicament loomed over the camp in every sense. Last time she had been shut away around the back of the main block, but now she was strung up for everyone to see. Some of the girls couldn't bear to look at her and covered their ears when they heard her sobbing. Esther shuddered every time she went outside and secretly wished the girl would die, to put an end to her suffering and theirs. Life here was bad enough without having to see and listen to that. Whenever Garrugaska patrolled the fence, the guard would pretend to take potshots at her and whichever Punchinello was stationed at the top of the tower would hiss down to her, making hideous threats. Jody was thankful for the times when she passed out and her mind wandered in dark places.

On the fourth day she was cut down. No one could quite believe she was still alive. There had been more rain. She had tipped her head back and the drops she had caught had saved her. She had also been able to ease the agony in her arms by putting her weight on one of the cross-timbers behind her. But she was much weaker this time and her hands were almost black from the tightness of the ropes. Nicholas and Drew carried her frail body to her cabin and Alasdair and Christina sat with her.

She had a fever and didn't come round for another two days. Her body recovered slowly, but she was never the same again. Her spirit was defeated. She had endured too much and seen things none of the others had. Every night she had heard those melancholy 1930s tunes playing and in the cold morning saw strange creatures exit the cabins to be shepherded into vans, which were driven away, long before any of the other children stirred.

Jody withdrew into herself. She wouldn't look anyone in the eye and kept hers on the ground or fixed to a spot on the wall. She wouldn't speak and Alasdair worried incessantly about her. It was heartbreaking to witness the pitiable transformation. He tried to engage her in conversations about music or books or anything before this had happened, but there was no answering spark. Nothing could kindle her interest. She stopped brushing her hair and had to be prompted to wash. Even Christina was shut out. Jody could no longer bear to be touched and flinched whenever the seven-year-old tried to hug her.

Captain Swazzle was greatly pleased to see the change that had come over her and would swagger by, singing her name slowly to send her cowering into the nearest corner.

The weeks rolled over. The two graves grew green with grass. No flowers brightened Anchu's plot, but Jim Parker's became covered with daisies. Spencer suggested to Maggie that a headstone for Marcus would be a good idea, even though he wasn't buried there. It would be a focal point, somewhere she could go to think about him, and if anything happened to them, one day other people would know that a boy called Marcus had died here. Maggie agreed. They salvaged some wood from the demolished cabin and she wrote what they knew about him on it then placed it in the ground close to Jim's grave, together with a tearful goodbye. A simple stick, with a curved Punchinello hat placed on top, marked where Anchu was interred.

The felt-tip scribbles finally wore off and the girls' faces returned to normal. Maggie's vibrant fuchsia hair faded and the dark roots grew, while her weight dwindled. No one could accuse her of eating secret supplies of food any longer – but not one of them apologised.

Gradually the soap and toothpaste ran out and they had to resort to brushing their teeth with charcoal. Their clothes became grey and ragged and they looked more and more like scarecrows. They were still expected to work as hard as ever, but the unvaried diet was beginning to take its toll on their health. Skin rashes became common, cuts and scratches took longer to heal and one of the girls in Esther's cabin complained of thinning hair.

Lee thought about the food he had stashed beyond the wire, in the woods. They really needed it now, but the guards were more trigger-happy than ever. He would never make it out there and back again. With a sinking heart, he realised the only way to bring food in was to return to Mooncaster. The prospect filled him with dread, but what else could be done?

"Not yet," he told himself. "Don't be goin' back there yet."

One morning, just before the first reading of the day, when Jangler was smugly informing his young prisoners of the latest news, they wondered why the only guard on duty was Garrugaska. Where were the others?

"… and the Midwest of the United States is now one with the words of Austerly Fellows," Jangler told them. "They welcomed *Dancing Jax* with euphoric celebrations when it was read to them from the pulpits of their churches. Even the Ismus was surprised by how swiftly it was received there. How eager those poor lost souls were to join the ranks of the blessed. Only a handful of states remain stubborn, but that won't last. The civil war that has broken out across America will be short-lived. Soon the resistance will be quashed and the burning cities will find joy and peace within the sacred pages. Praise to the Dawn Prince, hail to the Holy Enchanter."

The children remained silent. They didn't even bother listening to these vainglorious speeches any longer. They had no way of knowing how true they were and talk of distant countries might as well have been about other planets. All that mattered to them was how to live through the coming day, here in this evil place. Only Spencer let his thoughts dwell on the violence that was undoubtedly raging on the other side of the Atlantic. He wondered how the places he had always wanted to visit were surviving the effects of that book and he prayed no aberrants like himself would have to experience a camp such as this.

Then the door of the Punchinello cabin opened and the other three guards came strutting out. An audible gasp issued from the prisoners' lips. Spencer's mouth fell open. He didn't trust what his eyes were showing him.

Captain Swazzle's demand for a completely new wardrobe had finally been granted. Rigged out in their new clothes, the guards paraded up and down, and the children gaped at them in blank surprise. Having one of those creatures dressed as a cowboy was disturbing, but now…

The guards had each chosen a certain distinctive look that appealed to them, for one reason or another. Their previous yellow tunics and ruffs had made a certain warped sense, and matched those hideous faces and high, humped shoulders. But these new garments were utterly preposterous. The absurdity reinforced just how inhuman they were and they appeared even more frightening than before.

Bezuel was decked out like a gangster rapper. He wore a red tracksuit with the word BEZ emblazoned in diamanté letters across the stomach of the baggy black sports shirt beneath. Custom-made mirror shades concealed the cruel eyes and an oversized beanie covered his large bony head. Those strong fingers were adorned with chunky gold rings, studded with diamonds, and fat gold chains and medallions were hung about the thick join where the head met the chest. A luxurious coat of silvery grey chinchilla was draped over his shoulders.

The Punchinello sauntered past, posing and grinning to display the gold grills on his teeth. The children's eyes flicked from him to the two others.

Captain Swazzle was dressed like Al Capone, in a dark blue, pinstriped, double-breasted suit, tailored to fit that deformed figure. The corner of a white silk handkerchief poked neatly from the breast pocket and a platinum watch chain was strung across the waistcoat. A white fedora was wedged on the Captain's head and pearl-grey spats covered handmade Italian boots. Swazzle brandished the machine gun as a fashion accessory and the cigar in that wide mouth waggled slowly from side to side.

It was Yikker who drew the most attention. The guard who had despised Marcus and made his brief life here as painful as he could was dressed in the long black cassock of a Catholic priest, with a biretta perched on his pockmarked skull. He held a leather-bound copy of *Dancing Jax* in one hand as though it was a bible and his automatic pistol in the other. Lee found that outfit particularly repugnant and the disgust showed on his face.

"As you can see," Jangler announced, directing a slightly uncomfortable, almost embarrassed, glance at the guards, "the Punchinellos have decided to dress differently. Don't let their new attire confuse you. They are still Warders of the White Castle and you must continue to obey them with the same deference as previously. Failure to do so will result in punishment."

"Punishment…" Captain Swazzle echoed, looking across at Jody and flicking cigar ash on the ground.

The journey to the minchet thickets took longer that day. The three Punchinellos were enjoying their new outfits too much to march the young prisoners at the usual brisk pace. Bezuel and Yikker promenaded as though the paparazzi were watching and took photographs of each other with the mobiles confiscated months ago. Captain Swazzle affected a rolling tough-guy gait, hunching those humped, vulture-like shoulders even more and scowling at the surrounding countryside. Garrugaska grumbled at them impatiently and took a simmering temper out on Spencer.

When the work parties divided and reached their separate destinations, the guards made the children work twice as hard to make up for lost time. Yikker had brought the lash along and applied it whenever one of them appeared to sag or take too long a breather.

By now the internees were a familiar sight when they were out working. New Forest locals and tourists alike would drive slowly by, to jeer and scream abuse or throw objects at them. Occasionally a car would pull up and the angry driver would bribe one of the Punchinellos with cigarettes or cash so he or she could get close to one of the prisoners. Then they would either spit at, hit or shove them into the minchet thorns, while denouncing them as the lowest abominations in creation. It was deranged, brutal behaviour and there was nothing the children could do to defend themselves from it.

That day was no different. In the afternoon a peppermint-green Beetle parked at the edge of the road and a man in his forties came out. His unbalanced hatred for the aberrants had flushed his face. As he crossed the road, his fists tightened and his knuckles blanched.

Bezuel nudged Yikker to go and see what the man could give them before allowing him any contact with their charges. Yikker uttered a gargling cackle and the cassock-clad figure went scampering over, eager to haggle.

Bezuel slipped away, silent and unnoticed, the hem of the chinchilla coat skimming noiselessly over the grass. The minchet grew dense in this part of the forest. It choked and clotted the trees and the guard had to skirt round and thread a meandering way through. Bezuel had noticed one of the older prisoners had become separated from the rest and was now out of sight. It was this stray internee the Punchinello was keen to pursue, while the attention of Yikker was distracted elsewhere. Bezuel had waited a long time for this moment to present itself. The guard licked his lips in eager anticipation.

The smaller girls were foraging deep within prickly caves. They had to crawl on their stomachs through heaps of sharp spines and needles, to search for the largest fruits that grew in the shade. The danger of encountering a Doggy-Long-Legs' nest was ever present in there and the children squirmed forward fearfully. Clouds of bluebottles buzzed everywhere. They pollinated the stinking minchet flowers and bred swiftly in the fruit's sloppy grey flesh.

Pushing a shopping basket before her, Christina wriggled through on her elbows. The thorns scratched her arms and snagged her hair, but she could not get out of there until the basket was full. Squeezing between two thick stems, she winced when a woody spike raked across her neck. Then she saw a cluster of ripe grey fruit in the gloom ahead and forgot about the pain.

It was the largest crop she had seen – enough to fill the basket and more. Pulling a determined face, she pressed on. When something brushed against her forehead, she swept it aside and reached for the fattest minchet. It came away from the stalk easily and she placed it carefully in the basket. Then she stretched for another, but her fingers broke through a covering drape of sticky gauze.

The girl let out a startled breath and drew her hand back. Wispy brown strands clung to her skin. It was the web of a Doggy-Long-Legs. She had crept into one of their nests.

Christina's eyes widened and she stared around in the gloom. It was so dark in there it was difficult to make out anything other than the overhanging minchet. Those horrors could be anywhere. The chaotic jungle of branches and twigs that surrounded her could easily conceal spindly legs and any one of those leaf bundles might be a tensed body, waiting to pounce.

Not daring to make a sound, she pulled the shopping basket towards her and started to inch backwards. There was a faint, dry rustle and a tiny movement in the corner of her eye. Christina halted and turned her head. There it was!

A small distance away, suspended in a hammock of gnarled, twisting vines, and concealed beneath old leaves and dead grass, was a Doggy-Long-Legs. The black, bulging eyes were fixed on her. A withered leaf turned over and came twirling down, followed by the tip of a thin, curved claw.

Christina tried to edge away, but the back of her dress became caught on that woody spike, pinning her like a butterfly. She couldn't move.

A second, third and fourth leg stepped out of the leaves. Then the savage, hairy face emerged, the mouth already open.

The little girl tugged and heaved, but she only pushed the spike further into her dress and it hooked on to the collar. She was completely stuck. Frantic, she reached behind her head to tear the fabric free, but it was no use.

The Doggy-Long-Legs pulled its body clear and the four back legs came arching after.

Christina went limp and looked into those baleful eyes that were already feasting on her. The creature advanced stealthily. The sharp fangs ground together and it made a gloating, clicking sound in its throat.

Then a change passed over the girl's face. She stuck out her chin and she bared her own teeth.

"You will not," she growled. "You will not!"

The Doggy-Long-Legs kept on coming.

"Stay back!" she commanded.

The beast was very close now. She could smell its foul breath. Rearing up on its hind legs, it paddled the air with the four front limbs and saliva dripped from its hungry jaws.

"Stop!" she shouted.

It was as if she had hit out with a sledgehammer. A violent jolt shook the Doggy-Long-Legs and it staggered back in dismay. The black eyes burned with fear and it stared at the child in panic and terror.

"Go away," Christina said.

The creature covered its face with its forelegs and backed off.

"Go!" the girl demanded. "Now!"

The Doggy-Long-Legs scuttled about. It sprang into the low branches, climbing as far, and as fast, from the seven-year-old as its eight legs could take it.

Christina closed her eyes. The quality that had driven the predator away left her features and she indulged in a small, secret smile before resuming the tussle with the woody spike.

Outside the thicket, at the outer edge, Charm was humming tunelessly to herself. She hadn't realised she had wandered so far from the others. She was trying to think what to do for the girls in her cabin. What treat or entertainment could she contrive to take their minds off all this? Maybe a talent contest? She and Lee could be judges. Perhaps they could even put on a little show for the others? Rehearsing for something like that would be a welcome distraction. It might even be a lot of fun. She gave herself an imaginary pat on the back and resumed humming.

Standing on tiptoe, she pulled a fruit from the stem and placed it with the rest, in the shopping basket they all carried. She grimaced as she always did when touching that sweaty flesh and wiped her fingers on her skinny, and now very shabby, Armani jeans.

"No wipe," a guttural voice said suddenly.

Charm jumped and spun around. Bezuel was there. The thin lips parted in a foul leer, displaying the gold grill bridging those yellow teeth.

"You frighted the life outta me!" she gasped, dipping into the obligatory curtsy. "I were miles away."

"No miles," the Punchinello corrected, ogling up at her. "But far from others, yes."

The girl looked over the top of his beanie and realised they were quite alone. It was a situation she had been careful to avoid till now. She was instantly wary.

"Best be getting back then," she said. "Don't want 'em finkin' I run off or got lost."

She began retracing her steps, but the Punchinello caught hold of her hand.

"No go yet," he gurgled. "Stay."

"I gotta put these 'ere minchets in the truck," she explained, trying to ease herself free.

The guard's strong grip held firm.

"Stay," he repeated, breathing heavily.

Charm was anxious to get away, but she didn't dare show how scared she was. "Just for a minute then."

Bezuel lifted her hand and caressed it. "You no need wipe," he said.

"Yes, I do," she answered with a forced light laugh. "That stuff's 'orrible sticky and attracts all the flies."

"No need wipe," the Punchinello said again. Then, before she could stop him, the squat creature put her fingers in his wide mouth and started sucking them.

Charm almost gagged and tried to pull away. The Punchinello refused to release her. She felt his cold, fat tongue squeeze and probe between her fingers and his lips moved over and under her knuckles like twin slugs. Behind those mirror shades his beady eyes rolled back in his head.

Eventually he grinned and loosened his grasp. The girl tore her hand out and thrust it under her arm.

"I'm goin' back!" she said, anger mixed with revulsion and alarm.

"No go!" the guard commanded, blocking her way. "Bezuel want speak. Bezuel like. You pretty."

"Fanks, but I…"

The Punchinello lifted the sunglasses and the intent in those eyes was unmistakable. Charm began to back away.

"You like Bezuel new threads?" he asked. "Is good, yes? Bezuel see on tellyscreen. Bezuel learn much from tellyscreen. He know skanks crawl over bling bling like maggots on minchet. You hoes like shiny gold and ice, yes? Bezuel let you touch gold – you let Bezuel touch you."

"Not wiv a bargepole, mate and you can stick your bling! I ain't interested."

The ringed fingers lunged at her. Charm yelled and ran. The guard caught her pink Bvlgari belt and snatched her back, pushing her against the thicket.

Charm cried out, but the Punchinello pulled the gun and thrust it against her stomach.

"You no make noise," Bezuel growled. "You no scream. If other abrants come to help, me shoot them in head, then me shoot you. You want feel lead, or gold? Bezuel want your booty, Bezuel get – before you go."

"Go?" she said. "Where'm I goin'?"

The guard sniggered at her. "You near birthday. You too old for stay in camp. No good. You must go."

The words hit her like a slap in the face. "My birthday?" she murmured. "Is it July already? Oh, my God. Where… where they sending me?"

Bezuel shrugged. "Me no care. Me want taste, before you go."

Charm trembled and twisted her face away as the guard lifted her T-shirt with the gun barrel and the pale tongue came lolling out of his mouth. She squeezed her eyes shut and Bezuel reached for the dropped shopping basket. It took one of the gathered fruits, to smear over her exposed skin.

Suddenly a dark blur sprang from the prickly branches behind her. It pounced on the minchet in the guard's hand and sank its teeth in deeply.

Bezuel screeched in shock and pain. He waved the arm about, trying to shake the Doggy-Long-Legs off. But it wrapped its spindly limbs around the fist, chewing and gnawing greedily.

As Bezuel shrieked and whirled about, Charm ran. Not looking back, she pelted through the trees, heading for the road and the others.

The Beetle was just moving off when she rejoined them. Yikker was swigging from a bottle of Merlot the driver had handed over and Alasdair was picking himself up from the ground. The imprint of a shoe was stamped on one shoulder. The other children were standing around him. Charm's girls helped him to his feet and he mumbled a thank you whilst glaring at the cassocked Punchinello.

Three gunshots rang out. Yikker lowered the bottle and stared at Charm questioningly.

"Spider fing," she explained, trying not to let the horror of what she had escaped sound in her voice.

Yikker's hooked nose sniffed the air and when Bezuel emerged through the trees, nursing a bleeding hand, he hooted with mocking laughter.

Bezuel snatched the Merlot and guzzled it down. Although the mirror shades were once again over those eyes, Charm could feel the Punchinello's lecherous stare boring into her.

She spent the remainder of the afternoon dodging the guard's advances, making certain they were never alone together. Foremost in her thoughts though was the bombshell he had dropped. She desperately wished Maggie and Lee were here. What was she going to do? She didn't want to be moved from the camp. Her girls sensed something was the matter, but she didn't want to upset them and pretended it was merely a headache, but inside she was absolutely devastated and horribly afraid.

Somehow she got through the shift and the long march back. After the evening soup, she quietly invited Maggie, Lee and Spencer outside. The graves and Marcus's headstone had become a favoured spot to sit and talk. The other kids usually respected your privacy if you went there to discuss serious or personal stuff, or needed time on your own. Charm led her friends there and sat down.

"Now," Lee began. "You gonna tell us what's eating you tonight?"

Charm had made up her mind not to tell them what Bezuel had tried to do. She feared Lee would attempt some form of retaliation and wind up getting himself shot. She'd cope with Bezuel in her own way. She'd managed so far. She'd just have to be extra vigilant from now on. At least she wouldn't have to put up with the creature's disgusting attentions for much longer.

"It's me birthday soon," she told them.

"Aw, babes," Maggie said. "I'd stick a candle in your soup if I had one – and if the soup was thick enough."

Lee's face fell. "Hell, no!" he said. "When?"

Charm fanned her eyes. "On the seventh. I dunno what today is, but that Bez said it were near."

Lee scowled. He hadn't been keeping track of the date either and his watch didn't display it. He looked at Spencer. The other boy shook his head apologetically. Lee turned around and stared at the camp. Some girls were playing a clapping game in the middle of the lawn, others were washing clothes in buckets, one or two more were sitting on their own. Would any of them know?

At that moment, a shrill scream sounded in one of the cabins and Christina came running out, followed by Alasdair. The Scot caught up with her and gave her a hug. Jody's ranting voice was still calling after them. She was getting worse.

"Dinnae be upset," Alasdair said soothingly. "Jody's no well. You ken that? She doesnae mean it. She wouldnae be nasty to you for the world."

Christina wiped her eyes. "I miss her," she said.

"Aye, me too."

"Will she get better? Will my old Jody come back?"

"I cannae say. But we'll keep our fingers crossed, yeah?"

"You can only cross them on one hand!"

"Ah, but I can cross my toes too! You didnae know that, did ye?"

The girl laughed.

"Hey, Alasdair!" Lee called, waving him over.

The Scottish lad looked across in surprise. That clique didn't go out of their way to speak to him these days. He didn't blame them. He had behaved like a titanic jerk and some things were impossible to forgive.

Holding Christina's hand, he wandered over.

"What you guys doin'?" he asked uncertainly.

"You know what the date is?"

It was the last question Alasdair expected. It took him a few moments to think about it.

"Sit down, man," Lee invited.

Alasdair and Christina sat. Christina glanced at Maggie shyly. Since the attack on her with the ripped pages, she had kept out of her way. The seven-year-old teased a daisy from the ground and concentrated on trying to fashion it into a ring for her finger.

"Is it no July?" Alasdair asked after some minutes' pondering.

The others groaned. Alasdair thought again.

"How many days since the last delivery of leftovers?" he asked. "No this present lot, the one before."

Maggie counted back. They were on their fourth day of this batch; the

420

previous one had been a very long eight days prior to that.

"That's it then," he said. "That were when I gave up keepin' score. That were the day after midsummer, the last time the guards had one of their boozy blowouts. Remember, they lit another fire and sang dirty songs round it, then shot at empty bottles late into the night. So that makes today July the third. Why do ye want to know?"

"It's Charm's birthday on the seventh," Spencer told him.

"I'm real sorry," he said.

"I don't get it," Maggie butted in. "What is so wrong about having a birthday?"

"I'll be sixteen!" Charm answered.

Only then did Maggie realise. "They... they're going to ship you out of here?" she stammered. "Oh, no! They can't!"

Alasdair held up his useless hand. "They do whatever they want," he said bitterly. "Dinnae kid yourself otherwise."

"Didn't Jangler say something about an adult camp?" Spencer asked. "You'll be sent there. Might not be so bad as here."

"Aye an' it might be a ton load worse. If oor lot can kill wee kids and torture lasses till they crack, what do ye reckon they'll be doin' to them folk?"

"Coat it with sugar why don't you?" Lee muttered.

"He's only sayin' what I've already been finking," Charm said. "I ain't fick."

The stress and pain began to show on her face. Turning away, she gazed at the trees in the distance – beyond the wire. Perched on top of a high fence post, a blackbird was singing. It was a pure, liquid sound, filled with hope, freedom and praise for the late sunshine. Charm's eyes began to swim.

"Sixteen," she murmured. "Me sixteenf. That were gonna be like so crucial to The Plan. The day before, Uncle Frank were gonna sort a studio session an' I'd have some real tasteful glamour shots done. They'd be published in the red tops on me birthday. That were gonna be the start of it proper. It were all gonna kick off huge after that. The Charm brand were gonna get mega. By the time I were twenty I was gonna have me own fashion range an' perfume... so many fings..."

The others didn't know what to say. It was Alasdair who broke the silence and voiced what they were thinking.

"Glamour shots? Is that no topless and such? So, technically, the papers would've printed photos of a fifteen-year-old girl for blokes to slobber over? That's no right."

"But I'd be sixteen, innit?"

"Not when the photos were taken, you wouldnae be."

"When they was printed I would be though. What's the difference?"

"A lot," Lee said softly.

Charm couldn't understand what the big deal was. "I've done loads of modellin' before. Pukkah professional. Uncle Frank got me plenty of jobs – he had contacts all over – always sending me photos and CV to people on the Web he was."

"I wouldn't get my kit off for the camera," Maggie said. "Mind you, it'd need a wide-angle lens!"

Charm gave her a prod. "You ain't that big no more. And I didn't mind, honest. I just wish I had bigger boobs. It's not like I'd be scared or nervous nor nofink, Uncle Frank's been coaching me for years and got me well used to sessions like that, so I'd be ready and relaxed when the proper time came."

"He what?"

"Well, I'd be no use otherwise, would I? A model what's jumpy and shy ain't no good to no one. It's what they all do in this game, so he said."

Lee lowered his eyes. Maggie put her arm round her.

Charm was confused by their reaction. Was it pity, shock, disappointment, unhappiness? To an outsider, someone who wasn't in the business, she supposed it must sound quite odd, but she had been grateful to her manager. He had done a lot for her career. She trusted his judgement entirely. After he first met her mother and took an interest in her daughter's ambitions, things had really started to happen.

For some reason the image of Bezuel's eyes that afternoon flashed into her mind again and she shuddered. Why did it suddenly remind her of Uncle Frank? She stared across at Christina who was admiring the daisy on her finger. The first glimmer of doubt flickered in her mind. Charm shook herself.

"Well, The Plan's been truly flushed down the bog now," she said, hurrying to fill the silence and chase that unpleasant memory from her head. "On me sixteenf I'll be out of 'ere. I just wanted to say a whoppin' fank you, from the bottom of my heart, to you guys, for making this place survivable. Wivout you, it'd have been millions times worse. I never had no proper friends before – mad, innit? I reckon you're the best mates I'll ever 'ave and I'm gonna miss you summink fierce when I have to go. Just promise you'll look after my girls, yeah? They're a blindin' bunch."

She paused to catch her breath and gulp back the impending tears.

"What about us?" Maggie murmured. "What am I going to do without you? You've been brilliant. Always there when I was rock-bottom. You've been such a good friend to me – to all of us. You never let us down."

"Shut up or me waterworks'll start!"

Maggie was determined to be upbeat. It would have been so easy to give in and cry, but that could wait until the day Charm went through those gates for the final time.

"Hey," she said. "Remember that picnic? The day we all had to wear Mooncaster clobber?"

Charm laughed. That was the first time she had spoken to Lee. "He didn't wear none of it," she said, pointing at him.

"And I spouted a load of garbage about *Dancing Jax* not being such a bad thing," Maggie continued. "And Lee ripped my head off for it. Well, I'm saying the same right now and he can go off on one again if he likes cos, without that book, I'd never have met you lot and I'd never have met Marcus, and the thought of that never happening scares me."

"Likewise," Lee said quietly.

"You're closer to me than my real family ever was," Maggie rattled on. "I've finally stopped hating on my stepmother. Why did I ever let her get to me the way she did?"

"Cos you weren't happy," Charm said.

"That's bonkers, that is; must mean I'm happy here. That makes no sense."

"It's other people what make you happy," Charm told her. "Not being famous, not having loads of money and a mountain of flash stuff. Never thought I'd hear meself sayin' that. I am so gutted I'm goin'."

"You won't be on your own in that new place for long," Maggie said brightly. "We're all going to turn sixteen one day. When's your birthday, Lee?"

"November."

"Oh... well – that'll be here before you know it!"

He dragged his fingers through his hair. "You think there's a unisex camp for adults? Cos, you know, that'd be a first."

"Hope they'll send a car," Charm said, not wanting to think about it, but trying to be practical. "Don't fancy walking all the way to wherever the new place is. I'll never make it wiv them two humungous cases I got."

Alasdair had felt uncomfortable during this mutual appreciation. None of those nice words were meant for him and he felt he was intruding on their special time together. They had been incarcerated here for two months and he hardly knew these people at all. He found himself envying their closeness. Most of his spare hours had been spent with Jody and Christina, and now Jody had retreated into herself. He wished it could have been different, but Jody had been a 'them or me' type of person. He didn't regret any of the time he had spent with her, but it had been at the expense of other friendships.

Lee raised his eyes and studied Charm's face, trying to capture every detail. The spray tan had worn off long ago and real sunburn had replaced it. She looked better to him now, less artificial and factory-made. She wore hardly any make-up, preferring to save it for the pampering nights in her cabin. Her blonde hair hung loose over her shoulders and the honey-coloured light of the summer evening made each strand glow golden. He had never felt so close to anyone outside his family before. He wanted to protect her, but he couldn't even do that here. He felt angry and useless. There were so many things he wanted to say to her and now there wasn't time.

This was how he always remembered her, bathed in that gilding light. When the agony and horror of what was to come had passed, he conjured this precious time and saw her smiling at him.

"What you finkin'?" she asked. "You'll wear your eyes out, ogglin' at me like that."

Lee blinked and realised the others were sniggering.

"Just wishin' I could take you out on a date, is all," he mumbled, suddenly awkward.

Maggie looked away. That was what Marcus had said to her. She glanced at the wooden marker that bore his name and gave it a wobbly smile.

"A date?" Charm chuckled. "Ooh, so many flash places round 'ere. Was you finkin' about the dinin' hall, or maybe over by the gates or the tower? I dunno if I got the right gear to wear. I'll have to melt some plastic an' get summink brand-new."

Lee's grin froze. The most fantastic idea hit him. He couldn't believe he hadn't thought of it before. His face lit up and he almost blurted it out in excitement. He checked himself just in time.

"Hey, Alasdair," he said bluntly. "Could you take Christina back? Must be getting on, be eight soon."

The Scot didn't reply. He knew exactly what this was. Lee wanted to get rid of him. He wasn't part of the group and couldn't be trusted with whatever he was going to say. He stared at the other lad a moment, just so Lee knew he was fully aware what was going on here. It hurt to be sent away on such a flimsy pretext, in fact it was insulting, but Alasdair had built that wall of suspicion himself and couldn't expect any other treatment. Grudgingly he rose and told Christina to come with him.

"I don't want to go yet," she objected. "Jody's still cross."

"You're comin' in, noo," he said flatly. "It's turned cold oot here."

The little girl pouted and trailed after him.

"God, you're rude," Charm scolded Lee.

"I got summat to say," he explained simply. "Didn't want him to hear. He understood fine."

Spencer and Maggie stirred uneasily. "If you two are going to get sloppy," she said, "we'll leave you to it as well."

"Hell, no," Lee told them. "You stop right there. I know I can trust you. You's family to me now and what I got to say... it's important. It's the biggest damn secret in this whole camp."

The gravity in his voice made them sit up and they leaned in closer.

"Now this is gonna sound crazy," he whispered, taking a quick look around to ensure no one was within earshot. "But it's gospel truth. I ain't got no time to invent up stuff to make me seem..."

"Oh, spit it out!" Charm said.

"I've been to Mooncaster."

He waited for them to say something, but they only stared back at him.

"You hear me?" he asked.

"I'm just waiting for the punchline," Maggie said.

Lee shook his head. He knew it was an impossible thing to believe, but he had to try and make them.

"OK," he said. "From the top. When this first started, way, *waaay* back, months ago, before the riots and fires, I was hanging with a bad crowd, real rudeboys. Man, we thought we was the business and I thought I was it. Thinking back, I ain't proud, but when you grew up on my estate, there weren't much else to make you feel good about yourself. We had our own war goin' on and didn't pay no attention to stoopid news scares about a kids' book. Anyhow, one night there was gonna be a tussle – us and another gang. Was gonna be real messy. We went to the party with blades and bats, and yes, one of us had a gun – but no, it weren't me."

He paused a moment, recollecting that night at the beginning of the year, stepping into that underground car park, high on adrenalin and keyed to do serious damage to whatever moved.

"Yeah. We got there, tooled up, but... them other kids. All they brought was a book – that was it. 'Fore we knew what they was doin', they started readin' at us. We just laughed at first. Then my bruvs stopped laughin'. They was noddin' their heads like they was on summat. I freaked and tried to run, but my heart felt like it was gonna pop and it was as if I was drownin'. That's when I passed out – but I woke up in Mooncaster."

"You were a Jaxer?" Maggie breathed. "It got you? You were one of the affected? How did you break out of it?"

"No!" he said. "I said *I* woke up, not some peasant or some knight or any of that fairy-tale crap. I woke up as me."

"That's not possible," Spencer countered. "No one wakes up there as themselves. That's the whole point."

"I did and I do every time I goes back."

"You're serious, ain't ya?" Charm murmured.

Lee nodded. "For a long time I was just invisible when I was there. No one could see or hear me – I couldn't even touch nuthin'. That was so weird, but I got used to it – fact it were addictive. Man, I couldn't wait to go and see all them things in them pages and when I was near to someone new who got turned, I got dragged there too. Still happens that way, there ain't no brakes. Then one day I started leavin' footprints in the snow. Another time I was a blurry shadow, getting more and more solid and stronger every trip. So now, if I go, them deluded zombie folks see me, same as you do."

The others let this sink in. If anyone else but Lee had said this, they would never have believed a word.

"Now you know where them apples came from that one time," he said, amused by their stunned faces.

Maggie rocked back. "No!" she hissed. "They were from there? I got into trouble over them! Jody thought Jangler gave them to me."

"Wait," Spencer said. "You can actually bring objects back from there? That's… incredible!"

"It's a real place, same as this, sometimes feels more real than here."

"Hang on," Maggie butted in. "How come we're starving, if you can nip there and back so easy?"

"Cos it's not like droppin' down to Sainsbury's! That place is crazy mad. It's like nuthin' you ever saw. That book don't give you a clue what it's really about. There's all kinds of dangerous stuff goin' on the whole time, in every corner. Last I was there, I had the bones scared right outta me and haven't dared go back since."

"If Jangler and the guards ever found out what you can do," Spencer uttered worriedly, "they'd kill you straight away. They'd have to. You're a rogue element, a free radical in their blessed, Jaxy world. You're a massive danger to all of it, do you realise that? The things you'd be able to do… I don't understand why you've told us. You shouldn't tell anyone."

Lee wiped his forehead and sighed. "Some secrets is just too big for one person to keep," he said. "I had to get it outta my dome before it burst. Been burnin' me up the whole time we been here. 'Sides, I'm gonna need your help. Maggie's right. We ain't gonna make it on the slop they give us. I'm gonna have to go there again and bring food back. But there's summat else I wanna do first…"

A curious smile played across his face and he looked over at Charm.

"What?" she asked.

"I wanna take you on that date," he told her. "I wanna take you with me – to Mooncaster."

24

WHEN THE INITIAL shock of his invitation subsided, there wasn't time to discuss it. Spencer checked his watch and was dismayed to find it really was almost eight o'clock. They barely had time to hasten back to their cabins before the curfew.

High on the fence post, the blackbird continued to sing. When Garrugaska came patrolling the perimeter, the guard raised his gun and shot it.

In their separate cabins, Maggie and Charm's minds were spinning. How could they sleep after hearing that? On the mezzanine of their own hut, Lee and Spencer whispered together for hours and worked out a plan.

The next morning, Lee didn't get a chance to speak with Charm alone. Someone was always there and they couldn't get away. It was only when the two work parties met up on the way home, much later, that he told her what had been decided. They were going to attempt it that very night.

Straight after the soup, which she was much too nervous to eat any of, Charm hurried back to her cabin. There she wrapped, in a tight bundle, some of the re-enactment clothes she had been given for that picnic, so long ago now, and raced round to Lee's. Spencer was waiting by the stairs.

"Good luck," the boy said earnestly.

Charm gave him a hug and ascended.

She had just reached the mezzanine, where she burst out laughing, when Alasdair entered. He didn't think anything of it until he noticed Spencer standing like a sentinel at the foot of the stairs.

"What's goin' on?" he asked.

"They want some time together," Spencer answered truthfully. "I'm making sure they don't get disturbed."

The Scot raised his eyebrows. "So they've got you being their bouncer noo? Aye, well, she'll be away soon. S'pose they should make the most of it, but I'm no gonna stop in here, listening to them two bonking. I'm off oot."

Spencer smiled and told the same to Drew and Nicholas when they came in.

The moment she saw what Lee was wearing, Charm had a fit of the giggles. He looked ridiculous. He had borrowed Spencer's cloak and jerkin and sneaked the green cowl Alasdair had worn on that picnic from under the Scot's bed. His lower half still retained his usual trackie bottoms and trainers.

"You look mental," she giggled.

Lee was sitting on his bed. He pulled at the laces of the cowl grumpily.

"Gotta blend best we can there," he said. "You got yours?"

She cast her bundle down and told him to turn around whilst she changed.

"Shy girl," he chuckled, facing the far wall. "Don't take forever. It's half six already. We gotta get our asses back here before lights out, remember – so we don't got much time."

As she threw off her ordinary clothes and stepped into the long undershirt and kirtle she had brought, he reminded her what he had said earlier.

"I so can't believe we're doin' this," she said. "If this is a wind-up, I'll jeffin' frottle you."

"Just stick close and do whatever I say."

"Ooh, you're a bossy beggar!"

"Cos it's dangerous, Sweets. Can't stress it enough. First sign of trouble, or even summat I don't like the look of, we're outta there. If we get an arrow in our neck in that place, we bleed here just the same. If we die there, we're croaked here too. And, when I'm trying to get us back, if you let go my hand, you'll be stuck there. This ain't no joyride. This is deadly. For real. Am I makin' this plain?"

"I hear ya," she tutted, fastening a belt round her waist, with a leather purse attached. Then she donned a linen coif.

"All done," she declared. "You can look now."

Lee turned and couldn't stop himself smiling. She looked lovely, like a princess masquerading as a servant girl. He patted the bed and she sat next to him, expectant and trusting.

"I reckon the safest place to be," he said, taking her hands in his, "will be out in the fields – away from the castle, the forests, the village and the witch's tower. Course out in the middle of no place still ain't no guarantee – there's all sorts of surprises under every stone. And then we have to watch for that Bad Shepherd – he is one sick piece of psycho trash. He's the last person you ever wanna tangle with and has a nasty habit of poppin' up just when you ain't expectin' it. OK, you set?"

"No," she answered.

"No? What you mean, no?"

"I was finkin'. What you're doin' is lovely, it really is. An' you're so sweet to wanna take me on a date and everyfink, but – I don't wanna see no countryside nor nofink like that. We got enough of it 'ere."

"Then what? Don't ask for no big crowd events, or dumb-ass royal parties. There ain't no nightclubs there. If the Ismus guy spots us, we is dead for sure."

Charm shook her head gently. "That's not what I want. There's only one fing I wanna see. Only one sight I got my heart set on. Please let me, please take me there."

"Why do I know I'm not going to like this?"

The girl looked beseechingly at him.

"Please," she said. "I wanna see me ma. Can you help me find her? She works in the castle wash house."

Lee let go of her hands.

"What?" he cried. "Is your name Jody, cos you're sounding just as crazy?"

"It's all I want in the world," she begged. "Just to see her again. Please!"

It was an insane idea. Going to the remote countryside of that twisted Kingdom was hazardous enough, but to walk around, inside the White Castle itself, was suicide.

And yet Lee could hear the desperation in her voice. How could he refuse her? In a few days she'd be gone and he'd probably never see her again.

"I'm not makin' no promises," he sighed. "We might not even make it there. My aim sucks. What I said before goes double now. We get out soon as I say."

She nodded readily.

"Let's do this," he said, taking her hands again. They were hot and pink with excitement now. "But if you do find your old lady, don't go hopin' she'll know who you is. She'll be livin' that make-believe life to the max. You hear me? Don't stoke yourself for no happy ending; them's for different storybooks, not *Dancing Jax.* "

"Yes, I know," she whispered, her eyes sparkling.

The boy told her to close them and hesitated before closing his own. His gaze lingered on that beautiful face. He really would do anything for her. He'd never felt that way about anyone before.

"Hey," he murmured shortly. "Open your eyes."

"Summat gone wrong?" she asked. "Ain't it workin'? Have another go, please."

"Open them."

Charm looked up, hesitantly, and blinked in the sudden bright sunshine. Then she covered her mouth with her hands.

"OMG!" she squealed through her fingers. "I can't believe it! I can't believe it! I didn't feel nothin'. It's amazin' – you're amazin'!"

She threw her grateful arms round his neck and kissed him ecstatically.

It was a warm summer's day in Mooncaster. They were in a beautiful, ornamental, walled garden. Low hedges of neatly clipped box formed tidy borders to hem in the abundantly flowering roses, peonies, calendula, lilies, foxgloves, irises, violets and campion. She had never seen such brilliant, singing colours or such full, blousy blooms. The mingled scents that wafted through the air were indescribably sweet and the bees seemed drunk as they droned from plant to plant.

Charm inhaled the sights and smells joyously. Even the grass beneath her feet was a vivid emerald green and the freckling daisies shone out like stars. A cloud of pink butterflies rose up and flew about her as she stepped forward. They fluttered in formation, forming a large heart shape in the air that passed over and around her.

"It's like that bit in *The Wizard of Oz*!" she exclaimed, with childlike wonder. "Where the bungalow drops on the old bag and Doroffy goes all colour and meets them scary toddlers."

"Well, we ain't in that place," Lee reminded her sharply. "This ain't no fairyland you ever saw on TV or the movies. This is like Narnia on crack. You just remember that. Ain't nuthin' safe here."

He nodded past her shoulder and she turned to see the turrets and towers of the White Castle dominating the sky. They were within its three concentric walls, inside the royal gardens.

Charm had spent many months longing desperately for *Dancing Jax* to work its spell on her, but now she gazed up at that huge castle and despised every stone, every fluttering banner.

"We is deep in the enemy's turf," Lee said. "This is not desirable. If we're seen, we is out the exit, soon as – you hear me? No matter what's goin' on, no matter if you've only just found your mum, right? If we're caught here, we's deadsauce."

She nodded and he pulled the cowl up to conceal his face. "Remember," he warned. "I can't get back to the real world – *our* real world, 'less I'm outside. For some reason it don't work if I'm indoors. You say what you gotta say to her then we skip. Now stay close and let's find this laundry. If it's where I think it is, we ain't too…"

He paused and pulled her behind a trellised arch, festooned with perfect, pale pink roses. There was a movement in the flower beds. The blooms and leaves were pushed aside as something came forward, towards the low box border.

Lee put a finger to his lips. "Don't you make a sound," he whispered to the girl. "This might be nuthin', might be just an animal, a squirrel or summat – but even they ain't to be trusted. There's no 'normal' here. Just cos it's cute an' fluffy don't mean it ain't gonna try and kill ya."

Charm peered through the latticework of the trellis and reached for Lee's hand when she saw a small ladder poke up above the flower bed. What was carrying it? She couldn't see yet. Surely even here the squirrels didn't need ladders? Suddenly its progress halted and it jerked and jiggled. The other end was snagged on something. A white foxglove shuddered and a small voice grumbled and grunted with effort. The ladder tugged violently and the tall mast of the foxglove toppled down like a felled tree.

"Oh, stuff me sideways!" the voice cried. "That's done it! You're in hot water now! She'll notice that, she will."

The ladder came speeding towards the low hedge. It stopped, angled forward and rested against the top. Then a preposterous little creature in a straw hat came scampering up.

Lee squeezed Charm's hand urgently. They had to go, his expression told her. They didn't dare hang around now. She'd have to try and find her mother tomorrow.

The girl agreed and was about to run with him, when she gasped and let go of his hand. Lee whirled about. What was she doing?

Charm was staring at the figure that had climbed on to the hedge and was now pulling the ladder up after.

It was a little man, dressed in a green leather jerkin and short breeches. His head was out of proportion with his body and his arms and legs were short and thin. Hanging from the straps and belts, fastened around him, were many tiny jars and bottles, full of different coloured liquids. A silver trowel was secured under the straps across his back.

"We gotta get outta here now!" Lee hissed at her.

Charm caught his sleeve and pointed through the trellis. "Look!" she said. "Don't you see who it is?"

Confused, the boy stared at the strange little man, who was now climbing down the other side of the box border.

"No way!" he muttered. "Can't be!"

His voice was louder than he intended. The small man started at the sound and slid down the remaining rungs, rolling backwards on the grass and losing his hat. Jumping up again, the alarmed creature turned fearfully towards the rose trellis.

"Who's there?" he demanded. "Who's that spying in the floribunda? Come out! Or I'll whistle for the guards! They'll jab you out of there soon enough."

Without the hat, there was no doubt about it. Lee and Charm both knew that face. It was a distorted caricature of one they were only too familiar with.

"Marcus!" the girl called, breaking cover before Lee could stop her. "We thought you was dead!"

The little man leaped back as she came running towards him and whipped out the trowel, wielding it as though it was a sword.

"Who are you?" he cried. "What are you doing in the Gentle Garden? 'Tis for Under Queens and Jills only."

"It's me, Charm!" she answered, kneeling to speak to him.

"A charm you're wanting, is it?" he said. "You most likely want the Physic Garden, thataways. You done strayed into a private royal retreat here. You maids ought to know better than to come prying and trespassing. What if one of the Majesties had been out, perambulating? They'd have had you beaten and boxed black and blue, they would. Most partic'lar about who they lets in here they is – specially the Queen of Hearts. Thinks this is just for her personal private pleasure she does, the way she carries on. As if she didn't have a Garden Apart, all her own!"

He looked around cautiously. "Now don't you go telling no one I broke that there digitalis purpurea and I won't give you away neither. Very fond of the foxgloves is the Queen of Hearts – uses them in her tinctures and concoctions she does."

"Marcus," Charm said. "Don't you know me?"

"Crocus," he corrected, pointing to a golden brooch, shaped like a flower, on his jerkin. "Crocus Weedy be my name, goblin to this here Gentle Garden, I be. Today that meddly Queen has got me making sure all her prize beloved beauties smell right for her. Their own perfumes aren't whiffable enough according to she. Here, have a sniffy of this."

Putting the trowel down, he untied one of his jars, pulled out the cork stopper and held it up. The fragrance of lily of the valley flooded out and wrapped around Charm.

"Pretty pong, isn't it?" he said, tapping the stopper back in. "A teeny dab in each flower's mouth, that's what I'm tasked with. Got every whiff there is, about my person – each one a hooter's dream."

"You don't remember me?"

"Not for the likes of me to know the likes of you," he replied, putting his hat back on. "Garden Goblins don't mingle with tall folk much; we don't even mingle with each other much neither. I sleep up in the dovecot, sharing my nights with the birds. Old Juniper, who tends the Lordly Garden, kips under a broke flowerpot and Greengage, of the Physic, holes up in the woodpile."

"What about Maggie?" the girl said. "You must remember her? And the tunnel you was digging? What about them 'orrible worm fings?"

"Tunnel? Digging?" he cried. "I don't do none of that heavy toil! That's what serfs and moles is for. Us Garden Goblins are the ones who clean their mess after. A bit of weeding and turning the loam over is the most my trowel blade does and I got no quarrel with worms if they stay out my lawn, spoiling it with their squiggly heaps. Prettying up is what us Garden Goblins is for: shining leaves, painting dew on the webs each morning, rolling the ferns into tight scrolls, keeping the hedges clipped and trim, opening out buds and training butterflies to flutter in patterns when the

Majesties come strolling by. Never enough hours to squeeze it all in."

The girl hung her head. It was no use.

"We gotta get going," Lee's voice called to her.

The goblin with Marcus's face glanced crossly at the trellis. "No man is permitted here!" he shouted, hopping up and down angrily. "Get you gone! Shoo – both of you!"

Charm rose and left him. Crocus looked at the flattened grass where she had been kneeling and threw his hat down again.

"I'll have to get my big comb and groom that!" he grumbled. "The Queen of Hearts demands it perfect! Just look at your big, clodhoppy footprints in the velvety sward. Go away – go away! As if I don't have enough to keep me busy this day. Leave me to mind the Gentle Garden in peace."

Charm returned to Lee and they ran through an archway, leaving the garden behind.

"It *were* him," she insisted. "It *were* Marcus."

"Marcus is dead," Lee reminded her.

"I don't get it. Is this what happens? When you die, you turn into summink freaky here, not even a proper person, and don't know who you are?"

"Freaky is right," he told her. "That was a twisted joke – a parody of who he was."

"Were it a ghost or real or what? Were it his soul?"

"I dunno and I dunno what this place really is – or where. Unhealthy is all I'm sure of."

"What's Maggie gonna say when I tell her?"

"You think it'll make her feel better knowin' he's here, like that?"

"No…"

"Then forget what you just saw. Marcus is gone. Keep it that way, for her."

"I hope I don't end up here, like him," she said with a mortified shudder. "What would I be? A dragon or a statue or summink?"

"I won't let that happen," he promised.

Charm began to wonder if trying to find her mother was such a good idea. Could she really bear it if she didn't recognise and remember her either? Was she strong enough for that? It took all the courage she had to press on. In thoughtful silence, they passed through courtyards and covered walkways – always on the lookout for sentries and Punchinellos. They encountered no one. The place seemed deserted. Lee didn't like it.

"This ain't right," he muttered. "We should've seen someone by now. Where is everybody?"

Charm wasn't listening. Through the next arch, she caught sight of linen shirts and woollen hose pegged out on slender ropes strung between the walls. This was it.

Her heart in her mouth, she hurried forward and ducked under row after row of dripping washing. Then, through the lazily flapping laundry, she saw a dumpy figure, stooping to take the last item of damp clothing from a large basket.

The woman was dressed in long skirts covered by a wide apron. Her shirtsleeves were rolled up past her ruddy elbows and she pegged the final garment on the line wearily.

When Lee caught up with Charm, he whispered, "Is that her?"

The girl shrugged. She didn't know. Covering the woman's head was a knight's steel helmet, with the visor down.

A trilling song began echoing inside that startling headgear. The woman took up the basket and plodded into the nearest outbuilding.

"Go after her," Lee said. "But the first sign of trouble, we get ourselves straight out here and back to the camp, yeah?"

"You stuck on repeat or what?" Charm asked.

Hurrying under the washing, they made their way to the door of the building the washerwoman had disappeared into.

"There now," the laundress said as she removed the helmet and set it down. "I'd like to see Haxxentrot's gorcrows peck my nose off, like she threatened, when I've got that on. It was so generous of Sir Darksilver to loan me one of his old helms. I shall take extra care with his bundles in future – only the best starch on his linen."

Easing herself into the rocking chair by the ingle, she looked round the washhouse with the satisfaction of having done a hard day's work. It wasn't over yet, but she felt she had earned a brief sit-down. The coppers were steaming on the fires, waiting for the next load of grubby garments, but she kicked off her wooden clogs and rubbed her aching feet. Then she examined her chapped red hands and blew on them.

"Is that her?" Lee murmured in Charm's ear as they peered inside.

The girl shook her head. "That's not me ma," she answered with bitter disappointment.

"So go aks where she is."

He nudged her in and made certain his cowl was down over his eyes before following.

"'Scuse me," the girl began.

The laundress looked up from the cracks and splits in her fingers and rose from the rocker.

"What may I do for you, m'dear?" she asked. "Got tired of the jousting, have ye? Don't know why they bother, 'tis always the Jack of Clubs who wins, him and that special horse of his. Never was much of a one for tournamenting myself. I knowed how much work it makes for the likes of me I suppose. Them bloody tunics and undershirts will all come through these coppers. Bring them here straight away, I tells the squires every time. But the daft lads never do and so they have to be steeped in salted water for a week and slapped about something brutal before the stains start to lift. 'Tis murderous work for these poor hands; there's no helpful brownie to do the work for me, more's the pity."

She looked expectantly at Charm then squinted with curiosity at the hooded figure who stepped in behind her. She couldn't see his face and his hands were tucked inside his sleeves.

"I were lookin' for Widow Tallowax," the girl ventured.

The woman's puzzled features brightened. "Then look no further," she declared. "For I am she, a lowly matron but of good character. Is it a kirtle spoilt or some soiled braies? I'll get the sin boiled clean out of them, my pretty maid."

Charm stared at her blankly. "You can't be her," she said. "You're not me ma – you can't be Widow Tallowax."

"Your ma?" the woman repeated, pattering forward in her bare feet to take a closer look at her. "I don't be nobody's ma. But I'm who I say I am, as sure as tar don't never scrub out of a velvet cape."

Charm shook her head and backed into Lee. "It's not her," she stated unhappily. "Where is she?"

The boy took his hands from his sleeves and touched her shoulder gently. He should have spoken about this earlier.

"Yes, it is," he said. "She's in there. Remember, there's only so many characters in that damn book and millions of zombie people all thinking they're one of them. What we got here is the prime version, just like the Jacks and Jills we see are the prime versions of them. You gotta concentrate. Look close – think real hard about who you want to see."

Charm didn't really understand, but she turned back to the laundress and pictured her mother's face in her thoughts.

Widow Tallowax looked at them uneasily. "What is it you want?" she demanded, eyeing the hooded figure's black hands with surprise and unease. "I don't got time to squander in idle chatter, or whatever game you be having with me. If you don't have nothing for my seething waters then be off – and shame on you for confounding a poor honest matron at her daily duties. I'll fetch my tongs and put them to the backs of your legs if you don't leave."

As she spoke, the woman's shape began to flicker. Charm drew an incredulous breath. Before her eyes, the washerwoman blurred and changed, growing taller or wider, thinner and shorter. Each instant showed a new, different person. Only the clothes remained the same; the arms, torso, face – everything else altered. It was like skimming through the pages of a flick book. All manner of people jumped in and out of those long skirts: different ages, different sizes, different races, until finally Charm let out a squeal and grabbed the woman's hand.

The face of her mother, Mrs Benedict, had appeared. As soon as the girl touched her, the rapidly switching images stopped.

"Ma!" Charm yelled, throwing her arms round her. "Oh! I missed you so much. So much. Why didn't you come get me like you said?"

The Widow Tallowax leaned back in surprise. Who was this strange, weeping maiden? She pulled those desperate arms from about her neck and stepped away, flustered and speechless.

"It's me," the girl said. "Charm, your daughter. Charm Benedict. You know me, you got to!"

The woman wrung her hands. The girl was obviously overwrought, but this display was most unseemly.

"Please, Ma," Charm implored, the tears streaking down her young face. "Don't do this. You can't not recognise me. You was painting this face wiv slap since it were two years old. You don't forget summink like that."

"Put an end to this!" the widow snorted. "My eyes have never seen you before this day. Why do you maltreat me in this fashion? Is it a trick of the Jill of Spades or the Jockey? If either of them were not content with one of the garments I returned, this is a cruel revenge and ill deserved."

"Remember The Plan!" Charm continued. "Remember the times we went shoppin'. How about that night out when we went to that club, wiv them footballers in it? I was only fourteen, but got in dead easy and when that bloke hit on me, you gave him a right smack. I was dead narked cos he were famous and we rowed all the way home in the cab. How about them stinkin' gherkins? You must remember!"

The washerwoman bit her lips and moved away. She realised now this was no trick. The poor maid was moon-kissed.

"Forgive my harsh words earlier," she said. "They were spoken in alarm. Now I see you have a brain fever and your hooded companion must be your physician. Take great care of her, sirrah. How sorrowful it is for one so young and fair of face to be so tormented."

"I'm not nuts!" the girl cried. "What can I say to make you see? What can I…?"

Thinking of something, she tore at her bodice and threw it down, then wrestled out of the woollen kirtle. Widow Tallowax raised her hands at this scandalous behaviour.

Standing in her long undershirt, Charm unfastened it to expose her bare stomach. The pink diamanté stud in her navel twinkled in the firelight.

"Look!" she said. "You came wiv me when I had it done. You went green and nearly fainted."

The laundress covered her eyes at so shocking a spectacle.

"We was best friends, you an' me." The girl wept. "It weren't like what other girls had wiv their mums. We was special, real close – like sisters. We were never apart. You must feel that, deep down. Somewhere in your heart, you do know – you got to. There's a big empty hole in there, I know it, cos that's what's in mine."

Charm's anguish and frustration became too much and she broke down, sobbing.

Lee cast the hood back and put his arm round her, but she pulled away, too distraught to be comforted.

"Suds alive!" the washerwoman exclaimed when she saw the boy's face. "From what foreign land have you journeyed? One where the sun burns hotter than here, that much is plain."

"Yeah, that's right," Lee humoured her. "I'm from a long ways off, from the Peckham desert. I'm part of a religious order who worship the almighty Nike, in the holy temple of Footlocker."

Widow Tallowax listened with fascination, but was distracted by Charm's distress. She didn't like to see anyone upset and this poor child was beside herself with grief. It was impossible to witness without feeling pity for her. She was too tender-hearted to see anyone suffering such despair.

"There, there, my dear," she said, coming close to pat the girl's hand. "Don't take on so. A lovely face such as yours should never be rained upon. Sunny smiles, that's what cleans our faces best. Whoever your true mother may be, I'm certain she'd not want to see you so wretched."

"Why don't you give her a hug?" Lee prompted.

"I couldn't do that," the woman declined. "I'm not in the habit of embracing strangers. I am not the Jill of Hearts."

"Please," Charm whispered through her tears. "Hold me."

Widow Tallowax hesitated, but what harm could it do? Stretching her arms, she wrapped them about her. Charm rested her face on her mother's shoulder and closed her eyes. For one precious moment, she imagined they were back in the real world, and *Dancing Jax* had never devastated their lives.

"I love you, Mum," she said.

The widow moved away shyly. The contact had been strangely affecting. Almost as if the girl's tears were contagious, a large drop rolled down her own cheek and she brushed it away hastily.

"If it's a mother you seek," she said, "why not go to Hunter's Chase and look you there for Malinda's cottage? She's godmother to all unhappy maids."

"It's my real mum I want, not a fake one. There's been enough fake in my life."

"But she could aid you in your search. 'Tis said she's beneficent and generous and her magick is still strong, for all the talk of her retirement. I oft-times think I should ask her for a spell to enchant the washing so it can scrub itself."

"A good cuddle's the best magic there is," Charm said. "I don't want nofink from a fairy godmother."

Widow Tallowax didn't know what else to say. The sound of horses and babbling voices drifted in through the open door.

"The tournament is over," she told them. "They're coming back from the tilt yard. Such a day of it they've had. The whole castle was out there."

"We'd best go," Lee suggested softly.

Charm nodded. There was nothing else for her here. She had tried her best and had experienced one final, blissful hug. The memory of that would have to sustain her, in whatever ordeals were yet to come in the new camp. Picking up the leather purse she had discarded with her kirtle, she handed it to the laundress.

"This is for you," the girl said, wiping her eyes. "I always promised I'd come find you if the book ever worked and give you money. Well, I ain't got no dosh, but this is loads better."

"A gift for me?"

"Yeah."

The noise of the crowd was coming closer. They could hear shouts and cheers for the Jack of Clubs and praise for Ironheart, his magnificent steed. Lee was anxious to escape this place. He pulled the cowl over his head once more and waited impatiently.

"I do not know what I have done to warrant your charity," the widow said, unbuckling the purse and looking inside. "What manner of curios are these?"

Charm managed a faint smile. "Rimmel and Max Factor, lippy and eyeshadow," she said, "Olay and Garnier body and skincare – all the moisturiser I got. You said you missed Boots' make-up counter most when you was here. Do your chapped hands the world of good them creams will."

"Such treasures!" the washerwoman breathed. "They put even the Queen of Hearts' own ointments to shame. How can I thank you?"

"If a girl can't treat her muvver, what's the point of anyfink?"

"We have *got* to go, now!" Lee stated.

Widow Tallowax held the purse close to her bosom and watched them hurry to the door. She didn't understand what any of this had been about, but she knew the poor girl was in turmoil.

"Young maid!" she called suddenly. "If I was your mother, I should be so proud to call you daughter."

Charm looked back at her one last time. "If you even remember this when you wake up next," she said in cracking voice, "get rid of Uncle Frank. He's… he's not what you fink he is."

The words meant nothing to the laundress. The two strangers departed. As she returned to the rocking chair to inspect the amazing gifts more closely, a sudden sense of loss overwhelmed her. The purse dropped from her fingers and she clutched at her chest. It was as if someone had torn the heart from her breast. That unhappy girl's sorrowful face filled her thoughts and she ran back to the door.

The courtyard was empty, except for the gently swinging washing.

"Come back!" Widow Tallowax called, running forward and getting tangled in the drying linen. "Please, come back! Stay a moment more, child."

Tears ran down her face. She staggered back to the washhouse, her mind racing and thundering, battling to get free. She had seen that maiden before, somewhere many miles from here – in a different existence…

"Cookie dough," she murmured vaguely. "My flavour is cookie dough."

As soon as she uttered those unusual words, she collapsed against the wall, like a knight struck down in the joust.

"Oh, God!" Mrs Benedict screamed, staring around wildly. She remembered. She knew who she was. She knew everything.

"Charm!" she cried frantically. "Charm! Where are you? Baby!"

She bolted forward, tearing the washing from the line as she yelled her daughter's name.

"I'll come get you! I promise!"

Then she shivered as tremendous forces seized her. The shape of Widow Tallowax blurred once more and Mrs Benedict's face faded from Mooncaster forever. The woman who was the prime version of the laundress slipped back into that long skirt and apron and swayed unsteadily for a moment. Then she pulled herself together and stared at the wet clothes strewn on the ground about her.

"Who's been flinging my good clean washing about?" she demanded crossly. "That Jockey – he's naught but mischief!"

Charm and Lee opened their eyes. They were back on the bed, in the cabin. The girl gave him a feeble smile.

"Thank you," she said.

He kissed her and they held one another until Spencer came upstairs, shyly, to warn them it was getting close to eight o'clock. Charm rose and returned to her cabin.

Lee rolled on to his back and stared at the ceiling. He didn't know then, but tomorrow would be the darkest day of his life. He thought he had seen the worst pain and evil *Dancing Jax* could inflict, but he was wrong. That was yet to come and it would haunt him until he died.

25

THE FOLLOWING MORNING Lee was up early. He didn't want to miss a moment of Charm's company. Pulling on his clothes, he hurried outside. The sky was sullen and grey, but he didn't notice. He ran to Charm's cabin and stuck his head round the door.

The girls were groggy. No one had got used to the intense sleep that the Bakelite device induced and most of them were still lying on the floor. They groaned at his cheerful face and one came running out, to make use of the bathroom in Esther's cabin because theirs was still boarded-up.

Lee tilted his head to one side.

"Hey, where is she?" he asked.

They all knew who he meant and tittered among themselves.

"You want to hold her, you want to kiss her..." one of them sang.

"She might've gone the bog as well," another suggested.

Lee chuckled and strolled about the lawn, waiting. He saw Maggie go running to the main block to get the breakfast started and, soon after, Esther followed her. Time ticked by. A nasal cackle sounded above. Yikker was on duty in the skelter tower. The Punchinello was staring down at him. Lee ignored him. The sight of that thing dressed as a priest made him feel sick.

Gradually the camp awakened. Children emerged, scratching their heads and yawning. Cold water coursed through the showers and the other girls from Charm's cabin went to queue outside neighbouring bathrooms. But where was she?

After twenty minutes, Lee began to worry. He asked in every chalet, but no one had seen her and she wasn't in any of the bathrooms. He went to the kitchen and asked Maggie. She was dying to know what had happened last night, but Garrugaska was there and she wouldn't have mentioned it in front of Esther anyway.

"She must be somewhere," she said, frying the guards' sausages.

"I'd try the bathrooms again," Esther suggested with a sneer. "She's always hogging ours."

"No speak!" the Punchinello ordered. Jabbing a hostile finger at Lee, the guard told him to get out.

The boy left the main block, making sure Charm wasn't in the lecture hall. A horrendous suspicion started to form and he ran back to her cabin. No, her two pink Louis Vuitton cases were still there. That calmed him a little, but where could she be?

When Jangler rang the bell for the prisoners to line up for the morning reading, Charm had still not appeared. Maggie and Esther hurried to join the ranks and, whilst Captain Swazzle did a headcount, Lee cast about for her.

Jangler consulted his clipboard.

"Firstly," he began.

"Wait!" Lee spoke up. "We ain't all here yet."

Jangler looked at Swazzle.

"Ten and nine," the Punchinello reported.

The old man ticked something on his list. "Jolly good, all present and correct."

"Hey!" Lee shouted. "What's goin' on? Where is she?"

The other children shuffled miserably. The girls from her cabin were now desperately unhappy.

"If you're referring to Charm Benedict," Jangler said, with a dismissive sniff, "she's gone. And if you address me in that insolent tone again, I will have you whipped."

Lee choked back a cry. "What? Where's she gone? What you done with her?"

"She was transported a couple of hours ago. This camp is for aberrants under the age of sixteen. She couldn't stay. I made that perfectly clear when you first arrived. I fail to see what you're puling about."

"But her birthday's not till the seventh!" Maggie objected.

"I thought it far better to send her away early. Much kinder, in my opinion. There's a lot less mucus and snivelling hysterics when it's done suddenly and quietly – nice and efficient."

"You what?" Lee yelled. "You're dead! You hear! You're dead!"

Blinded with anger, the boy lunged forward. He wanted to wring that old creep's neck and beat the ghost out of him.

At once Bezuel slammed Lee to the ground and trod on his face. Lee grabbed hold of his foot and twisted it violently. The guard squawked and was thrown sideways in a flurry of chinchilla. Lee was about to spring up and fly at Jangler when Garrugaska pressed the revolver to his head.

"The hell you will," he growled.

"Don't move!" Spencer urged Lee.

Lee slumped back on the ground and let out a rasping cry of despair. The Punchinellos thought the sound was hilarious and instantly copied it. Bezuel scrambled to his feet and brushed dust from the fur coat. Then he gave the boy a savage kick in the ribs. The other children winced and looked away.

Maggie raised a shaking hand. "Please," she asked Jangler. "Is the adult camp nearby? Could we write to her?"

"The girl's a fool," he muttered to himself. "Don't be stupid. She's gone and that's an end to it. You've had two whole months to say whatever you wanted. If you didn't say it then it's your own silly fault. Now before the first chapter of the day, here's an interesting tidbit of news. The Jill of Spades' trial is to commence this morning. Will that dark-hearted girl be acquitted of causing the Felixstowe Disaster or will she be found guilty? Europe is agog; crowds are already massing outside the Old Bailey. And some glorious tidings – the Lord Ismus's High Priestess the Lady Labella…"

As he droned on, Christina tugged at Jody's sleeve.

"Barbie's gone away," she whispered. "She's not coming back. You can be happy now and get better."

Jody turned an unfocused gaze upon her. *"You ought to see Sally on*

Sunday," she sang softly. *"Dressed up in her dainty Sunday clothes. With her hat on one side, she's a picture of charm... of charm... of charm..."*

Christina looked at Alasdair. The boy shook his head. There was no getting through to her.

Lee felt annihilated. He couldn't believe Charm had been taken from him like this. Maggie knew how he felt.

"Least she's alive," she told him later, during breakfast.

"Why's her luggage still here?" he asked.

"You heard what he said. It was all done so quick. They'll probably send it on."

"I woulda killed that guy if I'd got my hands on him," he said. "Really wanted to."

"You think I haven't?"

Lee didn't remember the march to the minchet thickets that morning. He barely even felt the lash when it swiped across his back as Captain Swazzle chivvied him along.

Brooding, he harvested the squelching fruit, hardly realising what he was doing. He told himself he should have stayed away from Charm. He shouldn't have let her get close to him. He almost wished he could go round the bend like Jody. Least it wouldn't hurt so much. He wondered if Charm was thinking about him, wherever she was.

Spencer was in the same work party and kept a concerned eye on him. A little after midday, a car pulled up. The children had grown to dread this. Which of them would the driver select to abuse this time?

They didn't dare turn round. They didn't want to draw attention to themselves. They heard the car door slam and a strident female voice called the guards over.

"I'll give you a bottle of whisky and two packets of unfiltered Turkish cigarettes if I can go tell that piece of filth over there what I think of him and slap his face – the dirty, reject scum!"

Captain Swazzle agreed eagerly.

The woman's heels came crunching over the forest road. Spencer held his breath. He was a preferred target for these enraged tourists. Swallowing nervously, he continued putting the minchet into his basket and kept his eyes lowered. The footsteps drew closer. Yep, here she was…

"You disgust me!" she shrieked. "Turn around, and look me in the eye, you despicable freak!"

Spencer blinked in surprise. She wasn't addressing him. Slowly he looked to the left and saw a middle-aged woman thumping a handbag into Lee's shoulders. Spencer bit the inside of his cheek. She really shouldn't do that. The state Lee was in, he was set to explode.

"Face me – you scumbag, you steaming pile of dog dirt!"

She smacked the back of his head. That did it. Lee whirled around, ready to smash her nose into jam with his fist. Then he spluttered and stopped himself, just in time. The woman gave him a crafty wink.

"You wouldn't dare, you coward!" she taunted, for the benefit of the guards. "You aberrants make me puke!"

Lee couldn't believe it. The woman was smartly dressed in a cream skirt and jacket. But the last time he had seen her face it was wearing a linen cap and was flushed from the steaming coppers of the washhouse. It was Charm's mother.

"What the…?"

Mrs Benedict glanced quickly at the Punchinellos. They had waddled over to the truck where they were dividing the cigarettes between them and squabbling over the whisky.

"I don't have long," she whispered quickly. "I've driven through the night to get here. Soon as you left me yesterday, I remembered. I remembered everything and found myself back at home. By heck, I've been busy since then!"

Lee stared at her in wonder.

"How dare you look at me, you insolent cur!" she snapped, slapping his face.

"I'm so sorry," she hissed. "They were watching. You have to look at the floor."

"Ow," he muttered. "You got some right hook on you. But listen, about your…"

"I know," she said bitterly. "I found the other work party first. One of the girls there told me they sent my baby away this morning."

She threw a wary glance back at the truck. Captain Swazzle had pulled rank and taken sole possession of the bottle. Garrugaska was smoking two cigarettes at once and ambling back this way.

"I should've brought more drink," she scolded herself. "I had to give some to the other guards just now. I don't know who you are, but I could see my Charm trusted and liked you – a lot. That's more than good enough for me. I believe there's something incredible about you, some power to enter that awful world whenever you want, without it taking you over."

Lee nodded cautiously.

"Then use that power properly!" she implored him. "You're the only person I've heard of who can do that. You're unique. It's a fabulous gift – a miracle. You've been given it for a reason. Use it! Help me find my baby and I'll get you out of that camp."

"How you gonna do that?"

"Trust me," she insisted. "I can."

"You're talkin' large an' empty, lady. Those guards got guns an' my Kevlar vest is in the wash."

"Guns? Is that all? You've no idea what it's like out there in the rest of this country now. You wouldn't recognise it. Things, monsters – miles worse than these ugly midgets – are everywhere. God knows where they came from. It's a vision of Hell out there. What do you think all this muck you pick every day is for? What do you think eats it?"

"You!" Garrugaska's harsh voice interrupted as he came stomping up. "More Red Eye – give!"

Mrs Benedict assumed a haughty manner.

"You've had all I've got," she said. "There is no more."

"Me want Tarantula Juice!" the guard ranted, stamping his boot, making the spur jingle and spin. "Me want Coffin Varnish!"

"Then go make your colleague share that bottle," she instructed. "It isn't fair he should hog it."

Garrugaska blew a smoke ring from both corners of his wide mouth and studied her dubiously. Something about her wasn't right. Her eyes weren't as dark and glassy as they should be.

"You go now," he drawled. "You move. Go in car."

"I haven't finished!" she cried indignantly.

"You too quiet with abrant. What you mutter mutter? Garrugaska say you go. Ride off, Greenhorn."

"I was reciting the sacred text to him, you fool!" she retorted. "I want my money's worth. I haven't even kicked him in his privates yet! I'm not budging till I do that – the evil, ungrateful beast!"

The Punchinello snickered. "You do it. You kick hard. Me watch."

Mrs Benedict turned back to Lee, a deeply apologetic look on her face. She couldn't back down now. The boy took a step away.

"No chance!" he said.

Garrugaska pulled the gun from its holster. "You move, you dead," he warned Lee.

Charm's mother prepared to kick him. At that moment, Captain Swazzle called Garrugaska's name. The imp turned and Mrs Benedict's kick went wide. Lee thanked whatever angel was watching over him then started a performance. He uttered an agonised groan and fell to the ground, clutching his crotch.

Captain Swazzle was beckoning Garrugaska back to the truck. The silver-nosed guard enjoyed the sight of Lee rolling on the floor for a few moments then went to see what the Captain wanted.

"Tonight," Mrs Benedict whispered as soon as she dared. "At eleven o'clock, there'll be a lorry waiting at the junction of the road that leads to your camp. It'll take you, and whoever you want to bring, to a safe place."

"No way I can bust outta there!"

"You've got to! There's someone on the outside desperate to meet you. I've arranged everything. But first you've got to find out where my daughter's been sent."

"She's gone to the adult camp. Can't you Google it?"

The woman looked across at the guards. Captain Swazzle was holding one of the confiscated mobiles and trying to operate it with those fat fingers. A picture message had beeped in and wouldn't open. Garrugaska poked at the phone and they started arguing again.

"There is no adult camp," she told the boy. "At the end of May, the last few adults in this country who were immune to that book were rounded up and shot. So you see, I really need to know what has happened to my baby."

Lee sat up. "Sure," he promised. "But I don't see how I can get past those guards and their guns and jump a barbed-wire fence."

"You must be a very nice lad," she remarked dryly. "Because my baby obviously doesn't like you for your brains."

She opened her handbag and threw something heavy to the ground.

"For the fence," she said.

Lee had just enough time to realise they were a pair of wire-cutters before he stuffed them into his pocket. This woman was as surprising as her daughter.

"Say, does Charm like Brazil nuts?" he asked suddenly.

"What?"

"Don't matter."

"Just you think on. Like I said, you've been blessed with this wonderful gift for a purpose. Don't waste it. Go to that evil place and bring back something that will help you – and maybe all of us."

"I already thought of that, but spears and shields ain't no use against bullets."

"Ee, lad, is your brain powered by cheap batteries from the market? I really will kick you in the plums if you don't turn all the lights on in there. Mooncaster's strongest weapons aren't swords and crossbows."

"Hang on… are you…?"

"At last!"

"That's crazy. I can't do that. Most I done is sneak a few apples from a tree. You ain't serious."

"Get your frightened, lazy backside over to Mooncaster!" she told him angrily. "Go there and, by whatever means necessary, it doesn't matter how, murder someone if you have to, bring back something really important – bring back Malinda's wand."

Captain Swazzle finally managed to open the attached picture. The message was from Yikker, who was with the other work party. The Captain squinted at the photo. It showed that same woman whispering to one of the girls, just under an hour ago.

The Captain pushed the whisky into Garrugaska's hands. Who was that female? What was she up to?

"You!" Swazzle shouted to Charm's mother. "What you do? Why you talk so much?"

"I've got to go," Mrs Benedict said hurriedly as the Punchinello came stamping over. "Get the wand, find out where my baby is and be out there at eleven! No later. The lorry won't wait, it's then or never."

"Wait, I never!"

"You've got to!" she said backing away, across the road to her car. "It's your only chance. Maybe the world's only chance! Remember, eleven sharp."

"Hey, you didn't say, who's so desperate to meet me?"

She was already starting the engine and didn't hear. Reversing sharply, she caused Captain Swazzle to dive out of the way. Then she wound the window down. As the tyres screeched, she yelled, "Yes! She absolutely loves Brazil nuts!"

Lee threw back his head and laughed.

Trying to look absorbed in the work, Spencer sidled over.

"What was that about?" he asked. "Who was she? She looked familiar."

"That there," Lee chuckled, slightly bewildered, "was the mother-in-law."

He spent the rest of the day thinking about her lunatic plan. The more he considered it, the stupider it got. How could it ever be expected to work? There was no way he was going back to Mooncaster to try and steal a fairy godmother's magic wand. There probably wouldn't even be a lorry waiting at the junction anyway. Where was Charm's mother going to get one from and if everyone who wasn't a Jaxer had been shot, who else was there to drive it? And just where would a lorry head for? There had been checkpoints on all major roads and rigorous controls at every ferry port two months ago. It was probably ten times worse now. He wasn't going to risk everything for a half-baked idea, born out of desperation and no proper planning.

By seven o'clock that evening, something would have happened that would make him completely change his mind.

When they weren't busy in the kitchen, Maggie and Esther were obliged to ensure the camp was tidy. They scrubbed the steps of Jangler's cabin and did his washing. At about five, Maggie was wiping a damp cloth over the windows she could reach. The sun had come out and was gleaming in the clean glass. Reflected in one of the panes, she saw a van arrive. It was the latest consignment of cigars and cigarettes, alcohol, DVDs and sausages for the guards. Even though they were greedy for smokes, liquor and violent movies, they never lost that gleeful enjoyment of sausages.

As with every other delivery, Jangler oversaw the unloading and made a great show of unlocking the fridge. He enjoyed any excuse to rattle the iron hoop of keys that hung at his waist.

"The Jill of Spades has walked free from the Old Bailey," he told Maggie. "I've been watching the trial, broadcast live on the television. What an uproarious circus it was in the courtroom. The princess was dressed in the most audacious fashion and pleaded guilty to every charge. Her contrition and repentance were most heartbreaking. The families of those killed in the Disaster were crowded in the public gallery and heckled the judge and jury to acquit her. They threw ribbons and glitter down then started singing until everyone joined in, including Jill herself and the judge. There are celebrations in the streets this very moment. Astonishing day!"

"Nice for her then," Maggie muttered.

Jangler clasped his hands in front of his portly stomach.

"I am not unmindful of the distress caused by your friend's departure this morning," he said with uncharacteristic empathy. "It now appears to be a tradition here that when one of your number leaves, for whatever reason, I grant you the right to share in the guards' sausages. The same shall be true of this evening. You may have one sausage each, in memory of your friend and in jubilation at the Jill of Spades' release."

"You're very generous," Maggie said unconvincingly.

"I'll get them started!" Esther volunteered. She was too hungry and sick to death of soup to turn her nose up at Jangler's offer.

The old man smiled indulgently and counted out the required nineteen sausages before locking the fridge once more.

"I hate that old git," Maggie said when he had gone.

Esther began frying. "Oh, cheer up, Chunky! You'll be stuffing your face with one of these bangers, same as the rest of us – and be glad of it."

"I hate you too," Maggie mouthed at her back.

When the work parties returned, the water jugs, soup and Jangler's special treat were served as usual in the dining hall. The exhausted children filed in and assumed their customary places. Jody no longer sat at the tables. She preferred to crouch in a corner and eat on her own. Nothing Alasdair could do would persuade her back among the others. She was getting progressively worse.

Lee sat down, surprised to see the extra ration on their plates. He was still thinking about Charm's mother and her farcical scheme, and was anxious to speak to Maggie about everything that had happened. Suddenly he realised no one was eating. That was odd. They usually tucked in immediately. Then he saw why. The guards had followed them inside.

Normally the Punchinellos left them to it while they went to guzzle their own meals in their cabin. But not tonight. Captain Swazzle paced around the tables, tipping his white fedora back, with his machine gun resting on one high, hunched shoulder while smirking at the others. Yikker was standing in a beam of sunlight that slanted in from a window and clasped his large, strong hands together as if in prayer. His beady eyes flicked over the children's apprehensive faces. Garrugaska and Bezuel both blew tobacco smoke from their mouths. What were they waiting for?

Maggie came from the kitchen with the last two bowls of soup and set them down. She sat next to Lee and eyed the guards uneasily.

"What is this?" she murmured. "Feeding time at the zoo? They going to start chucking stale buns at us? We should be so lucky."

"Another long day's toil over," Jangler declared as he came striding in. "I just wanted to tell you how pleased I am with your diligence and progress, out there in the minchet orchards."

"Orchards?" Alasdair snorted under his breath in disbelief.

"A joyous day for us, in this grey dream," the old man continued. "The Jill of Spades is pronounced innocent and so we shall make merry this night. Please, don't let your food go cold. Bon appétit!"

"Squassages…" Captain Swazzle cackled. "Lovely, lovely squassages… eat – eat!"

The children returned their attention to the meal. The guards and Jangler did not depart, but their repulsive smiles grew ever wider. What were they doing? Why were they suddenly so interested in watching them eat? It was unnatural and the youngsters were mystified. Tentatively they began. In the corner, Jody bolted the chewy sausage down. Her vegan days were over. She devoured every sweet morsel like a hungry beast and licked her fingers. Then she started on her soup.

Lee pushed his food away. Those big-nosed goons were putting him off.

"You should get that down you," Maggie told him. "The protein will do… ugh!"

Her teeth had crashed into a small nugget of bone. She fished it from her mouth and dropped it on the plate.

"Cheap bangers," she grumbled.

"Squassages…" Captain Swazzle and the guards chanted. "Sticky, pinky, meaty squassages – yum yum."

Lee caught an expectant, agitated expression on Jangler's face. The old guy was psyched about something and was trying to suppress it. Lee had given up second-guessing the lunacy that went on in this place. It truly was an asylum. Everyone was crazy, from Jangler, to the Punchinellos, to Jody and every other inmate, including himself. At least he wasn't mad enough to take any notice of Mrs Benedict's moronic plan. His stomach rumbled and he gave in to it.

A bright gleam of rosy light sparkled across his eyes. It dazzled him and he moved out of its path. Wondering where it came from, he cast his curious gaze down, till it rested on Maggie's plate. The bone fragment there was bouncing the evening sunshine around, glittering like a…

Lee jolted upright and snatched it up. Wiping it clean, he stared and his mind crashed in horror and disbelief. Behind him, the guards screeched with disgusting laughter and Jangler clapped his hands.

"Little Jack Horner!" he joked.

The Punchinellos hopped up and down, whooping.

Lee spat out the contents of his mouth and retched. Then he went berserk. He hurled the plate to the floor and slammed the table as if he was possessed.

"Stop!" he screamed at everyone. "Stop eating it! Stop! Stop! Dear God! Stop!"

The others stared at him in fear and confusion. He was shivering and gagging and tears were streaming down his face. Unable to say any more, he held up the tiny object in his quaking fingers.

It was a heart-shaped, pink diamanté stud.

Moments later, the dining hall was filled with shrieking children. They ran from the tables, coughing and choking, swilling their mouths with water and spitting it on the floor. Some of them threw up; others forced themselves to do the same.

Maggie lurched from her seat and staggered to the door. She stumbled outside and collapsed on the grass. Lee fell to his knees and howled. His fingernails bit deep into the wood of the table. This couldn't be real. It couldn't be happening. Life couldn't do this to him.

The shrill hilarity of the Punchinellos confirmed everything.

"Wasn't that a dainty dish!" Jangler sang.

Crouched in the corner, Jody observed the pandemonium, confused and uncertain. Gradually a slow smile tugged the corners of her mouth and she understood. She watched the spluttering girls weep uncontrollably as they hugged one another and saw Alasdair sitting aghast in his chair. Spencer was on the floor, bent double and crying like a baby. Close by, Christina was wailing. The front of her dress reminded Jody of the first day they met.

Jody began to snigger as she recalled something else from that day.

"She was right after all!" she laughed dementedly. "She really does froth on the tongue – ha ha ha!"

Alasdair heard her and covered his shuddering face.

Through watering eyes, Lee glared at Jangler.

"I am gonna kill you!" he swore, lumbering to his feet and rushing at the old man. "You sick son of…"

With a fierce yell, Yikker sprang forward and cracked the boy across the back of the head with a pistol butt.

Blackness roared in Lee's brain and he fell, unconscious.

Jangler applauded and the four Punchinellos linked arms to skip in a circle.

"Allow them fifteen minutes," Jangler instructed, nodding at the inconsolable, traumatised children. "Then get them to clear up this mess. Fun's over – it's a disgrace in here. Bottles of hard liquor all round for you chaps later."

The guards swapped arms and danced in the other direction.

Jody crept forward, catlike, towards the tables. She grabbed the gruesome, uneaten food from the plates and crammed it in her mouth like a wild animal. She didn't waste a crumb.

Alasdair sobbed into his good hand.

26

Lee was out cold for the best part of an hour. When he awoke, his head felt like it had been hit with a wrecking ball and there was a lump the size of a potato at the base of his skull. He was still lying on the floor of the dining hall. Sounds of mops, clattering buckets and scraping plates echoed inside his mind. Then he remembered.

Gritting his teeth at the physical and mental pain, he uncurled and sat up. Only one thought burned fiercely. He was going to watch Jangler die, by his own hands.

"Hey," a voice said gently. "Don't get up yet. That's a nasty lump you've got."

Lee twisted round. Maggie was on a chair nearby. Alasdair and Spencer were beside her. They looked pale and ill.

"Where is he?" Lee demanded.

"Jangler's ootside," Alasdair said. He couldn't call that vicious old sadist Mainwaring any more. It was too affectionate a nickname for the likes of him.

"Don't go out there," Maggie pleaded. "The guards are drinking. They're waiting for one of us to flip out and attack the old sod, so they can start shooting."

"They can shoot me after I've torn his head off and kicked it over the wire. I won't care then. But that's what I've got to do. Don't you stop me."

He lifted himself up and shuffled towards the door.

"You can't even walk!" Maggie told him.

"I'll manage."

Spencer ran after him. "This isn't the way!" he said. "You know what is. If you go out there now, you're just killing yourself for nothing!"

"Nothing?" Lee growled at him.

"Yes! Nothing. *She* wouldn't want you to chuck it in now. You're angry and want the hurt to stop. I felt the same once, but Marcus talked sense into me. You have to carry on. You have to keep going. You owe it to those who can't. You owe it to *her*!"

"Get outta my way, kid."

"You'll have to knock me down first. If you go out there and attack Jangler, you'll be dead in seconds and you'll have thrown away our one chance of striking back and actually making a difference. You've been told what to do, so do it."

"You're crazy if you think there's a hope in hell of that plan working."

"Yes, I'm crazy. We're all crazy. There's nothing sane any more! That's why it's got to be worth a go. There's a real possibility it could work. It's so stupid it's brilliant! And that's the best revenge you'll ever get. But there's no hope of anything ever again if you get shot to pieces out there! This isn't just about you. Stop being so selfish! What happens to us, to the rest of the world? To those girls in *her* cabin, the ones *she* asked us to look after? What would *she* want you to do?"

Lee stared into the younger boy's eyes. Spencer was frightened, but he was right, dammit. Lee let out a shout of frustration and he kicked the wall. Then, with a phenomenal effort of will, he doused the raw grief that was torching his insides. Ice, he had to be ice. Bury all that rage in an arctic place, deep, deep down. Lock it away until the right time. Here, now, he had to be cold. He had to think.

He closed his eyes and took long breaths. His head was throbbing and his mind was in chaos, but he steered through it.

"OK," he whispered hoarsely.

Suddenly Mrs Benedict's plan didn't seem so laughably stupid. In fact, Spencer was right about that too: it was the only thing that did make sense now.

He put his hand on Spencer's shoulder and thanked him.

"Let's do this," he said grimly. "That's what she'd want."

They returned to the others.

"Tonight," he told them. "We get out of here."

"What?" Maggie and Alasdair said together.

Lee realised Maggie still knew nothing about last night or meeting Mrs Benedict today. He was about to relate the basic facts when he gave Alasdair a cautious look.

"You still dinnae trust me," the Scot said, reading him correctly. "Are we no beyond that? I already ken you're plottin' on doing a flit somehoo. Tell you what, I'll leave ye to it. But you wilnae know if I've gone straight to Jangler and told on ye till they nab you later."

Before Lee could answer, out on the lawn, the bell started clanging. Spencer looked out.

"It's him," he said. "He's got the book with him."

"Time for the last communal reading of the day," Maggie breathed. "He can't be serious. After what he just put us through, what he did…"

"The man is criminally deranged," Alasdair said. "Always was."

Lee wiped his mouth.

"Come on," he told them. "I'm gonna look that evil pig in the eye one last time. Cos when I get back later, that's when he's gonna wish he'd never been born."

"Back?" Alasdair asked. "Back from where?"

Lee snorted and left the dining hall.

"Don't let them provoke you," Spencer warned.

"No danger of that, kid," he said with a deadly smile. "Right now I'm glacial – I am Jack Frost."

Jangler and the guards were waiting impatiently. The children came shambling from their cabins and the main block. Charm's girls were holding hands. They had taken items of her clothing from the suitcases and were wearing them in defiance and remembrance. They had loved her with all their hearts. Esther and her crew lined up sulkily. They were still clutching their stomachs. Esther's face was graven with shock. Drew and Nicholas felt nauseous; they stared at the ground, trying not to pass out. Jody was at the back. She had almost totally shut down. Only the long habit of obeying the bell's summons had drawn her out here. She stared emptily into the distance, not seeing the trees. Christina came to stand next to her. The seven-year-old had been washed and changed by one of Charm's girls.

Lee, Maggie, Spencer and Alasdair were the last to join the assembly.

"Hurry!" Yikker scolded. "In line – in line."

Lee looked at the guards. They seemed disappointed he wasn't ranting and raving and lunging at Jangler. He saw their hands twitch over their guns. Yes, Spencer was right, this was a better way. They so wanted to pull those triggers. He could see the resentment on their ugly faces. It was almost painful for them.

"Another *charming* evening," Jangler greeted them, emphasising the adjective with callous relish. "For tonight's text I've chosen a delicious passage, concerning the midwinter banquet held in the Great Hall. It contains such vivid imagery of the mouth-watering dishes we are served at Court. I'm certain you'll savour every word."

He commenced the reading, rocking backwards and forwards as always. The children began to feel sick again. They couldn't think of food without heaving. The descriptions of the feast made Esther light-headed and she fainted. Another girl followed and then Nicholas crumpled to the ground.

The Punchinellos quacked and cackled. This was better entertainment than a horror film. They swigged from their bottles and bet each other which prisoner would fall down next.

A sharp spasm clutched at Lee's heart. His eyes widened and he felt a sudden cold surge through his veins.

"No," he grunted. "Not now!"

The back of his throat began to burn and he looked around wildly. He recognised what was happening to him. It meant only one thing. Someone here was falling under the spell of Austerly Fellows' words for the very first time. They were going to Mooncaster, and they were dragging him with them.

465

Maggie was alarmed. She saw Lee trembling and sweat begin to pour down his face. She took hold of his hand. It was freezing and covered in gooseflesh.

He wasn't aware of her. His eyes were locked on Jody. Her head was nodding to the rhythm of Jangler's voice. Then she began to shake violently and flung herself down, writhing and convulsing. Alasdair cried out and pushed through the crowd.

"She's having a fit!" he shouted. "Help me. Someone hold her arms and legs before she hurts herself!"

The guards laughed at him, struggling with his one good hand while Christina tried to catch hold of Jody's flailing legs.

Lee's stomach lurched and his eardrums were splitting. The breath wheezed out of his lungs. Then he toppled over. Spencer caught his arm as he fell and Maggie kept hold of his hand.

Captain Swazzle ceased laughing at Alasdair's hapless antics and turned to see Lee, Spencer and Maggie drop to the floor. The Punchinello elbowed the other guards and they guffawed at them sprawled in a heap.

Jangler stopped reading and sighed wistfully as he returned from his other life. He viewed the fallen children and tugged on his pointed beard. Nine of them had fainted. Jody's feverish movements ended and she grew still.

"Is she dying?" Christina asked Alasdair.

The boy didn't know and he gently arranged Jody in the recovery position.

Jangler tucked his copy of *Dancing Jax* under his arm. Then he stepped between the unconscious children and chortled, feeling very pleased with himself. His Lord had commanded him to make them suffer. They were certainly doing that. There would be no shortage of nightmares tonight.

Standing over Lee, Maggie and Spencer, he thought it most peculiar the three of them should faint together like that. He nudged the girl with his shoe. She was as still as a stone and could easily be mistaken for dead. The other two were the same, completely insensible. It was exceedingly strange.

Nearby the other children began to groan and stir as they came round.

Suddenly Alasdair gave a shout of dismay and he scrambled away from Jody in a panic.

"What is that?" he yelled. "What is it? Dinnae touch her, Christina!"

Jangler and the guards hurried over and looked down at the stricken girl. Her eyelids had fluttered open, but the eyes beneath…

"Good gracious!" Jangler exclaimed. "I've never seen the like of that before. Whatever can it mean?"

The Punchinellos muttered unhappily and didn't get too close.

"You tell me what it means!" Alasdair snapped. "What is up wi' her? What've you done to her noo?"

Christina gazed down at Jody's face. Her eyes were no longer human. They were transparent orbs of bright blue glass.

"Most irregular and unexpected," Jangler commented. "I do believe she has crossed over into the Kingdom of the Dawn Prince at last. She is no longer an aberrant. She is one of the blessed. What a sensational occurrence! After all this time being worthless scum. Well, well."

Alasdair couldn't get his head around it. "So she's one of you Jaxers noo?" he said. "But why them eyes?"

The old man stroked his moustache. "This girl was always a troubled creature," he said thoughtfully.

"She wasnae afore she came here!"

"I believe she has become wedged halfway between waking and sleeping. I have no idea who she is in our real world, but it must be a very unusual personage."

Alasdair knelt beside her again and stroked her hair.

"Jody," he called softly. "Can ye hear me?"

There was no response. The blue glass eyes stared fixedly up at the evening sky.

"It's no use," Jangler told him. "She can't respond. She's still awake, back home. Dear me, she'll get awfully tired not being able to sleep there and dream these silly fancies."

"Can ye no do something for her?"

"I'll call for an ambulance. The poor child needs a doctor. I'm only a gaoler and she is no longer one of my charges. I can't keep her here."

He disappeared inside his cabin to make the call. Alasdair drew Christina towards him.

"Time to say goodbye," he told her sadly. "Jody's going away noo."

The little girl crouched beside Jody and slipped her small hand into hers. Alasdair looked around. It was only then he saw Lee and the others.

"Och, no!" he cried.

Running across, he dragged them clear of each other. At first he thought they really were dead until he checked their pulses. Then he tapped and slapped their faces and spoke their names. Not one of them moved.

"What is going on here?" he uttered in despair. "Help me get them indoors."

The Punchinellos flicked their fingers at him and returned to their bottles. Drew came over, but Nicholas didn't feel up to it. Charm's girls stepped forward.

Lee touched the back of his head. The lump was still there and sore as anything. He sucked the air through his teeth. It was freezing and made them ache. Then he realised that his knees and arms were freezing too. He opened his eyes.

"Oh, what?" he cried.

"I didn't see that bus coming," Maggie moaned groggily. "Am I in one piece? I'm too scared to look. It's gone all cold. That noise – the horrible falling feeling…"

Startled to hear another voice, Lee stared down at her. Then his astonishment doubled when he saw Spencer lying close by.

"Damn," he muttered.

"Is it that bad?" Maggie asked, shivering.

"There weren't no bus," Lee told her. "Open your eyes, you're in one piece. Hey, Sheriff Woody, wake up."

Spencer blinked and both he and Maggie looked up simultaneously.

The vapour cloud of the girl's breath steamed like an old-fashioned train as she turned the air blue with her incredulous, technicolour language.

They were in the middle of a wood. The trees were bare and icicles spiked down from the diamond-dusted boughs. Deep and unspoiled snow covered the ground and they were lying in it.

Lee rose and brushed the stuff from his knees.

"When I said I was Jack Frost, this is not what I meant," he said, rubbing his bare arms then helping Maggie to her feet.

"We're here, aren't we?" she marvelled, her teeth chattering with the cold and the excitement. "We're in Mooncaster!"

Spencer was speechless. He stared about them, overwhelmed. This place wasn't like any of the real woodland he had seen in the New Forest. This was like being inside the most chocolate-boxy, picturesque Christmas card, complete with silver glitter. Everywhere he looked was a painter's dream. The sky was a pale gold; all it lacked was a church spire in the distance, with a light shining behind a stained-glass window. But there were no churches in the Dawn Prince's Kingdom.

"Er… why… how did we get here?" he stammered.

"Didn't you guys see Jody back there?" Lee asked. "She was being converted. That book was finally working on her. When a newbie turns, they always drag me with them if I'm near. I can't stop it. You two just got in the way an' I pulled you in with me. Sorry."

Maggie blew into her cupped hands. "Don't apologise," she said. "It's amazing. But we're not exactly dressed for it. We're only in T-shirts. I'll turn purple in a minute."

"I gotta get you back to the camp soon as. We'll just be lyin' on the floor there and can't wake up. That is way too dangerous. No tellin' what could happen to us in that state."

"I saw other kids fainting," Spencer said. "They're in the same boat."

"Difference is, they'll come round. We won't, long as we're here. Gimme your hands. We're goin' back."

"Hang on!" Spencer argued. "This is perfect, don't you see? You were going to have to come here tonight anyway. We can be your posse!"

"You is kidding me."

"The three of us together stand a better chance of finding Malinda's cottage and stealing her wand than you on your own."

Maggie's jaw dropped. "We're doing what?" she cried.

"No way!" Lee told them. "You have not the smallest clue what this place is like! It's a fairyland war zone here. I don't even trust these trees!"

"The trees can talk?" Maggie asked. "That's bloody fabulous!" She ran over to the nearest and knocked on it. A hammock of snow dropped down on her head and she squealed, jiggling up and down to shake it out of her T-shirt.

"I've not seen them talk," Lee admitted. "But all sorts of weirdness lives in them, and under them, an' if you keep foolin' around like that, you ain't gonna last long."

"Sorry," she said contritely. "I'm just so gobsmacked to be here. It's real – it's actually real! And it's gorgeous!"

"Visitin' time is over," he said decisively. "Grab my hands. I'll come back after eight o'clock on my own, properly geared up, and find that thing."

Spencer refused and folded his arms.

"Them Big Noses could be putting your sorry ass on a fire right now, for all you know!" Lee said crossly. "Cos they is more than capable of that, and worse – or do you need reminding what they just did? Do you, really?"

"Alasdair is there," Spencer replied. "He won't let them. He'll look after us."

"Ya think?"

"Yes – I trust him, and you should too. It's time you did. I've seen his face each time he's excluded. I know what that feels like, even before

Dancing Jax. Whatever he did and said, Alasdair's really sorry for it."

"That changes nuthin'! He can't stop those…"

He spun around suddenly. There had been a noise – music. It was nearby.

Lee hissed at them to crouch down. They peered over the snow-covered roots and caught their steaming breath in their hands.

The wood was on a gentle slope. A little way down there was a gap between the ice-draped trees, forming a winding path through the forest. Figures were travelling along it and Maggie clamped her lips together to stop herself exclaiming with delight.

It was a procession of woodland folk: animals and strange creatures who dwelt in the forest. Leading the way, the beautiful almond hind carried the three gnome miners on her back. They were brothers who tapped for moon pearls and wish stones beneath the earth. For once they were not bickering amongst themselves but playing instruments – a flute, a drum and a hurdy-gurdy. After them marched a badger on a long silver leash, held by a thin character in a plum-coloured gown and stovepipe hat, decked with matching ribbons. A pair of weasels followed then a group of squirrels, stoats, foxes and rabbits and several wild cats. All of those animals were walking on their hind legs, clutching twigs of evergreen in their front paws, which they waved about in time to the gnomes' midwinter song.

> *Gud masters give ear to our pleading*
> *Wherever ye may abide.*
> *Come, see where we will be leading*
> *To doorways far and wide.*
> *The sun, she has slept long enough, love*
> *'Tis the darkenmost time of the year.*
> *So sing out loud, beat the drum, love*
> *Awake and bring the gladdest of cheer.*

Maggie was mesmerised. It was the most enchanting, yet bizarre spectacle she had ever witnessed. Outlandish creatures went parading by. Some were odd, stunted people with long, beak-like noses along which icicles were forming or robins hopped; others could barely be seen beneath oversized hats or were muffled in scarves or beards. A small, whiskery, barrel-shaped woman rode on a wild pig that was garlanded with scarlet berries. Amidst all this, a very solemn-looking twig imp in a russet cloak strode up and down carrying a staff, topped by a golden sun symbol, keeping them all in line and reminding the animals not to devour each other on this special day.

Tramping on all fours at the rear of the column was an enormous bear, whose shaggy fur was a rich shade of cinnamon. Nobody dared ride on its back. It turned its snout towards the place where Lee and the others were hidden and sniffed the cold, sharp air. Its wild, amber eyes glinted. Then it tossed its head and continued on its way.

When the music faded in the distance, Maggie's eyebrows lifted as far as they could go.

"Wow!" was all she could say.

"Shh!" Lee whispered. "It ain't over yet."

There was a rustling in the trees beside the path. The snow was shaken free and the ivy that grew around the trunks ripped itself clear. It slithered to the ground. Then the evergreen vines moved like serpents and twined and twisted themselves together, forming a rough human shape. Then there came a leathery, swishing, crackling sound and a stocky being made entirely of holly branches strode on to the pathway. It stood before the graceful ivy form and bowed low. The Ivy Girl gave an answering curtsy and raised a leafy hand. The Holly Boy took it and together they went waltzing through the forest.

"Er... none of that," Spencer remarked in a stunned monotone, "was in the book."

"Whole heaps of stuff goes on here what ain't in them pages," Lee informed him.

"No wonder you got addicted to this place," Maggie breathed. "I just seen it with my own eyes and I don't believe it."

"Still want to go mug a fairy godmother?"

Maggie looked at Spencer and they nodded in unison.

"If the guards were going to do something to us, back at the camp," she said, "we'd have felt it by now, wouldn't we?"

"And it's got to be done," Spencer added.

Lee didn't feel like arguing any more.

"It's your funeral," he said.

They picked themselves up and stamped their feet to get the blood circulating again.

"Do you have any idea where we are?" Maggie asked, rubbing her hands. "Is this where she lives?"

"Like I know one wood from another!" Lee answered impatiently. "There's lots of woods in this mad place. Could be any one of 'em."

"But there's only one Cinnamon Bear," Spencer said. "And it lives in Hunter's Chase, same as Malinda. Come on, how many times have you read that flipping thing? Didn't any of it sink in?"

"And that," said Lee, "is why the geeks shall inherit the earth."

They felt the best way to go would be to head left, travelling parallel to the path, but not walking along it, in case they encountered other peculiar creatures. As they journeyed, Lee told them to look out for fallen branches or stout sticks, something they could use as a weapon in case something unexpected leaped out at them.

"I wish an unexpected hot-water bottle, an extra-large fleece and a Tibetan hat would jump out at me," Maggie muttered, scanning the snowy surroundings. "I can't feel my ears."

Apart from the cold, this place was a constant indulgence for her other senses. The scents of the forest were keen and captivating. She could smell the pines growing higher up the hill, the tantalising rumour of sweet woodsmoke from a distant chimney – even the glossy leaves of the evergreen. It was so intoxicating she began to imagine she could smell the snow in the clouds moving over the golden sky.

Then there were the sounds. The crisp crunching of their footsteps, the soft flopping of snow out of trees, a slushy stream trickling thick and slow, the light scudding of solitary birds, the furtive foraging of unseen wild animals, hidden under white canopies, the tinkle of sleigh bells…

"What's that?" she murmured.

Lee had already halted and pulled them behind a tree. A little way ahead, the path joined a second wider track and the junction was in a clearing. The ringing grew louder. The teenagers held their breaths and waited. Then, at last, the sleigh came into view.

The body was carved from a single piece of oak, painted jet-black. The high, pointed prow was shaped like the head of a horned demon whose wings swept back, forming a frame around the seat. Six raven-black, muzzled hounds drew it and the occupant was swaddled in heavy sables, its head hidden in a hood and hands in leather gauntlets.

"I don't know this from the book either," Spencer whispered.

"It's not Father Christmas," Maggie assured him.

They watched as the rider alighted. It turned right and left, as if searching for something. Then it strode past the panting hounds and called out.

"Where are you? Get out here, you craven rats. Show your ugly faces. How dare you keep me waiting?"

Lee looked at the others in surprise. That was a girl's voice.

"She doesn't mean us, does she?" Spencer asked.

Lee didn't think so.

"Cease skulking this instant or I'll loose my hounds and they'll hunt every last one of you. I always keep them hungry – they run faster with an appetite. Their jaws will shovel you up and they'll crunch your puny bones."

Petrified yelps and alarmed chirrups sounded from the trees and snow-covered undergrowth around the clearing. Then tiny figures came creeping out of countless hiding places, stealing forward timorously.

The Jill of Spades cast back the fur hood and her lips curled in derision as she surveyed these base, fearful creatures.

They were the Runtlemen: a scavenging, beggarly tribe that infested Hunter's Chase like cockroaches. They were no bigger than hedgepigs, and it was believed they interbred with them, for many were covered in spines and had a passion for slugs. Other sickly specimens sprouted tatty feathers and were clawed of foot. Some had rodent-like features. They were dressed in rags, or tufty with fleabitten fur, or were naked under clods of dirt. No one had dealings with the Runtlemen. Time and again they had proven themselves to be the lowest form of walking filth. They were dishonest and sneaky, treacherous and merciless – but only if the victim was weaker than themselves. Because foremost in their character was a profound, inherent cowardice. Without that, the Runtlemen would have been a terror to travellers through the wood and their great numbers would have emboldened them to invade neighbouring farms and dwellings, maybe even to assail the village of Mooncot.

And so the Jill of Spades eyed them with the contempt they deserved. She despised having to traffic with them, but she had no choice. They had something she wanted.

She grimaced at them. The vermin surrounded her and the virgin snow made them appear even dirtier.

"Where is your chief?" she demanded.

One of that pestiferous horde took a hesitant step forward. He leaned on a gnarled staff. There was more nose than face on his wizened head.

"Here am I, Your Highness," he squeaked, blinking nervously. "We received your message."

Jill didn't disguise her revulsion. "Then where is it?" she asked. "Where is the thing you claimed you had in your possession? Would you dare try to deceive me?"

The chief tapped his nose. A speck of dirt fell out.

"We have it, to be sure!" he told her proudly. "Found it lying way yonder, deep in the forest – the snow all around crimsoned with blood and the frozen corpses of wolves and sundry portions of another beast we weren't quite sure of."

The multitude smacked their lips at the memory of that hearty feast.

"Yes, we have what you want. Have no doubts about that, but what of your end of the bargain? We Runtlemen are ever scorned and played false by such as you."

"Such as I?" she said, highly insulted. "There are no others such as I in this entire Kingdom. Never forget that."

The chief grovelled apologetically.

"Even so," he wheedled, "where is that which you were to bring in exchange?"

The Jill of Spades walked back to her sleigh. A smaller sled had been trailed behind it. The bulky object this carried was hidden beneath a large piece of sacking. Jill pulled the cloth away and at once the clearing erupted with thrilled chirps and clicks and yips and caws and the stamping of little feet.

On the sled, trussed in ropes and in great discomfort, was a great silver swan. It was the King Swan, from the moat around the White Castle, and the only creature who dared challenge Mauger, the monstrous Guardian of the Gate. It was said to own the most fearless heart in the whole Realm.

The bird's head was bound close to its body. Its bright, flame-coloured eyes were open now and ablaze with fury. The sleeping potion she had captured it with had worn off and it strained and pulled on the ropes.

The Runtlemen streamed eagerly towards the sled.

"One moment," the girl said, standing between it and them. The look on her face was enough to cow their fervour and send them skittering back again. "Where is what you owe me?"

The chief tilted his head and blew a high, skirling note through his nose.

Soon Jill heard the grunts and puffing wheezes of many voices, as fifty more of those squalid forest lice came trudging into the open. But above their heads, the new arrivals were carrying what she was so desperate to have. With it, she could keep the bargain Haxxentrot had forced upon her, the night of the autumn revel.

The Runtlemen brought into the clearing the skull of an animal. It was larger than any of them and they had attached it to a long stick, which was more like a tree trunk to their eyes.

The Jill of Spades pulled the sables close round her throat and nuzzled into them. This was a glorious moment, for that was no ordinary skull. A long, tapering horn spiralled up between the eye sockets and the remains of a wispy beard still clung to the jaw. It was the skull of a unicorn.

"We cleaned it out real tidy," the chief boasted. "Gnawed and licked every last bit, every shred, 'cept the beard, thought it looked prettier with it left on – and we was full from the wolves."

"It's exquisite," she declared. "Give it to me – I must have it."

The chief signalled to the bearers to bring it closer.

"Might a low-born bogworm such as me dare ask what you want with such a totem?"

She arched her brows. "What do you want with a swan?"

"Ah, that's easy answered. We're going to eat it alive, Your Highness. There's no braveness in our hearts you see, so if we eat the savagest critter in the land, we're sure to get some. We was hoping the unicorn would've helped there, but it were too late by the time we found it. A maiden had tamed the fight clear out of the beast – and it were dead o' course. The King Swan is a different kettle of rhubarb! Ho – we'll be a-feared of no one, once we've gorged. Then we'll make some heads ache and see about some grievances!"

Jill stooped and took hold of the stick, shaking off the Runtlemen whose hands had stuck to it with the cold. She lifted the unicorn's skull level with her face and ran her hand down the horn.

"This," she told the chief, amused to share her black secret with one such as he, "is a key. With it, I shall be able to pass through the enchanted fence of Malinda. No one with malign intent may enter there, but the virtue of this will guide me through. The dweller of the Forbidden Tower has tasked me with delivering unto her the Fairy Godmother's wand — and this night she shall have it."

The chief scratched his nose. "We never meddles with Malinda," he said. "Nor even dare look on her cottage. Strong magick she got."

The girl laughed. "Not after I steal it from her," she said. "Besides, you and your sordid mob will have the courage of a thousand knights by then. Come, feast on the swan, eat your fill – I never liked it."

She stepped aside and the Runtlemen surged at the sled, swarming up the runners and clambering over the ropes. The swan hissed at them, but could not move. Thousands of tiny, gore-hungry hands tore at the silver feathers and half as many little mouths prepared to feed.

Jill unhitched the sled from her sleigh. Those creatures were disgusting. Once she had delivered the wand, she would return and really would loose the hounds. They made her skin itch.

At that moment, three voices came bawling from the trees, where the track forked left. Jill spun around and saw a large girl and two boys belt towards the clearing, brandishing sticks and hollering bloodthirsty yells. The skin of one was almost as dark as her sables. It astounded her and she wasted precious moments staring. Then she jumped into the seat, but before she could crack the whip and command the hounds, the mysterious boy had stormed up and was reaching in.

"This is a sleighjacking, princess!" he declared, wrenching the skull from her.

"No!" she cried. "Who dares assault me? I'll have you drawn and quartered for this!"

Maggie and Spencer had charged at the small sled and were swiping their sticks through the Runtlemen, whacking them off the stricken swan. The squealing host retreated before those formidable, battering weapons and they leaped from the bird's back, clutching handfuls of downy feathers. Yammering, they bolted into the trees, shaking their fists at being cheated of their prize and swearing vengeance on humankind. One day they would be as ferocious as lions; one day they would strike and lay waste the works of man and everything he held dear. Maggie darted after them and they fled, screaming.

The Jill of Spades was incensed. Tearing off her gauntlets, she jumped from the seat and ran to the hounds, unbuckling the harnesses and ripping the muzzles from their jaws.

"Get them!" she commanded, dragging two of the great dogs around and pointing at the three strange bandits. "Go – attack – kill!"

The hounds bounded away. Spencer staggered back at the sight of them and the stick fell from Maggie's hands. The hungry dogs ran, swift as the wind, and their baying boomed through the forest. Their dark mistress grinned wickedly.

But Lee had not been idle. He still had the wire-cutters Mrs Benedict had given him in his pocket. They were brand-new and the blades were sharp. One by one he snipped through the restraining ropes and set the King Swan free.

"I hope you know whose side I'm on," the boy told it as the final cord was cut.

The bird's head reared like a cobra over the back of the sleigh. It hissed far more rancorously and the hounds slithered to a halt. The great wings shook and unfurled to an immense span and the dogs whimpered. The bird's flaming eyes burned terror into them and they kicked up a snowstorm as they wheeled about and ran, yelping – with their tails clamped between their legs.

The King Swan glided from the sled, ran along the ground and lifted into the air, flying straight for the girl who had tormented and brought it here. The other four hounds yowled and flattened themselves into the snow as it swept low over their heads. The Jill of Spades uttered a horrified wail and raced into the trees, pursued by a wrathful, avenging, silver-winged angel.

Lee gripped the unicorn skull tightly.

"We've wasted enough time here," he said sharply. "I know where we are now. I been this way before once. There's a little cut-off just down that way. Malinda's cottage ain't far. Let's go rob, or scam, or tie the old lady to a chair if we have to. That damn wand is mine tonight."

27

LEE CHECKED HIS watch. Back in the camp, it was half eight, long after curfew. He was amazed their unconscious selves hadn't been kicked, or worse, by now. If this was down to Alasdair then he owed that boy a huge apology – if they ever made it back.

"Am I the only one who thinks it's incredibly convenient to have got here just when that deal was going on?" Maggie asked. "I mean, here we are wanting to do the exact same as the Jill of Spades and now we've got the one thing that'll help us do it. Isn't that a bit… well, unlikely? Shouldn't we be worried?"

"That always happens in fantasy," Spencer told her. "It's one of the tropes. The hero always finds a magic plot device that'll turn out really handy later. That's why Westerns are better."

"I'm not a hero," Lee said darkly. "I just wanna kill someone – and this is gonna help."

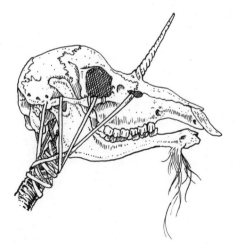

This time they kept to the track. It curved around in a long arc, where the trees grew more densely than anywhere else in Hunter's Chase. The topmost branches met, high above their heads, forming a natural tunnel. If it hadn't been winter, and without the sparkling whiteness of the surrounding snow, this part of the forest would be eerily dark.

"Isn't Malinda supposed to be one of the few goodies in the book?" Maggie muttered, looking around uneasily. "It's a bit doomy gloomy. She should sell up and move."

"Evil things are always prowling round her cottage," Spencer explained. "Her goodness is a magnet for them, and the witch has lots of her spies watching. That's why Malinda needs the magic fence to keep them at bay."

"I used to be a cake magnet," the girl said. "That was a lot easier."

Lee gave them a stern look that told them to be quiet. Maggie's instinctive stress response was to crack feeble jokes, but this really wasn't the time for it and certainly not the place.

The path made a sharp turn and they stood stock-still when they beheld what lay beyond. There, in a glade, only a short distance away – was the home of Malinda.

It was every child's ideal of a cosy country cottage. Built of mellow stone, crystals and curious objects hung in every mullioned and leaded window, which were bordered by pretty shutters with hearts, spades, diamonds and clubs cut into them. A single climbing rose, bearing blooms of different colours, including blue, grew round the arched door and the thatch was pleasingly untidy and in need of renewal. Another window, hung with gold lace, peeped out of the centre and a straw owl at one corner of the roof seemed to regard with disapproval the two straw hares dancing at the other. From the quaintly painted pot, at the top of the one stout chimney, pink smoke climbed leisurely into the sky.

No trace or breath of winter touched that dwelling. Within the white picket fence that ran all around the impossibly twee cottage and its well-tended garden, not a fleck of snow had fallen. Early autumn still lingered there; even the light that bathed the stonework and shone in the windows was soft and romantic and considerably warmer than anywhere else in Mooncaster that day.

Outside the fence, the snow was deep and startling footprints had been made in it by prowling fiends. But someone, perhaps daring children or maybe even Malinda herself, had built a jolly-looking snowman, with coal eyes and twig arms raised in friendly welcome.

"I could so live there," Maggie breathed.

"We got company," Lee whispered. "Over there."

He indicated with his eyes and they glanced to the right of the path. In the distance, through the trees, something was moving. It was a tall figure, three times their height and clothed from head to toe in flowing grey, spectral robes. They couldn't tell what manner of creature it was. All they could see of it were six clawed, bony fingers sticking out of each long sleeve. A pointed hood concealed the face and its movements were oddly stiff and jerky.

"Keep movin'," he said.

They tried not to look at it and hurried on, towards the cottage, but Spencer couldn't help turning round. The grey figure was keeping pace with them. The next time he looked, it had moved closer.

Then Maggie spotted two more, through the trees on the left. Their long strides bore them quickly over the snowy ground. When they raised their arms to clatter and rip their claws through the branches, they were just blackened bones.

The teenagers ran and the towering spectres let out shrill screeches as they broke from the trees and gave chase into the glade. They moved with frightening speed and their claws came reaching.

Maggie felt them catch and pull at her T-shirt and she ran faster than she ever had. Spencer still had his stick and he brandished it desperately. One swing of a skeletal hand knocked it from his grasp and sent it flying. Lee held the unicorn skull at arm's length, hoping it would ward the attackers off, but it had no effect.

The snow grew deeper quickly and running became difficult. Maggie could barely drag her feet through it. Then a hand punched her in the back and she fell. Spencer stopped and tried to help. Another shove sent him diving into the snow next to her. Two of the grey figures stomped closer and stood over them menacingly, whilst the other went after Lee.

Lee heard the cries of the others, but he wouldn't stop. He had to go on. He had to get to that cottage. Only the death of Jangler and those Punchinellos mattered to him. Maggie and Spencer shouldn't even be here. He'd told them to go back to the camp. They weren't his responsibility. He always looked after number one. They knew the risks.

"No, they didn't!" his conscience shouted at him. Even he didn't know the risks here. Besides, *she* would have gone back to help them.

Snarling, he spun around on one foot. The third spectral figure came rushing up and its claws seized him by the throat. Lee was forced to his knees then thrust on to his back. Insidious, snaky laughter issued from the darkness within the pointed hood and the figure stooped over him.

"That will do!" a scolding voice rang out abruptly. "Fie on you! Shame!"

The grey figures reared up and stared across at the cottage. They hissed in annoyance and their hands made bony fists. Lee heard someone clapping in irritation.

"Shoo!" the voice said as though reprimanding naughty children. "I know who you are. You don't affright me. Just what are you supposed to be? It's the most guileless tomfoolery I've seen in many a mumming season. Now be off with you!"

Lee craned his head back and saw a sight that made his heart leap.

A brisk, elderly woman, in a pink and gold gown, gathered a spangled shawl about her shoulders and stepped through the garden gate. The silver walking stick she leaned upon to wade through the snow was tipped by an amber star.

The tall figures wavered uncertainly. The one standing over Lee took a hesitant step backwards and started chattering unhappily to itself.

The boy bared his teeth and kicked out with brute force. His feet struck one of the spectre's legs. To his astonishment, it snapped. The figure warbled in dismay and tottered unsteadily before the robe fell away and Lee gaped at what was revealed.

The tall, sinister figure was a contraption made from wood. The legs were stilts and the claws were attached to long sticks, operated via strings by a small creature with a wobbly white head and yellow eyes.

Jub, the Bogey Boy, looked shamefaced and embarrassed to have been discovered. He gave the arms a final, feeble wave and tried to hiss and sound frightening, but it was no use. Looking down at Lee, he grinned sheepishly, showing all his babylike teeth. Then he dropped the false arms and hopped from the one remaining leg. The snow reached up to his nose, but he scampered away from the approaching old woman, burrowing a trench towards the trees.

The other two figures knew the game was up and they were striding as fast as their stilts could take them, until the one at the back tripped and went crashing into the other and they both collapsed in a bundle of splintering sticks and flapping volumes of grey cloth.

Slapping one another and cussing, only the tops of their heads were visible above the snow as they scurried after Jub.

Lee uttered some cusses of his own.

"Such silliness," the old woman tutted. "What did they think they were doing? Oh, but look at you, poor dear. You must be frozen to the marrow in such inadequate attire. Why, the village boys wear more when they swim in the millpond in June!"

She leaned over to offer Lee a mittened hand, but he got up without her assistance.

Spencer and Maggie were still shaking their heads at the wreckage of the Bogey Boys' costumes.

"How gullible are we?" the girl asked. "We'll be scared of glove puppets and cut-outs next."

"You must all come inside and warm yourselves by my hearth," the old woman called. "I insist."

Maggie and Spencer stared at her with keen interest and came trudging up.

"You invitin' us in?" Lee asked, giving the suddenly redundant unicorn skull a disappointed glance.

Malinda smiled. She had the sort of face and demeanour that won friends and inspired confidence. Her eyes were the palest blue and framed by fine webs of wrinkles. Her cheeks were like October apples and her hair could have been spun sugar. Lee knew Charm would have loved her instantly.

"But of course," she replied. "I dare say you'd like something to warm you. 'Tis a most unforgiving chill out here this day."

"As long as it's not soup," Maggie said.

Malinda gave a silvery laugh. "No," she replied. "But there are pikelets to toast and smother with butter and preserves, and a cheery herbal infusion to lift your spirits. I'm sure those mischievous Bogey Boys made their harassing antics most convincing and alarmed you most dreadfully."

Her eyes fell on the skull and her mouth twitched with amusement.

"What are you doing with that smelly old thing?" she asked. "It's not true what they say about it, you know. I don't know who started that nonsensical rumour, probably the Jockey – it smacks of his oafish drollery."

The mild reprimand made Lee feel almost as foolish as the Bogey Boys had. Using the skull as a magical key seemed ridiculous now and he lowered it self-consciously.

Malinda led them towards her gate and Maggie noticed the stumps poking out the back of her bodice. They were bound in clean bandages, but spots of blood still seeped through. The wings would never heal completely and she would never be free of the pain of that vicious assault on her.

As they drew near to the fence, the retired Fairy Godmother halted and an impatient frown puckered her forehead. She looked crossly at the jolly snowman and set her toe tapping.

"You may as well go with the others," she told it tersely. "There's no point you hanging around here now. I don't know why you stayed this long."

Maggie wondered if the snowman was alive. Was it going to wiggle that carrot nose and wave the twiggy arms before walking away, singing a song? She would believe anything of this place now.

Nothing happened.

"Be off with you!" Malinda said. "Or do you want me to lose my temper?"

She lifted the wand and a faint glimmer flickered in the amber star.

With that, the coals dropped off the snowman's face, disclosing a pair of real yellow eyes behind. The ginger lashes blinked and a disgruntled voice mumbled inside the head.

"It's no use moaning about it," Malinda said. "And you've most certainly gone and caught a most shocking cold and stored up no end of sorrow for your joints. If you get lumbago like mine, you'll rue this folly."

The snowman gave a judder. One of the twigs fell out and the coal buttons popped off. Then the head split apart, exposing that of the fourth Bogey Boy.

Rott scowled at them petulantly. Then he elbowed his way out of the body and hurried after the other servants of Haxxentrot, into the trees.

"They'll be back later," she sighed in resignation. "Disguised as something else. I don't know why they do it. They've never fooled me yet and never learn anything of value to tell that unhappy wretch in the tower."

Moving to the gate, she swung it open and ushered the teenagers inside. The leap in temperature was instantly noticeable, especially to Spencer, whose spectacles steamed up the moment he stepped through.

The garden was everything they expected. Topiary animals had been clipped into the bushes and herbs grew either side of a stone path. Lupins and ox-eye daisies hugged the walls, buttercups splashed the lawn with gold and the air was warm and fragrant. There was even a real wishing well and an inquisitive frog studied them from the bucket as they walked by.

"You've got a lovely house," Maggie said.

"Oh, do you like it?" Malinda asked, greatly pleased. "Some people, who ought to have better things to do in my opinion, think I should live in a place made entirely of gingerbread, with barley-sugar twists either side of the door. Can you imagine how impractical that would be? Every bird, mouse and squirrel, from here to the Northern Marches, would be flocking to literally eat me out of hearth and home. And then the first drop of rain and it's a soggy disaster!"

When they reached the front door, hanging above the brass knocker a primitive calico cat doll, with painted eyes and wearing an embroidered smock, greeted them.

"Welcome home, good Mistress," it said through the stitching of its mouth.

"Oh, tush, Cartimandua," Malinda said. "I've only ventured a few steps beyond the garden gate. Anyone would think I'd been sailing the Silvering Sea in an eggshell for seven years, the way you carry on." She turned to her guests. "Come you in and welcome."

The door opened by itself and they entered.

Inside, the cottage was comfortable and snug. Samplers, carvings and testimonials, bearing good wishes and gratitude from former clients, ingénues and apprentices, hung on the walls. Shelves crowded with leather-bound books and parchments filled one alcove; a dresser piled with jars, bottles, pots and leather vessels filled another. Lanterns of coloured glass were suspended from the oak-beamed ceiling and rainbows, cast by the crystals in the windows, trembled on every surface. Two overstuffed wing-backed chairs were angled towards a fireplace in which silver flames crackled and sparkled.

Malinda guided them in and bid Maggie and Lee take the chairs, inviting Spencer to sit on a large velvet cushion between them. She hung her wand and shawl on a wooden peg. Then a thought struck her.

"Oh!" she warned hastily. "Please be careful of Gilly; she may be hiding. It would be most unfortunate if you sat on her – she might break. That really would be a calamity."

"Who's Gilly?" Maggie asked.

"She's a very clumsy bunny," Malinda said loudly, addressing the corners of the room and any place this Gilly might be concealed. "Who ought to know better than skulk about and get herself into scrapes. She knows very well what the consequences would be if any mischance befell her. Always trying to climb on to things, or running too fast round corners. I normally keep her in a well-padded hutch, but this is her exercise hour and I wasn't expecting company."

Maggie and the others eased themselves down, eyes peeled for a fluffy rabbit.

Lee was agitated and fidgety. What were they doing sitting down? They should just take the wand and go back to camp. He still held on to the skull on the stick and considered threatening the old lady with it. But she was so gentle and endearing. She reminded him of his grandmother, before she had been turned by the book. He didn't want to threaten her unless it was genuinely necessary. If the stories about her were true and she was warm-hearted and benevolent then perhaps she would lend them the wand willingly for a little while? He sucked his teeth and couldn't believe he had actually thought that might be a possibility.

"I have an infusion made up already," the old woman said, taking a pot from a trivet and pouring the contents into four earthenware goblets. "This should revive your spirits and go tingling down to your littlest toes."

"Herbal tea!" Spencer declared, cupping it in his hands and inhaling the curling steam.

"Tea?" Malinda enquired, putting a pikelet on to a toasting fork and holding it close to the flames.

"It's a drink we have at home. Doesn't taste anything like this though. This is lush."

Maggie added her enthusiastic appreciation. "I wouldn't swap this for a chocolate milkshake. I can feel it going to my ears! It tastes like a sunny day. If we had this at home, it'd be a sell-out."

"Ah," the Fairy Godmother said, toasting another pikelet. "Now we come to it. I should like to hear about that place, for I know you are not of this Kingdom – nor indeed this world."

"That don't surprise you?" Lee asked.

"Bless you no, dear, not much does. I know that one of you is the Castle Creeper. I'm not sure which of you it is yet, but that can wait till after you've eaten and thawed yourselves. Now be careful you don't get chilblains."

Impaling a third pikelet on the tines, she set about buttering the first two, leaving the toasting fork hanging in mid-air all on its own.

"Blackberry preserve, my dears?" she asked. "I've some freshly made gingerbread – far better to put it on a plate than use it as roofing – and nigh on a whole seed cake, as well as bread and honey, if you wish?"

"I could definitely live here!" Maggie reiterated emphatically.

After the harrowing ordeal earlier in the camp, Lee and Spencer didn't want to eat anything. A hot drink was the most they thought they could manage. But Maggie could not resist the sights and scents of the scrumptious spread placed before them and she needed to totally obliterate the taste memory of that vomitous nightmare. The boys watched her take the first few bites, and saw the melted butter running down her wrist. Then they had to obey the loud demands of their shrivelled stomachs and joined in.

"There now," the Fairy Godmother said, beaming, as they made short work of it. They had forgotten what real food tasted like and this was more delicious than anything they could remember. She crooked a finger at a three-legged stool in the far corner. It gave a hop and came hobbling over for her to sit on. "That's better; you looked as though you hadn't eaten in days."

Clasping her hands across her lap, she regarded each of them in turn as if searching for something in their faces.

"It's been a long time since the Night of All Dark," she said. "I tried then to…"

A furtive scuffling interrupted her and she turned to see something shiny and blue dash across the rugs. "There you are!" she said. "Don't be so rude when we have visitors. Come say 'how do'. Where are our manners today?"

Presently a little face came peeping out from the shadows beneath a side table.

Maggie exclaimed in surprise and the face pulled back again. Malinda coaxed it some more and Gilly the rabbit crept forward.

It was not an ordinary animal. It was made entirely of clear blue glass. The fur and features were merely modelled into it and perfectly smooth, yet it moved like any real, living rabbit of flesh and blood. The ears flipped up to catch the astonished sounds these three strangers made and its feet waggled when Malinda scooped it up and put it on her knee.

"Gilly's painfully shy with people she doesn't know," she said, stroking its ears flat and causing the cute little nose to wrinkle with pleasure. "To look at her now, you wouldn't believe there are days when she won't stop chattering about all sorts of subjects. Yikkety-yakkety, so opinionated it can be quite tiresome. But I mustn't decry her; she's simply overtired – she never sleeps, poor pet. Part of the bewitchment I suppose."

"Bewitchment?" asked Maggie.

"Once this was a maiden, just as you, who had the ill luck to chance upon Haxxentrot in a meadow one morning and ate a forbidden sweetmeat. The witch transformed her into this form, and did more besides…"

"More?"

"Alas, yes. The glass is hollow and, although it appears empty within, it is not. There is a badness in there. Haxxentrot filled it with a virulent plague of her own brewing and cursed Gilly with a reckless disposition. That is why she must never break. If that were to happen, the plague would be set free and the denizens of Mooncaster would surely perish. A padded hutch is the best comfort I can give her."

She continued stroking and returned to what she was saying before.

"On Ween Night, I tried to tell you I wished to be of assistance. But you melted into the dark. I have hoped and waited for your return ever since."

"Why would you help?" Lee asked.

"I am Malinda," she answered, smiling. "Everyone knows I strive to give aid where it is needed. And there is another reason… for too long now this land has been afflicted by the presence of an unstoppable evil. It is a canker that none can withstand. It is a blight on our lives here."

"The witch?" Maggie asked.

"Not her!" the Fairy Godmother said. "Haxxentrot spins her schemes and daunts the unwary and ensnares poor damsels like Gilly here, but she dare not contest against the Ismus directly. She did barely escape their battle through the sky on Ween Night with her skin intact. No, there is but one true terror that stalks this Realm and all fear him, yea even I – I more than most perhaps, for I have suffered cruelly at his barbarous hands."

"The Bad Shepherd guy," Lee murmured.

Malinda shivered and the stumps of her wings trembled. "The very mention of his name fills me with loathing and dread. He is hate in human form, driven only by the impulse to murder and destroy."

"Can't you cast a spell on him or something?" Maggie suggested. "Why doesn't the Ismus hunt him down with his knights?"

Malinda smiled sorrowfully. "Would that we could," she replied with regret. "But the Bad Shepherd is not of this Kingdom. He too hails from a different world and is amongst us, uninvited and unwanted. Our magick has no sway over him and we cannot destroy him. We can chase him to the borders, but we cannot rid ourselves of his malignant presence entirely. Always he comes slinking back to bring fresh torment, fresh grief."

She gazed into the hearth and tears welled up in her pale blue eyes. "I fear very soon he shall do his worst wickedness yet and I am powerless to prevent it. Only one person can."

"The Castle Creeper?" Spencer asked.

Malinda nodded. "It is written that only 'the unnamed shape, the thing that creeps through the castle and the night' can bring about a final end to the Bad Shepherd's destructive dance. One of you three darling young people must rid us of this baneful scourge. I beseech whomsoever is the Castle Creeper to come to our aid and save us. Please, I implore you, as our darkest hour approaches."

Lee glanced uneasily at the others. "What do you think one of us could do against him?" he asked.

The old woman paused before answering and bestowed her most benign, sugary smile upon them. Silence seemed to swell inside the cottage, broken only by the crackle of the silver flames in the hearth. A rainbow from the window crystals settled on her face. The shimmering patch of lurid colours made the rest of her appear dark, almost dirty.

"I want you to kill him," she said sweetly.

Maggie and Spencer drew their breath and they looked at Lee. Malinda observed them. Her smile became a triumphant one as she guessed.

"So, at last," she addressed him. "You are the one. I should have known."

Lee didn't bother to deny it.

"I ain't killin' nobody for you, lady. I got my sights set elsewhere. I'm only holding it together for that. It's the last fight I've got in me an' I ain't wastin' it."

Malinda set Gilly on the floor and the glass rabbit went scooting off under the table again.

"I wish you would reconsider. Perhaps we could strike a bargain? Is there aught you would ask of me?"

Lee's eyes flicked over to the wand, hanging on the peg. Malinda chuckled, but now it didn't sound quite so friendly.

"That won't be of any use to you in your world," she told him. "It would just be a pretty stick."

"Maybe I'll find that out for myself."

"You would be wasting your time – and the goodwill of Malinda should not be spurned or cast aside so lightly. I could make life so much more agreeable for you."

"My life is so far deep down the toilet, there ain't no way out and I don't think I even wanna get out, cos it's too damn painful an' I can't face it. But I'm gonna take some pieces of crud down with me in the final flush."

"Hope always gleams when least expected."

"Any hope I mighta had, got snuffed out – and the scuz responsible is gonna pay. That's all I care about."

"But what of your friends here? Surely they deserve consideration? I could help them too. Their hearts' desires could be granted."

"No thanks," Spencer said. The atmosphere in the cottage had changed. What had seemed so snug and cosy now felt oppressive and sinister. Maggie agreed with him. The shadows deepened. In spite of the fire, a chill flowed over them. The soft wrinkles around Malinda's face hardened into severe lines. Lee's hands tightened round the unicorn stick.

"I have an ointment that could banish those repulsive blemishes and pustules that inflame your face," she told Spencer. "And just one draught of a potion will dissolve this fat girl's unsightly excess. Don't deceive yourselves. How oft have you dreamed to cease being quite so grotesque as you are."

Spencer and Maggie stared at her. The pretence of kindliness was over. It was as if a different person was speaking through her. A smell of damp crept about the room.

"We're leavin'," Lee said, rising from the chair, pointing the unicorn's horn at the Fairy Godmother. "You want someone dead – you bloody your own hands. Ten minutes from now, mine are gonna be red enough."

"You have no idea, do you?" Malinda snorted. "Still, after all this time, none whatsoever. But then you're only a child. You don't even realise what it is I'm asking you to do. You don't understand who the Bad Shepherd is."

"You got so many psychopaths in this damn place, I don't care."

He nodded to the others and they moved to join him.

"Oh, but you do care!" Malinda insisted. "And you do know him. All your life you've heard his words, all of you have – most especially your grandmother."

"You don't know nuthin' 'bout my family!" Lee snapped. "Spence, get the wand – tea and cakes with Tinkerbell is over."

"I know all there is about your families," she said. "I made it my business to do so. Lee Jules Sherlon Charles, I know that your grandmother had a painting of the Bad Shepherd hanging in her precious front room. A painting she hid from view, the moment she became one of the blessed."

Lee lowered the skull.

"Wait," he murmured. "What exactly you sayin'?"

"What's she on about?" Maggie mumbled.

Lee thought he knew, but he couldn't dare bring himself to believe it.

"That painting on my grandmother's wall was of Jesus," he said cautiously. "Which she replaced with a nasty print of your White Castle. You's talkin' bull."

"The Bad Shepherd has many names where you come from," Malinda informed them. "Prophets in dusty sandals are so numerous there. They infect the place like a virus. Even in this Realm we were not immune: an aspect of him came seeping in. But, fortunately, his presence here is a malady that can be cured. I made sure of that; every eventuality was considered."

"Damn – you're one of the biggest loons of the whole bunch!" Lee declared. "You're telling me that homicidal wack-job, the off-his-meds schizo what tried to chop me up with an axe that night, is really Jesus Christ? Oh – I heard it all now."

Malinda inclined her head. "But of course. How else would such as he appear in the Dawn Prince's Kingdom – the distorting prism of the Devil's own playground?"

"Oh, she's totally nuts," Maggie broke in.

"The joy of it is," Malinda continued, "by invading this Realm, and assuming the role of the Bad Shepherd, the Nazarene has had to agree to… how shall I say? My terms and conditions. Therefore, if he dies here, he has to die in every other world also. His power and influence will perish out of existence entirely. Only the Creeper can bring this about. That is what I want you to do for me. This is what you *must* do."

Lee struggled to find what to say. "You is aksin' me to kill Jesus? Seriously? You want me to do that? You expect I'd even think about it for a second?"

"That is why I have waited so long to meet you. Why you are so important. This mighty victory is in your gift alone. So much pain and unpleasantness could have been avoided if you had declared yourself sooner."

Maggie had heard enough. "Let's get out of here," she said in disgust.

The girl reached for the door, but Malinda twirled a forefinger and the lock snicked into place.

"You cannot leave," she said. "I am not done. The deal is not yet made."

"Stuff you!" Maggie snorted. "We don't need to use the door. Lee can take us back to our world from in here."

"Tsk, tsk, he can only return if he's outside. It doesn't work indoors, does it, my dear?"

Lee didn't answer. He'd had enough too and was revolted by what he had heard. She wasn't keeping them here. Striding to the nearest leaded window, he smashed it with the skull. Malinda tapped her fingers and the wooden shutters outside came slamming to. He pushed and beat his fist against them, but they were like iron.

"You'll never get out, without my permission," Malinda said and now her voice was different. It was deeper, crueller – almost masculine. A speck of black mould bloomed on her cheek.

"And I'm not about to let you return to the camp to murder my devoted Lockpick. His family have served me faithfully for three generations and he's done such a thorough job of keeping you so abjectly miserable in that place. I've found it far more amusing than I anticipated. Watching your little arguments, the backbiting, the budding romances – most diverting. But here we are at last."

The teenagers turned to her.

"How'd you know about the camp?" Maggie asked. "And how do you know so much about us? Who are you really?"

The Fairy Godmother rolled her eyes. "Haven't you worked it out yet, you cretinous lard depository?"

With a rustle of taffeta, she turned slowly on the stool, wheeling around in a circle. By the time it was complete, her face had changed and the gown no longer fitted. The aged back was straight and the rounded shoulders were broader and defined. Sinewy forearms protruded from the sleeves and the legs had stretched. The eyes weren't blue any more, but immeasurably dark. The features were gaunt and the spun-sugar hair was now sleek and black. Empty bandages fell to the floor.

The old woman was gone. Sitting in her place, but wearing the same clothes, was the Ismus.

The trademark crooked smile appeared.

"That's much better," he said, unlacing the cuffs and rolling them back. "Speaking through a pensioner's mouth, long distance, isn't exactly high up on my list of pleasures. This is much more comfortable… well, apart from the frock. Not really my colour. Now then, isn't this nice? I feel I know you so well, apart from you, Spencer – you're a bit of a repressed oddball and keep to yourself far too much. It isn't healthy. But Garrugaska has taken a real shine to you, it's rather adorable really. When a Punchinello wants to kill you, it's practically a declaration of love. So, in a way, all three of you have had a romance in the camp. Isn't that splendid?"

The teenagers were too taken aback to respond.

"Now I can finally stop house-sitting inside the head of one of your fellow aberrants. Another grave for someone to dig there, when I vacate possession, I'm afraid. You really did take an inordinately long time to show yourself, Creeper. It's been months since your last visit to these shores. What kept you? I'd have thought you'd be making regular raiding trips to selflessly steal food for your chums. How thin did you want them to get? Even the body I was hiding in was starving and it's been dead for two months!"

Lee recovered from the shock and took an angry step forward. "This is Christmas and birthdays rolled in one," he said with a dangerous grin on his face. "You, me, here, on our own – with no blacked-up minders watchin' your back. Couldn't be sweeter. First, I'm gonna make sure you know real hurt, then I'm gonna cut off your head and burn it. Let's see what that does to this 'playground' you got goin' here. I'm bettin' it'll fizzle to nuthin'."

"But you haven't even heard my offer yet," the Ismus said calmly. "You know what I want you to do; let me tell you what I'll do for you."

"Ain't nuthin' you got I want, Dead-meat."

The Ismus laced his mittened fingers together and leaned back on the stool.

"Charm was such a lovely girl, wasn't she?" he said appreciatively.

"You do not get to say her name!" Lee bawled.

"Oh, wouldn't you like to see her again?"

"What?"

"This, my dear Creeper, is the bargain. It's very simple. You dispose of the Bad Shepherd for me, and you get to live happy ever after, here, with the pretty Miss Benedict – and all her whimsy."

"She's gone – you stinkin' pile of crap!"

The Ismus raised his eyebrows. "Come now," he said. "You of all people realise that doesn't matter here. Tell me, did your previous random explorations ever take you to Battle Wood, atop the southernmost hill?"

Doubt and uncertainty swamped Lee's anger.

"Probably not," the man continued. "No one ever goes there now and there's not a great deal to see. It's almost impassable anyway. Thorns and ivy and brambles have taken over, but once, long ago, there was an ancient stronghold on that lofty summit. I imagine it's crumbing into ruin now, but there is an old tale of a fair maiden who lies in enchanted sleep within its topmost chamber. Only her true love can break the spell, with a kiss."

Lee stepped back, breathing hard.

"You shut up," he said.

"That maiden could so easily be Charm," the Ismus tempted him. "I could make that happen. This world is my creation. You could be the valiant prince who rescues her. Think of it, the life together you wanted – better even. I will give you a princedom. You will be equal to the Jacks and Jills."

Lee's stocky frame sagged. The unicorn club slid through his fingers. He stumbled back against the doorway, his heart and mind whirling.

"Don't listen to him," Maggie cried. "It wouldn't be real. You know she's dead. You know what Jangler did to her! It wouldn't be Charm! It would be a lie – like everything else here!"

"This is no lie, far from it – just a different reality. Imagine, a whole lifetime with her – and one day, if you so desire, children too. Could you truly abandon that? Did she mean so little to you?"

"Stop it!" Spencer shouted suddenly. "Open this door and let us out!"

"Don't interrupt me, boy," the Ismus growled at him. "This is between the Creeper and me."

"Oh, really?" Spencer said, stooping quickly to pluck something from the floor. "You sure about that? Cos I think you need to do what I say right now – or else…"

In his hand he held the glass rabbit that had come snuffling by. Its legs paddled the air and its ears were waggling.

"Put that down," the man ordered. "I said, put it down!"

"Not a chance! I'm going to count up to three and if that door doesn't open, this Easter refugee gets smashed to bits and out pops that plague."

"You'd never do it," the Ismus scoffed. "You'd never condemn everyone here to such an agonising death. You're no mass-murderer.

You'd be killing everyone you know, everyone who is currently under the spell of *Dancing Jax*. If they die here, they die back in your world too – including yourself and Lee and Maggie of course. That takes a certain amount of abandon and backbone you simply do not have."

Spencer's mouth was dry. "Maybe *I* wouldn't," he muttered timidly. Then he gave an insolent wink. "But Herr Spenzer can."

The Ismus looked startled, almost impressed.

"And what of you, Gilly?" he asked the rabbit. "Have you nothing to say?"

The glass animal squirmed in the boy's grasp and its little mouth quivered open.

"Please don't shatter me!" it pleaded. "I may be reckless and clumsy, but that isn't my fault. I don't want to die. I didn't want this badness inside me. I can't help it. Eating the forbidden sweetmeat made me this way. Please don't!"

"Oh, God!" Maggie spluttered, recognising the rabbit's plaintive voice and staring at it in horror. "It's Jody!"

Spencer almost dropped it in alarm and Lee raised his eyes, surfacing from the conflict boiling inside him.

The Ismus grinned. "Yes, poor mad Jody. This is what she became in Mooncaster. Her conversion was a complete surprise to me. What a rotten old time of it she's had. Jangler really broke her in the camp. Would you do the same to her here?"

Spencer lifted the rabbit higher, as if to hurl it down. Her piteous wails were heartbreaking. The boy wavered. Then he began to shake and knew he couldn't do it.

The Holy Enchanter relaxed. The boy was weak.

"You see," Lee said abruptly as he snatched the glass animal from Spencer, "I never actually liked the girl. She were a royal pain in the ass from day one. So I got me no guilt about crushing her blue bunny head under my Nikes. Don't care 'bout no plague neither, cos I've sworn I'm gonna take out Jangler and as many of them guards as I can, even if it kills me. This won't be as up close an' personal as I'd like, but it'd get the job done. It's win-win for me – how about you?"

He held the whimpering glass rabbit out in front of him and met the Holy Enchanter's hostile glare, and matched it. They both knew he wasn't bluffing and he was grimly amused to see the smirk wiped from the Ismus's face.

"One…" he began counting.

"Two…"

"Thr—"

"All right!" the Ismus shouted, mould breaking out across his pale, perspiring skin. "But when you reawaken at the camp, you'll be dead within minutes. I'll see to that."

Lee laughed bleakly. "Them minutes is gonna be glorious an' messy though," he promised. "You're gonna have to audition you a new Lockpick, cos that one's just reached his expiry date. Now open the goddamn door."

The Ismus raised a finger and the lock clicked back. Maggie wrenched the door open and she and Spencer dashed outside.

"A life with Charm," the Ismus reminded Lee as the lad retrieved the unicorn club and backed out. "That's what you're throwing away."

"As you so rightly called it, my life is gonna consist of minutes back there – an' real busy ones at that. Guess I can deal with any regret in whatever time I get spare. Now go put some guy clothes on, you dumb-ass!"

With that, he threw the glass rabbit into the cottage and slammed the door behind him.

The calico cat above the knocker jiggled madly on its nail. "Call again soon!" it warbled dizzily.

"Gimme your hands," Lee told the others. "Keep tight hold of that wand, Spence."

"But he just said it'll be useless there!"

"Maybe – but do the guards and Jangler know that?"

The cottage door was torn open and the Ismus stood there, clasping the glass rabbit he had barely managed to catch safely.

The teenagers had already gone and the frog on the bucket fell into the wishing well in wide-eyed surprise.

Back at the camp, all hell was about to break loose.

28

I⟨T WAS ALMOST⟩ ten o'clock and the light of the July day was finally failing. The ambulance bearing Jody away had departed almost an hour ago, her blue glass eyes still staring upwards. Not knowing what to do for the best, with the help of the other kids, Alasdair had the three unconscious bodies of Lee, Maggie and Spencer brought inside his cabin as it was the nearest to where they fell. Jangler had been too preoccupied to fuss about a girl remaining in there after lights out and the guards were making a night of it, celebrating the acquittal of the Jill of Spades.

Punch-drunk again, the Scot thought. *Any excuse to get bladdered. They're worse than I was.*

Christina had begged to stay, but he didn't want to risk getting her into trouble. Once Jangler realised his precious rules were being broken, there was no knowing what he'd do. Alasdair passed her into the care of the other girls in her cabin and the seven-year-old shuffled away unhappily.

The cacophonous din of the guards in the hut next door was worse than usual. Two TVs were turned up full, one showing a violent Western, the other blasting out hip hop. Yikker was on duty in the skelter tower, guzzling red wine, otherwise the other TV in there would have been showing a slasher flick.

Nicholas and Drew had to sleep on the mezzanine because their beds downstairs were being occupied. Alasdair sat on his own. He couldn't understand what had caused Maggie, Lee and Spencer to pass out like that – and simultaneously. It was well weird, but then what wasn't here? He had checked under their eyelids and was relieved to see they were human, but the pupils were unnaturally large. That happened when the book took you over. Had they become Jaxers now too? What would happen if they didn't come round? They couldn't lie there indefinitely.

The questions and the stress were giving him a headache. He bowed his head and rested it in his hands. This place was killing them, one by one. Who was going to be next? He thought of the first young lad. It was two months since Jim Parker had been murdered. Alasdair blamed himself for not doing more to help him. If he had only spared the time, that first weekend, to sit him down and talk. Could that have prevented his death? Alasdair reproached himself bitterly, because he was certain it would have.

Suddenly the three figures on the beds around him kicked their legs as though they were running and let out wild yells. The Scot raised his face in astonishment and saw them sit up sharply, panting and gasping. Spencer put his arms out as if to save himself from falling and Alasdair did a double-take when he saw the thing he clutched in his hand. It looked for all the world like a magic wand and had not been there a few seconds ago. Then he saw the stick Lee was holding – and what was fixed to one end of that.

"What?" he cried, jumping up and staring – a hundred questions firing in his mind and getting tangled on his tongue. "What the… how… what? Just what?"

The others swayed on the beds, disoriented. Lee gazed around blankly, until he recognised the familiar shape of the cabin. Then he sprang up and ran to the door.

"What are you doing?" Alasdair asked, dragging his eyes off the unicorn club left behind on the bed. "It's ten o'clock. You cannae go oot there! You've been dead to the world for hours."

"Ain't goin' out," the boy answered. "Anyone gone by here just now? You see anyone? One of the other kids?"

"No – I didnae – I wasnae looking. Where the hell have you been? Cos you were no just flaked oot, I ken that noo! What is…?"

Lee hissed at him to be quiet. Further along the row, a cabin door had opened, just as he knew it would. He put a finger to his lips and waited, pulling as far back into the dim shadows as he could whilst remaining close to the door. Stealthy footsteps were approaching. Someone was walking this way, heading for Jangler's chalet at the end – to alert him.

Lee held his breath as the figure passed by and he stole a wary glance up at the tower. Yikker had slumped down, out of sight, and was gargling vulgar songs. Perfect. Then Lee moved with a speed and agility greater than Alasdair ever thought he was capable of. He yanked the door open and darted out. An instant later, he returned, dragging someone with him, his hand clamped firmly over their mouth.

Maggie and Spencer were still feeling groggy, but they understood what was happening. Alasdair didn't.

"Hey!" he shouted in outrage. "What you doing? Let go o' her!"

Lee didn't answer. He swung the person he had caught, like a sack of potatoes, and slammed her against the wall violently. With his other hand, he grabbed the girl by the throat and lifted her off the ground.

"Christina!" Alasdair bawled, leaping forward to pull the insane Lee off her with his good hand. "What are ye doing? Get off! Let her go – you lunatic!"

Lee shook his head fiercely and the little girl choked in his strong grip. Pleadingly, she looked over to Alasdair and stretched a feeble arm towards him. The Scot charged at Lee and threw his weight against the boy. They went crashing to the carpet and Christina fell to her hands and knees, coughing.

"You madman!" the Scot yelled as he struggled and fought, one-handed. "What do ye think you're doin'? She's but seven years old! You out of your mind?"

Lee tried to push him off, but Alasdair's fury gave him strength and he punched Lee in the face. The two of them vied with one another and Christina picked herself up. Not looking back, she hurried to the door again.

"Stop her!" Lee shouted.

Christina opened the door, but was snatched back by Maggie, who hauled her further inside. The young girl clawed and screamed like a wild animal. By now Drew and Nicholas had heard the commotion and were running down the stairs. Spencer ran at them with the wand and the skull club.

"Stay there!" he told them.

"What's going on?" Nicholas cried. "What's she doing to Christina?"

Maggie shoved the girl on to a bed and tried to hold her down. Christina pushed back her head and screamed at the top of her voice.

"Jangler! Jangler! Help me!"

The noise of the Punchinellos' TVs drowned out her screeching. Nobody outside the cabin heard her.

Lee finally managed to overpower Alasdair and came lurching to help Maggie.

"You goin' no place!" he told Christina.

The child glared at him. Then she called out to Nicholas and Drew, sobbing in anguish.

"I'm scared. They're hurting – save me! I don't understand! What have I done wrong?"

The boys on the stairs tried to push past Spencer to help her, but he struck one against the head with the skull and kicked the other in the stomach. Both of them stumbled to their knees. Spencer took a deep breath. He didn't know he could do this sort of thing. He kind of enjoyed that. But he hoped they weren't badly hurt.

Alasdair was back on his feet and came running. Spencer pointed the unicorn's horn at him and the Scot skidded to a stop before it.

"You're all mental!" he raged. "You've woke up crazy. Let her go, for heaven's sake! She's only a wee lass!"

"Alasdair!" Christina wept. "Make them stop."

"In God's name!" he begged.

Lee stared down at her, revulsion contorting his face.

"This ain't Christina," he said. "That little girl ain't been around for a long time. What we got here is a spycam."

"What?"

"You always thought we had an informer in here with us. You was right, but you was lookin' in the wrong places."

"Dinnae be absurd, man. You're no makin' sense! Listen to yourself! That's Christina there. Can ye no see that?"

Maggie shook her head. "Christina's dead," she told him.

"You're out of your minds! She's right there!"

"That's just her body," Lee insisted. "He's been inside it all along!"

"What? Who?"

"The Ismus! Watching and laughing at us. Makin' us fight ourselves, telling tales to Jangler, grassing on Jody, making her do stuff – pushing her over the edge."

"Christina wouldnae ever do that!"

"Oh, open your eyes! Look at her!"

Alasdair gazed down. The seven-year-old had stopped struggling, her energies spent. He wanted to rescue her from these mad people, but with only one good hand it was impossible. He felt such a failure. He failed everyone – Jim, then Jody, now her – as he had failed to save his parents, that night in Edinburgh.

The boy caught his breath.

A change had come over Christina's face. The eyes were darkening and her trembling chin set hard. Her mouth became cruel and severe. She turned her head and those black, glittering eyes regarded Alasdair with scorn.

The Scot swore and retreated fearfully.

"Och, no…" he breathed.

Christina's lip curled and she opened her mouth to speak. But the voice was not her own, it was that of the Ismus. Christina's voice was gone forever.

"You and Jody were so easy to delude," the man snarled. "It was too easy really, there was no challenge there. You got boring very quickly. What a dreary pairing you made. Is it any wonder I spiced it up a little? At least Fatty and Muscleboy had comedy value. A shame he got digested by one of my Lord's pets. I used to enjoy pretending to faint so he could carry me. Do you realise what a chore it is, making these dead legs walk?"

Alasdair staggered away. "Make it stop!" he said. "Shut its filthy mouth afore I do."

"This body had served its purpose anyway," the Ismus continued as inky spots peppered across the forehead and the mould came sprouting out. "You won't be able to stop me when I leave it. I might even pounce on one of you and take you over, for a laugh."

The pitiless eyes fixed on Maggie. "I wonder what it feels like, being a walrus in a dress?" he sniggered. "I might crawl inside you. Mmmm... nice and roomy – I could throw a party."

The head lifted to stare at Spencer. "Or how about you, Cowpoke? I'd make you run outside and give Garrugaska a rootin'-tootin' treat by letting him gun you down like an outlaw – or maybe he could hang you. It'd be the first dance you were ever good at. Aww, don't look so nervous. It's what you wanted a while ago."

Then the Ismus's attention rested on Lee. "And what of you, Creeper? Shall I invade your head and see what makes the tocks go tick? Not quite the nice boy your proud mummy thought you were, are you? See, I did my research very thoroughly. A gang member – tut tut, blud. And that night, when you were going to mete out some hard justice to those other lost youths... who was it really had the gun? It was yours, wasn't it? I'd like to know if you fired it before you were dragged to Mooncaster that first time. If I rummage around in your stubborn head, will I discover what truly happened in that underground car park? How many did you shoot as they read my sacred words to you and your bruvs?"

"You won't climb inside my head," Lee stated coldly. "You need me alive. I'm the only one can kill your Bad Shepherd and that's way too juicy a peach for you to chuck. You daren't get rid of me – case I change my mind and do it."

"Lee!" Maggie cried.

The Ismus laughed.

"I knew my offer didn't fall on closed ears!" he chuckled foully. "What I said can still be yours – you and the delectable Charm, together…"

Lee lifted the girl's body from the bed.

"Yeah, but like I told you, next few minutes of my life gonna be real busy."

"I won't allow you to kill Jangler!" the Ismus warned.

Lee carried Christina to the bathroom and thrust her inside, pulling the door shut.

"Time to advertise for a new gaoler," he muttered.

"You can't keep me in here!" the Ismus yelled, heaving on the handle. Black mould foamed from Christina's eyes and ears.

On the other side, Lee told the others to grab the duvets and force as much of them under the door as they could to seal the gap.

"He can't get through there, surely?" Spencer said.

"You better be glad there ain't no keyhole in this," Lee replied. "Now find somethin' to keep this door shut with! And if you see any stuff crawling through, jump the hell away from it. Don't let it touch you."

There wasn't much time. He told Drew to hold the handle then claimed the unicorn stick and Malinda's wand from Spencer.

"You can't just go kill the old man," the boy told him.

"Come watch me."

"But it's quarter past ten now. There'll be a lorry waiting for us at the top of the road at eleven. We can get out. It doesn't have to end here!"

"Ended for me when he butchered her. No going back from that. And he needs to pay."

"Stop feeling so sorry for yourself! You've got this amazing gift that no one else has and you're the only one who can stand up against that devil in there! How dare you think of throwing it away!"

Maggie left Drew stuffing a duvet under the door and barricading it with pillows.

"Spencer's right," she said. "We've got a chance to escape from this place. The only one we'll ever get. What do you think is going to happen to us? Me and Spence are good as dead if we stop here after what we've done. And what about Charm's girls? She'd give them this. She gave them everything she had."

Lee hated it when other people were right. Even so, there might be a way to accomplish both… He glanced out of the door. Yikker was still singing up in the tower. But Captain Swazzle was making a drunken patrol of the perimeter, armed with the machine gun.

"How we gettin' past that?" he asked.

"Marcus worked that out," Spencer remembered. "He knew how long it took one of them to walk the fence. The speed Swazzle's going, it'll take a bit longer tonight. There's plenty of time to dodge him completely."

"Not long enough to get eighteen kids outta here," Lee stated. "We wouldn't make it."

Alasdair stirred. "If we could cut the wire," he spoke up, in a stilted, grief-cracked voice, "I've got an idea."

Lee reached into his pocket and fished out the cutters.

Two minutes later, one end of a sheet had been tied to the handle of the bathroom door and the other to a railing of the banister. It wasn't going to open any time soon.

Inside, the splinter of Austerly Fellows had evacuated Christina's body and she was lying on the floor, finally at peace. The bubbling mass of mould sat on top of her. It gave a frothing chuckle when the edges of duvet came squeezing under the door. It didn't even need to get out of here. There was a far simpler, faster way of warning Jangler.

In a New York penthouse suite, the Ismus opened his eyes and called for a telephone. One of the Harlequin Priests bowed and went to attend to it.

Back in the camp, Alasdair and Maggie waited till Captain Swazzle disappeared beyond the main block. Then they crept out. Crouching in the shadows, they hurried in turn to the other cabins and roused everyone from sleep, then hurriedly explained what was happening.

The girls were frightened but excited. Some were reluctant and didn't

Hertfordshire Libraries

Customer ID: *****0733

Items that you have borrowed

Title: Freax and Rejex
Due: 11 January 2020

Title: The rest of us just live here
Due: 11 January 2020

Total items: 2
Amount outstanding: £0.00
19/12/2019 11.51
Items on loan: 2
Overdue: 0
Reservations: 0
Ready for collection: 0

want to take such a terrible risk. These were mainly in Esther's cabin. Cracking her knuckles nervously, the thirteen-year-old refused to leave and said anyone who did was mad. They'd all be shot. Maggie and the others tried to tell her it was their only hope, but Esther was adamant. She was stopping.

In what had been Charm's cabin, the girls there were only too eager to escape this horrendous place and listened carefully to what they had to do.

"If you've got dark clothes, put them on," Maggie said in her own cabin. "But don't bring anything. Leave your bags and the rest of your stuff behind. We're going to have to run through the woods and can't take anything that'll slow us down."

"Where will the lorry take us?" a girl asked.

"We don't know, babes – but it's got to be better than here."

"Hey," Alasdair said. "What happened to Marcus's belongings? They still in the wreck of his hut?"

"No, Lee and Spencer collected most of it for me. In a bag over there. Why?"

"Och, he had a long-sleeved navy blue shirt. Would ye mind if I had a borrow of it? My gear's no dark enough for slinkin' aboot."

"Sure."

Alasdair opened the bag. He found what he was looking for and closed his eyes momentarily. Some lines from one of his favourite songs came whispering from his lips like a valediction.

"When darkness comes and pain is all around, like a bridge over troubled water, I will lay me down."

The significance of what he was about to do weighed heavily. Yet it was the only way – the others wouldn't have time otherwise. One last hopeless chase and sacrifice, to try and atone for the mess he'd made.

"Great," he told Maggie, making sure she didn't suspect what he was up to. "We're ready."

29

IN THE END cabin, Jangler had fallen asleep in the armchair. The detailed report he'd been writing of the day's events was on his lap, unfinished. His mobile phone was ringing fiercely on the desk, but he didn't hear the Ismus's urgent summons. The Punchinellos next door were so loud he had taken to wearing earplugs. He snored peacefully and dark, oily dreams dripped through his subconscious.

Almost sixty years peeled away and he was in flannel shorts, being led down a long, sickly-smelling corridor. Hushed, funereal voices spoke over him. He was shown into a large yet stuffy bedchamber where the curtains were drawn and black candles burned either side of the deathbed. His grandfather lay there, expiring, worn out in his Lord's service – a parched husk waiting for the end to come.

The very first Jangler, who had been present at that fateful Beltane gathering in 1936, was too weak to rise. His failing eyes looked on the young boy who had been ushered in to see him, one final time.

"Initiate him into the faith," he whispered in a phlegmy croak to the lad's parents. "There must always be a Jangler. Mr Fellows will return. The world will ripen. The vigil must continue, unbroken. Jangler must be here, for him to depend on."

"Rest easy, Father," the younger man said. "Little Maynard is already one of us. I have shown him a photograph of the Grand Duke and he worshipped it. The legacy will endure."

Old Mr Hankinson raised a trembling hand to the boy, who reached up and took it in his. The grandfather's last breath wheezed out and the candle flames were extinguished. The boy turned to his solemn parents.

They were dressed in black robes, just like the other ten people in the room.

"Grand'da is lucky," the boy said. "Now he is with the Dawn Prince."

"Not until the rites are performed for him," the new head of the family said.

"One day I shall be the Jangler," the boy said precociously. "Hurry up and die, Daddy."

In the cabin the mobile stopped ringing. Presently a text beeped in. And still he slept.

Alasdair's cabin was crowded with everyone, except Esther. She had stayed resolute and remained in her own hut. No argument would budge her.

The girls were horribly afraid. Maggie tried to assure them it would be OK, but even she wasn't a hundred per cent certain this would work. She just prayed that it would.

Alasdair's plan was to cut two holes in the fence. One would be just behind the graves. The other would be closer to the opposite side of the camp. The hope was for Captain Swazzle to discover it on his way around and assume an escape had been made that way. This would give everyone time to make use of the first hole. It was going to be tight – there were only twenty-five minutes till eleven o'clock. They would have to race through the trees to reach the road and meet that lorry – if it was there.

They watched, hearts in mouths, as Captain Swazzle went stumbling past the gates.

"Get a move on," Alasdair urged, under his breath.

Swazzle waddled further along until only his white fedora could be seen in the darkness. It drifted from side to side then turned.

Impatient, Alasdair opened the door before the Captain disappeared behind the main block, trusting to the drink to dull those sharp senses.

"Good luck," Maggie told him.

"Aye," he said, slipping out into the night.

Wearing black jeans, Marcus's dark shirt and a torn length of black material tied round his head, to hide his sandy hair, the Scot flitted like a shadow past the two end cabins. Garrugaska and Bezuel were still boozing and watching their TVs and there wasn't a sound from Jangler in his. Alasdair ran over the grass, towards the grave markers, and immediately set to work, snipping through the fence. It was tougher than he expected.

Presently Maggie joined him, with the first of the younger girls and carrying Malinda's wand, in case they encountered one of the guards or Jangler.

"It's taking too long," she hissed, watching him struggle with the steel. "You can't manage with that hand."

"Yes, I can! There – it's done. Get the lasses oot of here – I'll go start on the other one."

"Be quick!" she said. "You don't have to make it as big as this. Just enough to make them think someone's got out that way. Hurry back!"

"Dinnae worry about me," he said with a mysterious, remote look on his face. "You guys be careful. I'm sorry – to all of ye, most of all to you. I was wrong, aboot so much, and made lives worse than they already were."

Maggie stared at him, alarmed by his words. "What's going on? Alasdair?"

The boy grinned. "Your pal, Marcus, wasnae such a choob after all," he said, showing the can of body spray he had removed from the bag at the same time he took the navy shirt. "He's going to give you time to get away. See – I was wrong aboot him too. I'm so sick of being wrong. Time to do something right. Something to make up for all them mistakes."

"No!" she hissed.

"I'm doing this," he said softly. "Just tell Lee, I was worth trusting."

"The guards will slaughter you! It's pointless! You won't last a second when they catch you. Don't do this!"

The Scot glanced at the board that marked Jim Parker's grave. His eyes crinkled as he smiled.

"A hero never chooses his own battles," he said, repeating words the dead boy had spoken to him so long ago now. "They choose him."

He darted off down the fence, leaving Maggie distraught. But she couldn't call after him and already the next pair of girls were running up, together with Drew and Nicholas. Pulling the wire back, she guided them through.

Alasdair followed the corner of the fence around and ran as far as he dared. Swazzle still hadn't emerged from behind the main block.

"Probably fallen over," the boy murmured to himself. "Hope he flattened that massive conk, the lightweight milk jockey."

Even as he said it, the white fedora bobbed into view. Alasdair applied the cutters feverishly. It wouldn't be long now. He wrenched at the steel mesh, making a hole just large enough to crawl through. Then he turned the aerosol on himself.

"Halt!" Captain Swazzle shrieked in the distance. "Stand and disclose!"

Alasdair was already on his stomach, worming through the fence. A strand of sharp steel he hadn't bent properly ripped through the shirt and gouged along his back. He stifled a cry and hauled himself clear.

Squawking, the Captain came running. Alasdair scrambled to his feet and hared into the trees, squirting a trail of body spray as he ran, in the opposite direction to the one the others were going to take.

Swazzle halted in front of the damaged fence. The hideously wide mouth gibbered with rage. The Punchinello glared at the trees beyond, then let the machine gun do its screaming.

On the skelter tower, Yikker heard the weapon blasting into the night and lumbered to his feet. The great hooked nose trembled as the sensitive nostrils caught a familiar and much despised scent on the air – one that Yikker had thought never to smell again.

"Stinkboy!" the guard growled.

Yikker had been sorely disappointed not to have been the one to kill Marcus. The guard had always been suspicious that there had been no corpse found and harboured a secret belief that he had somehow managed to escape during the appearance of the tentacled monster that rainy night.

Now the night air was giving proof to that belief. Stinkboy was back!

Whooping, Yikker turned the searchlight on, directing the beam towards the gunfire. Then the guard went clomping down the tower stairs, his own pistol in hand.

Lee and Spencer were still in the cabin with the last three girls when the shooting started.

"Could just be firing at nuthin'," Lee said, trying to make the girls less terrified. "You know what them big-nosed goons is like."

Suddenly the TVs were switched off next door and the abrupt silence was more frightening than the gunshots. Garrugaska and Bezuel came rushing out, eager to see what was going on. They scampered between the cabins and ran to the rear fence.

"Now!" Lee said. He opened the door and looked around. He saw the searchlight pointing towards the back of the camp and breathed a huge sigh of relief. He hoped Alasdair's little diversion would detain those bloodthirsty monsters just long enough.

Behind them, the bedding stuffed under the bathroom door darkened and furred with mould as the splinter of Austerly Fellows emerged.

Lee and the others ran past the end cabins. There was more gunfire and the guards were quacking shrilly, revelling in every moment of the chase. Lee turned. That Scottish kid did all right and those Punchies were stupider than he imagined, if they were beyond the fence, chasing empty shadows in the woods.

Spencer and the girls ran on, to where Maggie was waiting. Lee was about to follow when he caught sight of Esther sobbing in fear on her step, too afraid to move. She had changed her mind. She didn't want to be left here on her own. But now the guns petrified her.

"Hell," Lee mumbled, doubling back to fetch the stupid girl.

"I can't move, I can't move!" she snivelled when he reached her.

"Now you can," he said sternly, grabbing Esther's arm and

frogmarching her towards the graves.

"We're going to be killed!" she wept.

"Don't tempt me," he replied, brandishing the skull stick in his other hand.

They rushed to the fence. Maggie and everyone were now on the other side, waiting anxiously.

It was ten to eleven.

Lee pushed Esther through then stepped away and held up his hand in farewell.

"What are you doing?" Maggie asked. "There's no time. Come on!"

"Ain't comin'," he answered. "Least, I got me summat to do first. You go find that truck and get the hell outta here. Look after my sweet's girls for her."

"Lee!" Spencer called. "Don't do it!"

He was wasting his breath. Lee was already striding back over the grass, towards the end cabin. The unicorn club swung menacingly in his hand.

Spencer turned to Maggie. "You heard him," he snapped. "Get going."

"What are you going to do?"

"Stop here till the guards come back – till he comes back – I don't know. Now get lost – go on!"

Maggie hugged him quickly then ran into the trees with the rest, heading for the main road, the wand still in her grasp.

Lee's brows hooded his eyes. His mind was calm. What he was about to do was going to be in cold blood. He'd enjoy it more that way.

"What anarchy is this?" a familiar, pompous voice spoke out. Jangler's portly shape was standing outside his cabin, staring sleepily around at the camp and listening to the gunfire in the distance. In his hand he held his mobile and he adjusted his spectacles as he read the latest text.

"Old man!" Lee called out. "You an' me got business."

Jangler turned to him and put the phone into his pocket.

"So," he declared. "You're the one. I did wonder if the spotty cowboy lad was the Creeper, or that Esther girl; they're both skulkers by nature. What is that you have there? Been to a jumble sale, have you?"

Lee tapped the skull against the palm of his hand. "This is what I'm gonna beat your sick brains in with," he promised.

"I think not," Jangler said and he called for the guards.

Lee took a step nearer. "Oh, them's way too busy chasing nuthin', back there in the woods," he said. "Jus' you an' me here."

From Lee's cabin, the splinter of Austerly Fellows came bubbling and seething. It pulsed on the doorstep, viewing the showdown between the gaoler and the Castle Creeper. It tensed, preparing to intervene and protect the Lockpick's life.

The old man took his hand from the pocket. He had exchanged the mobile for a small pistol. He wasn't stupid enough to arm the guards and not take precautions of his own.

"You, me and my gun," he told the boy. "Now drop the white elephant."

Lee hadn't anticipated he'd be armed. It showed in his face and he let the skull club fall to the ground.

On the step the pulsating black mould quivered in amusement. The danger to Jangler was over. That wily old man was more than capable of looking after himself. But it was time the guards returned to hunt down the escaped aberrants. This camp had ceased to be of worth. New and larger camps in other countries would be opening soon. Spilling on to the ground, the mould streaked through the grass, rushing swiftly towards the back fence to summon the Punchinellos back. The woods were full of moving targets for them to gun down.

"You ain't gonna pop that thing at me," Lee said, eyeing the gun. "Your Ismus guy needs me alive."

A callous smile tweaked Jangler's moustache.

"I hold a different view," he said. "The Creeper is far too dangerous to be allowed to live. You could wreak havoc in Mooncaster if unchecked. I suggested massacring the lot of you right at the start to be sure, but Mr Fellows disagreed. I would never presume to correct the Grand Duke, but it would seem my opinion was the correct one. You should have been slaughtered then. That is an omission I shall now set right, and balance the account to my satisfaction."

Holding the gun at arm's length, he braced himself for the recoil.

"*Beyond the Silvering Sea…*" Lee said suddenly. "*Within thirteen green, girdling hills…*"

The old man started and gaped at the boy incredulously. What was he doing?

"*…lies the wondrous Kingdom of the Dawn Prince…*"

Jangler's head began to nod and he started to rock backwards and forwards, slipping into that other existence. He felt a cold breath on the back of his neck and the will ebbing out of him. The gun fell from his fingers.

Lee came stampeding forward with his head down. Yelling ferociously, he dived at the old man, his hands grabbing the gaoler's throat. Together they fell, but by the time Lee hit the ground, Jangler was nowhere to be seen and the boy was unconscious.

Jangler looked up. It was still night but it was cold. He saw the stars blazing brightly in the sky, the way they burned in…

"Get up, you lowlife. I wanna knock you down again."

Lee was standing over him. Jangler sat up and fumbled for the gun. It wasn't in the grass and the ground was wet and boggy. He stared around fearfully.

They were on a strip of spongy ground. Around them was a fetid swamp.

"Where…?" he spluttered.

"Don't you recognise the neighbourhood?" the boy taunted. "Guess you castle guys don't make it out this way too often."

"I'm… in Mooncaster?"

Lee seized the collar of the Lockpick's costume and hoisted him roughly to his feet.

"Yeah!" he roared right in his face. "I brought you home!"

Jangler blinked and shuddered. "It… cannot be," he stammered. "How can I be here and know who you are – and know of that dream life in the camp? It's… it's not possible. I'm not still asleep. It doesn't make sense."

"Awww, shoulda brung your clipboard. You coulda worked it out on there."

"I… I don't understand this."

"You won't have to get used to it for long," Lee told him, taking the phone from the old man's pocket.

"That device!" Jangler cried. "It has no place here! It doesn't belong!"

"Ain't no coverage neither," Lee remarked. "That's OK. I weren't gonna ring no one. Mmm… nice sealed unit, looks waterproof to me, does it to you? Let's find out, yeah? Just setting the alarm to vibrate."

He gave the old man a contemptuous shove that threw him off balance and sent him tumbling. His hands splashed into the brackish bog and he only just saved himself from tipping head first into the swamp.

"See," Lee said, squatting on his haunches to stare him in the face. "Beating your brains in really weren't enough. What you did to her – that deserves something a bit more special. A bit more off the hook."

He tossed the phone in the air then jumped up and caught it. Reaching back, he threw it into the middle of the dark, sludgy water. The mobile floated on the thick slime for several moments then it sank slowly down into the cold darkness.

"Now get up and go fetch it."

"What?"

"I said, GET UP!"

Lee hauled him to his feet again and pushed him into the slime. But the old man's initial shock at being dragged here had faded and he refused to be pushed around. He was Austerly Fellows' most trusted servant and had led the Inner Circle for many years in his absence.

Squelching back on to the bank, he raised his fists.

"Oh, you just made this so much more fun for me," Lee said, grinning.

Jangler ran at him and Lee learned his appearance was deceptive. The old man was strong and solid. He dashed the lad's hands aside like straws and came barrelling in to smash a punch on his jaw and follow it with an uppercut under the chin.

Lee reeled sideways, stepping into the mire. Jangler shrieked wildly and kicked out with his foot. Lee sprawled into the marsh, but he reached out and pulled the man with him. In the sucking mud, the pair of them slugged it out.

Down in the deep, the mobile began to flash and vibrate.

Caked in filth they battled. Hammering blows were dealt on both sides and blood mingled with the ooze. Jangler's thumbs reached for Lee's eyes and began to push them into the sockets. The boy bawled then slithered and slipped out of his hands. The marsh was pulling them further down. They were going to drown here.

"OK," Lee accepted grimly. "Long as he goes down with me – I'm cool with that."

He launched himself at the old man and tried to duck him under the surface.

In the centre of the wide swamp, large bubbles began to rise and break in the air.

A great disturbance was travelling up through the reeking mud. Lee and Jangler were lifted on the swell. The boy used it, thrashing his arms and legs to try and catch hold of the grassy clumps that grew around the edge of the bank. Clawing at the sod, it took every ounce of strength to trawl himself clear and he dropped, exhausted. Gripping one of Lee's ankles, Jangler pulled himself out after and staggered upright.

The old man's dripping face was plastered in scum and algae. He spat it from his mouth as he addressed the boy one last time.

"You want to know how she died?" he tormented him. "Screaming and slow, screaming and slow." Throwing back his head, he laughed repulsively.

Lee pressed his face against the wet ground and his fingers raked through the soft clay. He couldn't go on. He couldn't live with this. Tears fell from his eyes, but he knew he had to make one last effort. He raised himself on his elbows and started crawling away.

Jangler's foul laughter reverberated over the swamp. Then his voice changed and the laugh became a strangled shriek. Lee didn't turn round, he kept on moving.

Jangler howled. A pale, mottled tongue, as thick as his arm, was coiled about his middle. It tightened and squeezed the old man's stomach then pulled and tugged him around. Jangler's spectacles were lost in the mire, but he could still see the immense horror of the Marsh King. The tawny eyes bulged out at him and the tongue began to tow him back into the mud.

The third generation of Janglers screeched in terror.

Lee stumbled to his feet and forced himself to look, for her sake.

The massive jaws opened and Jangler was drawn out, across the bog – towards those needle-like teeth.

"Screamin' an' slow," Lee uttered bitterly.

The boy stared into the bloated frog's speckled eyes.

"Make sure you chew that proper," he told it. "No gulping it down. Make it last."

Jangler's frantic screams intensified. Lee lingered a few moments more, just to make certain.

"Bon appétit," he said.

Spencer knelt over Lee's unconscious form and looked around in bewilderment. Where did Jangler vanish to? He had seen Lee charge at him and saw them both fall together, but the old man had simply disappeared.

Spencer shook his friend urgently. They couldn't stay here. It was eleven o'clock. The lorry would be leaving.

It was no use. It was as if Lee was dead. Spencer didn't know what to do. Should he abandon him and run for the road, in the hope the lorry was still there? He couldn't do that. Seeing the stick with the unicorn's skull, lying close by, he reached for it. Then he saw Jangler's gun.

Across the world something remarkable was happening. The hundreds of millions of copies of *Dancing Jax* were smouldering. In people's homes, in their bags, in their hands as they were reading, in huge container crates awaiting distribution, the pages in which the Lockpick of the White Castle was mentioned began to burn. Every reference to Jangler, the gaoler of Mooncaster, glowed with scarlet fire. The ink was scorched clean off the paper, leaving blank spaces behind. The line illustrations depicting him as a portly man, with a waxed moustache and pointed beard, sizzled and flared, leaving no trace on the page.

In New York, the Ismus felt the old man's death, like a knife in his own heart. Letting out an agonised yell, he collapsed into the arms of the Black Face Dames.

"Jangler!" he wept.

This was the power of the Castle Creeper. There was no character called Jangler in the book any more and none of the others would remember there ever being one.

Surging through the woods, chasing after the guards, the splinter of Austerly Fellows also felt the old man's death. The frothing mould crackled and juddered. Rearing up, it shook, weeping in sync with the Ismus in New York. Then, when that man collapsed, the splinter exploded.

"Please wake up!" Spencer called to Lee. "Please come back!"

Growing more and more fretful, he decided to drag Lee over to the fence and pull him through the breach. He didn't think he was strong enough to lug him through the trees to the road, but he'd try his damnedest.

And then he heard a sound that turned his blood to water.

A pair of spurs came clinking between the cabins and Garrugaska turned a delighted face upon him.

The silver-nosed Punchinello removed the cheroot from his mouth and spat on the ground.

"Get ready, little lady," he drawled, quoting the Outlaw Josey Wales. "Hell is coming to breakfast."

He nudged the Stetson on his head, and licked his lips. Then his large hand moved to the holster at his side.

"Prepare to do a whole lot of dying," he snickered.

Spencer couldn't breathe. A shot rang out across the camp and he was thrown back.

Garrugaska grinned widely. Then a trickle of dark blood dribbled down the silver nose and the beady eyes swivelled round.

"Awww... darn it..." he groaned as he crashed into the grass.

"Ow! Ow! Ow!" Spencer yelped, astonished by the recoil of Jangler's gun. He waggled his hand and shook his arm. Then he ran over and tentatively touched the guard with his foot. He was undeniably dead.

Spencer grimaced and took the Stetson from him.

"Mine," he said, wiping the hat on his trousers.

At that moment, Lee's legs started to kick. He let out a woeful cry and snapped back into his body. Suddenly he was covered in stinking mud, his eyebrow was bleeding and he was choked with emotion.

Spencer hurried back to him.

"We've got to go!" he said. "Before it's too late!"

Lee shook his head. He'd done what he wanted. He didn't have anything left. This was it for him.

"You go," he said in a hollow voice. "Leave me here."

Spencer thrust his hand under Lee's slimy arm and heaved. "Shift yourself!" he ordered.

"Can't," Lee answered. "I got things in my head I can't get rid of. Don't wanna live with them in there."

Spencer pulled him to his feet. "I've just shot my first gunslinger!" he yelled. "So don't mess with me!" And he pushed him to the fence.

Alasdair couldn't run much further. The camp's rations didn't furnish the energy for chasing around. He was out of breath and light-headed, but he could hear the Punchinellos crashing through the trees behind him. They were getting closer all the time.

Captain Swazzle moved swiftly. Bezuel had cast the cumbersome chinchilla coat aside, but Yikker had the lead. Stinkboy was close. The guard's hooked nose could smell the sweat and the fear on the air.

Alasdair was almost spent. He hoped the others had managed to get away. But when he heard the distant shot as Spencer put a bullet in Garrugaska's brain, he didn't dare try and guess what that signified.

And then Yikker came springing out behind, hollering in his pinched voice, the cassock flapping round his stunted legs.

"Stinkboy!"

There was a crack like thunder and Alasdair's right leg went from under him. The next moment he was rolling on the ground. His leg felt hot. He clutched it. Blood was soaking through his jeans. The hunt was over.

Lying there, he saw Yikker prowl closer, sniffing and eyeing him dubiously. He ripped the black material from the boy's head and Alasdair's sandy hair was shaken free. Yikker screamed and stamped his feet in a fury.

"You not Stinkboy!"

Captain Swazzle and Bezuel came scuttling to his side. Their savage eyes flashed at the wounded lad and they stroked their guns.

Alasdair glared back defiantly and, in a loud, undaunted, clear voice, he began to sing.

Oh flower of Scotland,
When will we see your like again

That fought and...

The woods flared and shook as the Punchinellos emptied their guns.

On the other side of the camp, on the main forest road, the lorry driver heard the crackling barrage of gunfire and threw his hands up.

"That's it!" he barked. "I can't stay any longer! They'll be here next – and so will most of the nearest village. It's twenty past. I've waited too long already. I've got to go! Get in the back with the rest."

Maggie caught his arm. "Please!" she implored. "Just a few minutes more. They'll be here, I know it!"

"Should never have believed it in the first place," the driver blamed himself, pulling away and marching round the rear of the vehicle. "It was a stupid bloody risk. Do you know what it took to mobilise and set this up so fast? Do you know how far we've come? And for what?"

He peered into the darkness in the back of the lorry, where the escaped children were huddled together. The man softened.

"Least we got you out," he said kindly. "That's something."

He gestured for Maggie to climb up with them.

The girl hesitated. She'd kept him waiting here far longer than he was supposed to. She had to face the truth. Spencer and Lee hadn't made it.

Maggie nodded slowly and was about to climb up, when she heard the sound of someone running through the trees.

She turned apprehensively. It could be the guards. No – it was them!

"Lee! Spencer!" she cried, running to meet and hug them. "Oh, you're filthy!"

The driver stared at the newcomers, intrigued. One of them was carrying a strange skull attached to a stick. He had thought Maggie's wand was an unusual thing to bring out of an internment camp, but that was even more peculiar.

"Which one of you is the Castle Creeper?" he asked.

Lee frowned at him.

"You're in the front with me," the driver said. "You two, in here."

Maggie and Spencer clambered into the back and he closed and locked the doors.

Lee got into the cab and the man started the engine. The lorry rumbled off.

"We're not going far in this," the driver told him, keeping his eyes on the dark road ahead.

"Don't mind where we's going," Lee muttered. He didn't know why he'd let Spencer drag him to this. He was dead inside.

"There's an army helicopter waiting for us, just under a mile away."

Lee didn't answer.

"Not our army," the man explained, plugging the silence. "This country has had it. So has most of Europe. Any day now, America is going to follow."

"You don't say."

The man's gaze left the road a moment. "You can't imagine how exciting this is for me," he said.

"What?"

"Meeting you, the Castle Creeper. When they told me you were in that camp, I just wouldn't believe it. Couldn't get over it. It's an honour and a privilege!"

"Autographs later, yeah?"

"Sorry, it's only – I never really thought you'd even exist. Just another false hope. But you're the first genuine, tangible hope we've had so far."

Lee took something from his pocket and cleaned the mud from it with his fingers. The owner of this pink diamanté had been his hope. The doors to painful memories began to swing open in his mind. It was unbearable.

"You look exhausted," the driver said. "You can sleep on the flight. There'll be plenty of time. We're going a long way away. One of the last few places on earth still safe from the book and that Ismus maniac. Fingers crossed we don't get shot down by the RAF. What's that you've got there?"

Lee turned the heart-shaped stud over in his fingers. "Belonged to a friend of mine," he said.

"I'm sorry. They didn't make it?"

The boy returned the stud to his pocket. He had made up his mind.

"She's just fine," he said, staring out at the night. "I'll be giving it back to her real soon."

The lorry bumped and tore down the forest road.

Lee looked more closely at the intense, scruffily bearded man behind the wheel. By the dim glow of the dash lights, he could see how thrilled the guy was.

"So what's your name?" he asked.

The driver reached over and shook his hand.

"My name's Martin Baxter," he said.

3am. 200 metres above New York City

Standing on the balcony of the Ty Warner Penthouse suite of the Four Seasons Hotel, a cashmere blanket wrapped round his shoulders, the Ismus leaned on the glazed railing and breathed deeply. The air up here was invigorating. The pain had abated, but not the anger. He looked down on the raging fires.

It was a magnificent, torrid spectacle. There was practically one in every block and too many to count in Central Park. The night sky was aglow with ruddy flame and the skyscrapers of Manhattan flickered with angry light. Over the East River a subway train was burning on the Williamsburg Bridge. Appropriately enough, the Statue of Liberty was in darkness.

This was one of the last cities in America to surrender to the power of *Dancing Jax*. Only Boston, San Francisco and Las Vegas still resisted with any sizeable force, but nowhere as violently as here. The National Guard had been called out, but now even they were battling among themselves. The Ismus listened to the shots, explosions, wailing sirens and screeching tyres a while longer with a rapt expression on his face, as if enjoying a symphony. Then he returned inside, closing the French doors behind him.

The disturbances of New York were silenced immediately and the air-conditioned opulence and serenity of the suite welcomed him once more. He gazed around at the members of his Court. The three Black Face Dames were stationed outside the private elevator, although the hotel itself was defended by a cordon of police, who each wore a playing card pinned to their uniform. The Harlequin Priests stood either side of a marble fireplace and the Jockey was on the telephone.

"Haw haw haw," the Jockey laughed into the receiver. "I don't care who you are, Mr President, the Holy Enchanter is a very busy bee and not taking any more irksome calls. Now stop pestering him or I shall have to come play pranks on you and be fearsomely naughty. You won't like that!"

Hanging up, he skipped to one of the other windows and flung the handset over the balcony.

"What a pushy nuisance!" he remarked. "Just because he's discovered he's a knight of the House of Clubs he thinks he can annoy you at any hour. That's his fourth call since midnight. I'll be so glad when the castle replica is completed in England and we shall be free of these freakish contrivances. How they annoy one."

He glanced at the plasma screen above the mantle. The news reports showed crowds of the newly converted marching through the streets and fighting with the misguided idiots who dared oppose the spread of the sacred book. Kate Kryzewski was there, doing pieces to camera, with the chaos and pitched battles fulminating behind her. She was dressed from head to toe as the character Columbine, in pretty, patched rags, with a tambourine at her waist. The Jockey licked his lips in appreciation.

"Where is the Lady Labella?" the Ismus asked abruptly.

The Jockey started then grinned. He tittuped to the master bedroom, beckoning all the way.

The High Priestess was lying on the bed within. She was sound asleep. The Queen of Hearts and the Queen of Spades were sitting with her. They rose when the Ismus looked in and curtsied.

The Holy Enchanter stared at his consort, sleeping peacefully on the bed, and covered her with the blanket from his shoulders. Then his attention shifted to the infant in the crib close by.

"The young princeling is quiet as the Jack of Diamonds' magic slippers," the Queen of Hearts said, beaming. "Why, he's a delight to watch over."

The Ismus ignored her and stared down into the cot. The baby was awake. Livid stains of minchet juice discoloured his plump, innocent face and his wide blue eyes roamed over the tall, gaunt figure who peered in at him.

A crooked smile hooked the man's mouth. He knew the child was not his. It was the son of Labella's previous partner. Before *Dancing Jax*, Labella had been called Carol and the man she abandoned in order to become the High Priestess of Mooncaster was Martin Baxter. This was the dissident maths teacher's son.

The Ismus chuckled softly to himself. It amused him greatly to have the enemy's child in his power. A sudden, impulsive idea occurred and he glanced purposefully at the window. The penthouse was on the fifty-second floor – a truly dizzying height. He reached into the crib and let the baby's tiny fingers close about one of his own. Then he broke into harsh laughter.

The Jockey and the Under Queens could not begin to guess what was so comical.

"No," he told himself, becoming solemn once more. "That would be a waste of resources. You're going to prove very useful, aren't you, my little princeling? Very useful indeed."

He swept out of the bedroom and the Jockey followed.

"Fetch me another phone," the Ismus told him. "I want to speak with my publisher."

"More foreign editions?" the Jockey chortled.

"No, I wish to discuss something new with them."

"New, my Lord? I do not understand."

The Ismus turned his dark, glittering eyes on him. "*Dancing Jax* was always conceived as the first volume in a two-book sequence," he said. "Every bestseller must have a sequel. The public demand for the continuation of a blockbuster product must be satisfied. I'm going to give my readers what they want."

The Jockey's eyes almost fell out of his head. "A sequel?" he spluttered. "How can there be a sequel? It is a chronicle of our lives there – our gateway to them."

"Then call it a furtherance to the world of Mooncaster. The first took only nine years of my life to write. I have been planning the follow-up for eighty years."

"This is stunning news."

"Oh, it will be more than stunning," the Ismus promised. "Much more. *Dancing Jax* was only the baited trap; the second book is when the jaws close and bite down hard on this dirty little world."

"My Lord?"

"Don't you worry, just fetch me a phone."

The Jockey moved away uncertainly, the caramel leather of his costume creaking with every step. He halted then wheeled around. "May I ask," he began nervously. "What will this furtherance be called?"

The Ismus stared out at the troubled night. "I would have told the title to Jangler first," he said with profound regret.

"Who, my Lord?"

The Ismus was about to dismiss him, irritably, but sighed. Not one of the converted remembered the Lockpick. He had been completely erased.

"The next book," he told him, "will be called *Fighting Pax*."

The Wyrd Museum, Book One:
The Woven Path

**Dare to enter the Wyrd Museum, where fantasy
meets the seriously sinister...**

In a grimy alley in the East End of London stands
the Wyrd Museum, cared for by the strange Webster
sisters – and scene of even stranger events.

Wandering through the museum, Neil Chapman, son
of the new caretaker, discovers it is a sinister place
crammed with secrets both dark and deadly. Forced
to journey back to the past, he finds himself pitted
against an ancient and terrifying evil, something
which is growing stronger as it feeds on the
destruction around it.

HarperCollins *Children's Books*

The Wyrd Museum, Book Two:

Raven's Knot

Brought out of the past, elfin-like Edie Dorkins
must now help the Websters to protect their age-old
secret. For outside the museum's enchanted walls, a
nightmarish army is gathering in the mystical town of
Glastonbury, bent on destroying the sisters and their
ancient power once and for all...

**Revisit the chilling, fantastical world of the Wyrd
Museum in this sepell-binding sequel to**
The Woven Path.

HarperCollins *Children's Books*

The Wyrd Museum, Book Three:
The Fatal Strand

The thrilling conclusion to the chilling trilogy.

Something has come to disturb the slumbering
shadows and watchful walls of the Wyrd Museum.
Miss Ursula Webster is determined to defend her
realm to the last as the spectral unrest mounts. Once
again, Neil Chapman is ensnared in the Web of Fate,
facing an uncertain Destiny. Can he and Edie avert
the approaching darkness, or has the final Doom
descended upon the world at last?

HarperCollins *Children's Books*